Safe In the Arms of God

Volume One of the Story of the Nutt/Landers Family of Granbury

By: Melinda Jo Ray

Historical Novel tracing the stories of the interwoven lives of
the Nutt and Landers families and their migration to Hood County, Texas
from Neosho Missouri, told primarily through the marriage and love story of
Jesse Franklin Nutt and Elizabeth E. Landers.

ISBN 978-0-692-611234
U. S. Copyright 2016
First Edition Printing
By Print One of Granbury

Table of Contents

DEDICATIONS

To Ama, the best grandmother in the whole world, you told me the first stories and through your memories the years of the past became real. You also sang and played for me the first songs of our Lord. That music and Faith became the melody of the rest of my life. For all you did and for all your love I am forever grateful. See you in the choir Upstairs!!!!

To Mother and Daddy - You taught me so many things about love and respect and honor and family and caring for others. But most of all you showed me what unconditional love looks and feels like and instilled in me the ability to believe in God first and myself second, no matter what. You know this was always my dream. I so wish you were here to share it with me! Daddy, it would take you one night to read! Mom – you it would take a little longer - you would read each and every a, an, the, and but! LOL!

To Jesse, Jacob, Lizzie, Abel and Sally and all the rest, thank you for giving us a legacy to be proud of! Thank you for the vision you had even through the darkness, and most of all thank you for witnessing the Faith you lived to the community you loved. I am so honored to be the one to tell your stories to a new generation. Thank you for building us a home in Los Brazos de Dios.

To Dr. Samuel Patel and staff for all you do to save the vision of so many, including this author, every day. Without your work this story might not have been written, and without your daily efforts so many would be walking in darkness. Thank you for being some of the healing hands of God in our world.

To those who loved me enough to walk with me through my own days of darkness and wondering what God had in mind-
Duncan and Kathy and Ruth.
You three are still those thousandth men in my life.
Thanks be to God for putting you there.

FORWARD and ACKNOWLEDGEMENTS

In October of 2006, I embarked on a great adventure. I was part of a group of partners who bought the Historic Nutt House Hotel in Granbury, Texas. Located on the historic downtown square of a small Texas town, the hotel occupied most of a two storied limestone and cypress structure known in the historic record as the J. and J. F. Nutt Building. At the time, all I knew was that "The Nutts were some of the founders of the town, and their granddaughter Mary Lou Watkins was largely responsible for the preservation and restoration of the downtown of our little city." - That of course is a gross over-simplification, and says nothing really about all the most compelling reasons why I came to feel theirs is a story that needs to be told!

As the knowledge and the desire to tell this story grew in me I bothered a lot of people! I am sure to miss someone. But to all who so generously shared the pieces of the tale- Karen Nace, Diane Lock, Mary Kate Durham, my Mom, Bert Johnson, Cody Martin, Melba Hoover, Maurice Walton, Glen Ward, Joan Nutt Veale, Sassy Papasan, and all the Nutt and Landers descendants who have let me adopt your families- I owe so much gratitude!!! To the folks at the Hood County Jail Museum, and the Hood County Historical and Genealogical Society, Preserve Granbury, the Bridge Street History Center, the Hood County Library, and the Paluxy Baptist Association for putting up with all my questions, phone calls and emails - THANK YOU!

These men and their families – through their stories – have much to tell us that we need to hear – about Faith, and courage, and honor, and integrity, and community, and patriotism, and what it took to build and keep this nation. I hope I have preserved the essence of those stories here. It is styled a work of Fiction, because Time refuses to yield all of her secrets, no matter how diligently we look for them. There are simply things we do not know, and assumptions we must make. But the truth of finding the extraordinary in the ordinary way these people lived their lives is what I hope to share here. There is love, there is laughter, there is hope, there is vision, but most of all there is Faith- Faith that brought a family westward into an unknown wilderness- and instilled them with the assurance of being ever "Safe in the Arms of God".

Prologue

The sound of my steps echoed in the emptiness of the little white cottage in the woods as the gray and silver light of dawn spread a soft glow through the windows. Each room was empty of furniture, but full of memories. It had been our first place – ours together –just us. It had been our place of refuge and a haven for healing. And finally, it had become a place for new beginnings and the coming of joy.

I held joy close, as I walked through those rooms, remembering. Steps, strong and sure, sounded up the steps and into the room behind me. "Lizzie?" said my husband softly, "It's time to go."

I crossed the room to where he stood. He reached for my hand and I met his hand with mine. As our fingers intertwined, he breathed deeply, "Honeysuckle…. Whenever I smell it from now on…I will remember this place."

Jesse paused and I stood still with him in the moment, waiting. "Lizzie," he breathed, "my sweet Lizzie. I know what a leap of faith this is for both of us – this- this journey. But, your brother reminded me this morning of something I should have remembered all along. In all our talk and apprehensions about this choice and about this journey, we've forgotten where we are going," he said.

Puzzled, I replied, "What do you mean Jesse?" picking up on his quiet…excitement?

"The Brazos River…" he said, softly, "Lizzie after all this, we are really going there- to our safe place.- Remember, that first night, I told you it's name…., the river named Brazos by the Spanish – El Rio de Los Brazos de Dios – The River of the Arms of God." The stillness was all around us, as he continued, "We, all of us, are going to spend the rest of our lives settled right where we should always know ourselves to be – safe-- in the Arms of God." Jessie squeezed my hand and led me outside to where the wagon was waiting. And finally, for the first time in years, like the settling of a dove, true peace came.

It had been a long time since I felt that peace. The last five years (Dear Lord – had it really been only five?) had begun with such joy, then been shattered by such heartache. And now, at last we were beginning to find joy again. There had been so many moments when I had questioned…. Not my faith….but the WHY of it all… and what God would have me do. But what I kept realizing, again and again, was my absolute certainty that this man was mine- given to me to love and help and cherish, no matter what. So, as the wagon lurched into motion – I remembered….

Section I : Neosho

Growing Up Cousins 1844 - 1853

Jesse and I had known each other all our lives. Our fathers were best friends as boys, growing up on adjoining farms in Tennessee. Then Jesse's father had fallen hard for his best friend's sister, and they became brothers by marriage.   With that marriage the link was formed that would bind our families together for all the years to come. My aunt Sarah and her David had 12 children, and my parents 13, and we all grew up together. Our land in Tennessee had been sold to my uncles, and in 1844 our two families traveled together to Missouri, where more land and a freer life beckoned. I was eleven at the time, and for all of us children that journey had been a grand adventure.

The past ten years in Missouri had flown by, all of us children meeting on the road after morning chores for the walk into Neosho to school held in the Masonic hall, the biggest building in town. We all attended church there too with other Baptists in the area- our two families occupying four whole rows of seats on one side of the room. The services were usually followed by a fellowship meal and afterward by joyous hours of fishing and fun stolen amid the hard work by everyone in the daily life of a large farm.

Even in the closest of families, there are members who seem to share a special bond. Something about them and the essence of who they are just mesh. Sometimes it is a grandparent and grandchild, sometimes a pair of siblings, sometimes a child and a parent. And sometimes, very rarely, when the ages and circumstances are just right, that bond can happen between three people, and so it had been with my cousins Jesse and Jacob and I. From an early age they were thinkers, those two. Because we were so close in age we were often together, and miraculously for me – they invited me into their world. They didn't seem to mind that I was a girl and that I had ideas too. They accepted me as an equal in our little society of thinkers and dreamers.

Every day after school we would run from the front door of the old Masonic Hall down the road and around the bend in the river to where the downtown of our brand new county seat was being built. We would sit on the rocks on the river bank and watch as builders built and measured and the great men of the area would come and stand, and wave their arms and point, until the bricks and mortar, and lumber and nails became a temple of justice and government, and houses for business and commerce. At night, the boys would sit at the top of the stairs and listen when their father, David Nutt, along with other men from the area (both the ordinary and the Great) came to call on my father, who for many years had been their representative to the Missouri Legislature. He had also helped most of them as a lawyer and friend, drawing up wills, dealing with land sales, and legal disputes, and so on. The plans for the new downtown Neosho had mostly been sketched out amidst much robust discussion right down there on our dining room table. Sometimes they would be joined by visitors, like my father's old friend Amon Bond from Tennessee, and they spoke of weighty and great matters, and hard issues and choices- of the beckoning promise of the great western frontier, and the gathering storm of national division and states' rights and slavery.

And on the banks of the creek on Sunday afternoons, with scripture and hymn ringing fresh in our ears, we sat with hooks in the water and talked our own talk, of how one person can make a difference, how working together people of little means can do great things, how this new country gave every man the chance to aspire to greatness, and how our Christian duty called us to behave toward others. We debated the different things people could do, the choices of life. Was it better to teach, or preach, or build, or grow, or heal, or explore the unknown? Could a person do more good as a leader of men or as a servant of the poor? What was that thing called destiny and legacy, and how did a person know what to do about one or the other or both. And because I was there we even talked about where a woman's place is in all this, and whether they could truly be wives and mothers who helped raise up new leaders, if they had no education themselves. Then one day discussion became life lesson, and a boy became a man.

One Sunday when we were all about fourteen or fifteen, we were sitting on the bank of the creek behind the Nutt farmhouse. Jesse and Jacob both had fishing poles and had lines in the water, but the fish weren't biting, and they both stared morosely at the water passing over our bare feet, a welcome coolness in the warmth of the hot August day.

"You all surely are quiet today," I finally said. "Is something amiss?"

"Papa and Mama had a go to last night," said Jesse without looking up.

"A go to? Oh, you mean a *fight*?" I said, incredulously. *"Aunt Sarah and Uncle David?"*

"Yeah," said Jacob, "and knuckle-head here thought he should get involved." He didn't look up either.

"Oh, Jesse," I breathed, "whatever were you thinking?"

"I was thinking it's wrong, that's what," said Jesse passionately, finally looking at me with eyes that were moist, yet blazing with the righteous anger of the young.

"Well, I think Papa is wrong too," shouted Jacob hotly, "but I'm smart enough to keep my mouth shut. Now he'll be watching, and neither of us will be able to do a thing about it!" He shoved his brother in the shoulder, and the next thing I knew the fishing poles were on the ground, and there was a wrestling match taking place before my eyes.

I scrambled to my feet to get out of the way. Having six brothers myself, I knew better than to try to intervene right away. I let them both get in two or three significant blows before I grabbed one of the cane fishing poles by the smaller end, drew back, and swung. The larger end of pole connected with a single solid "Thwack" across two sets of ankles. They both leaped back grabbing at their feet, and each emitting a very satisfying "Ow!" of protest.

"Dang, Lizzie!" shouted Jesse, "That hurt!"

"You're darn right, it hurt!" agreed Jacob. "Good Lord, Lizzie! What're you doin'? Trying to kill us!?"

"You'll both neither curse nor use the Lord's name in vain in my presence, Jacob and Jesse Nutt." I said indignantly. "And you'll conduct yourselves like gentlemen, or you'll have no further conversation with me!"

It took a moment, but a heartbeat later they were both scrambling to their feet, tugging at their disheveled clothes, and looking down with embarrassment. Jesse was the first to meet my eyes. "I'm sorry, Lizzie," he said simply. "I lost my temper. I surely know better." He and Jacob exchanged a look I didn't understand, *then*.

"It's my fault," said Jacob, "I'm the one who started it. Lizzie, I'm sorry. And brother, I know you were just trying to get Papa to do right. That took guts. I was sure he was going to wallop you!"

"I was too," said Jesse, "When he took that big breath, I thought I was done for."

"What on earth is this all about?" I asked, sitting down on a log in the shade nearby.

They both came over and settled on the ground on either side of my feet. I waited, but neither of them spoke, they just looked at each other. Finally after several seconds had passed, I said, quietly, "Jesse. Jacob. I can tell it's important. And it's troubling you both. Please. Tell me."

"Papa's not a bad man," Jesse began defensively.

"I know Uncle David is a very *good* man," I said, firmly. "My father would tell you that too. But he also says he is stubborn, pig-headed and proud. Not to his face that I've ever seen, but he does say it to my mother on occasion."

Jacob nodded, "I suspect Uncle Abel knows," he said to Jesse. "Aunt Sally and Mama probably told him years ago."

Exasperated beyond bearing, I said, "Told him what, for goodness sakes? *Tell me.*"

"Papa won't let the girls go to school." blurted Jesse.

"Won't-... What do you mean?" I said blankly.

"The girls, our sisters, he won't let them go to school." said Jacob.

"He says book-learning (as he calls it) is a fine thing for a man," said Jesse, "but a woman has no use for it."

"But that's- I mean, I know lots of people feel that way, still," I said, bewildered. "but not Uncle David, surely? Why- wh- wait a moment- Elizabeth and Phoebe can read!"

"Because Mama had Aunt Sally teach them before Papa could find out!" said Jesse. "Think about it Lizzie, did you ever see Phoebe in school?"

Dumbfounded, I stared at him, "I- well- I.... No." I said, in amazement. "How could I not have.... My own cousin..."

They both nodded vigorously. "There are so many of us and so many of you, and since after Phoebe we've all been boys, till Susan, nobody really noticed." Jesse said. "And if they did, since Mama can't read and write, they probably just thought…. If they thought anything… that Aunt Sally was teaching the girls at home. And Mama and Aunt Sally did too, till Papa found out. They fought about it then too. I was six and fixing to start to school, and Mama wanted Phoebe to go with me. And Papa said no, and it was the first and only time I ever heard them raise their voices at each other until yesterday. I was scared to death, *then*. Yesterday I was just mad."

"But why yesterday? Why after all--," I stopped. "Susan. Susan will be six in the fall."

"Yes," said Jacob, "and Papa refuses to let her go, and has forbidden anyone to teach her."

I was silent, just trying to take it all in, when Jesse said, "When I heard them yesterday, I listened for a while out in the hall. They just kept getting louder. Papa was yelling and Mama was begging, and then Papa called Mama a fool. That's when I walked in and stepped right between him and Mama, looked Papa in the eye, and said, 'Papa, I love you, but you are wrong sir. You are wrong on two counts. You are wrong to deny my sisters the same education you have provided for me. And you are also wrong, sir, for raising your voice in anger towards my Mother and your Wife. You promised before God to cherish her, and I believe cherish includes respect."

"I was standing in the doorway, watching," said Jacob, "and there was Papa, turning a deep beet red, and Jesse standing there dead white and eyes blazing like some avenging angel, and poor Mama looking like she couldn't decide whether to faint, or cry, or applaud. And there is just this absolute total silence, and then Papa takes this huge breath, and I am thinking I need to find a place to hide, and Papa turns to Mama and says, 'Sarah, you have my profound apology for my conduct. I hope you will forgive me. On the matter under discussion, my decision stands.' And then he takes another big breath…"

Jesse jumped in, "And I just knew I was gonna get thrashed! But he looks me in the eye, and I swear he almost looked proud. And he gave me this little bow, like men do, you know? And he said, 'I thank you sir, for your defense of my Wife and your Mother, and for your most just correction of my conduct toward her. On the matter of discussion we will, as gentlemen, simply have to agree to disagree.' And he held out his hand, and I-I shook it, l-like his equal. And then he turned to Mama and said, 'My dear, if you will excuse me, I have matters to attend to.' And he walked past me and Jacob here, and straight out the back door."

Stunned, I looked from one of them to the other and then back at Jesse, "Oh, Jesse…" I breathed. "So, now…"

"So, now, none of us can teach poor Susan anything, because, God bless her, she is such a little talker, it's bound to slip out!" said Jacob.

"Maybe not now," I said, "but surely later…" I stopped, and looked at Jesse. "I am proud of you, cousin. You did your best. Meanwhile, in four years little David will be six and Susan still just ten. If not before, maybe *one of us* will be in a position to do something then- when David starts school."

Jacob and Jesse both nodded, and Jesse said, "I guess you're right Lizzie. We'll just have to wait." A splash sounded in the creek nearby, and he grinned suddenly, as he said to me and Jacob, "Well, come on then. If Lizzie hasn't broken my fishing pole, maybe we should go catch some fish!"

As the months turned into years, the boys I loved continued to grow into men. Good men, visionary men. Jacob spent more and more time in the company of Brother W.H. Farmer, working with the poor and the orphans' home our church had founded in Neosho. Jesse read voraciously, and began spending more and more time with my father and Mr. Bond, and his own father – who had been the son of a sheriff, talking about law, and civic leadership. And he cultivated friendships with local merchants, and set about to learn the ways of business and commerce.

And although I learned and even took some little pride in my growing knowledge and skills in the household realm, it was those Sunday afternoons that I still looked forward to most. But changes were coming, and as I was to learn, there were choices to be made that would affect our lives forever.

Choices February - April, 1853

As time passed- more and more often it was just Jesse and me who met by the river to walk and talk, as Brother Farmer grew more and more dependent upon Jacob's help. Finally the day came when Jacob told us he was considering whether God was calling him, not to the ministry as we had expected, but to be a physician. Brother Farmer was going to arrange for him to study with a doctor in St. Louis, a process that would take several years.

"Have you told Papa and Mama?" asked Jesse.

Jacob nodded. "Mama already knew." he grinned. "She reminded me of all the hurt and sick animals I used to bring home to nurse!" He paused. "Papa- wants it for me, - but he is worried about the money. He is distressed that I will be dependent on Dr. Harding's charity. But I explained that I would be like any apprentice, learning my profession while working as a helper to my employer. It is an honorable path."

"Well, brother," said Jesse, his eyes moist, "I am most pleased you have found your calling. But I will miss you!:"

"We will both miss you," I said, "Greatly."

"And what of you, Lizzie?" asked Jacob. "What path do you choose?"

Standing there on that path in the woods, between my two cousins, these two boys I loved dearly, it came to me that they were now men and I was a woman. My heart broke with the realization that no matter how much love I had for them both, the time had come when I must make my choice. Time stood still, and I looked from one brother to the other, and tears ran down my cheeks.

"Oh, Jacob," I said brokenly, "I am so sorry." I took a step back as Jesse's hand gently found mine. "My- my place is here." I finished softly.

His eyes bored into mine, and then flicked down to our joined hands. His face closed, and he looked from me to his brother, and said, "Then I wish you every happiness. Take care of her, Jesse," he whispered. And he turned, and walked away.

We stood there in stunned silence, Jesse and I, holding hands. Blinded by tears, I turned into Jesse's arms. For a long time we just held each other. Then Jesse stepped back, and looked intently into my eyes. Finally he asked, "Elizabeth, are you sure?"

I nodded, looking down at our still joined hands. "Yes, Jessie. I'm sure."

And so the dye was cast. The next week Jesse appeared on the front porch, hat in hand on a Sunday afternoon asking to speak to my father. My mother trained a gimlet eye on me and said, "Well, Leatha, looks like you may have a suitor. Are you going to give poor Jesse a chance at least?"

Knowing how frustrated she had been these last years at my seeming disinterest in encouraging the courtship of several young men, I smiled as I said, "Why of course I'll give him a chance, Mama. It's him I've been waiting on all along."

For a moment she stared at me in silence, and our eyes met across our sewing hoops. She returned my smile gently as she pulled a thread taunt, and said, "Ah, so that's the way of it, then..."

18

The back door opened, and my father came in. "Daughter, young Jesse Nutt has asked to pay court to you. Now, I know he is very young, but I believe him to be a man of no little promise. I think you would do well to consider his suit." He looked expectantly in my direction.

"Well, Papa," I said firmly, "it just so happens that I totally agree with you! So, yes, I think that could be arranged." And I rose from the table, put on my bonnet, kissed my father on the cheek and went to answer the knock that was already sounding at the front door.

I opened the door, and there was my Jesse, smiling his sweet smile. As I placed my hand in his, he said softly, "Thank you, Lizzie, for being such a blessing in my life."

"Thank you, for loving me for who I am." I replied.

We took our next steps together with the sure knowledge that wherever the path led we would walk it together. Over the course of the next few weeks Jesse and I prepared for our wedding. Mama and Aunt Sally were awash in plans for food and festivities, Jesse and his brothers were busily working on completing a small house for us on the Nutt family farm, and one day my father summoned us both to his library. It was actually Jesse he summoned, but Jesse insisted I come too. Papa looked a little startled to see me there, and said as much as he invited us to sit.

"Uncle you need to understand that Lizzie and I are partners in this marriage. She has a fine intelligence and a good head for figures. You said you had a business proposition for me and as it will affect both of us I thought she deserved to hear your proposal first hand," said Jesse firmly.

Seeing the thunderclouds gathering on my father's brow I said, "Papa, I can leave…"

Jesse reached over, and stayed me with a gentle but firm hand on my wrist. "Elizabeth," he said, never losing eye contact with my father, "It is my wish that you stay."

"Oh, stay, girl," said my father, his eyes flickering to me and then back to Jesse "No harm in it." He continued, addressing Jesse, "It has come to my attention, nephew, that you have a good head for detail, an understanding of business, a keen sense of some of the intricacies of civil matters, as well as a good solid Christian understanding of morality and fairness."

"I am flattered, sir" said Jesse, sincerely.

"Don't be." snapped his Uncle Abel, "You are also stubborn, willful, and naïve." He paused to be sure that sunk in, and I tucked my head to hide a smile. "But we can work on that," my father continued. "It occurs to me that you might be well suited and have some interest in pursuing a practice of the Law. Should that be the case, I am in need of a clerk in my downtown office. You could take the post and thereby have gainful employment. At the same time I am prepared to offer you such instruction as I may in that arena. With due diligence and proper study, I see no reason you should not be prepared to take exams and receive a license within a year or two. I am prepared to pay you the same salary as my last clerk, Mr. Jedidiah Sims - $20 per week at 50 weeks per year. Should you receive a license to practice, I will make you a partnership agreement with you taking the practice upon my retirement, - which, I might add, will not be for many years, yet."

Jesse's eyes met mine met mine briefly, then solemnly met my father's gaze, as he said, "It is a most generous offer, sir, and one I am most happy to accept. I appreciate the opportunity, and will do my utmost to prove worthy of your trust."

"Just spell the words correctly on your copy work to begin with," said Abel gruffly, as he and Jesse shook hands. "Sims never could spell worth a damn. Begging your pardon my dear," he added, belatedly remembering my presence.

"It's alright, Papa," I said blandly, "I've heard worse- from you!" I added with a smile.

He had the good grace to look embarrassed and said, "You two can go now. I'll expect you at nine o'clock sharp Monday morning, Mr. Nutt."

As soon as we reached the front hall, we turned to each other, big grins on each of our faces. "Oh, Jesse, I'm so glad! It's what you've wanted to do!"

"He probably just wants to be sure I can support you, " said Jesse, with a rueful smile, "but I think there's a good chance I may have a knack for it. ... At least I can spell!" We both laughed as we left the house to walk into town, talking all the way of our new plans for the future.

*****   ******   *****   *****   *****   *****   *****   *****

It was a room filled with memories and friends that Papa and I stepped into two weeks later on that sunny April afternoon in 1853. Jesse was there waiting for me, tall, dark haired, and slender, in a brand new suit. I gave thanks to God at the sight of his two closest brothers, Jacob and Abel standing up with him. Jesse's beautiful hazel eyes shined with love as my father placed my hand in his and we made our promises to God and each other surrounded by the joyful love of family. "I, Elizabeth Eleanor, take thee, Jesse Franklin, to be my wedded husband, to have and to hold from this day forward- to love, honor, and obey, for better, for worse, for richer, for poorer, in sickness and in health, keeping myself only unto him for as long as we both shall live." And his to me, "I Jesse Franklin take thee, Elizabeth Eleanor, to be my wedded wife, to have and to hold from this day forward, to love, honor and cherish, for better for worse, for richer, for poorer, in sickness and in health, keeping myself only unto her for as long as we both shall live." Afterward we stepped out into the spring sunshine to begin our lives together.

Four hours, much food, and countless well wishes later, Jesse and I climbed into the carriage my father had loaned us to travel the short distance to the little cottage Jesse had prepared for us on his parents' farm just at the edge of Neosho. The white paint gleamed through the trees in the gathering dusk, and the scent of honeysuckle filled the air from the two huge mounds of the stuff on either side of the steps. It had been a mild winter and spring, so the white yellow blossoms were already in full bloom. Jesse assisted me down from the carriage and drew me into his arms. "Welcome home, Mrs. Nutt," he smiled, kissing me gently before leading me up the steps. He paused to left the latch, and then in a swoop I was laughing in his arms as he carried me across the threshold. "Jesse!" I laughed, "Put me down! This dress must weigh 50 pounds!"

"Ah, but a beautiful 50 pounds it is! And even more beautiful is the woman wearing it!" he responded, setting me gently on my feet in the middle of our little parlor. "I hope you like the house! Mama and Aunt Sally both gave us all kinds of things, and they've spent hours over here setting things around."

"Oh, Jesse of course I like it! It's perfect!" I said, taking in what I recognized as pieces Jesse and I particularly fancied from our childhood homes.

"Come with me," he said, "I have to show you the most special thing." He led me to the bedroom, and my eyes were immediately drawn to the beautiful double wedding ring quilt on the bed. "Our two mothers made that quilt for us together. I am reliably informed that it contains a piece of material from every garment you or I have ever owned in our entire lives."

"Really?" I gasped, "That's amazing! But, oh, look, there's the sky blue silk I wore for my sixteenth birthday! And there's that wonderful navy blue wool from your winter coat you had."

"Oh, and look there is that ugly yellow and brown plaid from that shirt that our Grandmother Landers made me for Christmas that time!" said Jesse, "Lord I hated that shirt! Especially after Jacob said it looked like a horse blanket to him!" Jesse's laugh faded at mention of Jacob.

"I was so glad he was there today," I said, "I didn't know if he would..."

"I didn't have a chance earlier to tell you what he said when I asked him to come and stand up with me," said Jesse.

"That can't have been easy," I said, softly. "He's gone so much with Brother Farmer, and when he is around, he's hardly spoken to me."

"I know," said Jesse, "but I'd made up my mind to ask. It's what I'd always thought of... having him and Abel with me." He paused for a moment, remembering. "I left it as long as I could. I waited till he came home last Monday night. I was waiting on the porch as he came up the walk. I could tell he'd had a hard day by how exhausted and haunted he looked. So I stepped out into the moonlight where he could see me, and asked if he'd had a tough day. And he answered, 'Hard enough, brother. There's all kinds of grief in this world.'"

Jesse shook his head at the memory, and continued, "I agreed with him, saying I was sure his work seemed overwhelming at times. And then I gathered up my courage, and said to him, 'Jacob, I don't want to add to your burdens. And I will understand if you- if you cannot. But as you know Lizzie and I are getting married on Saturday, and I am sure hoping you and Abel would honor us both by standing up with me that day.' Well, Lizzie he hesitated and I just knew he was going to say no. But then he looked up and nodded, and said, "Jesse, you are my brother, and Lizzie is my cousin and now good-sister, and I have loved you both all my life. I will be there.'" Jesse swallowed hard and continued, "So I said 'Thank you, Jacob.' I held out my hand, and he shook it and went in the house without another word."

"Well, I am so glad he was there," I said, "and I love this quilt," I continued, looking down at the bed once more.

"Me, too," said Jesse, taking my hand and kissing my palm gently. "I think it's time we try out the other side of this quilt – by getting under it."

For the first time in my life, I felt shy with Jesse Nutt. I looked down at our hands interlocked together there on that wonderful quilt, and felt a blush burning my cheeks. A moment passed and his other hand came up gently under my chin, and brought my eyes up to meet his. "Sweet Lizzie, don't be afraid…. It's still just me, Jesse. You know I've always loved you and I promise you I always will. God has given us to each other for joy." He leaned in to kiss me once more and we gave ourselves to each other, covered by a blanket made of love.

Amon Bond and the Grand Scheme of Things   April 1854

It was on a stormy spring Monday almost a year later that my father came home for luncheon with news. "Sally," he said to my mother, "Amon Bond is coming to visit. He will be here for the usual gathering of gentlemen tomorrow night, but I thought we might expand on the normal refreshments for that evening by inviting a few of the gentlemen and their wives to come for dinner. You ladies can get better acquainted over dessert, while we gentlemen retire to the library along with some of the usual group."

My mother turned upon my father a look that would best be described as deeply suspicious. "Amon Bond? Surely he must be dead by now. What plot are you and that old fool hatching now?"

My father's bushy white eyebrows climbed, "Now, Sally you know as well as I do that Amon Bond is neither dead nor a fool. Nor will I concede to old, as he is only two years senior to myself." He puffed mightily at his pipe for a moment, and then continued, "And as for the hatching of plots…. You should know by now that whatever joint enterprises Amon and I have embarked upon have never been "hatched" but rather carefully considered and thought out endeavors with great potential benefits to all concerned."

"That may all well be," said my mother, acerbically, "but the end result has in my experience often been highly disruptive for me. The last time I ended moving almost overnight from a comfortable home in

Tennessee to one still under construction here. As I recall, your dear sister Sarah Nutt was the only thing standing between me and absolute insanity."

"Sally, that is all water under the bridge, as you well know," said Papa, gruffly. "Amon writes a fine hand, but I must admit his letter is a bit confusing. He mentions his boy Benjamin has come into some land (how I cannot imagine- as he is all of 23 years of age). But come into he has and so Amon has in mind to get a group of like-minded souls together with the idea of going with young Benjamin to form a new settlement."

"And what godforsaken corner of the earth is this land located in, that there would be room for all these people?" asked Mama, almost, but not quite rolling her eyes.

"Why my dear, I believe it is down along some river," said Abel Landers, his eyes sparkling with amusement, "in the great new State of Texas!"

My mother was silent a moment, staring intently at her husband's face. "Texas." She breathed, "Oh dear, Lord." Then she turned, took her apron from its hook, and headed for the kitchen saying, "Lizzie, get out the good china, polish the silver service, and after breakfast tomorrow be ready to set the table. It appears there will be sixteen to dinner. I'd best go consult with Cook about what will be needed, and then get to market to prepare." The door did not shut quietly as she stepped inside.

***** ****** ***** ***** ***** ***** ***** *****

Amon Bond arrived the next afternoon. A small-boned short individual with voluminous amounts of wiry white hair, a beard to rival Kris Kringle's, and eyebrows that made my father's own bushy brows look tame by comparison, he was like my father in that he had a personality that instantly filled a room. He and my father together were a formidable force indeed. I had just finished setting the table on Tuesday afternoon, when Mr. Bond and my father came noisily in the front door. The house immediately seemed smaller somehow, and my father smiled broadly as he caught sight of me. "Amon, you remember my daughter, Elizabeth- now Mrs. Jesse Nutt?"

Mr. Bond smiled too, and nodded courteously, saying, "Of course, Miss Elizabeth! Allow me to congratulate you on your marriage, my dear. I renewed my acquaintance with your husband but a short while ago at your father's office. He appears to have grown into a most able young man, and, I might add, one of sterling character!"

Bobbing a small curtsey of acknowledgement, I said, "I thank you, sir. Welcome to Neosho. I hope you had a pleasant journey?"

"Most pleasant indeed, my dear," he said, "And where, pray tell is your dear Mother? I am most eager to renew our acquaintance, and to share with her and your father the remarkable opportunity I have recently been so fortunate as to be apprised of. I understand your father has spoken of it to you as well. You and your young man will no doubt be interested to hear the details of this opportunity. I do hope you are both invited to attend the festivities this evening!"

By the time Amon Bond finally paused to draw a breath, my father was looking rather unamused at his blatant salesmanship. "Amon," he said, "Elizabeth is not the one you have to sell. It's Sally. And trust me, she is going to be a much tougher nut to crack than anyone else involved here. She and everyone else I've invited tonight have a serious interest in this thing, and serious reasons for considering it. Save your standard sales pitch for another audience. This one will demand better."

Struggling to keep my composure in the face of this outspoken outburst, that was rude even by my father's own admittedly political standards, I stammered, "I-I am sure that my mother will find whatever you have to share of the utmost interest, Mr. Bond. Father, I believe you will find Mother has retired to the library to await your arrival."

My father turned a gimlet eye on me, and said, "Ah, lying in wait is she. Well, Amon, you might as well come try your magic on Sally now. If we can't persuade her, there's not much point in the rest."

"Be ye not faint of heart…" quoted Mr. Bond, placing his hand on my father's shoulder in a comradely fashion. "Come my friend, let us visit the lioness in her den." They nodded farewell to me and turned toward the library, like two old soldiers off to battle, leaving me speechless in their wake.

As I returned to my work, I couldn't help but think it was likely to be an….interesting…. evening.

Two hours later I had finished dressing for dinner, and Jesse had just arrived. We were standing in the hallway near the stairs when the library door opened, and my mother appeared. She had the stone-faced look of someone who has just received shocking news and is still processing how to deal with it all. She nodded vaguely at me and Jesse, and said as she walked past us toward the stairs, "Elizabeth, I must go and change for dinner. Should any guests arrive before I return, please see to them until I come down."

"Mother," I said, worried, "is everything all right?"

She paused on the stairs, and looked down at Jesse and me as she said, "No. But it may be someday. I must say, the most extraordinary thing has occurred. I actually find myself in agreement with Amon Bond. And that scares me to death."

She disappeared into the upstairs hallway, and I turned to Jesse. "What on earth…?"

"I don't know," he said, mildly, "but it must be big." He nodded toward the front window, which showed the first group of guests coming up the front walk. "Look who's coming to dinner."

I looked, and with a stifled gasp, I began to poke at my hair. "Oh, dear Lord, Jesse! Is that who I think it is?"

Jesse nodded, "I think so, Lizzie. I've only seen him once. He came with your father and Amon Bond to our house in Tennessee, when I was about six or seven years old. It's one of my most vivid memories. I've seen drawings since- in the newspapers and such." He reached out and took my hand and said, "Stop poking, Lizzie. Your hair is fine."

"Who's that with him? " I whispered, "The older couple…?"

Before Jesse could answer, the knock sounded at the front door, and my father came out of the study, followed closely by Amon Bond, both of them looking uncharacteristically resplendent in their dinner dress. My father opened the front door, bowed smartly and then reached out and grasped the hand of the tall gentleman standing before him. "Senator, it is good to see you again! Please come in! Welcome to Neosho, and to my home. And you as well, Senator Benton! Mrs. Benton, welcome! I believe you all know Mr. Amon Bond?" Pleasantries were exchanged all around.

And then my father was turning to me and Jesse, saying, "Senators, Mrs. Benton, I would like to introduce my daughter, Elizabeth, and her husband, Mr. Jesse Nutt." As I dropped a curtsey, and Jesse bowed and extended his hand, my Father continued, "Children, I would like you to meet an old friend, Senator Sam Houston - of Texas, and former Senator Thomas Benton – of Missouri, and Mrs. Benton."

Feeling totally inadequate, I stepped into the role of hostess, inviting everyone into the parlor. My father valiantly rescued me at that point, smoothly sending me to greet other arrivals as he began to work the room. Jesse's parents arrived next. I almost gasped at the sight of them. They had obviously been forewarned about the guest list. Uncle David was nicely turned out in his best Sunday suit, and Aunt Sarah looked genteel, but slightly stern in the deep gray gown she kept only for the most important of occasions. Mother came down soon after, and I was grateful she was there to greet the remaining guests as they arrived. Mother's deep navy blue silk gown flattered her immensely, and I caught my father's fleeting look of pride and affection as she came down the stairs. When she had finished greeting Amon Bond's family, and his sons-in-law Thomas Lambert and Austen Yeats, my father arrived at her elbow to escort them all into the crush of the parlor to meet the two senators, and Mrs. Benton.

An hour later, I sat at the long dinner table next to Jesse, listening to Senator Houston graciously exchanging stories about the intricacies of Washington society with Mrs. Benton and my mother, and mentally taking stock of just who was who at this little dinner party of ours. My father sat at the head of the table, with Senator Benton and Uncle David on his right and Amon Bond and Amon's friend Thomas Lambert on his left. Sarah Bond, Amon's wife was seated just to the left of Mr. Lambert. She was a tiny little thing, with hair even whiter than Amon's, and a determined attitude which I suspected was a result of constantly worrying about what her husband might do next. If Senator Benton felt any umbrage at being seated next to a man who made his living as a farmer and blacksmith he certainly gave no sign. The conversation at that end of the table appeared to be most amiable, as Jesse's usually quiet and sometimes stern father laughed heartily at some humorous tale being shared by that illustrious gentleman.

My aunt Sarah, herself not a naturally outgoing woman, was making a valiant effort to engage Mrs. Bond and her daughter, Mrs. Yeats in conversation. My younger brother Henry had slipped in at the last minute, obviously fresh from a bath, shave and haircut. He was seated next to me, and like Jesse was hanging on Senator Houston's every word. Young Benjamin Bond, one of Amon's younger sons was seated across from Jesse, next to the senator. Although much of an age with Jesse and me, he was clearly intimidated and miserable, a situation not helped by the fact his only possible outlet for conversation was his own brother-in-law, a Mr. Yeats, who was also deeply enthralled with Senator Houston.

Cook and Callie did an admirable job of serving such a large gathering, and dinner passed pleasantly. Father and Amon behaved themselves and didn't bring up anything inappropriate, like politics or business, and mother kept the conversation going quite well considering the diversity of the group. But there was an undercurrent in the room, particularly among the older men, of something akin to excitement or anticipation. I wondered what on earth was going on, and wished, not for the first time, that I could be privy to the after dinner meeting of the men that was surely coming. As we left the table, and the men headed to the library while we ladies moved toward the parlor across the hall, I caught at Jesse's sleeve, and I whispered , "You and Henry had better listen well, because I expect a word for word report!" He smiled impishly, "Your wish is my command, ma'am!" he winked. "Come on, Henry," he said, "we've got an assignment to carry out!"

They hurried away and I turned to the parlor, fully expecting an interminable evening of observing niceties with the other ladies. Instead, I walked into the female equivalent of a Council of War.

My mother stood in front of the fireplace, and as I came into the room she said, "Elizabeth, please close the doors." Startled, I stopped in my tracks and quickly turned to do as she asked, pulling the big pocket doors together with a click.

"Ladies, our gentlemen are having their own version of this meeting across the hall. I do not know what you know about what is being discussed in this house tonight, but my husband and Mr. Bond and Senator Benton have asked Mrs. Benton and me to speak with you so that you may know the reasons behind what may be coming, and be ready to assist your husbands in doing what is safe and prudent for all of our families. Senator and Mrs. Benton have served our state in Washington for many years. During their time there they have had ample opportunity to hear all sides of many political debates and issues. The senator lost his senate seat a few years ago because of the stance he took on several hotly debated issues. Those issues continue to plague our nation, and our division becomes greater every day. Some of us may even have division in our own families. That makes this all very, very difficult.

Our husbands meet tonight to discuss our options, and most particularly to discuss a new option that Senators Benton and Houston have made them aware of. I am going to ask Mrs. Benton to tell you about that, but first – one thing.

What is discussed in this house tonight, the true reasons our husbands may choose to take the advice of the Senators, must never be breathed outside the privacy of communication between you and your husbands. If those we call friends and neighbors came to know about any of this, our husband's livelihoods, and perhaps even their lives could be in danger. So ladies you must promise silence for the sake of your families and your husbands. Does everyone here so promise?"

Shocked we all nodded, and Elizabeth Benton stood and began to speak, changing the course of our lives forever.

"Ladies, my husband and Senator Houston did not announce their coming here tonight. This visit is not on either of their "official" calendars, they did not notify their staffs of their whereabouts, nor were local government officials apprised of their coming. Officially, publicly, -tonight never happened. We were all at home. That this subterfuge is necessary saddens me and my husband greatly. I will also tell you it mostly just makes Senator Houston angry. But nonetheless, because both men have a genuine concern about where our nation is headed and what may be coming for all of us, they have determined to help as many like-minded individuals as they can in the coming years. They intend to help them keep their families safe. Ladies, let me be blunt. The issue tearing our country apart little by little is black slavery. Many of us come from families with a tradition of slave ownership. Each of us older ladies, I am sure, remembers a time in our early marriages when our husband owned slaves. Yet, I am informed that every one of us – you, Mrs. Landers, and you, Mrs. Bond and Mrs. Nutt, have watched your husband struggle with his conscience on this issue over a period of years. And every one of you has watched your husband, with God's help, find ways to quietly free those souls under his "ownership" in an honorable and safe manner. None of you now have slaves in your households. And you younger women, who grew up in these families, grew up without the horrible reality of slave ownership being a part of your personal lives.

Needless to say, my husband and Senator Houston share your husbands' convictions about the slavery issue. They are both determined to find ways to see to it that as America expands westward those new areas are populated by people who simply do not own nor intend to own slaves. They are seeking out like-minded individuals, men of character who only want to be allowed to live as their conscience dictates, and making arrangements for these families to be the next wave of settlers moving west in to Texas and onward.

Mr. Houston was unable to prevent Texas from becoming a slave state, but he is determined in its frontier regions to build a new majority of citizens, who, when the time comes, will have the votes necessary to keep Texas aligned with the United States of America, and to vote Texas to be slave free in ten years. That is his dream for the state he loves. That is his and my husband's hope for our nation as well. There is land in Texas ripe for the taking. The Texas Homestead Act was signed into law again just this year, and Senator Houston is fighting to get it expanded to encourage more settlers. There is resistance to this- some of which is tied to the slavery issue.

Both Senator Houston and my husband feel there may be a limited window of time to take this action. The legislature could repeal the law at any time. Those already possessing land would be safe, but those who wait may find they have waited too long. Each individual may claim at this time 160 acres. Family groups may work together to acquire large tracts of land and then sell it to others who come later once they have clear title. You ladies all have large and hardworking families of high moral character. You are the kind of people Texas needs. You are the kind of people our nation needs.

This is the proposition our husbands are discussing tonight. I know the prospect of pioneering this new land is daunting and will not be without hardship. But we offer you a place where you can live free according to your convictions, without fear of persecution, and hopefully a place somewhat sheltered by sheer distance from the turmoil and heartache that we greatly fear is coming. I do not know what decisions your families will make in this matter. It is your free choice. My job is to help my husband make the offer. We consider this project a sacred trust to the nation my husband has served for over thirty years. We pray you will join us in this effort, but if you cannot, we implore your confidence. Missouri has been good to us, but times are changing, and my husband has lost his senate seat, many friends and colleagues, and has even had his life threatened because of his pro-union, anti-slavery views. We don't ask Missouri to change. That is for her people to decide. Neither Senator Houston nor my husband favors forcing slave states to become free. We want to preserve the Union. We hope with time more can be persuaded to see the evils of this horrid institution so it may be abolished by the will of the people- in time- not now while the extremists hold sway. Meanwhile, we simply seek to help those of like views to find safety and to support our country." She paused and then said, "Ladies thank you for your attention."

Silence reigned for a good minute, and then my Aunt Sarah raised her bowed head and said, "Ladies, will you join me in prayer, for our husbands in their deliberations?" There was a brief flutter as we all joined hands, and six voices sounded as one. "Our Father, which art in heaven, hollowed be Thy Name. Thy Kingdom come, Thy Will be done on Earth, as it is in heaven...."

It was a mostly subdued and thoughtful group of gentlemen who emerged from my father's library several hours later. Mother offered to make room for everyone to stay the night in our big rambling house, but all agreed it was best to be on their separate ways. Jesse and I had already planned to stay the night. As we watched the others leave, I was shocked to realize that the men were seeking the cover of darkness as our gathering broke up.

I was standing alone, near the door to the parlor when Jesse found me. "Come on up to bed." he said, gravely. "We need to talk."

I nodded, "I will be there as soon as I have helped mother tidy up," I assured him.

Almost an hour later, I was brushing the tangles out of my hair, trying to find some sense of calm when Jesse entered the room. He was dressed for bed and I wondered where he had been. I didn't have to wonder long. "Sorry," he greeted me with a kiss on the cheek and took my hand. "Your father wanted a last word. I hope you aren't too tired. We've much to discuss."

"I'm fine," I assured him. I climbed into bed and waited, filled with an anticipation bordering on dread, but willing to let him take the lead. "I am told," he said, "that Mrs. Benton spoke to the ladies last night. So... you know at least the bones of what Amon and the senators came to propose last night."

"Yes," I said, thoughtfully, "On the surface it is fairly straightforward. There is land in Texas for the taking, and they are looking for good folk to go there and settle. But we've land here Jesse, and a good life. But that's going to change, isn't it? - Soon. That was the real reason they have come to us. Not only are they offering land, it is…a safe haven… of sorts, from at least some of what is coming?"

"That's part of it," he agreed, "But there is more than that. I think perhaps Mrs. Benson did not go into detail, and just as well, as open discussion of any of this could have serious consequences if heard by the wrong folk. Of course, we're all right now. We'll not be overheard here. But during the day- we must be mindful of the servants. Elizabeth, you know where both our father's stand on the slavery issue, right?"

I nodded and answered, "I know our grandparents in Tennessee had slaves. And I know that when both Papa and Uncle David came of age and got their own land, they had slaves too. Papa has told us how he and Uncle David were friends and they talked and prayed together about the course of their lives, and then became brothers when Aunt Sarah and your Papa married. He said they both realized over the course of years just how wrong it is for one man to claim ownership over another. And that they both gradually taught their people the things they needed to know to be independent, and freed them. And if any died they were not replaced. And that by the time we came here in 1844, neither of them had slaves anymore."

"Yes, exactly," said Jesse, "well one reason they came to Missouri from Tennessee was because although Missouri allows slavery, there are lots of people, especially in this area who don't have slaves, and it would not be a problem. But now…." His voice drifted off and for a moment he stared out the window at the late rising moon.

"What now?" I asked, puzzled. "What has happened that makes everyone think bad things are coming? Mrs. Benton wasn't very clear on that part."

"For years there has been friction here in Missouri over the slavery question, especially in the counties north of here. But it's been local things- people refusing to help look for runaway slaves, or folks with slaves moving in to a community without slaves and it causing fighting and even gunplay between one or two neighbors," explained Jesse. "Well, the law that made Missouri a slave state way back in 1820, also states that the territory west of here- called Kansas Territory is supposed to remain free. That was done to keep in balance the number of free states versus the number of slave states."

I nodded, "Yes, I knew that."

"So, maybe you aren't aware so much, because we haven't seen it much right here, but there are organized groups on both sides Lizzie, who have supporters from all over willing to give them money and arms, to promote either slavery or abolition. And now, right now, before Congress in Washington is legislation that would abolish the Missouri Compromise, and create a new law. That new law is called the Kansas-Nebraska Act. It divides Kansas territory into two states, and gives the citizens of each the right to *vote* whether to be slave or free. That means both sides will be stampeding to get people in there to try to win a majority vote. And many think there will be those who will lobby for Missouri to get to vote too- since the Compromise is revoked. The extremist factions of both points of view are armed and ready to do whatever it takes, by any means necessary, to see that their side controls the outcome of the elections whenever they might be held."

I sat for a moment, stunned, and then I said, "J-Jesse, that's crazy! W-why it's an open invitation for –for…"

"- Slaughter." Jesse finished grimly. "Yes, it will be.- Neighbor taking up arms against neighbor, outsiders coming in and trying to seize control of certain areas. It will most likely be civil war on a local scale. And who is to say that somehow it won't spread into surrounding states, until the whole of the nation is engulfed. That is an extreme scenario, granted, but it could happen. And Lizzie if one group or the other were to gain strong control at the national level and try to bend all the states to their will... it won't matter who is right and who is wrong. We will simply be a nation engulfed in flames and a fuselage of bullets, where brother will fight brother, and ... and..."

"...and In Rama was there a voice heard, lamentation, and weeping, and great mourning, Rachel weeping for her children, and would not be comforted, because they are not." I quoted softly.

The seconds passed as we sat silent. Finally, I found my voice and said, "Jesse, where can we go? Where is there anywhere safe?"

"That is why Senator Houston came." Jesse said, quietly. "He has a vision, you see. There is a place in the valley of a great river in Texas where there is land for the taking under the new homestead law. He and Senator Benton and others like them want us and others like us to go there, far away from the guns and the drums, and plant a seed. A seed that will grow into a community of men of common belief that can someday help him to see that Texas stays in the Union, and that someday *ALL* of her people are free. He wants us to be one of those seedlings, growing safe in the wilderness – in our case protected and fed by the waters of a great river named by the Spanish almost 300 years ago. It is El Rio de los Brazos de Dios, the River of the Arms of God."

Family Matters   May – December 1854

The next few days passed in a blur, as Jessie and I assisted our parents in getting the word to all of our family households in the Neosho area. The messages called for a family gathering hosted by David and Sarah Nutt at their sprawling farmhouse outside Neosho. The gathering was set for Sunday after church services, so our clan all falling in and heading to the farm for a meal together was unlikely to attract anyone's attention.

Unaccustomed to the need for secrecy, I privately thought it rather silly of my father to emphasize it so much.   But then the weekly newspaper arrived. Jesse's face was grim as he silently handed me the paper when he came home on Friday evening. The featured headline "Kansas-Nebraska Act Passes Congress" was sobering enough but a highlighted quote from Senator Seward sent a chill up my spine, "Come on, then, gentlemen of the slave states. Since there is no escaping your challenge, we accept it in the name of freedom. We will engage in competition for the virgin soil of Kansas, and God give the victory to the side which is stronger in numbers, as it is in right."

"And so it begins," said Jesse, shaking his head.   "Engage in competition! The man cannot possibly be naive enough to truly think it will be a "peaceful" competition, surely? There have already been reports of both pro- and anti-slavery folks being harassed for speaking their minds in town meetings and such in towns on both sides of the border.   A colleague of your father's, who lives in

Springfield said a big bunch of free-staters, as they call themselves, just sent word from Vermont. They are sending settlers by train to St. Louis, and then on to Springfield. They had wealthy sponsors willing to send money for hotel rooms and such and wanted to alert local merchants to have in stock such supplies as they might need, to stock up and head into Kansas to settle." Some of the hotel owners are pro-slavery and don't want to rent to them, while others just want the dollars no matter who they rent to. And the pro-slavery faction is threatening reprisals against the hotels who do rent anti-slave free staters rooms, and against the merchants who sell them goods. He says it's already caused hard feelings and in one case, fisticuffs in – of all places – a prayer meeting."

"It's already beginning then?" I said, putting aside my supper preparations to come sit by him at our little kitchen table. "I never dreamed it would start so soon!" I paused, gathering my thoughts as I sat down. "Jesse, is there time? With my father's practice and both our families' holdings, leaving is going to be a complicated process. How long will that take, and will we be able to leave soon enough? Before it somehow lands on our doorstep? My father is a prominent man. His views on most everything are well known." I ended with a grimace.

"Papa and I tried to have a talk with your father today, about that very thing," said Jesse. "He was well known as being free-state and anti-slavery as a three term state representative. Indeed his views reflected the views of most folks here in Neosho for a long time. But things have changed. Most of the newer folk own slaves, and the numbers have changed. That's part of why he decided not to run again and retired to private life."

"Yes, I knew that," I agreed, "but he still speaks his mind publicly and often."

"Yes, and if we are to have the time we need to put our affairs in good order before we leave," said Jesse, "it is he who is going to have to change. He simply must not engage in ways that draw attention to us from the various factions."

"That is going to be very difficult for him," I said.

"Yes, it is," acknowledged Jesse, "and he knows it. He and Father and I agreed that it will take at least a year and that during that time he will simply have to step back somewhat from his public activities. "

"Well, he is of an age where many men begin to do just that," I said, "so it shouldn't cause much comment."

"But meanwhile," said Jesse, "we have to get the families on board. Most of your lot will probably be in agreement, but some of my older siblings- they have deep roots here, and some have married into pro-slavery families. I don't think any would turn against family, but they may choose to stay."

I nodded. "Oh, Jesse, it's so scary to think of how this could go. With the country I mean. Not to mention right here in Neosho with our own kin, with people we love on different sides of this thing."

Jesse nodded grimly, "My oldest brother, Henry- his wife, Celina's folks have always had slaves on their farm. He thinks we should have them here. My father and he have had words about it many times over the years. If it came to armed conflict here, which it will, I cannot imagine someday facing him...l-looking down the barrel of a gun!" Jesse closed his eyes in pain at the thought, and shook his head, "No! Best we should leave and go elsewhere, agreeing to disagree!"

I squeezed his arm in sympathy, and said, "Surely, we all can agree on that as the best course of action? You would think that any pro-slavery folks would be glad to see free-staters leave."

He nodded, and said, "You would think so, right? But... and this is where it gets crazy... not if they think we are going somewhere with the intention of making another area more likely to be a free-state area someday, which we are. And...., other free-staters in the area are likely to look on it as 'abandoning the just cause' and hold it against us as well."

"But that's...." I shook my head, "crazy!"

"Yes," he agreed, "and my dear, if you are suddenly feeling your world has been turned upside down and wrong side out, join the crowd. Judging by the atmosphere in town today, it is likely to get a whole lot worse before it gets better."

I shook my head, and said, rising from my chair, "There's a frightening thought. Well, as my old Grandpa Shipman used to say, when you need something to bring people together – there is always food! We'll have dinner for the whole family over at Uncle David's place, and see what happens. Meanwhile, I have food here. Shall we have some?"

"Sounds like a good idea, especially if we can have some "coming together" time afterward," he said, with a sudden grin.

My heart lifted as I batted him with the dishtowel as I headed for the stove. "Jesse Nutt, you are incorrigible!" I laughed, thinking this might just turn out to be a very good evening after all.

***** ****** ***** ***** ***** ***** ***** *****

The week passed as through notes and word of mouth we got word to our various family members about the gathering at David and Sarah Nutt's farm after church on Sunday. If anyone asked, we were celebrating the five family birthdays for May, not that I anticipated anyone asking.... But... just in case....

So it was on Sunday, after a particularly rousing set of hymns, and a very appropriate sermon from Brother Farmer about Moses and the

Exodus, that we gathered for Sunday dinner – all forty-three of us – on the lawn of David and Sarah's home. Everyone brought food, and all of our women had a reputation as fine cooks, so the trestle tables groaned with the weight of succulent meats and tasty desserts, and freshly prepared vegetables from spring gardens. The little ones played and chased one another, and squealed with delight when scooped up and hugged close by a grandpa or aunt or uncle. The house was surrounded by huge oak trees, which shaded the lawn, and a breeze kept the early summer heat at bay.

Every one heaped food on plates, and scurried like ants before finally settling on blankets spread across the lawn, in their various family groups. My father and Uncle David crossed to the porch steps, stepped up a couple and waited. Gradually heads turned and talking ceased and all was still. Uncle David, as host, spoke first, "Welcome, our dear children, and family! We are truly blessed to be together as one today. There are important matters we must discuss today with you all. But first, the good Lord has blessed us with a bountiful feast. Let us give thanks to him and enjoy the meal and the great pleasure of company. Afterward, Phoebe Landers and Celina Nutt have volunteered to take the younger children into the house for their naps, while the rest of us consult with one another on matters that affect us all. Abel will you lead us in prayer?"

All heads bowed, as my father's big orator's voice echoed across the yard:

"Dear Lord and Heavenly Father, we come together today as one family to give thanks to Thee for the great blessings Thou hast bestowed upon us. We thank thee for the bounty of our fields and the benevolence you have shown to us in our abundance of family and our love for each other. We give thanks to you for this food- a portion of your great harvest granted to us. We ask that you bless it for the nourishment of our bodies, and we ask that you keep us ever mindful of your Love and Grace towards us. In Jesus name we pray. Amen!"

With our great Amen, Jesse murmured, "And let the feeding begin!" which got him a giggle from two nieces, and a look from his mother. All was great fun as food was consumed, family news and recipes exchanged. As with all such gatherings from time immemorial, the children wolfed down their food, and were soon off to run and play in the nearby creek, while their elders took a more leisurely time, enjoying not only the food but one another's company.

In time the ladies rose, and cleared away the remains of the meal while the gentlemen clustered in bunches divided by age or interest to smoke and talk of crops, local events, and politics. Out of the corner of my eye I watched as Uncle David, my father, and to my surprise, Jesse, moved among the groups, quietly listening- interjecting a remark here or there to steer conversation, getting the lay of the land. I must confess to a swelling of wifely pride as I saw my young husband already growing into the talent for leadership I knew my father hoped to nurture in him.

Distracted for a moment by a crisis involving a roving four year old and a milk pitcher left too close to the edge of a table, when I looked up next it was to see Jesse and Jacob disappearing into the grove of trees beyond the house. My first instinct, as it had been my whole life, was to abandon all and follow them. But things were different now, so I bided my time and sure enough some few minutes later I saw them emerge from the same spot, heads bent together in that way I knew so well, still deep in conversation. We ladies were winding up our chores, and I moved with my mother and Aunt Sarah toward the blanket where we had shared our meal. Jesse and Jacob stopped as they reached the end of the house, and my eyes filled as they started to shake hands, and then pulled each other into a quick embrace before Jesse turned to join our fathers at the porch steps. Blinking rapidly, I dug in my pocket for my handkerchief.

Thankfully neither my mother nor Aunt Sarah noticed my discomfiture, their eyes already busy watching their husbands and

Jesse stride toward the porch steps. Jacob joined my brother Henry, his younger brother Abel and the other half dozen or so young single men between the ages of thirteen and twenty who had their own gathering spot off to one side. My younger sister Phoebe, who was already teaching school at the orphanage in Neosho, was helping Celina herd the dozen younger children aged 3 to 11 into the house for naps and parlor games. She marched the last of her charges in front of her through the front door and closed it behind her.

With the sound of the closing door as their signal, my father and Uncle David mounted the front steps, while Jesse stood to one side and rang Aunt Sarah's dinner bell once to bring everyone's attention. My father began. "Children. I call you that because all of you belong to my dear friend David and me in one way or another. We are- all of us here – family. During this past week David and I, along with young Jesse here, and a few others, met with two great men who came to us with important news.- Tidings that will have a bearing on the lives of every person here for many years to come. As we, as a family and as individuals, make decisions about these matters going forward, we will – more than ever – need the help and guidance of Him who made us. With that in mind, I have asked young Jesse here to lead us in prayer."

Jesse stepped forward to stand on the first step in front of both our fathers, and said, in a clear voice that carried easily over the yard,

"Heavenly Father, you have blessed us to be born citizens of a great nation. But we are living in times where we see that nation and her people being torn asunder by great divisions of conscience. Those divisions are so deep and so awful that they threaten to turn neighbor against neighbor and even brother against brother in a searing flame of hatred that has the capacity to destroy entire communities and leave utter desolation and despair in its wake. Father today we are met to talk of the course we, as a family, will take in the face of this great calamity. We ask you, Our Great Shepherd, for your clear and

45

perfect guidance for us, your imperfect sheep. We ask that you lead us to wise choices for ourselves and for our families. We ask you to show us what you would have us do in the world. We ask that you keep us safe in your everlasting arms. And finally, Lord, we ask that you bring us through these times ever faithful in our witness to your great Love for us and for all mankind. We ask this in the name of our Savior, Jesus the Christ. Amen."

There was a stunned and very subdued quality to the Amen this time, and all eyes were fixed on my father as he began to speak. He described the situation both as Senators Houston and Benton had laid it out, and also told what he and Jesse were already seeing in the reports from all over the state that were coming into his office in Neosho. Jesse stepped forward to personally describe the situation shared by his friend from Springfield, and Uncle David described the unheard of happening of an argument that degenerated into fisticuffs after the Masonic lodge meeting in Neosho just two nights ago. Other men present, grown and young both, told of incidents witnessed or heard of in recent days from friends in neighboring towns.

My oldest brother Christopher's wife Mary told of a group of ruffians who came to her front door wanting water for their horses, obviously intoxicated, talking of going to fight for freedom in Kansas. Freedom for who was not specifically mentioned, she added. Upon further questioning, she admitted that she had been very frightened indeed, as some had made ribald remarks regarding her person. By the end of this testimony, my father had extracted a description of the men, and their horses, and every man present wore a look of grim determination.

As if this was not enough, Jacob spoke up to report of harassment of some of the free blacks who worked for the Neosho Baptist Orphanage. These workers lived in Neosho, and worked at the orphanage which was at the edge of town. Their persons had been threatened and their homes vandalized on more than one occasion in recent months.

"So, my children, you can see the time of trial is already begun," said my father. "I will tell you that David and I have already decided that this opportunity is one we must seek. Even if all was well here, this would be a once in a lifetime opportunity to be in on the start of building a permanent and lasting legacy for our families in a brand new place. But given the circumstances, we see no better option for our families but to go. Now some of you older children have ties here. - Jobs and families and in-laws and so on. We want each of you to carefully consider, and to do what is right for you and yours. We love each and every one of you no matter what you decide. You do not have to decide now, or even within the next few days and weeks.

Amon Bond has left this past week with his family and a few other hardy souls, to blaze a trail for us. They will be possibly the first white settlers to reach the land Senator Houston has recommended to us. Amon will be back in the fall to report to us. Each of you will have the opportunity to visit with him and hear that report. Those of you who decide to go should do so by the end of this year. Our plan at this time is to travel to Texas in the early spring of next year. If you are going you must have your affairs in order, your land sold, and so on.

Meanwhile, we must cope with the situation here as best we can. My recommendation to you is live quietly, make arrangements to watch out for each other. Do not travel alone. And under no circumstances is any woman to be left alone on a home place without at least one able bodied husband, brother, cousin, or father there for her protection. We will not have what might have happened to Mary happen to any of our womenfolk. Is that clear? We will work together to rotate field work, and the women can also arrange to go visit while you are away. Stay in touch with each other, and do not hesitate to let me know if you are in any kind of difficulty. Pride has no place in family, and if you need funds for more hired help or to buy needed items they will be there.

Now, last, and importantly, we must not discuss this outside the family. At least not until the decisions are made. And in every situation, avoid if you can, taking sides. Whatever your personal convictions on slavery, the Union, politics, and so forth, be friendly to all but confidants of none. If Amon's report is favorable, barring unforeseen disaster we have a year here, no more. Stay alert, stay together, and stay safe. And pray for our state and our nation. Now, questions?"

There were surprisingly few questions, and some that could not be answered until Amon's return. But, there was a sense, as we hugged and said goodbye that evening, that for most of us the dye was cast. We were going to Texas and our lives would change forever. Little did we know that change was coming much sooner than next spring - coming tragic and unexpected, - and very definitely forever.

  ***** ****** ***** ***** ***** ***** ***** *****

"Jesse," I said, as we were walking from David and Sarah's house to our cottage later that evening, "forgive me if I am being nosy, but, what did you and Jacob talk about?"

He grunted, "I was wondering if you were going ask."

"I'm sorry," I began, but he cut me off with a squeeze to the hand.

"It's all right," he said. "It was – a good conversation, and one we needed to have. He wanted to know what was going on. That didn't take long, as I told him he'd have to wait like everyone else. No way was I going to get on the fathers' bad sides by letting the cat out of the bag early. Then he wanted to know about my job with Abel and what my plans were there. He was excited for me that I am reading to be a lawyer. But mostly, Lizzie, he wanted to know – how it is with us- if

48

we are happy and well. He apologized to me Lizzie, for n-not being able to stop loving you. He said he hopes to find a cure in time, but meanwhile he hopes we understand why he isn't around much. I told him it was all right, that God knows I can understand someone loving you Lizzie! I cannot even think about how I would feel if you had chosen differently!"

"Oh, Jesse, it just breaks my heart to come between the two of you! Do you think avoidance is the answer? I almost followed you today. I've been with you two for so much of my life- it seemed so strange for you all to go off and me not be tagging along." I smiled sheepishly.

He stopped in the middle of the path, and turned me to look at him, "Sweetheart, I know what you mean, and sometimes I feel the same way. But Elizabeth you must understand that there is a difference, and we must respect that difference. What Jacob feels for you is real, as real as what I feel. And for the three of us to put him in the position of constantly having to battle with that I fear would just lead to tragedy for us all. So, give this thing some time. My hope is that maybe if Jacob goes to St. Louis and studies medicine, he will meet someone. If that were to happen, then perhaps later on they can join us in Texas.   God knows I am sure we will have need of doctors there."

"Well, I am glad you had a chance to talk, and it looked like you parted on good terms." I said. "Your relationship with each other is what I worry about"

"We'll be all right, Lizzie," said Jacob, "We understand one another, my brother and I. And I will say this." He smiled at me tenderly, in the fading light, "We both have excellent taste! We both fell in love with the most wonderful woman in the world!" With that proclamation, his lips met mine, and we were somewhat delayed in finding our way home.

     *****   ******   *****   *****   *****   *****   *****   *****

There was a knock at the door, and Jesse looked up from the brief he was copying to see Abel Landers' secretary, Tad Jenkins standing at the door of the tiny private office his father-in- law had installed him in a few weeks ago. The receptionist/secretary now employed by Abel Landers to handle the Law Office visitors and correspondence was apologetic. "Pardon the interruption sir, but your father is here to see you."

Jesse rose as he said, "My father? Well, certainly Jenkins, show him in." He stepped around the desk to greet his father with a firm handshake as he entered. "Papa! Welcome! Come in and have a seat! To what do I owe this pleasure?"

David Nutt returned his son's handshake warmly, and settled himself into a nearby chair, as he explained, "Well, Jesse, I've a legal matter to discuss, and it involves family, so I've come to you."

"A legal matter? Papa are you sure you want me and not Uncle Abel?" said Jesse, feeling compelled to honesty. "I'm still very much new at this and learning."

"If you feel a need to consult with Abel, then you certainly have my permission to do so. He has handled most matters for me in the past." said David, amiably. "But because this involves an agreement between myself and your brother Henry, I thought I would come to you to oversee the matter."

"All right," said Jesse, a small warning bell going off in his head- David Nutt and his oldest son had what could best be described as a tempestuous relationship. "Go on. What kind of agreement are we talking about?"

"Well," said David, "as you know, Henry and I have shared the running of the farm these last several years with you younger boys helping out more over time, as you got older. Then in the last couple of years, you and Jacob have helped less, as you began to pursue other things. Daniel and Abel are finally old enough to be of real help, but the truth

50

is son, I am not as young as I once was. The smithy takes all my time and energy. I've simply nothing left to work the farm, even part time. Henry has offered to take over the running of the farm in exchange for he, Celina, and their children living with us on the place, and a one-quarter share of the profits."

"Well, I can certainly draw up an agreement to that effect," said Jesse, "if that is what you want. For both your protection and Henry's, I'd like to include some details you didn't mention. For example, is he to be autonomous in decision making? That means does he have to get your approval before hiring a new worker, or buying equipment, that sort of thing. And how do you keep track of the money? Will money from sale of crops go to you or him? Who pays who? What kind of report does he have to present to show you what he is doing… and so on? Give me a moment. We have some similar contracts we have drawn for other farmers in the area. Let me pull one, and we can use it to draw from."

Two hours later, they had an outline of an agreement: For the aforementioned ¼ of the profits and room and board for himself and his family, Henry would run the farm. He would present written quarterly reports with documented listings of income and expenses. Those reports would be reviewed by David, Jesse, and Jacob. Henry was required to come to David before encumbering any debt or spending more than $25 on a single item. All laborers must be free men, and their number and pay must be approved beforehand by David.

"Make no mistake," said David, "Henry and I have been round and round about this. I'll not have slaves working that land as long as Sarah and I own it. That land was paid for with her dower money, and she feels even more strongly than I do about the morality of the slavery issue! Now Celina and her folks, they are big pro-slavers, and they have worked hard on Henry to bring him 'round to their way of thinking. Both he and that wife of his think nothing at all is wrong with owning other human beings. I swear, Jesse, if I could figure out a way to do this differently, I would!"

"Well, Papa, maybe you and Mama should reconsider doing this. Certainly with them feeling as they do, living together will not be very pleasant for anyone," Jesse said, wondering just what it was his father wasn't telling him.

The mystery was solved a moment later when David Nutt said, "Well, Jesse, I don't think we have much choice. As you know, Henry has been working up on the old Ellis family place keeping it up for them since old Mr. Ellis died last year. They've been living up there as part of their pay and thinking they might get a chance to lease the place. Well, James Ellis has suddenly decided he wants it for himself and has given Henry and Celina thirty days to get out. I told Henry not to take that deal to begin with. The Ellises change their minds with the weather- the whole lot of'em."

"What about Celina's father?" asked Jesse. "He's got a big property, as I recall, and a couple of cottages on it, - in addition to his slave quarters." Jesse trailed off dubiously.

"To be honest Jesse," said his father pensively, "part of it is that I know in my heart that if they ever go there, Henry and those children will be lost to us forever. The other part is that even though Henry has fallen in with their way of thinking, I just can't bear the thought of my grandchildren being brought up to think owning their fellow human beings as property is acceptable. At least if they're with us, your mother and I get a chance to give them an example to follow."

"And what about Texas?" asked Jesse.

"Oh, your mother and I are determined to go. The farm here is only forty acres, and that should bring around five hundred dollars. For that same money, in Texas, we can get over 300 acres of good rich river bottom land. Enough to carve a legacy for all of us who go," said David.

"And if you are going to sell the farm, where does that leave Henry a year or two from now? You are surely not thinking he will choose Texas?" asked Jesse.

"Oh, no," said David, "not at all. It is my intention to sell the farm to him if we all go. See, he is sitting on $350 of dower money from Celina. If he works hard over the next year or two, with few expenses, he can buy the farm from your mother and me, and once we are gone, I suppose will run slaves on it or not, as he chooses. But it will be his land then, not ours."

Jesse nodded, at last understanding his father's logic. "All right, Papa, I will draw this up. I will have to run it by Abel, as he will be the attorney of record. But I don't foresee any problem. You and Henry come by on Wednesday, and we will get everything signed and agreed. I will have Jacob here to witness along with Jenkins."

David Nutt rose, and held out his hand. "Jesse, I thank you son. And I want you to know, I'm proud of what you're doing here."

"Thank you, Papa," said Jesse solemnly, "That means a lot. Give Mama my love."

   *****   ******   *****   *****   *****   *****   *****   *****

Henry and David Nutt signed their agreement at the end of July and by the middle of August Henry and Celina and their three small children were living in the big white farmhouse with Mama and Papa Nutt. Amon Bond came back in the late September. He slipped into town quietly and rather than attract attention with a gathering in town, we once again adjourned to the Nutt family farm. Amon brought back glowing descriptions of green and fertile land with good water and plentiful game. There were a few white folk beginning to come in. A trading post was already thriving about 15 miles away. The Indians were still a problem in the area, but increased trade helped, and the new army presence only a few days away at Fort Worth was making an impact as well. Hand drawn maps were spread out and plans formulated. Amon left for his Texas home with promises to return in the spring. We would be ready was the assurance we sent with him.

Christmas was approaching and even though it had been a horrific summer and fall all along the Kansas border, for the most part the troubles in Neosho had been minor-, more incidents of unruly persons passing through, an occasional public argument turned fight, and a couple of minor fires set in the area down by the river where the river boats docked to unload supplies and arms. Christmas carols were being practiced and secret gifts being bought. I was in a tizzy trying to finish the new sets of monogramed handkerchiefs I was making for Jesse.

Jesse was busy working with my father by day and in the final throes of studying law books at night. Every day my father expected another set of questions answered on his assigned readings. Jesse laughingly said he was beginning to dream of case numbers and precedents, and many nights ended with me massaging his poor right hand, cramping from holding a quill for so many hours.

We were so happy those wonderful final days of the fall of 1854. In spite of the turmoil around us, Jesse and I always found a haven in each other. Late at night we lay in the bed in our little cottage and talked of Texas. We planned our house, his law office in the center of the town, and even talked of names for the children we hoped would come.

Over those fall months things grew easier between Jesse and Jacob as well. Jacob even joined us for dinner a few times, and it was a poignant reminder of days gone by as we all discussed our plans. Jacob continued his preparations to leave for St. Louis after the first of the year. He planned to start medical school finally, and if war came he was determined to serve as a doctor for the Union army. He hoped over time to continue his focus of helping the poor and needy and most particularly orphaned children. He was much in touch with his mentor, Dr. Reginald Harding, and in addition to his volunteer work at the orphanage, he was working for pay at any odd jobs he could get to save money for his travel to St. Louis in the spring.

Finally, Christmas week was upon us, and on the night of December 22nd I put the last stitch in the last of the set of six monogrammed handkerchiefs I was making for Jesse, and folded them into a brightly decorated box and tied it with a red ribbon. I hid the package away in the kitchen cupboard and checked the stew cooking over the fire. The sun was low in the winter sky, and a north wind was blowing in, bringing with it a bitter cold. I sat down by the fire, and took up the days mending, eager to get in the stitches in before it got too dark, and looking forward to when Jesse got home.

Through the Fire -December 1854

Jesse Nutt looked up at the sound of raised voices outside his office. Tad Jenkins was in obvious distress. "Sir, you cannot just go in there without an appointment!"

A hoarse voice rose amid sounds of a physical altercation. "He's my brother! I don't need an appointment!"

Jesse rose quickly, and pulled open the door, and stared appalled at the sight of his brother Jacob standing in the small lobby, his entire body covered in soot, his hair on end, and his fist upraised. "Jacob!" he snapped, "What on earth is this about?"

Jacob whirled to face him and, upon seeing him, visibly sagged in relief. Jesse leapt forward to support his brother, grabbing a black covered arm, and said, "Jacob, here man, come sit down!" He led him to one of the padded leather chairs in front of his desk. "Jenkins!" he shouted, "Get some water, and a shot of whisky!"

Jacob sagged into the chair, but immediately tried to rise, saying "Jesse, please, you have to come! We must go! There's not much time!"

"Take it easy," said Jesse, kneeling beside him. He grabbed the glass offered by Jenkins, and handed it to Jacob. With an exclamation, he reached out to steady Jacob's shaking hand as he raised the water to his lips. After a moment, he took the glass from Jacob and exchanged it for one containing two fingers of whisky- neat. "Sip it," he admonished, "and tell me what has happened."

"They've set a fire," said Jacob, his voice still rough, "up along the north bend. It's taken out several buildings- mostly red houses and dock workers housing." He paused to cough. "And there are the- the 'working' women, and – and their children, -T-there was already an epidemic of illness at one of the houses that Dr. Harding was trying to treat, and now th- those poor souls are just lying in the street, w-with burns and w-worse! The fire brigade is trying to contain the fire, but n-no o-one will help us move t-those poor souls! Dr. Harding and Brother Farmer are trying, but we've only the one wagon, a-and the fire is coming." He raised his eyes to meet his brother's. "They sent me for help. All I could think was to c-come to you!" His voice caught, and Jesse grabbed his hand.

"You did right, brother," he said, squeezing Jacob's filthy and bruised hand. "I wish there were more time. The cousins would all help." At Jacob's sound of protest, he said, "I know, I know. Come," he said helping Jacob to his feet, "Papa Abel keeps a wagon at the livery on the corner. Let's go!"

Ten minutes later the two brothers were moving through the streets toward the orange glow to the north. The afternoon sky was dark with smoke, and they had tied their handkerchiefs across their faces to make breathing easier. The streets were jammed with people and horses and vehicles of all kinds, headed south, fleeing the fire. After what seemed an eternity of going against the flow, they turned a corner into an open street. The fire was in view now, and they could feel the first of its heat even three blocks away. Between them and the inferno stretched the straight line of Dock St. and a block away, through the haze, Jesse could see the bodies laid out on the hard packed dirt. A lone wagon and team waited nearby, two young boys clutched determinedly at the harnesses of the skittish horses. Two men moved quickly carrying limp forms and placing them in the wagon bed.

Jesse struggled for control as the team he was driving balked at going closer to the roaring flames. Jacob jumped down, grabbed the harness of the lead horse, and moved determinedly down the street. Moments later he and Jesse were on the ground. "Toby!" Jacob shouted, to be heard over the roar of the fire, "Come hold the horses!" As soon as the boy got a firm grip, he and Jesse moved toward the nearest row of bodies. Sweat was already pouring down Jesse's back. He had shed his coat on the way, and he threw it in the wagon bed as he trotted by.

Dr. Harding met them in the road, and shouted to Jacob, "The children! We've got to try to get them out first! The wind has shifted and there's not much time! Grab as many little ones as you can, and go! We will meet you at the orphanage! It should be safe there. The creek off Main should protect us, even if the fire spreads to downtown! Then you can come back for the last of them!"

Jacob clutched the older man's hand briefly in farewell, and the four fell to loading the tiny bodies into the wagons. Jesse reached for the nearest bundle of blackened rags, and at his touch it became the body of a frail, tiny toddler, who whimpered in fear. The child began to scream in pain, as Jesse carried it as gently as he could to the wagon, all the while feeling the bones in one of the little legs shift with every step.

The next hour blurred into haze of tiny burdens, mostly babies under five years of age, all covered in black soot and rags, many near death or already gone with horrific burns. On the second trip back there were only six tiny bodies left forlorn in the superheated smoke filled street. Even worse than the ones before, these were not only burned, but also already deathly ill before the fire ever came. Skin and bones, their eyes and faces covered with sores, they were obviously in an awful state. Jesse and Jacob looked at one another in horror, eyes wide and white rimmed in blackened faces.

Jacob reached for the nearest child, and Jesse exclaimed, "Jacob, NO!" as loudly as his smoke clogged throat would allow. But he was too late. His brother cradled the small limp bundle against his chest, tears streaking the black of his face in the orange glow of the fire.

Jacob stood, looked at Jesse, and shouted back over the roar. "We have to try!" He sprinted away toward the wagon, as Jesse reached for the next tiny soul entrusted to his care.

Two hours later, as a smoke dimmed sun sank below the horizon, the inky black of night descended quickly on the streets of Neosho, broken only by the light of the fire still burning at the northern end of town. A lone wagon made its way slowly through the deserted business district. Jesse and Jacob Nutt sat next to each other on the wagon seat, leaning against one another for support. "Where should we go?" whispered Jacob, his voice a charred thread of sound. "We can't go back to the livery. This wagon has to be burned."

Jesse nodded, "We'd never make it all the way out to home. The horses are shot, we've no lantern, and there's no moon for the smoke." His voice was as cracked as his brother's and he ended this sentence with a spasm of coughing. After a few minutes of silence broken only by the slow clop of the horses' hooves, he said, "We'll have to go to Uncle Abel. He will know what to do about the wagon, and in that big house maybe we can stay – what's the word you and Dr. Harding used? – quarantined? – until we see what is going to happen..."

Jacob nodded weary agreement, and they turned the horses at the next corner toward the sanctuary of their uncle's home.

As the wagon rattled to a stop in front of Abel Lander's stables behind the sprawling white frame house, Thomas, the orphan Abel had hired as stable boy, appeared at stable doorway, armed with a pitchfork and a lantern.   As the light fell on the two blackened figures on the wagon seat, the boy drew back in fear and looked wildly toward the house. "Thomas, it's alright," said Jesse, straining his hoarse voice to speak above a whisper. "It's me and Mr. Jacob."

"Mr. Jesse?" queried the boy, incredulously, lifting the lantern higher, and stepping toward the wagon.

At Jacob's movement of alarm, Jesse barked hoarsely, "Stop! Don't come any closer!"

Confused, the boy froze in mid-stride and almost dropped the lantern.

"Thomas, I need you to go get Mr. Landers," croaked Jesse. "Tell him there's been a fire uptown and that Jacob and I are here and need his help."

"Yes, sir, Mr. Jesse," said the boy, nodding vigorously. He ran toward the house, pitchfork and lantern still in his hands.

In darkness once again, Jacob coughed deeply, and then said breathlessly, "We need to get down. If we don't move soon, we won't be able to."

"Stay put till Abel comes," said Jesse, tersely, "Harder for them to touch us that way."

Jacob nodded, then realizing his brother couldn't see him in the darkness, he agreed, "Good idea." His voice was just about gone.

Lights appeared in the windows at the rear of the house, the service entrance opened, and Abel Landers came striding toward the stables, lantern now held high. Lizzie's brother Henry and the boy Thomas followed closely, two more lanterns glowing brightly in their hands.

"Jesse?" Abel called, peering into the darkness. "Jacob?"

"We're here, uncle," said Jesse hoarsely, "Stop. Don't come closer yet."

60

"What is it, son?" he demanded, "Is someone injured?" He started toward the wagon bed.

"No! Don't touch the wagon, Uncle!" Jacob shouted, his voice cracking like shattered glass.

Abel Landers turned toward the sound, and raising the lantern high, he visibly flinched as the light finally found their blackened forms, and bounced off the whites of their eyes. "My God, lads! Are you burned!?" he said in horror.

"No, uncle," said Jacob, "we only breathed much hot smoke, so our throats and lungs are very sore. But Uncle, we were rescuing children from the wretched red houses near the docks. Many were badly burned, but they were also….diseased. It is very dangerous. The wagon must be burned where it stands. No one must touch it."

Jacob succumbed then to a fit of deep coughing, so Jesse continued, urgently. "We will strip and our clothes must be burned with the wagon. And the tack we have touched too. We've tried not to go near the horses."

Abel Landers nodded, and took charge. "Henry, go rouse the other servants and tell them to bring both hip baths out here. Tell Cook to start the water boiling and Thomas you fetch the buckets. We must get you boys clean and cared for, and then, never fear-, we will deal with the rest." He turned for a moment to see that his orders were being carried out, then asked Jacob, "Do I need to send for Dr. Harding?"

Jacob shook his head. "He was there, helping with the children. He will know to check here next. He said he would come when he can."

Abel Landers, unaccustomed to being anyone's second priority, digested that for a moment, then nodded, saying, "Well, the man's only human. That will have to do."

"Jesse, we've got to move *now*. My legs and shoulders are starting to cramp." Jacob rasped.

As Jesse pushed himself to his feet, his calves screamed, his head swam, and bright spots appeared before his eyes. Grabbing the back of the wagon seat for support he waited for the worst to pass, and then slowly planted a foot atop the front wheel rim, and lowered himself to the ground. He stood clutching the side of the wagon for support as Jacob followed the same steps on the other side. He and Jacob spent the next agonizing hour going through the necessary steps to get clean themselves and protect the others.

They met at the back of the wagon and helped each other strip to the skin, tossing what was left of the clothes they wore into the wagon bed to await the fire. Then Jacob called for two bottles of whiskey, and literally washed both himself and his brother in the stuff. He concentrated on their hands and faces using a soft cloth drenched in the strong liquid. Abel Landers was horrified at what he declared a waste of good liquor, but was mollified slightly when Jesse and Jacob both took several hardy swallows of the stuff as well. At last the baths were ready and each brother lowered himself into the mixed blessing of gloriously hot water and the sting of lye soap.

In the end, they at last allowed the other men to tend them, Abel and Henry enfolding them in dry soft towels with hands as gentle as any woman's, and supporting them as they staggered on rubbery legs to the two bedrooms that had been prepared for them. Jacob kept trying to give more instructions, but Abel said gruffly, "Hush, son. You've both done your best, and it's been a sight more than any but the best men I know. I'm proud of you both. Now rest yourself."

Jesse rallied one last time as his Uncle stopped at his doorway with the same admonishment. "Lizzie... Tell Lizzie..."

"You can tell her yourself son," said Abel in a choked voice, "I promise she'll be here when you wake up in the morning."

He pulled the door gently shut behind him, head bowed in thought, when a voice at the end of the hall brought him up short. "Abel? Henry? What's wrong?" asked Sally Landers in a hushed voice. Coming toward them, tying the ribbon of her robe, she continued. "Is someone taken ill?" She had heard voices and had already checked to find her younger children sound asleep in their beds.

"It's Jesse and Jacob," said Abel. "Walk with us, and I will explain. But we must go fetch Elizabeth, and the boys' parents. You will need to keep watch on them while we are gone." In spite of the cold night air, Sally followed her husband and son and listened intently to the story as they saddled their horses, and prepared to depart. "Be cautious, Sally. Until we know… don't you or anyone else touch them any more than needs be. And use lye soap on your hands if you do."

"I have nursed people before, Abel," she reminded him, not unkindly.

"Not like this, you haven't Sally. If this goes badly, it will be as bad as anything you or I have ever seen," said Abel grimly. "We must pray, Sally. Pray hard!"

"I will," she promised, eyes moist. "Now, go. And tell Leatha and Sarah I will keep good watch on the boys until they can do so themselves." Her husband and son both embraced her quickly, and Abel took her hand and kissed her knuckles gently, and they were gone.

***** ****** ***** ***** ***** ***** ***** *****

I sat in the rocking chair by the fireplace waiting. Something was wrong. In over eighteen months of marriage Jesse had never once been this late coming home without sending word. The mending lay idle in my lap, and I tried yet again to talk myself out of the large cold crystal of fear that had settled in the pit of my stomach.

The sound of pounding hooves sounded outside, and heavy steps trod up the steps to the porch. I was up and to the door an eternity before I heard my father's voice on the other side. "Eliza- beth," he called, the word breaking when I flung the door open before he could knock.

"Where is he?" I said, looking past my father for my husband, and seeing only Henry there instead. The clump of ice turned to jagged shards, and I clutched at my father's arms, saying again, "Where is he? What's happened?"

"He is alive, daughter, and when I left him, exhausted, but not badly injured." Papa reassured me quickly.

Relief washed over me. "Thank you, God." I breathed. Then I became conscious of my father's stillness, and Henry's silence. "There's something else, isn't there?" I breathed in deeply. "Tell me."

And when they did tell me- all of it – my heart broke with pride in these two strong, compassionate men I loved so deeply, and quailed in fear at the prospect before us all. "Papa and Mama Nutt- do they know?" I asked.

My father shook his head. "We came here first. Get your things. Henry will saddle your horse, and we will ride to their place together."

The next two hours passed in a blur. - The hard quick ride through the fields to the big Nutt farmhouse. - The crowd of generations, come to huddle in the cold front doorway as Papa again described Jesse and Jacob's courage, and the horrible price they might pay. All were exhorted to prayer, and loving hands made quick work in getting Mama Sarah and Papa David outfitted for the journey. The night had turned bitter cold, and the skies were starting to spit snow as we turned our horses toward Neosho, and the unknown future that awaited us.

The snow was coming down in force, and the hall clock showed 3 a.m. when we all stumbled into the front hall of the Landers house. My mother came to meet us, followed by Cook with a tray of cups filled with strong, hot coffee. As we all drank deeply, my mother broke the news. "Dr. Harding just arrived about twenty minutes ago. He is checking them now. They both started running a fever about an hour ago. Of course they both breathed so much smoke and got so hot, and then so cold... It could pass..."

"I want to see Jesse," I said, setting down my coffee.

"Dr. Harding implored me to let him do his job," said Mama. "He said he would come speak to us as soon as he has done his assessment."

"Well, surely he doesn't mean we can't see our boys," said Mama Sarah.

David Nutt was normally a taciturn man, but his voice was gentle as he said, "Sarah, we must wait a bit. The doctor doesn't need our presence to distract him from his duties."

Footsteps sounded on the stairs, forestalling further discussion. A wan and gray Reginald Harding entered the room. The look on his face told us all we needed to know. "Mrs. Landers, I see your family has arrived." He said, making an attempt at the courtesies.

Introductions were quickly made, and David Nutt spoke for us all when he commanded, "So Doctor, tell us about my sons."

Reginald Harding inhaled deeply, ended by coughing harshly, and I was reminded that he too had spent his day in the smoke and the heat and the cold, fighting for lives he could not save. The lines on his face were deep, and he seemed to think a moment before giving a reply. "First of all, sir, let me begin by saying that you have raised two fine young men there. Their courage and bravery and the gentleness with which they ministered to the most desperate among us today were truly the actions of the finest of Christian men." He paused, gathering his thoughts, and continued, "I will not lie to you. I am told you know of the risk they took. Of the danger they exposed themselves to. I am very much afraid they have both been infected. The particular scourge suffered by the poor children they rescued often results in very high fever, pneumonia type symptoms, and in a couple of days the development of infectious lesions or sores around the face and in the eyes and eye socket. It is life-threatening on several counts, the lesions are extraordinarily painful, and often the vision is affected drastically and permanently." The chasm of horror his words opened up stunned us to silence. After a moment he went on. "There is a possibility- I feel it is very slim- that the sudden onset of high fever and congestion they are both experiencing could be a result of the smoke inhalation, and the exertions of the day. If so, they are both strong, healthy young men, and should show marked improvement and indeed full recovery in a day or two. However, the degree of fever, and the fact that their eyes are already showing unusual sensitivity to light lead me to prepare you for the worst." He paused a moment, and said, "You must know, I am so terribly sorry."

Attempting to step back from the abyss, I struggled to form a question. "Doctor, what can we do?"

"A practical question, to be sure, Mrs. Nutt," he said, appreciatively. "First of all, I cannot emphasize strongly enough how contagious this can be – even taking the proper care. Mrs. Landers has graciously offered me accommodation on the premises, so I shall remain here as much as possible over the next few weeks. I have sent to Springfield for a colleague to come work with Brother Forester at the orphanage, and he should arrive tomorrow. We must limit contact with the patients to as few persons as possible. If you will forgive my presumption, I would suggest that since Mr. Landers has essential public duties that necessitate his attention, you sir should not be involved in direct care of either gentleman. I understand that Mr. David Nutt has sons who can run his farm for a time and women folk at the farm who can care for the young children. So I would suggest that the younger children from this household be sent there, and that

66

Mr. and Mrs. Nutt senior assist me with the care of their son Jacob. Young Mrs. Nutt and her mother can assist me with the care of Mr. Jesse Nutt. Young Mr. Landers here can act as a messenger between the households, and run errands as need be. He can also assist with his cousins' care if one of you is unable at some point."

He turned to my mother and said, "How many servants do you have on the premises ma'am?"

"Why, four – Cook, the stable boy Thomas, John our hired man, and Callie, our girl of all work," my mother replied.

The Doctor nodded. "They should stay and perform their duties as usual, with two exceptions. They are not, under any circumstances to enter the sickrooms. Nor are they to wash or handle any items used there except under my direct supervision."

My father nodded purposefully and said, "We will see to it."

"Both patients are sleeping now, but they have been left alone long enough. Why don't you four who will be giving the care come up with me now, and we will work out shifts and procedures to follow."

My mother, the Nutts and I rose to go after him. As we climbed the stairs I wondered if the others felt as numb as I did. I tried to gather my thoughts, and to prepare myself for the sight of my husband, but all I could feel was a sense of unreality, with sharp moments of mindless panic lurking around the edges. As we walked down the hall, my mother took my hand in hers. Never missing a step, she squeezed my fingers and said softly, "I'm right here Elizabeth. My darling girl, I'm right here."

Heartened, I placed my hand on the door knob of my old bedroom, and went to take care of my husband.

***** ****** ***** ***** ***** ***** ***** *****

Three weeks later I walked down that same hallway to that same doorway. It had been another long night, and I was vaguely aware that the dawn was coming. As I opened the door of Jesse's sickroom the bright pure light of the morning sun chose that moment to shine brightly through the open window and fall- on an empty bed. Panic washed over me in the few seconds it took me to see him, sitting sprawled on the floor, leaning limply against the wall beneath the window, one hand pawing weakly at the bottom of the window sill. "My God, Jesse!" I cried, moving quickly to kneel at his side, feeling his face frantically for the heat of returned fever. "What is it? What are you doing out of bed?" His face was wet, and for one horrible moment I thought the puss and drainage had come back. But the liquid sparkled clear on his pale checks in the sunlight, and I realized it was tears. "Oh, sweetheart, what is it?"

He grabbed my hand with surprising strength, and pulled me down to him. I went gladly, enfolding him in an embrace as he collapsed against me. His voice was a choked, breathless gasp, as he pleaded, "Oh, Lizzie, you've got to help me!" The last word caught in a sob.

I pulled him tighter against me, one hand clutching his head to my breast, my fingers caught in the waves of dark hair. "Oh, my love, my dearest, I am right here. "

He turned again, groping for the window, "Lizzie," he wheezed, begging, "Help me, up. I w-want .....t-the sunrise! Just o-one last time....." Frantically, he clutched at the window sill, as somehow I got to my feet, sobbing, and got my arms under his and around his chest and pulled up with all my strength. Somehow I got him standing for the brief second it took to grab a nearby straight chair and get it under him just as his legs gave way. He leaned against the window, sobs slowly subsiding, while I knelt beside him, clutching his hand as I struggled to watch his face through a veil of tears. Finally our breathing quieted, and as the white brightness of the morning sun warmed the room, Jesse stirred. He said quietly, "It's mostly gone now.

68

Only shapes and shadows left. Only with very bright light, like there is now can I see any detail at all. Dr. Harding says that in another day, maybe two, even that will go." He turned then, and looked at me, and said, "Lizzie, come stand by the window- with the sunlight on your face. I-I need to s-see you – this one last time." Wordlessly, I prayed for strength as I got up and moved past him into the full glow of the morning sun. He turned, his back to window, clutching the back of the chair for support, his eyes, once they found me, never leaving my face. "Oh, Lizzie," he whispered, "how will I bear it?" He reached a hand out to brush my check. "How will I live without seeing your sweet face?"

Unable to speak, I gently took his hand in mine, and kissed it, and held it, as my heart shattered, broken by his love and his pain. "Oh, God," I prayed silently, "Give me the words…." Eyes locked with his one final time, I said, honestly, "I don't know Jesse. I don't know how. And I don't know why either. All I know for certain is that we love each other, and we promised God to always be there for each other, come what may. And my joy in you and yours in me is not limited by sight or sound or any other earthly thing. We will find our way back to joy by simply being there for each other. Our hearts are broken right now, but God will mend them with love. I know he will."

"Lizzie," he whispered, "Come here, beside me." Summoning his strength, he lowered himself from the chair back onto the floor. We ended up leaning side by side against the wall. We sat close, our arms about each other, "I love you, Lizzie Nutt." He breathed against my hair.

"I love you, too, Jesse," I whispered back. But he was already asleep.

Exhaustion overtook me, and I slept too. I woke briefly, foggily aware that strong arms picked me up, and then the softness of a down mattress enveloped me and I slept once again.

I awakened sometime later, with no idea if it was day or night. I was in my shift, and my work-a-day dress, my stays, and other garments and shoes were neatly set and folded on the dresser near the bed, and the fire glowed cozily as if someone had just tended it. I glanced toward the window. No light showed around the edges of the neatly drawn drapes. Night then. I had slept through the day. And no wonder. It had been almost a month since Jacob and Jesse had driven into the stable yard out back. For more than twenty horrific days I had hardly left Jesse's sickroom, seizing a few minutes of half waking sleep now and again in the chair or in a pallet on the floor. Panic seized me, and I threw off the covers. What if he had wakened? I had promised him I would be there always! My bare feet hit the cold floor, and conscious of the hour, I once again walked rapidly and silently down the hall toward Jesse's room. Dr. Harding came out of Jesse's room, closing the door behind him. I must have made some sound of alarm, because he looked up startled. Seeing me, he hastened toward me, smiling as he came. "It is alright, my dear. He is sleeping well. I was here anyway, and thought I would check in."

Once again relief surged through me , and I said, "Oh, thank you, doctor! When I saw you- at this time of night, well I was afraid."

"Completely understandable my dear," he said kindly. "And I am glad to see you getting some much deserved rest as well."

I nodded and stopped as his presence and the probable reason for it punctured my mental fog. "Is it Jacob, then?" I asked. "Is he worse?"

Dr. Harding nodded. "Although his eyes do not appear to be as badly affected as Jesse's, he is having a much harder time shaking the fever." He shook his head regretfully, "I fear the poor boy had exhausted himself in assisting Brother Farmer and myself. It has made him more susceptible, I'm afraid."

"I should go, and offer to help Mama Sarah with his care." I said, turning to leave.

"No, my dear," said the doctor sharply. "We do not know enough about how these things spread, or whether they can be contracted again. Your husband needs you, Mrs. Nutt. We cannot risk your being infected, since you have not been already, and we also cannot risk you carrying the sickness back to your husband. He would not survive another acute episode."

"I have given strict instructions that the persons attendant upon Mr. Jacob are to have minimal contact with the rest of the household," the doctor added. "We have been incredibly lucky that no one else has been infected."

"Of course," I said, "I understand. "Please sir, do tell Mama Sarah, Papa David, and Jacob if you can, that we will be praying – without ceasing."

"I will, ma'am," said Dr. Harding, "I most certainly will."

***** ****** ***** ***** ***** ***** ***** *****

Dr. Reginald Harding said a heartfelt prayer himself as he walked toward Jacob Nutt's sickroom. He tried to stretch his aching back as he walked. Exhaustion was evident in the slump of his shoulders and the slowness of his gait. He was sick at heart over what had happened to these two brave young men, and the children they had saved. He had seen this horror before, and to save any was God's grace. To save half was a miracle, and he gave thanks for it. Of the twenty-two children transported by the two wagons that night ten still lived. Another week would finish the tale. How many would survive? And of those how many would live in darkness the rest of their days? "Dear Lord," he prayed, "help me – help them all."

At the sound of the bedroom door opening Sarah Nutt looked up from her handwork, and nodded as Dr. Harding entered the room. "Mrs. Nutt," acknowledged the doctor, inclining his head briefly. "How has he been these last hours?" he asked.

"Restless," she said, softly, her strong-boned face lined with worry and exhaustion. "He's been feverish all day, and this evening it's not let up. So far, the cool compresses seem to be just keeping it from getting higher."

"Has he been aware at all?" asked Dr. Harding, carefully beginning to unwrap the bandages that covered the upper half of Jacob's pale, drawn face.

Sarah shook her head. "Not really. If you speak loudly and touch him, he pulls away. Most times if I ask him to do something, like turn a different way to help me, he will try to cooperate. But when I ask questions he doesn't respond. When the fever goes up, it's a different story."

"In what way?" asked the doctor, a frown creasing his forehead.

"Then he gets just out of his head, crying out f-for Jesse mostly, and talk about being careful, a-and s-sometimes, doctor, h-he weeps," she whispered, her voice choked, and her eyes filled with tears, "he weeps for those poor children."

She stifled a sob, and shook her head as he patted her gently on the shoulder and replied, "Yes, Mrs. Nutt, I've no doubt he does. Your Jacob has a kind and tender heart, especially for the little ones. I've no doubt he would make a very fine physician someday, if---." Reginald Harding stopped, appalled, finding himself tight throated, and moist eyed as well.

He struggled for control, cleared his throat, but was saved further comment by Sarah Nutt, who turned and took his hand between both her own, and said, "Dr. Harding, I pray that my Jacob with have the opportunity to follow his heart and study with you. I have prayed without ceasing these past days for both my boys, but it will be as the good Lord wills. I-I know you have done your best..." Suddenly embarrassed at her familiarity, she stepped hastily back.

"I thank you, ma'am," said Dr. Harding, softly, "I only wish it were in my power to do more. I am glad report to you ma'am that your son Jesse is I believe on the mend. I have just come from him, and although he is sleeping now, when awake he is alert and clear minded. He is still much troubled in spirit, as you might imagine, as his sight continues to worsen. But otherwise he is much improved. His lesions have healed with remarkably little scarring, and he has now been free of fever for three days."

"Oh, thank God!" breathed Sarah, sitting down wearily in the rocker near the window. "I must confess- I was concerned. I thought I heard noises from down toward Jesse's room very early this morning. I was afraid he had the fever again...."

"No," the doctor said, coming around the bed, and coming to stand looking out the window, at the remains of what had been a particularly glorious sunset. "According to Mrs. Landers, who came in after the fact, your son had his moment of coming to terms- so to speak. His wife was attending him at the time, and was able provide him with some degree of comfort. In the end, both she and he have slept a very natural sleep of simple exhaustion and perhaps relief for most of the day. I have checked in on both of them several times and all is well as it can be. I met the young Mrs. Nutt in the hallway just now, after checking on your son, and she looked quite refreshed and indeed took a moment with me to inquire about Jacob, and asked me to assure you of her and Jesse's continued fervent prayer on his behalf, and for you and your husband as well."

Sarah nodded, and said, "Thank you, Doctor. I understand why it is not possible, but I do so wish I could see Jesse, just for a moment." Her voice broke.

"Mrs. Nutt, I do understand, and I am so very sorry, but until Jacob is free of fever we simply cannot risk it." He paused for a moment, thinking. "I am thinking, however, that perhaps tomorrow afternoon, if the weather is fine, I might encourage Mr. Jesse to sit in the garden briefly, to take some air. I could perhaps allow you to see him there as long as you keep physical contact to a minimum."

Sarah's eyes filled with tears, "Oh, doctor, I do thank you for understanding a mother's heart!"

A moan from the bed behind them brought an end to all talk as they both moved to Jacob's side. A brief assessment later, Dr. Harding said, "His fever is heading up again." He cast a worried glance over Jacob's thin form. "We've got to try to keep at least cool liquids going in. Could you go refill the pitcher here with fresh water, and while you are gone, tell Mrs. Landers to please have ice ready to hand."

Sarah reached for the water pitcher, as she replied, "Certainly, doctor. I will be back momentarily." As she left the room, and headed for the kitchen, Sarah once again began her now standard litany of silent and fervent prayer.

Hours later, Sarah leaned heavily on the arm of her husband, as they walked down the hall toward the room they were sharing in her brother's home. Suddenly the door they were passing on the left opened, and their daughter-in-law appeared. "Aunt Sarah, Uncle David, " said Elizabeth, "I was reading to Jesse, and we heard your footsteps. How is Jacob? We have been praying all day."

"Jesse? Is he awake then?" asked Sarah, eagerly.

"Now Sarah, we've just come from..." David began.

"Mama? Papa?" called Jesse from within. "Lizzie let them come in. I-I need to talk to them. Please!"

Elizabeth stepped back, "Please be careful," she whispered.

They both nodded gravely, "We understand, Elizabeth." said Sarah softly.

As they stepped into the room, Elizabeth hurried to the bedside and took Jesse's hand. "Dearest, your parents are here, but they have just come from Jacob. So they cannot touch you. I k-know you need more, but talk is all we dare allow right now. They are right here, standing on the other side of the bed."

"Mama? Papa?" said Jesse, softly, pushing himself up off the pillows, "Can you tell me... how it is with Jacob?"

Elizabeth felt the grief hit them like a hammer blow as they realized he truly could not see them. Tears ran silently down Sarah Nutt's face, as she buried her head against her husband's broad chest, struggling for control. David clutched her to him like a drowning man clings to a tiny fragment of bark off a ship, and said, "W-We were going to send word. Your brother is at long last better, God be praised!" He struggled to keep his voice steady as he continued, "His fever truly broke for the first time about three hours ago. He is now, the doctor says, in a normal deep sleep. The good man insisted that we retire for the evening. He said he will remain with your brother for the next few hours and be certain he has turned the corner. We are hopeful he will awaken in the morning much improved."

"Thank God!" said Jesse, in a choked voice, as he grabbed for Elizabeth's hand. She caught his in hers, and held on, knowing what was coming. "A-and h-his eyes?" asked Jesse, clearly bracing himself.

"W-we don't know yet, son," said his mother softly. There was a beat of silence, and then she took a deep breath, and said, "What we do know is that we are all still here, and we love one another, and we love the Lord and He loves us. He will not forsake us in our hour of need, nor will we forsake each other."

"Well said, wife," said David, "So son, as much as we grieve w-what y-you have lost, w-we are so grateful to the Lord that He has spared you to still be with us. The- the rest we will reason out in due time."

Tears were running down Jesse's face and the look of longing on his face was more than Elizabeth could bear. Grabbing two towels from the nearby washstand, she thrust them into David and Sarah's hands. Immediately divining her intent, they quickly wrapped one hand in the folds of clean white linen, and reached out to clasp Jesse's left hand between their own. His right hand still held tight to Elizabeth as he squeezed both of his parent's hands. Finally he found his breath, and said, in a choked but firm voice, "Mama and Papa, I do love you so! A-and I want you to know t-that we will be all right, Lizzie and I, f-for we have each other. B-but w-we must all p-pray for J-Jacob. I-I know him, as well as I know myself, and he – he will b-blame himself..." He sank back on the pillows as the weakness overcame him, and his parents stepped back quickly.

"Son, you must look to your own care, and regain your strength," said David firmly. "Rest assured we will see to your brother as your dear wife will see to you. And as soon as Dr. Harding feels it is safe we will all find a way together."

"Meanwhile," said Sarah, softly, permitting herself one last fleeting covered touch on his arm, "my dear sweet boy, rest you well knowing we all love you."

"Thank you, Mama," said Jesse simply.

"We will bid you good night now," said David, "Elizabeth, you as well."

She nodded wordlessly, unable to speak.

As their footsteps sounded, moving away toward the door, Jesse turned his face toward them both and said, "Sleep well and God bless."

"You too, son, you too," said David Nutt, as he softly closed the door.

Healing and Heartache   February – June 1855

I watched with a mixture of worry, resignation, and pride as Jesse and my brother Henry lifted the trunk into the back of the carriage. Jesse's hands were steady and sure on the rope as he tied the knots to secure the trunk in place, but his face was still pale, cheekbones still too prominent, and his eyes….. O, dear God, his poor eyes……. My own eyes clouded with tears, and I turned toward the horses at the front of the coach, stepping out of sight of the others, hiding my moment of weakness.   Leaning my forehead against the coarse hair of Tillie's mane, I struggled for control.

A gentle hand touched my shoulder. "Lizzie," said my husband, gently, "It's time."

A deep breath, and I turned to face him. "I know, Jessie." I said, forcing a smile onto my face, and into my voice.   His other hand stroked my cheek, feeling the wet tracks of my tears.

"Lizzie," he said, softly, "We will be alright.   With the Lord's help, we can make this work. I know we can."   His sightless hazel eyes, still so beautiful, flared with determination, and then softened, as he continued.   "But Lizzie, one last time, and then we'll not speak of it again. You can stay-."

"No, Jessie," I placed a gentle finger to his lips to stop him. "I am your wife. In sickness and in health, remember. For better or worse…..

My place is with you... always....no matter what. And we- you need to-go." My voice choked despite my best efforts, and he pulled me tightly to him.

He took my hand and turned, leading me to the padded carriage seat, his other hand touching the harness and tack lightly along the way for guidance. My younger brother Henry had already taken the driver's position, and as Jesse climbed in beside me, he said to us with a forced smile, "Now, you two just sit back there like royalty, and allow me to drive you to your castle in style!"

I gripped Jesse's hand tightly, and said softly, "Not quite a castle, but home nonetheless, and a haven Jesse." I reached up to stroke his hair lightly, "Remember... Moreover I will appoint a place for my people Israel, and will plant them, that they may dwell in a place of their own, and move no more; neither shall the children of wickedness afflict them any more...."

A real smile flickered across Jesse's wan face, "I declare, woman, you do have a bible verse for every occasion!"

"She surely does," said Henry, over his shoulder, "Used to drive Frank and me crazy! No matter what the situation, even if it was when we put frogs in Mama's lard bucket, she piped up with something about the plagues of Egypt! If you will recall, Mama tanned our backsides so bad, we stood up all day the next day at school!"

"As a matter of fact," said Jesse, making an effort, "I do recall something of the sort. Jacob and I wondered all day what you all had done...." His voice trailed off, and I gritted my teeth and fought back unshed tears as we rode on in silence.

An eternity later, the carriage pulled up in front of our little cottage in the woods, just as it had on our wedding night almost a year ago. Only a year? And only two short months since Henry and Papa had knocked on that door and my life had changed forever. Both seemed a distant lifetime ago. How much longer must it seem for my dear Jesse, I wondered.

Henry hopped down and opened the carriage door. He handed me down as Jesse carefully followed. "We are right in front of the cottage, cousin," said Henry, in a soft matter of fact voice. Three paces forward you are at the foot of the front steps. You built'em so I'm thinkin' you can take it from there."

A look of fierce concentration came across Jesse's face, his "wheels turning" look I knew so well. My heart soared as it transformed into a look of surprise and then determination. "By, George, I think you are right Henry!- I did. I built this house. I know every measurement by heart! " He took three steps forward and reached with a sure hand for the bottom post of the stair rail. He cocked his head in my direction and held out his other hand. "Mrs. Nutt, allow me to escort you – home." He said not quite choking up on the final word.

"I shall, indeed, Mr. Nutt ," I said, taking his hand. He stepped surely up the four steps to the porch, counting quietly under his breath, and then just as surely the three steps across the porch to the front door. I held my breath as he reached for the doorknob and found it with only the slightest of hesitations. He turned the knob and pushed the door open. He stopped for a moment, and turned back toward the carriage. "Henry!" he called.

"Here, Jesse" said his cousin from the bottom of the steps.

"Thank you – for everything." said Jesse. "Do bring word…. If there's any change."

"I will Jesse," his cousin assured him, "Good night, then, to you both. Sleep well."

He climbed into the carriage and drove away, as I turned to my husband.

Without a word he pulled me inside and shut the door.

*****   ******   *****   *****   *****   *****   *****   *****

Sarah Nutt knocked softly and at the barely audible "Come in, Mama," opened the door to the room her son Jacob had occupied for these past five weeks. She was startled to find her son out of bed and dressed in pants and shirtsleeves. In deference to his still weakened condition he was seated, not standing, by the window that looked out on the rising sun. "They've gone, then?" he said quietly, as she crossed the room.

"Yes," said Sarah, simply.

"Thank God!" said Jacob, explosively, as he buried his face in his hands. "I don't think I could have borne it another moment! I have begged God, day after day, as little by little things grow dimmer, that if he must have my sight, that he take it quickly! And yet here I am, at this window like a hungry creature, straining for the last sight of them both. And then quite unable to bear to see what I have done to them both, and even less able – may God forgive me – to bear seeing what they are to each other! I love them both so desperately, and yet I still look at her and all I feel is..... alone!" He was weeping openly now, and she moved quickly to him.

"Oh, my poor, sweet boy," said Sarah, pulling her weeping son into her arm, as her mother's heart broke and shattered yet again.

"And- and I know – a-all of this is my punishment! F-for what I feel... the horrible jealousy! - And yet, I love them both so much! And if it weren't for me and my g-going to Jesse for help that night- Oh, God, Mama- look what I have done to them! Both of them! – H- How can I l-live with the fact that it was m-me...." He continued to weep inconsolably, becoming more and more distraught.

Helpless, with no words that had any effect, and afraid to leave her son in this state, Sarah prayed silently that God would send someone. With the first impact of his fist against the glass windowpane, Sarah leapt forward with a hoarse cry. "No, Jacob! Please! Son!-"

Her cry broke off as he pushed her away with enough force to send her backward onto the floor with a thud - that corresponded with the sound of the bedroom door opening with some force. The next thing she knew she was cradled gently in her husband's strong arms, as Abel and Henry Landers moved to physically restrain her broken son. "Sarah!" said David, intently, "Are you injured, love?" His face was pale with fear.

She clutched at his arms frantically, and begged, "Please don't let them hurt him, David!" Tears were pouring down her face, and David Nutt turned her where she could see her brother Abel, with Henry's help, pull his nephew down to the floor, where Abel wrapped him in a fierce embrace and held him as the frail young body continued to shudder with sobs.

"Sarah," said David softly, "I want you to let Henry take you to Sally, while he goes to fetch Dr. Harding. Abel and I will stay here and tend to Jacob." She opened her mouth to protest, but no sound came. David helped her up carefully, and motioned to Henry, who came and put his arm about his aunt's waist in support. "Come, Aunt Sarah. I am sure Mama has something warm and soothing to drink in the kitchen."

Sarah fought to tear her eyes from the sight of her husband and brother as they got a much subdued, but still silently weeping Jacob gently up from the floor and helped him toward the bed. She finally turned their focus on her nephew. He flinched at the depth of sadness there, as she said quietly, "Yes, take me to Sally, and then you must go fetch Dr. Harding. - And Brother Farmer too, if he can come. I think Jacob needs them both."

As they moved toward the door, Henry assured her, "I will bring them both, as soon as I can."

*****　******　*****　*****　*****　*****　*****　*****

Abel Landers sat in the privacy of his library, and wept. Tears rolled silently down his cheeks as he thought of them all- his beloved daughter, Leatha, always the child who understood his heart, who reminded him so much of her mother. What was her life to be now? And young Jesse, who reminded him so much of his young idealistic self... such promise never to be realized... And his brother, with his healer hands and heart now imprisoned in a world of darkness... Both his sweet sister's sons- her brokenness this afternoon had shattered his hard old heart- and his stalwart friend David- how much more must he be feeling as father and husband....

The library door opened, then closed, and Sally Landers came wordlessly to her husband- for there were no words- and simply knelt by her husband's chair, laid her head in his lap and took his hand in hers, as his other hand gently stroked her hair. "Abel," she said softly, "I think you should know... that Jesse offered to let Leatha....go. He said he would go home, and she could take up her life here, and- and not be tied."

"What did our Leatha say to that?" he asked, a smile tugging at his lips, even as tears continued to wet his face.

"I think you know," smiled Sally, softly. "She loves fiercely, does our girl. Reminds me of someone else I know," she continued, reaching up to gently touch his cheek.

That did bring a smile, the gentle one only she ever saw from this, her lion of a man. "I guess that means you've been eavesdropping again?" he queried, bushy white brows on the rise.

"Only the kind all good mothers do." She smiled ruefully back. "Have I told you lately, Mr. Landers how much I love you, and how very proud I am of you? - Behind that curmudgeonly façade you show the world beats the heart of a mother hen! You want to take care of us all."

"Ah, sweet Sally," he said, the smile fading once more to tears, "you have found me out. I do try." He whispered in a choked voice as he buried his face in her soft hair, "I do try."

***** ****** ***** ***** ***** ***** ***** *****

15 February, The Year of Our Lord 1855
From: The Honoralble Abel Landers of Neosho, Missouri
To: Mr. Amon Bond, Esq. of Johnson County, Texas

Dear Amon and Family,

We are in receipt of your epistle sent prior to Christmas last, and apologize profoundly for the delay in our response to it. We are most happy to hear of your successful Journey home, and glad to hear that you feel secure shelter may be established for both folk and livestock before First Snow. We had our first bitter cold here just prior to Christmas-tide although the particulars of the event surely escaped our Notice.

Our families have been beset with most Devastating and Heartbreaking Calamities within these last months, and so we beseech your indulgence regarding the tardiness of this response. Two young men of our relation — both known to you- our son-in-law, Mr. Jesse Nutt, and his brother, Jacob Nutt, suffered most grievous injury just prior to Christmastime, and as a result of same have both lost their eyesight in both eyes. The young men were injured in the rescue of over twenty local children from a Great Fire in a burning building set Alight by those Nefarious and Licentious Factions who have caused Much Strife and Anguish in our locale over these past months. While some of those children have since Died, I am told that nearly half of the twenty-two little souls have survived and do yet Live. So, the Good God did not cause these two brave young Men to suffer in vain, but instead offers them and us the Solace that they have done Great Good, and will have those actions given to Some Good Measure in That Final Reckoning at the Last Day.

Needless to say our Families are in the midst of Great Grief and heartache. While we give Thanks that Both good souls are yet with us, their circumstance presents Itself with No Easy Solution for their future Livelihood and Vocation. Therefore, I must inform you that I Simply Do Not Know whether any of our Families here will endeavor to Embark upon The Journey to join you in the Most Promising situation you Offer to Share with me and Mine. We can be certain that No Such Undertaking will happen This Year, but are hopeful to send some to you by Spring of the Next – in April or May of 1856.

Please greet all in your community with whom I enjoy felicitous Relations and know that I ask for Their and Your Own repeated prayers On Behalf of our two boys. They have given much already to the Cause of Good and face No Little Burden because of it.

Your Most Obt. Servant,

Abel Landers

*****   ******   *****   *****   *****   *****   *****   *****

A knock sounded on his office door frame. Abel Landers looked up to see his secretary, Jenkins standing there with a most battered parcel in his hands. "What is it, Jenkins?" Abel asked, not unkindly.

"A letter, sir, from Mr. Bond." said Jenkins, handing it over quickly.

"So soon?" said Abel, "I can't believe the mail ran that quickly. It's only been three weeks!"

"A gentleman brought it, sir," said Jenkins. "He bid me inquire if you felt like receiving him. He said he'd rather not give his name, sir. But he asked most kindly about Mr. Jesse and Mr. Jacob, he did sir. He is waiting downstairs in case you were busy or indisposed."

"Well, Jenkins," said Abel, with a hint of his old spirit, "Don't be rude, show the man in!"

As Jenkins disappeared down the stairs, Abel carefully tore open the letter packet. Amon Bond's distinctive script filled the single sheet.

10 March, The Year of Our Lord 1855
From: Amon Bond, Esq. — Stockton Bend, Texas
To: The Honorable Abel Landers — Neosho, Missouri

My dear Friends,

We have received your epistle of this month past, and are all most Sorely Grieved to hear if the Great Misfortune to befall Mr. Jesse and Mr. Jacob Nutt. We shall certainly endeavor to Send Up most vehement Prayers to the Almighty on their behalf. We shall also include in those heartfelt petitions all of you who must be So Sorely Wounded in Spirit because of your great Affection for those Esteemed gentlemen. My own dear Wife Sarah sends especial good wishes to Mrs. Jesse Nutt, and to Mrs. Sarah Nutt, knowing their distress must be exceeding deep. Please also extend to Mr. David Nutt my assurance of my esteem of both Himself and of his Two Fine Sons, and assure him of our Firm Intention to render to him and his family Any Such Aid as we may be able.

We are all certainly cognizant of this Calamity having a Most Profound effect on your plans to travel to Texas and Join us in our Most Humble efforts to establish a settlement. We shall Consult with each other and send word to you how we might adjust our Affairs to Keep in Trust such properties as might be for your Future Acquisition, should you determine with time for Consideration that Your delay in Coming is only Temporary in Nature. This will allow you and your families to prudently consider All of the options available to you in this New Circumstance. Please assure all of our Continued Desire to have your party join us here. As I have reported before, the Land is fine and of great beauty, and presents a most Favorable Prospect for All.

We will await further communications from you, and Pray that they may find your Fortunes greatly improved.

Your most Humble and Obedient Servant,
Amon Bond

Abel Landers carefully folded the letter for safekeeping and placed it in his pocket to be shared with others later. He quickly donned his

85

jacket and turned to hold out his hand in greeting as the tall form of Senator Sam Houston filled his doorway.

"Sam!" exclaimed Abel Landers, shocked into informality. He shook Houston's hand heartily, and was further discomfited to find himself enfolded in a hearty hug.

A moment later, his old friend from Tennessee was pumping his hand, and Houston was saying with great sincerity, "Abel! It is good to see you! I am so sorry to hear about the Nutt boys! How do they fare? Is there no hope at all?"

Abel struggled to collect his thoughts as he motioned for Houston to sit, and met his gaze, as he shook his head regretfully. "I'm afraid not. They will both most likely regain robust physical health, but their sight is gone."

Sam Houston's eyes were sad, as he shook his head ruefully, "Such a loss. I know you saw promise in young Jesse. You were right too. I watched him that night you know. Still very young, but has that natural ability with people. Already can work a room like a pro. "

"You should have seen him at the family gathering we had. Almost fifty folks there, and fourteen menfolk aged 13 to 70, nine of them with wives, and the next day he sat right there in that chair and told me where each of them stood on the issues of the day, which ones would be leaning toward our plan, and which ones had ties here or wives that would cause them to want to stay put." Abel smiled at the memory. "And he also put in my hand a list of suggestions of other men here we might approach. Most I knew already, but some of the younger ones were not known to me, and dang it if he hasn't turned out to be dead right about every one I have checked."

"He also seems to have an aptitude for legal matters, " said Houston, casually. "He wrote to me a couple of times regarding some states rights research he was doing on his own. Mind like a steel trap- that boy has. And a fine innate sense of justice." He sighed. "God, what a waste!"

Abel nodded, still digesting the fact that Jesse had actually been conducting his own research, and had contacted Houston on his own. "Seems even more than I knew," he said softly, feeling a surge of sorrowful pride at the initiative shown by his young protégé'. "Sam… you don't suppose…. – no, never mind. What cannot be, cannot be. We all have to accept that."

Houston shook his head, "No, Abel, not in these times, and not here. In a big city back east, if he were already licensed, there is – a chance – perhaps- that he might be allowed to try to practice contract or probate law, using readers. But even then….., no…. although I surely wish it were so. What do you think he will do? I daresay I don't know him well, but I surely know enough to know he won't be content to do nothing."

"I don't think he is ready to think of that just yet," said Abel, "But I surely have. My daughter, Elizabeth, is an intelligent woman, and she can help him in whatever they decide to do. They both have fine heads for business, and I suspect that will be the direction they go. Perhaps a mercantile or dry goods or some such."

"And what of the other boy, Jacob? " Houston asked. "I've not met him, but I am acquainted with his mentor, Dr. Reginald Harding. We correspond occasionally about his observations of the situation here in Missouri. He has mentioned Jacob Nutt in most glowing terms as a man with a natural gift in the medical realm."

Abel shook his head in misery, and said, "There's certainly no more hope of him being a doctor than there is of Jesse being a lawyer at this point." Abel hesitated, and then added carefully, "Jesse has Elizabeth. She is like the Rock of Gibraltar, that girl. She will keep him whole. But young Jacob doesn't have that goodly anchor in his life and what's more also blames himself for what has happened.   We are ….concerned… about his state of mind." Abel finished softly.

"Well," said Sam Houston, thoughtfully, "he wouldn't be much of a man if he didn't have some sense of responsibility. But I understand what you are saying. Give it time Abel. They both have much healing to do yet."

"But, Sam, you of all people know… We don't have time!" said Abel, explosively! "This place is a powder-keg, just waiting to blow up! The whole damn country is! I don't really think even your paradise of Texas is gonna be far enough away to keep my boys safe! But, by God, maybe we can at least give the women-folk and children a place out of the line of fire! But not if we can't get there, and not if we can't all survive and make a living once we do get there! I'm well-off, but I don't have the kind of resources that can support 30 people or even 20 – indefinitely!"

"That's why I'm here, Abel. I have an idea." said the Senator from Texas, with a smile. "There's more than one way to skin a cat, as they say." And then went on to describe in detail exactly how to do just that.

An hour later, Abel grinned at Sam. "You have a genius mind my friend!" said Abel, "To send just a few to file the claims and begin to work the land, and plan to buy out others who make claim but decide later to move on….That could work. And we would have feet on the ground….." He set down the pipe he was chewing as Houston rose.

"Sam," said Abel, as he himself got up and came to stand before his friend, "I know you are a busy man. That you took the time to come here yourself, and concern yourself with our small situation….. Well, it means a great deal to me, my friend, and I do thank you."

Sam Houston smiled, and said, "Well, I was headed back to Washington, and Amon had been in touch. So I met him in Dallas, and then headed to St. Louis, with just a bit of a detour to see you here. That's my story, anyway..... But you see, Abel, I seem to remember a time back in Tennessee.....when there was a fella whose life kinda fell apart.... Wife left him and all.... And one night he'd had too much to drink- way too much, and fell off his horse at the side of the road and hit his head in the middle of a snowstorm. Well, I remember a couple of farmers who found that fella, and picked him up, took him to one of their homes and patched him up, warmed him up, fed him, and the next morning sent him on his way with his faith in human nature restored. And they never told the story, even though he was a man in the public arena..... Yes, Abel... I remember those good men – my friends Abel and David. So whatever I can do, whenever you need it, you tell me, and if it is in my power I will see to it. - Now, my friend, I must go. Remember what you have always said to me..... "Trust in the Lord.... He will show a way!"

***** ****** ***** ***** ***** ***** ***** *****

 "Jacob," said Sarah Nutt, gently, "it's time to go, son"

Her rail thin son got slowly to his feet, and reached a hand in the direction of her voice. Even though he couldn't see it, she shook her head in frustration, and said neutrally, "I'm right here at the doorway to the bedroom. You know the way."

He grimaced, but slowly made his way around the furniture and over to where she stood. "There, now," she said, taking his hand, "that wasn't so hard, was it? – Now let's go home."

At the top of the stairs, Sarah placed his right hand firmly on the rail, and his left on her shoulder. "Now, son, we go down side by side, with me one step in front. Remember, one step at a time. Just go slowly, and take your time."

Jacob could feel the emptiness of space yawning before him. Never before in his life had he been bothered by heights. Now that he couldn't see them, but only imagine them... they were terrifying. He fought the terror that made each slow inching of his foot over the edge of a step a sliding over the edge of a bottomless abyss. He gripped the smooth bannister and his mother's shoulder as if they were the crumbling edges of a cliff. It passed vaguely through the turmoil of his mind that he must be hurting her, and he tried to focus on loosening his fingers. But the distraction made him lose track of where his foot was on the step, and he froze in fear.

"It's all right son, you're doing great!" His father's voice said encouragingly from below. Not so far below now by the sound of it. Jacob gritted his teeth, and focused again on getting his feet to move. Finally, the carpet of the stairs gave way to the smooth hardwood of the hallway floor.

He stood there still gripping the curl of banister at the bottom of the stairs and found he was able to uncurl the hand on his mother's shoulder now. He gently petted the soft cotton of her shoulder, and said quietly, "Thank you, Mama. I hope I didn't hurt you."

His mother caught his hand in hers, and he felt the gentle squeeze, as she said softly, "Never you mind, Jacob. You hold on to me as hard as you need to."

He father was speaking to the Landers nearby. "So, Abel and Sally, we give you back your three youngest in exchange for young Jacob here. William, Sarah, and sweet little Martha have had much fun with their cousins these past weeks I think. But I know we will all be glad to be home once more!" He paused, and said, in an entirely different tone, "We owe you a great debt. There are no words...."

"And no words are needed!" said Sally Landers, firmly. "We are family. It's what we do."

While the other three embraced warmly, Abel Landers turned to Jacob and grabbed his frail hand firmly, "Boy, come with me. We'll get you settled in the wagon while these others say their sentimental goodbyes, eh?"

Propelling Jacob firmly out the front door, Abel gave no quarter at the porch steps, other than to grasp Jacob's elbow firmly, and say brusquely, "Three steps down". He kept right on moving as Jacob stumbled slightly and then righted himself quickly, buoyed by the support at his elbow. Coming to a stop beside the wagon a few feet away, Abel grabbed both Jacob's arms and said, "There now, that wasn't so bad, was it son? Sometimes in this life, even when you are so scared you can't even spit...you've just got to go ahead and live! That's what you've got to do now. You go home boy, and you find your feet again. And don't be afraid to fall on your ass a few times while you're doing it. But you do it, and you decide what you want to do with yourself, and then you come to me. Whatever you need to make it happen, we will see to it. That's a bargain, just between you and me. – And don't you think of it as charity. I'll expect to be paid back, with interest! - Here come your folks now. So climb on up. But you remember now. I'll be expecting you, Jacob." Jacob felt one final firm hand bracing him as he climbed to the wagon seat, and then Abel was gone.

His parents settled in on either side, and the wagon rocked as the horses began to move. Jacob was silent as Uncle Abel's words echoed in his mind...."Sometimes in this life, even when you are so scared you can't even spit- you just got to go ahead and live!" Jacob thought on it long and hard for the three miles of bouncing homeward journey. As his father announced their arrival at the gate to the Nutt farm, he prepared himself to greet his brothers and sisters. He couldn't find even a taste of spit in his dry mouth, but he scrambled and slid of the wagon seat and was standing on his own feet, when the loving arms of family embraced him and brought him finally home.

***** ****** ***** ***** ***** ***** ***** *****

Celina Nutt, his good-sister, wife to his oldest brother, Henry, came over to hug him when he entered the house. He heard her laughter as she made her way through the mob surrounding him, then her strong lean arms encircled him, and she brought with her the smell of fresh fried chicken, and creamy buttered potatoes, and behind it something sweet with caramelized sugar. "I've fixed all your favorites," she said in his ear. "Do you want to eat with this bunch of heathens, or shall I bring you a plate in your room?"

Finding his physical stamina was waning along with his courage, Jacob, returned her hug as best he could, and rallied as best he could summon. "Celina, bless you, the lunch smells wonderful. But I need to lay down for just a bit. Then I promise I will do it justice! The rest of you all go ahead. Don't wait on my account." He literally swayed on his feet, as a wave of light-headedness upset his already precarious balance. Immediately, there was a steadying hand on his arm, then a strong arm about his waist. "I reckon this lot can eat up plenty without your supervision, brother," said Henry. "Celina has my old ground floor room all fixed up for you."

As they moved away from the noise of the kitchen, and the press of people and voices, Jacob said, "Thanks, brother."

They turned through a doorway, and Henry led him to the bed. Jacob lay back with a sigh, as Henry said, "Don't know how much you remember. There's a night table by your bed. The dresser is just to the left of the door as you come in. There's a chair over there by the window, and the washstand with basin and pitcher and two metal cups is just across from the foot of the bed. Your clothes are on hooks on the wall to the left of the washstand and a new winter coat and hat are hanging on the right side. Your socks and such are in the top drawers of the dresser. Sarah made you some new ones for Christmas. You might want to check with Mama on those before wearin' em. They're a might colorful."

Jacob couldn't help but smile, remembering their younger sister Sarah's penchant for unusual color combinations. The muscles in his face felt stiff and unused. He ran a hand along his jaw, and said, "Thanks, Henry. I'm sure I'll get it all straight soon. Meanwhile, just try to ignore any crashes, eh?"

"Sure thing, Jake. Rest well, now. A-And Welcome Home." said Henry softly. Jacob heard the door click shut, and he lay silent, listening to the sounds of the house all around him. So many sounds and smells and textures, he thought, feeling the stitches in the quilt that covered him. It wasn't the same- so many sights never to see again- but it was home- at long last. His eyes closed, his body relaxed, and he was using those long unused jaw muscles again. When his mother looked in a few minutes later, he was sound asleep, his lips relaxed with corners turned up, in just a hint- of a smile.

***** ****** ***** ***** ***** ***** ***** *****

Jesse was sitting out on the porch, the gentle breeze of the warm March day, lifting the dark curls of his hair, as he sat motionless, obviously in deep thought. I walked out and took my seat in my own rocker, which sat companionably next to his. Reaching for his hand, I said, "Jesse? What's wrong? You've not been this quiet since we first came home almost a month ago."

"They took Jacob home today," he said.

"They did?" I said blankly. "But that's wonderful! He must be doing better at last!"

He nodded, "Papa came by this morning on his way to town, while you were out back working on the laundry."

"I wondered what happened to my help!" I said, with a smile. "Thought evil thoughts in your direction, I might add!"

He smiled ruefully, himself. "I would have rather been doing laundry with you…" He stopped, a look of profound sadness coming over his features. "Papa came to tell me that Jacob is better physically, and that they were bringing him home. He also came to tell me that Jacob has confided in Mama his feelings for you, and that both he and Mama feel it is best if we stay away for now. Apparently it's all muddled up now in his mind, his feelings for you, his jealousy of me, his guilt over what has happened, and his feeling that he has ruined our lives. Yet he feels so alone that not once, but twice, he tried to take his own life in these past weeks." There were tears running down Jesse's cheeks now.

Jesse's words and those tears set off the most extraordinary set of emotions inside me. I felt absolute agony for what Jacob was going through, but at the same time I felt a surge of pure white hot fury at David Nutt for finding it necessary to burden my husband with the weight of this knowledge. I was literally shaking I was so angry. I had forgotten I was holding Jesse's hand. "Lizzie, Lizzie, honey, what is it?" Jesse was turning toward me, and reaching for me with his other hand, even as he struggled to pull the hand I held free. I looked down wildly, and saw our joined hands, my knuckles white with the strength of my grip.

With an exclamation of horror, I let go, exploding out of my chair, to take out my molten anger out on the porch railing instead. "Damn him! How could he?!" I cried.

"Lizzie!" gasped Jesse, shocked and bewildered. "Who? Jacob?"

"No!" I almost screamed, as deep wracking sobs suddenly erupted from somewhere deep inside of me. "Your father!" I shouted hoarsely. "Can't he see that you've been hurt enough! You-you've lost as much as Jacob! You-you n-need your family too! A-and you have a life to rebuild too! And it's just as hard! And God knows I am so s-sorry about J-Jacob, but you shouldn't have to d-deal with his hurt n-now!

Y-you have your own! A-and yes- I have –m-mine too! For both of you!" The surge of anger spent, I finished hoarsely, my eyes spilling over with tears, "You don't need to bear the knowledge of Jacob's burden on top of your own. And they are w-wrong to expect you to!"

Footsteps sounded behind me, and gentle hands were on my shoulders, turning me, and then pulling me into a strong embrace. "Ah, Lizzie," Jesse sighed, his voice as shaken as mine, "My sweet tigress! Thank you my dearest girl, for your fierce love!" His lips brushed the top of my head, as he held me close. "Papa has to look out and care for all his sons and daughters, not just me. He wanted me to understand. And you see sweet Lizzie, Papa knows. He knows that Jacob does need them more than I do, because I am blessed with the one thing that will get me thru this and out whole on the other side. I have you, my love. Thank God! I have you."

***** ****** ***** ***** ***** ***** ***** *****

 "Jake," said a small female voice, at his elbow, "do you know where my mama is?"

Jacob turned in his chair and reached out carefully. A head full of curly hair slid under his hand, as Henry and Celina's four year old began to climb his leg. "Angie, my love," he said, reaching down to pull her into his lap, "I have no idea where your mama is right now. Will an Uncle Jake do instead?" He felt her sit still, considering this most serious of questions. Finally, the little head nodded as it lay against his chest.

"I's not sweepy." She confessed. Was she sucking her thumb again?

"And you're supposed to be taking a nap?" he asked.

Again the nod, and, yes definitely sounds of serious thumb sucking going on.

"Well, I tell you what," said Jake gently, "how about a story instead? Would you like that?"

Nod number three, "I wike stories!"

"Alright then," said Jacob, thinking furiously. "Well, once upon a time there was a beautiful princess with very, very long hair, and her name was Rapunzel....."

By the time the prince was climbing the tower... Jacob had two small bodies curled against his chest, and another sitting on his left foot.

By the time the prince and Rapunzel rode off into the sunset together all three were breathing softly, sound asleep.

When Celina and Sarah Nutt came in from hanging laundry to dry they were treated to the sight of three small children and one grown man, all sleeping the sleep of the blessed in one very sturdy rocking chair on their front porch.

Jesse Nutt was carrying yet another bucket of water to the vegetable garden at the side of the cottage, counting his steps carefully from the well to the porch rail, and then to the end of the porch, then three more steps to the end of the first row, then one long step sideways for each row.   The summer watering was one of several of the daily chores that he could now do unassisted.   And he thanked God again for Lizzie and her patience and ingenuity in helping him to learn each one.

He stopped at the sound of footsteps coming up the path to the house. He stood up and put the bucket down listening and waiting.   Two people. - Something funny about their gait.   He wondered if one was old or hurt.   The steps stopped at the edge of the yard.   "Jesse," said a boyish voice, "I've brought Jake to visit!"   It was his youngest brother, David's voice.

Without thinking, Jesse quickly lowered the bucket to the ground and took three steps in the direction of the voice, before he realized he had no clue where he was.   He stopped, and then a smaller young hand grabbed his and led him forward.   Then that same hand was guiding his hand into the grasp of one much the same.   "Jacob?" he whispered, at the same time, another voice whispered, "Jesse?"   And suddenly there were strong arms pulling each of them into the other's embrace.

After a brief time of tolerating the onslaught of tears, young David said, "Well, darn, if I'd known all you two sods were gonna do was snivel , I would've stayed home!"

The third brother was pulled into the embrace, and with the laughter of pure love and joy, the three proceeded to prove that vision is not required for a little rough-housing and brotherly teasing. Shortly though, they all sat on the ground, leaning against each other, and David said, "Jesse, you got anything besides that there water to drink? I have surely worked up a thirst."

"Why yes, I believe Lizzie made a fresh pot of coffee just before she left," said Jesse. "Come on inside and sit a spell. I could use a cup too."

"She left you here alone?" said David, disapproving.

"Davy," said Jesse, with a grin, "the last time I checked I qualified as a grown man. Lizzie and I are practical folks and we know what my limitations are. We are in agreement that losing one's vision does not mean losing one's good sense. As long as I am here at the cottage, and keep my bearings, it is perfectly safe for her to be gone sometimes."

"Did she come up with a bible verse to back that up?" asked Jacob, the grin sounding in his voice.

"No, she did not," I said, fighting to keep my voice light, as I blinked back tears, at the sight of the three brothers leaning against my porch rail, disheveled, and dirty and laughing! "And if any one of you three clowns thinks you are coming into my clean house without washing off first, you can just think again!" I actually forgot, and pointed as I said, "There is a perfectly good bucket of water right at the side of the house where Someone left it."

"My, my, Jesse," said David, winking at me, "I didn't know you'd married such a cross woman!"

"David?" said Jacob, with a shaky smile that broke my heart, "is she armed? T-the last time I heard that tone of voice, she almost beat Jesse and me to death with a fishing pole!"

"Really?!" said David, suddenly sounding like the eight year old he was.

His awed tone was just what was needed to save the moment. "Oh, she can be very fierce," Jesse assured him.   "We'd best go get ourselves decent.   Then we might be deemed worthy to have whatever that is that the lady is carrying that smells so delicious."

"That is Cora Beth Johnson's cinnamon bread, sirs.   Only clean gentlemen get to eat it." I called, as I went up the steps, and into the house, and quickly and silently fell apart.

My face was washed and the table set when Jesse, Jacob and David reappeared. I watched with interest as David subtlety guided Jacob through the unfamiliar surroundings. I saw Jesse listening, and knew he noticed too. Once the men had fallen on the coffee and sweets as men do universally, Jesse said with a casualness that fooled no one, "What brings you two up our way today?"

Jacob was still very thin, and I could see him swallow before he spoke, "Well, brother, since our sibling here has convinced me, by incessant pestering, to rejoin the living,..." at this point he and David both smiled affectionately in each other's direction, "he has brought to my attention something I think you need to be aware of. I am living in the house with it, and I am at a loss as to what should be done."

"What on earth?" I said.

"Jesse, you remember that contract you drew up last year between Papa and Henry, about Henry running the farm?" Jacob asked.

Jesse's head came up, and he leaned forward, 'Yes, as a matter of fact I do. Damn, I hadn't even thought of it since...well, since the fire."

Jacob nodded, and said, "Well since you and I were supposed to be helping Papa keep track of what Henry is doing and we've been......unable......" Jacob stopped for a moment, inhaled deeply and continued. "Anyway, when Henry submitted the reports in January as required – knowing Papa couldn't read them, mind- Papa turned to young David here, and had him read them aloud to him. And from what young David here tells me, those reports show Henry to have been a good manager, careful with Papa's funds, and a hard worker."

"Why do I sense a 'But' coming sometime soon?" asked Jesse, rhetorically.

David looked very young. "I don't want to make trouble, but it's wrong. And Henry shouldn't be lying to Papa!"

Jesse's head snapped up, and suddenly clear as day, I saw the great litigator he might have been. "Lying to Papa? How David? Be specific."

"Oh, he's been very specific," said Jacob, grimly. "Henry's running ten slaves on the place, having them work the north fields where Papa rarely goes."

I couldn't help the gasp of horror at the vista those words opened up. Jesse's hand covered mine, but his voice was all business as he turned his head toward young David. "How do you know this, David? Have you seen them?"

"Yes, sir," said David, nodding miserably, "I have. He's been using them since before harvest last fall. They came from Sister Celina's folks place."

"How do you know these workers are not free blacks? Papa has hired some from time to time." Jesse asked, patiently.

"Well mostly 'cause I heard Henry telling Celina that he'd bought'em from her daddy." David stopped, clearly not wanting to say more.

"But Henry can't afford slaves," I said, "He's supposed to be saving to buy the farm!"

"What else?" asked Jesse, well aware that there must be still more.

"David," said Jacob, gently, "you have to tell him the rest."

"You tell him," said David, almost in tears.

"David," said Jesse, his voice kind but firm, "come over here and stand by me."

The boy scrambled up and came to stand directly in front of Jesse. Jesse reached out and took both of David's hands in his, "Now, brother, tell me what you saw."

David took a deep shuddering breath, and blurted, "I saw Henry take a whip to one of 'em. He gave that black man twenty lashes with a horse whip right before my very eyes!"

"He knows you saw him?" demanded Jesse, sharply.

"N-no," said David, his voice trembling.

"Jesse…" I said softly, touching his shoulder.

I felt Jesse take a huge calming breath himself. "Where were you, David?"

"I wanted to go to town to go fishing with Billy Jenkins," said David softly. "We were both supposed to be at school. But instead of going to school, I hid in the wagon – in between the bales of hay Henry was taking to town to sell to old man Kruger. He went to check on the north field on the way. The s-slaves – they were supposed to all be haulin' rocks out of that field. He c-caught the man sleepin' under a tree instead of workin'. The man, he kept sayin' he was sick, and he was sorry, and H-Henry, h-he called him a-a lazy assed nigra, begging your pardon Cousin Lizzie, and he tied him to a tree and …."

Jesse's shoulders were hard as those rocks under my hands, and Jacob sat silent, pale as the cloth on the table between us. Jesse squeezed David's hands, and said, "Alright son, just one more question and we're done for now. Why in God's name didn't you go to Papa and tell him what you saw. Or come to Jacob or me or even Uncle Abel?"

"I-I was goin' to," he said, his voice trembling, "I really was. I-I had just walked into the kitchen to tell Papa I needed to talk to him private-like. But then there was a banging on the door, and Uncle Abel saying that you and Jacob was hurt...And then Mama and Papa went to stay at Uncle Abel's.... And Henry and Celina were in charge.... And...right there in the house, and I thought about what to do, I really did! But after January- I was scared. "

"What happened in January, David?" asked Jesse, his face like stone.

"Well you were both real bad. We all thought you were both gonna die. And Papa came out to the farm to- well to check on things – I guess." Said David, "And I was all torn up about whether I should go ahead and say anything or not, Papa being so upset and all. And I was there in the room when Henry gave Papa the report papers. Papa looked at the papers like he'd been hit, and said to Henry, "You know I can't read these." And Henry looks at him, and says, "Well, looks like for once you'll have to trust me, Papa, even if I'm not one of your favorite sons!" Well, Papa turned really red, and I thought for a minute he was gonna hit Henry. Then Papa looked up and saw me. And he said, "David, come here, son. I need your help." Well I got up and went and stood next to Papa, and he had me read that report to him, right there in front of Henry. And Henry sat there glaring at me the whole time."

"What happened next, David?" asked Jacob.

"Well I knew most of the words and the numbers parts were easy. So, after I read the reports, Papa thanked me kindly, and told me I had done a good job. And Henry just sat there, staring at me the whole time. And Papa told Henry he had some questions, and told me I could go on to bed. I wanted so bad to say something to Papa, but I just couldn't! And so I went. A-and later, I was laying there in my bed , wide awake, Abel and John snorin' like crazy across the room. And Henry comes to the door and just stood there for the longest time. I pretended like I was asleep. He never even looked over at Abel and John. He just stood there and stared at me. I don't know why I was scared, but I was. I kept remembering him whipping that man over an' over. A-and finally he went away, and I-I cried then, Uncle Jesse. I know it's not manly but I couldn't help it. I was s-scared, and- " His voice broke in a sob, and suddenly he was enfolded in Jesse's arms, a half a year of fear, and secret knowledge pouring out in a flood of tears.

My legs rubbery, I sat down hard in the chair between Jesse and Jacob. Reaching out to lay a hand on both their arms, I listened to Jesse's soft reassurances to David. "It's alright, David. You've done the right thing. You did good."

And after a moment, I breathed the words I knew were in each of our hearts. "Dear God, what are we going to do?"

Jacob turned his head to Jesse, and said, "You understand now why I had to come?"

"Of course," said Jesse softly, across David's head. "You are right. This has to be dealt with. And we have to keep it in family if we can."

"This is going to kill Papa," said Jacob.

"Papa is a strong man," said Jesse, "it is Mama I worry about."

"Oh, Jesus," said Jacob, "Is there any way…..?"

"David," said Jesse gently, "I need you to think now and answer two more questions. Think carefully, this is important."

The boy sat up and nodded, wiping his eyes, "Yes, sir?"

"First, and most important, does Henry have any reason at all to suspect that you know anything about any of this?" asked Jesse.

"No, sir," said David definitely. "He never saw me. I got out of the wagon when he went inside at Mr. Kruger's."

Jesse nodded, "Alright then. Now do you know if he is still using those men up at the north field?"

"Yes sir, I heard him tell Aunt Celina just the other day that he'd finally got her daddy paid off in full, and that it was gonna make a huge difference in how much money they could take out of the farm this year," said David. "They were in the barn, and I was in the chicken coop just outside."

"Are you sure?" said Jacob, sitting up straight, "He said how much money *they* could take?"

"Oh, dear Lord," I breathed, "this just gets worse and worse."

Jesse and Jacob both were stone-faced, and Jesse said, "That changes things, brother."

Jacob nodded, "We are going to have to involve Uncle Abel. We need his eyes, and his legal expertise."

"Wait a moment," I said, knowing what they were thinking, "Does Henry even keep an actual set of books? Since Uncle David can't read....."

"Oh, yes, there's books kept," said Jacob. "I've heard Henry and Celina going over stuff at the kitchen table at night."

"Papa can read figures, and Mama too," said Jesse, "Papa told me that, when we wrote up the contract. He always showed Mama the reports. She insisted on it."

"So is Mama not trusting Henry, then?" asked Jacob.

"According to Papa, it's not Henry, it's Celina. Mama never has liked her or her folks. Mostly because of the slavery issue," said Jesse.

"So maybe we can keep this in family," said Jacob.

"I think so," said Jesse. "Lizzie can we do six for dinner?

"Certainly," I answered, already adding to the stew in my mind.

"David, go down to the smithy, and tell Papa that Jesse and I are here and need to speak to him privately as soon as possible," said Jacob.

"So," I said, dubiously, "you hope to keep this from Mama Sarah?"

Jesse grimaced and shook his head. "I don't know, Lizzie," he said. "Mama is your father's sister. She is going to know something is going on. I think the best we can hope for is that we can keep her out of the direct confrontation that has to be coming. If we can keep at least that hurt from happening to her, I think we must."

"David," said Jesse, "Take Tillie, Lizzie's mare. Go first to the smithy, and talk to Papa, and then ride over to the farm. Find Mama, get her in private, and tell her Lizzie and Jesse are having her and Papa to dinner with Jacob and yourself. Tell her Papa is coming from the smithy, and that Lizzie says to come on over when she can."

"And what, pray tell, is to keep her from inviting the whole clan along?" I asked.

Jesse said, seriously, "Lizzie, again, remember whose sister my mother is. She is a Landers. She is going to know something is up, and will probably be here sooner rather than later."

"We will be lucky if she doesn't beat Papa here," said Jacob.

"Alright, David- go now," said Jesse, and then as the boy started toward the door, Jesse called after him, saying, "And David, you come straight back here. We know all we need to for now. Don't put yourself at risk, thinking to go sneaking up around the north field on your way back!"

The guilty look on David's face said it all. "Yes sir. I promise. I'll come straight back." He turned on his heel and ran out the front door, toward the barn.

Jesse turned to me, and said with a smile, "Was the look as guilty as the voice?"

"I refuse to answer, sir," I said, "on the grounds that I might incriminate that child."

Both he and Jacob released their tension with the bark of laughter I had intended. "Now," I said, pragmatically, "if you two gentlemen would adjourn to the porch, and try to stay out of trouble, I have a dinner to prepare."

Jesse stood and said, "Come along, brother. I know that tone. There's a good breeze on the porch, and we'll be less likely to get trampled."

Jacob stood too, and his hand found Jesse's shoulder with only the slightest of hesitations. "Lead on, brother. I am right here beside you."

As they left the room, I silently sank to my knees. In spite of the wretchedness of the situation at hand, at that moment there was no room in my heart for any tears save those of thanksgiving.

***** ****** ***** ***** ***** ***** ***** *****

I had just finished putting several wrapped potatoes into the coals of the fire to bake when I heard the hoof beats that heralded the elder

David Nutt's arrival in front of the cottage. I stood in the doorway watching as Jesse and Jacob stood to greet their father.

David Granville Nutt was still a fit man at age fifty-eight, but the last year had taken its toll. There was more gray than dark in his beard, and there were lines in his face that hadn't been there a year ago. He had eyes only for his two sons as he dismounted, and I thought I saw his powerful shoulders relax a bit at the sight of Jesse and Jacob standing side by side on the porch.

 "Papa!" said Jesse, "Welcome!" He extended his hand in his father's direction as David came up the porch steps. Papa David grasped it firmly, and pulled Jesse into a quick tight hug.

"Hello, Papa," said Jacob, as he too received his firm handshake and hug.

"Boys," said Papa David, his voice just a bit gruff as he struggled to contain his emotions.

With total sympathy, I stepped in to provide a distraction. "Papa David!" I said, smiling as I stepped out onto the porch. "Welcome!" In my hands I carried a tray with more of the cinnamon bread, and three glasses of freshly squeezed lemonade. "I brought you gentlemen some refreshment." I set the tray on the table between the rockers, and said casually, "Jesse, Jacob, the tray is on the table here between the rockers. Facing the house, drinks are on your right and sweets are on your left. Papa David, there's an extra chair just inside the door here. Feel free to set it where you are comfortable. "

"I thank you for your hospitality, daughter!" said David, with a smile. He reached past me and brought out the chair and sat down facing his two sons. There was a moment of food and drink being passed around, and then David said quietly, "Boys, I cannot tell you how glad my heart is to see you here- together. But I reckon, by the way young David was acting, that whatever it is that has brought you together also has the potential of trouble in some way? I pray I am wrong, but David did use the word urgent."

"Well, Papa," said Jesse, "I think urgent might be overstating things just a little. But young David has made us aware of a situation that warrants your attention, and since any way you look at it- there's going to trouble- family trouble- we thought it best to talk to you privately and quickly."

Papa David looked from one to the other of them, perplexed. "Young David, you say? What is it, and why didn't he just come to me?"

"He did, Papa," said Jacob, regretfully, "He had literally just walked into the kitchen to ask to speak to you privately, when they brought word that Jesse and I had been hurt."

David Nutt looked stunned, "But that was six months and more ago! And the boy spoke to no one all this time..... But why didn't he- if I wasn't there- why not Henry- I left him in charge....." At their stone-faced silence he stopped. "Henry. – Henry is part of the problem, then?" he asked. "What's he done?"

"David came to me, Papa, about a week ago," said Jacob, sadly. "As you know, Papa, David has – helped me...," his voice broke, and Jesse reached for his hand and found it, and squeezed hard. Jacob cleared his throat, and continued, "We- well things are better for me now, and a lot of it is because of David. We-we've grown close, and he came to me with this. He simply did not know how to tell you."

"Tell me what?" demanded David, his voice full of concern now.

Jesse took the plunge. "Henry is running at least ten slaves out on the north field. He owns them, and has been witnessed on at least one occasion seriously beating one of them. That is what we can prove with eyewitness testimony," he said bluntly.

His expression stunned, Papa David said, "David? Little David *saw* all this?"

"Not so little anymore, Papa," said Young David, coming up the steps.

All three heads turned quickly in his direction, but it was his father who spoke, and kindly too, "Come here, Davy, and tell me. What did you see?"

So young David sat on the raw white board of the porch rail and told his story again.

I was pulled away by the demands of my boiling stew, and the need to turn my roasting potatoes. But the sound of male voices in deep discussion was a quiet rumble through the open front door. An hour had passed, the table was set, and the food preparations finally complete, when I again heard the sound of another arrival in the front yard.

My mother-in-law didn't ride astride often. Indeed the only time I had seen her do it before was the night we received word about Jesse and Jacob. As I stepped to the door to greet her, I was forcefully reminded that she was a Landers too, and my father's sister. She stood in the yard, hands on hips, one eyebrow climbing, staring at the gaggle of obviously conspiring menfolk, and said, "Nice of you all to start the party without me." Balefully her gaze fell on me, "Leatha I must say I am disappointed that you didn't see to it that all invitations to your little party were issued equally."

"Sarah!" said Papa David, rising, and trying to sound outraged.

Young David's eyes were big as saucers, and Jesse and Jacob seemed to be trying their best not to smile.

"I am sorry, Aunt," I said, using her Landers title. "I admit that I should have sent a note with David, but I was afraid it would be seen by others."

That sobered her quickly, and she moved straight to her husband's side. "So what is it?" she asked simply.

"Mama," said Jesse, bowing to the inevitable, "this will make the third telling today of a tale I'd just as soon not heard in the first place. Why don't we at least do it inside over supper? That way maybe we can figure what's to do sometime before midnight?"

All adjourned to the kitchen table with dispatch, and when we were seated Papa David looked around and said, "Jesse, son, as head of house it is yours to say grace. But with your permission, I'd like to do it tonight, if I may?"

"Of course, Papa," said Jesse.

David Nutt's eyes swept over the five of us, waiting with joined hands, and then he bowed his head, and he said words that echoed those that had been in my heart all afternoon, "Dear Lord, we thank thee for the great blessing of family. We thank you for the great blessing of love that we receive from each other. We thank you for the blessings of fine sons and daughters who we have been blessed to nurture and to watch grow into good Christian people. Father, we thank thee for seeing us through our times of illness and trial with the constant knowledge of Thy Holy Presence. Lord we ask your blessing upon this food for the nourishment of our bodies, and we also ask that you nourish our minds with wisdom and compassion, that when our children stray we may be given the right words to lead them gently home to you. We ask this all in Jesus' Holy Name. Amen."

I groped blindly for my handkerchief, and smiled at my Uncle David through my tears. "All my life," I said, shaking my head. "All my life you Nutt men and your prayers can make me cry!"

His stern face was transformed by an older version of my husband's gentle smile. "Why, my dear, thank you. Thank you very much indeed."

***** ****** ***** ***** ***** ***** ***** *****

In the end, it was quite simple really. But the decisions made that night decided the course of our lives for all days to come. Especially Jesse and me, our course was set from that evening forward.

The next night, Jesse and I invited ourselves to dinner with my parents. David, Sarah, and Jacob had wanted to come as well, but for the sake of the younger children it was decided they were more needed at home.

We told my parents the whole tale, from the beginning. I told the first part, of what had happened at the cottage. Then, I gave the floor to Jesse to share the events of the next day.

Jesse was all business, as he told this part of the tale. "I took a liberty, sir, with Lizzie's help in the penmanship, to draft a set of documents for my father. He then traveled yesterday morning to meet with my brother Henry in his place of business. That would be the north field of my Father's farm. He took along as witnesses young David, myself, my brother Jacob, our brother Abel, my mother, and Lizzie. Since two of the adult male witnesses could not actually see what transpired, only hear, my father also enlisted two of his Masonic brethren as witnesses as well. He and we wanted you sir instead, but I advised my father against that, since as a current Justice of the Peace you could be called to render judgment should any part of this fall apart.

All ten of us arrived at the field on horseback. I am told that all ten field slaves were there in plain sight, along with Henry, and another white man named Perkins, who Henry had the audacity to introduce, *as his new overseer*.

Papa didn't mince words. He got off his horse, and met Henry at the edge of the field. He didn't even give Henry a chance to speak at first. He just started right in, Papa did, never speaking much above the volume needed for us all to hear. "Henry, it has been brought to my attention that you are running slaves on my property against my express wishes. I came here to ask if that was true. But the evidence before my eyes makes that question patently unnecessary. But just for the record, you are aware that this is still my property?"

"Y-Yes sir," Henry stammered, "P-Pa-"

"And you are aware, per our written and signed agreement, of my decision that I will not own slaves on moral grounds, and that I do not allow them to be used for work on any of my properties?" Papa asked.

"I know how you feel Papa, but-," Henry answered, and Papa cut him off again.

"And you are aware, are you not,' said Papa, "that I am adamantly against the physical mistreatment of ANY human being whether free or slave for punishment or discipline outside the realm of punishments for crimes meted out by duly appointed and elected Judges of the Law?"

Jesse paused for breath, and my father interjected softly, "Nice script. Wonder who wrote it?" Jesse blushed, but otherwise ignored him and continued.

"Henry caught on about then too, and settled down, and answered, "I am so aware." I could hear Papa's boots squish in the mud, and I knew he must be right up in Henry's face.

"And yet, sir, knowing that this was MY property, and knowing that I DO NOT allow the use of slaves, much less their mistreatment, and having signed papers to that affect, YOU have knowingly and intentionally done just that for at least the past eight months!"

"Well, I'll give Henry this much. He didn't cower. He came right back at Papa."

"And what if I have?!" he shouted, "You put me in charge! Basically said as long as the money was steady on your precious reports, that I was to run the farm as I saw fit! Well, I saw fit to run it using slaves! It's cheaper, and they work just as well or better than most of the lazy-assed paid workers- white or black! –Looking out for YOUR best interests by increasing YOUR profits! And this is the thanks I get! Public ridicule and embarrassment!?"

"If I had wanted to ridicule you and embarrass you in public," shouted Papa, "I would have called you out before the church and the whole town in court for breach of contract!"

"Well that would have been interesting! At least HALF of them would have been on MY SIDE!" Henry was practically screaming by then."

Jesse stopped, searching for words to continue, and I took up the story.

"I had been so focused on Papa David and Henry that I had really forgotten everyone else. And then the horse next to me moved, and I looked up, and there was Aunt Sarah, striding through the dirt, to step right between then just as I thought they might exchange blows! She planted herself right there in front of Henry, and she stood there with tears streaming down her face, and eyes blazing, and she reached up, and cupped Henry's face in her both her hands, and I-I knew she was remembering what he had looked like when she held him as a babe. And she said, so softly we could barely hear, "Today, you have broken our hearts. You have dishonored your father and his wishes. You have chosen a path we believe with all our hearts to be morally wrong. But worst of all, you have lied to us and betrayed the trust we had in you. We will always love you, Henry, and will pray to forgive you. But son, you have lost our trust. And that, once lost, can rarely be mended." And she dropped her hands, and turned to Papa David, and took his hand and said, "Come, David. Let Jesse give him the papers and we will go.""

Jesse continued, "I took the bundle of papers out, and told him, "These papers include the following documents, which will finally and forever settle upon you your share of our father's estate, to be distributed as follows: You receive immediate clear title and total control of this piece of property, heretofore known as the North Field of the Nutt Family Farm, consisting of 10 acres just north of the North ½ of the NW front Quarter of Section A & B of in Township No. 35 of Assay 89, per the attached survey of same. This property shall be registered at the Newton County , Missouri Courthouse as being under your sole ownership with Clear Title. In three years time, by sworn affidavit contained herein, David Granville Nutt does state his clear and irrevocable intent to sell the remainder of the property of 40.6 acres of the Nutt Family Farm, description and survey attached, to his Masonic brother, John Johnson, a resident of Newton County. At that time, on or prior to the date of March 15, 1858, all members of the Nutt Family shall have vacated said property in Newton County, and shall relinquish all control of same at that time. In exchange for housing and food during that Three year interim and a set salary of $25 per month, you will:

1. Continue to run said farm with the assistance of and under the direct supervision of said David Granville Nutt and his assigns, in such a way as to maximize the profitability of same.

2. You will use only free, paid laborers to assist in the operation of the remainder Farm.

3. You will not speak of this incident, this agreement, or of your feelings regarding same to anyone other than our father or your wife between now and the time you remove yourselves permanently from the premises of the Remainder Farm. The only aspect you may speak of publicly is the fact that you now own the 10 acre North Field.- A gift from our Father. Your wife, Celina Nutt is also to be bound in obedience to this oath.

Do you agree to the terms I have just set before you?"

There was silence. So finally, I leaned forward and said just to him, "Accept it, Henry. It's a generous settlement. It gives you time and capital to get your own place. And anything else is chaos, and you rip our family apart even worse than you already have."

Well, for a long moment nothing happened, and then Henry stepped up close enough my horse moved, and said loudly enough for everyone to hear, "I accept the terms so laid out."

I nodded toward him, and said, "Those are all signed already and witnessed by everyone here. We have signed copies as well. You will bring your copy to Uncle Abel's offices at noon tomorrow, to sign both copies before witnesses." "

Jesse sat back with a sigh, and said to Abel, "Sorry for the short notice. I hope your calendar is free."

"If it's not now, it will be," my father answered immediately.

He and my mother looked …. shocked. My father sat motionless, his head bowed. My mother stared at the table top. There was a very long period of silence. I searched their faces, looking for some clue to their thoughts. But for once, Jesse and I were equally blind.

Finally, Jesse could stand it no more. "Abel?" he said, softly. "Will it stand in court if need be? Did I do right?"

My father looked up, and his whole heart was in his face. He told me later that all he could hear was Sam Houston's voice saying, "What a tragic waste!". "Jesse, son," he said, "you did better than right. Yes, it will stand. Do you have David's copies?"

"Yes sir," said Jessie, pulling the smaller bundle from his coat pocket. "I told him you would need to see them."

Papa unfolded the papers and looked slowly through them, stopping to examine a line here and there. "Oh, yes, these will do nicely. Elizabeth, you do write a fine hand! Can you make me a third and fourth copy before noon tomorrow? We will need one for my files, and one to file with the county clerk in Neosho." He paused. "Jesse, I-"

I looked up, searching his face, but Jesse spoke first. "No, Uncle, don't. Lizzie and I talked about it as we were doing these papers last night. And again this afternoon- after this morning..."

He paused, gathering his thoughts, "Something like this, a document or advice to family or friends on a mostly informal basis. Together she and I could and can do that. In fact, my father and I want to talk to you about Lizzie and I going with Amon next year with just a few others, and filing the claims for the family and basically doing just that. "

He paused a moment to let that sink in, and then continued, "But Uncle, you know as well as I do that to practice law I have to be able to do two things- I have to be able to read people, and I have to be able to certify that the documents I produce are true and correct. I alone can neither look someone in the eye nor testify to the veracity of a written document. With Lizzie's help and her say so I can. But is that the same? I think not. At least in some circumstances, definitely not."

He shook his head, and went on, "A prime example. Suppose only I, or even Lizzie and I, had gone with my father this morning. Suppose the same events transpired. Suppose come tomorrow Henry claims that he never saw us, that we never spoke. That my father is a liar, and that he never agreed to the terms of this agreement? Could I as the only witness, or Lizzie and I (with her a woman and my wife) testify in court that the man my father spoke with was indeed Henry? Would it hold up in court? Especially a hostile court? The answer is no, it would not. So sir, I do thank you for your confidence in me. It means more than I can possibly say. But we both know my answer must be "No."."

My mother, silent all this time, finally looked up. "Jesse, you are very wise. And I applaud you for both your pragmatism and the honor of your stance. But, I hope you will forgive us the weakness of our pride in you. You and our Leatha are quite special to us, you know. – So, you have decided to go? With Amon, I mean?"

"Yes," said Jesse, "if he'll have us. He may not want a blind merchant with not much in the way of practical skills to offer."

"Well, Jesse," she said, "I don't think you need to worry. Amon needs good, strong, educated men to build what he is trying to build. And you are all of that. Amon Bond would be a fool to turn you down. And no matter what I think of Amon. One thing I know. I may call him names to Abel from time to time, but Amon Bond is no fool."

Her Father's Joy September 1855 to June1856

The ceiling above my head turned pearly gray white as the first faint hint of the coming dawn slowly changed the darkness into light. The sounds of trees moving outside joined with the constant gurgle from the nearby stream to remind me of all the reasons why I should get up and begin the day. Instead I permitted myself a quiet moment of cautious happiness. Between the mending of things with Jacob and the travesty of the situation with Henry, Jesse had his confidence back, and we were making plans at last.

Just the thought made me smile and stretch languidly. With the small movement I was suddenly awash in a cascading wave of nausea. My stomach seized, and a geyser of something surged upward. I flung back the covers and lunged for the empty basin setting on the nearby nightstand.

Jessie, startled out of a sound sleep, scrambled behind me, frantically saying, "Lizzie! Lizzie! What is it? What's wrong?" I felt his hands, urgently feeling along my spine as I half-lay, half-knelt on the floor heaving the remains of last night's meal into the heavy china bowl. One last spasm, and the feeling of being turned wrong side out, subsided. For a moment I just slumped limply against the side of the bed. "Oh, Lord," I croaked. Jessie's hands reached my head and gently pushed my hair back from my face, and felt the clammy dampness of my skin.

"Lizzie, sweetheart," he said breathlessly, "are you all right?"

Another deep breath and I felt a little steadier. "I-I think it's passing," I said, limply, wishing I could sound more reassuring. "It's better now."

His hands stilled, and he took a steadying breath himself, and said, "Just stay still. Don't try to move."

I closed my eyes, and tried to think steady thoughts as he crawled past me on hands and knees, brushing against me with his movements. There was a little fumbling noise, and then the sound of sloshing water. One hand touched my shoulder, and the other gently brought a cool, moist cloth to my face. His touch was feather light as he wiped first my brow and then my chin. Feeling much restored, I took the cloth from him and did a more thorough job of it. "Thank you, love." I said, softly. "I do think I am going to live."

"Do you think it is something you ate, then?" he asked. And I realized it was light enough I could see his brow creased with worry.

"I-I don't know, Jessie, I suppose it could be." I said. "But maybe not…"

"Ah…"he said. "I thought so."

My breath caught, "Y-you knew…?"

"Well, I hoped so…" he said, quietly. "But I-"

"And here I have been agonizing these last few days – how to tell you!" I said. "I was so afraid you would be upset. That it would be too much…"

He reached out and very gently gathered me to him. "Oh, Lizzie, a child is always a blessing and cause for joy! You are the heart of my heart. That hasn't changed. And to have a child with you…Oh, Lizzie, my only concern is for you and the child. Everything else God will grant us the wisdom to deal with!"

"Well, God will take care of us all, then! I just know it!" I declared, with a silent prayer. "He really is giving us a new beginning!"

"How long?" he asked, mind clearly already racing ahead. "Spring?"

"Yes, Mama says probably April." I said.

"So, you all have been conspiring behind my back, eh?" he smiled.

"My mother has had thirteen children." I said with a laugh. "She does recognize the signs!"

"Well, there is that!" he conceded with a smile.

Suddenly, serious, he stroked my hair, and said, "Lizzie, you must take care. Not all women have an easy time, and you have exhausted yourself this past year caring for me."

"Jessie, I am fine, and I will be fine! And I want to care for you!" I assured him.

"I know you do love, but life goes on. Already, it is so much... easier than it was. I think I have finally... I guess accepted it. I still have my moments of frustration- as you well know. But I have learned- thanks in no small part to you and your patience and ingenuity. And I am learning – every day – finding ways to do things," he said, getting to his feet. He reached with a practiced hand to the dresser top where I left his fresh clothes folded every night before going to bed. "As a matter of fact madam," he said, as he pulled his shirt on over his head, "my father and I are embarking on a joint project this very morning.- He's going to teach or should I say re-teach me to be a farmer!"

"And what, pray tell, might that involve?" I asked, intrigued.

"Well for this morning at least, it means that I am, my dear, going to re-learn yet another childhood skill," he said, with a grin. "I am going to milk a cow!"

With that announcement, he came back around the bed, gently raised me to my feet, kissed me thoroughly, and said, "And you, my love, are going back to bed and rest till I get back."

Ignoring my protests, he tucked me in, and said, "When I do get back, we will see what kind of wonderful breakfast we can concoct to go with the fresh milk! Deal?"

Placing his hand against my cheek, so he could feel my smile, I said softly, "Deal!"

***** ***** ***** ***** ***** ***** ***** *****

Jesse inhaled deeply, savoring the rich pine aroma coming from mantle of the big fireplace in his uncle's library. Funny thing, smells, he thought. As a blind man he had found his sense of smell becoming more and more sensitive, and he noticed the smell of things more now than he ever had... before. As the husband of a pregnant wife, he mused, he had also learned that smells could also be the Enemy. He smiled ruefully, and wondered what aroma would next set off poor Lizzie's now fickle stomach.

He was interrupted in his musings by the sounds of the library door opening, and of footsteps crossing the room, accompanied by the spicy aroma of a newly lit pipe. He stood, and turned toward the approaching steps, "Good afternoon, Uncle," he said, extending his hand. It was seized in a firm grip, as his greeting was warmly returned. He squashed the small twinge of regret that he felt over small things like that- that he always had to take the risk, that in every situation social or private he had to extend his hand- just put it out there in the general direction, and pray that whatever poor sod he was dealing with had enough sense to look down and grab it.

That momentary distraction caused him to miss what Abel had said after his greeting, and he turned toward his uncle's voice and said apologetically, "Uncle, I am sorry, I seem to be easily distracted today. What did you say?"

He heard Abel's snort followed by his good humored reply, "Living with a pregnant woman will do that to a man. Trust me, I know!" His uncle's footsteps moved away, and he said, "Come on over here, son, and have a seat by the fire. It's blasted cold out today! Your father assures me we'll have snow by tomorrow!" He moved confidently toward the warmth of the fire, lightly touching furniture whose placement he knew as well as he did that of the pieces in his own house. He lowered himself into the big overstuffed chair across from his Uncle, and prompted again, "You were saying, sir?"

"I received a letter from Amon Bond today. He finally managed to get a reply through to the one I sent him back in April after the episode with Henry," said Abel as he puffed deeply on the pipe, sending another blast of scent Jesse's way.

"Good Lord," said Jesse, "what on earth took so long?"

"Well as I told your father earlier today," replied Abel, "it is getting harder and harder to get mail through, if the rider happens to try going through Kansas!" He shook his head even though his son-in-law couldn't see it, and continued, "It is just a blood bath over there! Awful, awful things, no matter which side you are on! That Brown fellow- the abolitionist- he's every bit as much of a fanatic as the pro-slavery folks are, and they are just over there killing each other! It's a disgrace!"

Jesse nodded in agreement, "Yes, I know. Lizzie reads me the paper from cover to cover every time it comes. Thank God we haven't had any major incidents here in a while. Let's hope our luck holds out. Speaking of holding out, what does Amon have to say? Is our plan satisfactory? Are they willing to take us on?"

"He wishes more of us were coming sooner, of course," said Abel, "But yes, we are set to send a small group in the spring. I called you here today, because I want to discuss with you a change of plan. And I need you to help me sell it to Lizzie."

"What kind of change?" said Jesse, "and why?"

"We have prayed and prayed about this, my Sally and I," said Abel, "We both so passionately wanted to be a part of this first group, for many reasons. But this situation with your brother Henry has changed things. It ties your parents here in this volatile situation until April of '59 – 3 years from when we plan to go. That is a long time alone. Under the circumstances, Jacob and young David can help, but your father needs literate and mature eyes on the ground and ears to the grapevine, to protect not only his interests, but his safety and those of your brothers and sisters. All it would take would be one word – the wrong word – breathed by Henry to his father-in-law and his hot-headed pro-slavery friends and...." Jesse heard Abel heave another deep sigh, and could visualize that unruly white head of hair being shaken ruefully. "Jesse, I'm going to send my Henry with you and Lizzie. He can help you on the trail. And I have sent word to my nephew Logan. He wants to go. He is a good man, a fine farmer and a literate man, although not legally trained. You and he together can handle the land claims and legal matters until I can get there. Logan is actually near your oldest brother Christopher in age, but he married just a few years ago. I am told his wife is increasing, as is our Lizzie. Logan's child will be born in January. They hope to be here from Tennessee by March. "

Jesse sat, stunned, mulling it all over. He could feel Abel watching him. Finally, praying God would give him the gift of a glib tongue this night, when he had to tell Lizzie, he nodded. "All right, Uncle. I understand. I don't like it, but I understand. Damn Henry! I don't know that I can ever forgive him for what this has done to all of us!"

He heard Abel rise, and moments later he felt a hand on his shoulder. "Don't waste your energy on anger, Jesse. You and Lizzie are going to Texas. That's going to take all you've got. And we- all of us here are counting on you."

"Thanks, Uncle Abel. Thanks a lot." Jesse wasn't sure as he said it, if he was being sarcastic – or not.

*****   ******   *****   *****   *****   *****   *****   *****

Looking back on it years later, I never was sure how I survived those nine months of my first pregnancy. The first part is mostly a haze of nausea filled days, but that finally passed, and a good thing it was, as there was much to do. The fall and winter till Christmastime was taken up with physical preparations to go, being done early while I could still help. Belongings were sorted, to sell, to take, to give away. Furniture was sorted the same way. The things to be taken were carefully packed in wooden crates stuffed with straw and then stored away against the day they would be loaded into the wagons.

Logan and Fanny, two year old William, and tiny little Hugh, who had entered the world a month early, arrived in late January. Mama and Aunt Sarah were absolutely appalled that Logan had traveled so soon, but neither Fanny nor little Hugh appeared fazed by much of anything, Fanny being absolutely enthralled by her young son, and he being a most content and happy baby as long as he was fed much and often.

As February blew in, I began to resemble a very large clumsy sow, and my ability to help with physical preparations became nil. So I at last began to dedicate my long hours of waiting to stitchery. Tiny garments, blankets and booties filled my world, and as our child began to move within me, Jesse and I would spend hours sitting propped in bed, our hands covering my stomach, enchanted by the childish acrobatics taking place within.

We talked about names, but there was one I didn't mention. I thought of it often though, as I watched Jesse as he felt the child move. I prayed for a healthy child, and I lied when I told everyone I didn't care if it was a boy or girl, because I saw my husband's face whenever the child was mentioned, whenever the child moved. I heard the new vigor in his voice as he planned for our future. I saw the light in him I had thought forever dimmed, now shining bright on plans and hopes and dreams.

And on that day in April, when the sweeping pains came, and my child and I worked the hard word of every mother and child since Eve bore her sons- the hard work of being born- I waited, breathlessly, in that moment when I heard the child's first sweet cry – and my mother's voice said in glad wonder, "It's a girl, my sweet Leatha! You have a fine healthy girl!"

My mother placed my daughter in my arms, and at last I looked into the face of the child I had named in my heart all those months ago. I had named her for the look on her Father's face whenever he thought of her. "Hello," I whispered, "Hello our sweet Abigail." And then Jesse was there by my side, reaching toward the bundle in my arms. I gave her to him, a precious gift. I watched him touch her for the first time, watched again that beloved face transform. "Her name is Abigail."

"Abigail?" he asked, already enchanted.

"Yes," I whispered. "It's from the Hebrew. It means "Her Father's Joy".

***** ****** ***** ***** ***** ***** ***** *****

The sound of my steps echoed in the emptiness of the little white cottage in the woods as the gray and silver light of dawn spread a soft glow through the windows. Each room was empty of furniture, but full of memories. It had been our first place – ours together –just us. It had been our place of refuge and a haven for healing. And finally, it had become a place for new beginnings and the coming of joy.

125

I held Abigail close, as I walked through those rooms, remembering. Steps, strong and sure, sounded up the steps and into the room behind me. "Lizzie?" said my husband softly, "It's time to go."

I crossed the room to where he stood. He reached for my hand and I met his hand with mine. As our fingers intertwined, he breathed deeply, "Honeysuckle…. Whenever I smell it from now on…I will remember this place."

Jesse paused a moment, and I stood still with him in the moment, waiting. "Lizzie," he breathed, "my sweet Lizzie. I know what a leap of faith this is for both of us – this- this journey. But, your brother reminded me this morning of something I should have remembered all along. In all our talk and apprehensions about this choice and about this journey, we've forgotten where we are going," he said.

Puzzled, I replied, "What do you mean Jesse?" picking up on his quiet…excitement?

"The Brazos River…" he said, softly, "Lizzie after all this, we are really going there- to our safe place.- Remember, that first night, when I told you it's name…., the river named Brazos by the Spanish – El Rio de Los Brazos de Dios – The River of the Arms of God." The stillness was all around us, as he continued, "We, all of us, are going to spend the rest of our lives settled right where we should always know ourselves to be – safe-- in the Arms of God." Jessie squeezed my hand, reached up to gently touch Abigail's tiny head, and led me outside to where the wagon was waiting. And finally, for the first time in years, like the settling of a dove, true peace came.

Section II:

Stockton Bend

"Lizzie?" I whirled about, barely remembering to grab my skirt and keep it from the fire. My husband was standing near the wagon, and the flickering flames from our tiny campfire illuminated his face just enough for me to glimpse an odd half-smile, half-grimace that plucked at my heart, even as I started toward him.

"What is it Jessie?" I said, "Where's Abby?" I asked.

"Henry took her over to coo and babble at the horses, and to visit with her god-father, Mr. Bond. I told him I could manage. And that you were here, if I needed help." He stopped.

"And do you…" I said, carefully, "need help?"

That tentative little boy grin was back. "I don't think so," he said, softly. "Come and see."

His hand sought and found my elbow, and I said quickly, "Wait. I have to finish banking the fire. Just stay right here. I'll just be a moment." I strode back to the small stone circle I had laid and finished the job of putting sand on it to dowse the still burning branches.

As my eyes adjusted to the moon lit darkness I could see Jessie's silhouette against the white of our wagon canvas. A soft glow lit the canvas from within, and I knew he had lit the lantern for me. "You didn't have to light the lantern, Jessie."

"Yes, I did," he whispered, "You'll see."

As I stepped around to view the inside of the wagon, I stopped so suddenly that Jessie almost trod on my heels. The lantern hung from a long metal hook that hung down from the high arch of the wagon cover casting a warm glow over the interior. A straw tick mattress encased in white cotton cloth had been laid across the tops of the wooden crates of supplies, and two new looking feather pillows lay atop the double wedding ring quilt that had adorned our bed from the day of our marriage. A long narrow box-shelf built along the side of the wagon held our Bible, my small jewelry box, four other leather-bound volumes, and my small sewing basket. The trunk that held our clothes was at the foot of the bed platform along with another that proved to contain other bed linens and our small stock of medicinal items. And at the head of the bed platform, between it and the front of the wagon was a heavily padded wooden box, lined with tiny down stuffed blankets- a cradle for Abby.

My heart melted. "Oh, Jessie, how on earth did you...?" I exclaimed

"Henry helped some, before we left this morning. I could see in my mind how it could be, if we loaded the wagon right. So he just followed my instructions, and then, tonight, all I had to do was light the lantern, get it hung, and make up the bed." He stopped, and took my hand and kissed it gently. "I wanted to make a little piece of home for you Lizzie. – Did I get the right quilt? I thought it felt right but no one was here to say....."

Blinded by tears, I threw my arms about his neck and hugged him close. "Oh, Jessie! It's perfect! You are the dearest man...."

His armed tightened about me and his lips searched for and found mine. "Welcome home, Mrs. Nutt," he whispered. "I'll go ahead and confess now that Henry plans to keep our daughter occupied until her next feeding time. He and I both figure you would like a little break. So come on up and take a little nap. I'll be right here. Oh, and *do* put out that lantern." He smiled. "I don't think you'll be reading much later tonight."

***** ***** ***** ***** ***** ***** ***** *****

The next morning, I awoke to the song of birds chirping in the growing light of dawn. I rolled over reaching for Jesse, only to discover his spot empty. I squashed a surge of panic as the sound of his and Henry's voices, light in conversation, drifted in from outside. Reassured that all was well, I reached for Abby, who was beginning to fuss in her cradle. "Did you sleep good in the bed your Daddy fixed for you, my sweet girl? I whispered as I held her close. Her only response was a happy gurgle, as she latched on and began to nurse. I sighed contentedly, treasuring the last few minutes of quiet and solitude before beginning the rigors of the day.

I could smell coffee brewing, and when I came down from the wagon I saw that Henry and Jesse had already almost completed the reloading of the wagon with items taken down for overnight use, and were now in the process of re-hitching the mules for another day of labor. Jesse was still moving slowly and carefully and Henry – God bless him – quietly watching every move, every buckle fastened, just to be sure all was done as it should be. But Henry was letting his student learn, and Jesse made not a single error. Then they switched sides "to check each other".

By the time the sun was fully up we were moving. We soon found that to be the pattern of our days. Jesse, Henry, Logan, Amon and Benjamin up long before dawn making the coffee and rough breakfast, tending stock and readying wagons, while Fanny and I took a few precious quiet moments to nurse our babes and ready them and ourselves for the day. Sunup found us on the move, Jesse and I and Fanny and Logan taking turns with driving the two family wagons, while Amon, Ben, and Henry rotated driving the wagon loaded with supplies for the settlement at Stockton Bend, as the other two rode ahead and behind keeping an eye on the trail, and a lookout for Indians as well.

I was surprised when Jesse took the reins from me the first time. But he had handled teams of horses and mules his whole life, and his hands were steady and sure on the reins. "You just keep an eye out Lizzie," he said, "for the most part they will follow the team in front of them unless I tell them different. I just need you to keep an eye out for any tricky spots or to take over if we have to go faster or maneuver tight spots." As with everything else, we made a good team, and my heart was glad to see his confidence continuing to grow.

About noon, on our second day out, we stopped at a stream to water and refresh both the animals and ourselves. I had left Abby, content and sound asleep, in her little box bed in the wagon, and come down to the stream bank to sample its clear running waters. Poor Fanny could not so easily steal a quiet moment. The new baby, Hugh, was of course still tiny and needed constant warmth and almost constant feeding. William was, as my mother said, "already all boy", which basically meant he was into anything and everything- all the time!

As if to prove the truth of my thoughts, Fanny had just knelt by the stream and was washing her pale face, when young William came barreling down the path howling with glee, obviously escaped from his father's dubious supervision.. Before either Fanny or I had done more than look up from our ablutions, he passed airborne between us and landed with a mighty splash right in the middle of the stream. Amazing that one small body could make a large enough disturbance of the waters to totally drench two grown women, but that was certainly the case. Moreover, Master William had fortunately landed in the shallow water on his plump little backside, rather than his head, but found his dignity to be sorely injured nonetheless. His vocalizations promptly changed from screams of glee to wails of distress.

The fact that he was bouncing up and down and kicking mightily, gave ease to any concerns he might actually be seriously injured, but his cries were shrill enough to thoroughly spook all the animals in the area, including all of the horses and mules. I heard the startled exclamations of the men, and knew they had their hands full. I leaped into the water and scooped up young William, clapping a hand over his mouth even as my maneuver startled him into silence. "He's all right," I called to the world at large, mostly so the menfolk would know they could focus on the livestock.

Fanny came scrambling down the bank to meet me, "On, Elizabeth, I am *so* sorry!" she exclaimed, reaching out for her sodden offspring. I stopped long enough to make eye contact with the child, and said firmly, "No more screaming, understand?" He nodded, eyes still wide, and I took my hand away and handed Fanny her sodden, sniffling offspring. She clutched him to her, wet clothes and all for a moment, and then Logan Landers appeared out of the trees behind her, his month drawn in a thin line. He glanced at Fanny and William as he passed them, but he came directly to the stream bank and extended an arm to me. "Elizabeth, I do apologize for young William. It is my fault. He was left in my care."

I held on tight to his hand as I struggled up out of the stream bed. I was soaked from the waist down, and the front of my blouse was wet as well. It was amazing, I thought, just how much a skirt and petticoats could weigh when water-logged. So I was slightly breathless when I assured him, "It's alright, Cousin Logan, I know how quickly they can get away!"

I looked past him to see Henry and Jesse appear at the top of the bank above us. I saw Henry speak quietly in Jesse's ear, and his face relaxed into a grin. Henry also looked positively devilish, as he called down to me, "Well, Sister, if you wanted a bath, you should've said so. We would have stopped somewhere with a deeper pool!"

"You better wipe that grin off your face, Henry Landers, or I'll show you how deep it was!" I retorted, grinning myself. "Fanny, let me know if you need extra towels. We've a crate of older linens I brought along to cut into clouts for Abby."

"Thank you kindly, Elizabeth," she said, shyly, "I think we are fine for now. If you need a spare petticoat while yours dries, I've an extra one in my trunk."

"Oh, that would be wonderful," I said, thankfully, "My only extra is my dressy one and it's not well suited to the trail."

"I'll bring it to you, directly," said Fanny, turning toward her wagon, "Soon as I get William wrung out."

"Bring the children with you," I invited, "You can ride with us awhile, and we can visit while I change."

Jesse sensing what I was about, piped up and said, "Henry and I used to take my little brothers up on the wagon or horse with us all the time when they were little. Maybe we can give Master William a ride on the wagon seat while you and Lizzie visit."

Amon Bond looked at his son Ben, "You take the supply wagon then. I'll ride point."

We all scrambled to ready ourselves to move on. Minutes later, Fanny appeared at the back of the wagon with Hugh in one arm and a white petticoat in the other. Logan had brought William and planted him between Jesse and Henry with admonitions to behave or else. Fanny handed me the baby and scrambled up into the wagon unassisted.

"I didn't know if you'd be undressed yet, so I told Logan to go on," she explained. "The man's spent so much of his life just him and other menfolk, He forgets about the sensibilities of decent womenfolk sometimes."

"Logan?!" I said, incredulously. "I've known him all my life! I've never seen him be anything but proper!" I laughed, "Why, he always struck me as, forgive me, kind of starched and serious, compared to my father!"

Fanny flashed a smile, and I suddenly realized what a beauty she must have been before two babies and a miscarriage in the course of three years had turned her wan and pale. In the course of the next hour and a half, I discovered I didn't know the half of it. As the wagon began to move, I pulled the canvas openings at front and back shut and motioned her to put little Hugh in the box with Abby, who was awake but content. From the baby noises coming from the box, it sounded like they both were glad to have company. A brief glance to assure all was well, and I began to strip out of my soggy mess of clothes.

Fanny showed no embarrassment, but jumped right in to help me with fastenings, and I remarked, "I'm glad you don't mind my changing right here in front of you! I grew up sharing a room with two older sisters, so I didn't think of it till you were already here."

It was the first time I had heard her laugh, and she said, "Oh, Liz-Elizabeth! If you only knew! No, it's fine! I'm not the least embarrassed, I assure you."

"I do wish you and Logan would call me Lizzie," I said, smiling, "No one else calls me Elizabeth, except my father or Jesse, when they are angry."

"Angry? Jesse?" said Fanny, incredulously, "I can't imagine that. He is obviously in love with you!"

"Well, mostly my father is the excitable one in the family," I grinned, "but he's really all bark and no bite with us girls. Now the boys, he was more stern with them, but he was always fair."

"Logan's that way too," said Fanny, softly, "Stern sometimes, but fair always. Not mean like men can be."

Something in her voice caught my attention. I looked up in time to see a far away, haunted look cross her face, before she saw me looking, and lowered her eyes. Looking for something neutral to say, I said, "I've been wanting to talk to you about Texas." I smiled. "Papa told us that you and Logan were married there. So, I guessed you've lived there before. What's it like? Did you grow up there?"

The faraway look was back, along with a sad smile, and suddenly she seemed years older than I, although less than five years separated us in age. "Lizzie, honey, the Texas I know, you want no part of. But yes, I guess you could say I grew up there. If it weren't for Logan, I probably would have already died there too." She smiled, a real smile now, and said, "Logan told me about how your Jesse and his brother Jacob lost their sight. Guess that just goes to prove, heroism runs in the family."

"Heroism? You mean Logan?" I asked rather disbelievingly. "I mean-well, I'm sorry, but to me he's always just been Cousin Logan who was almost more like an uncle. He's actually two years younger than my oldest brother Chris."

Fanny nodded, "I know. He worships your father, you know. I do too. Things would have been very different for Logan and me if not for your father."

"Oh?" I said, intrigued. "How so?"

"Well, you know how your father is about family. Well, he more or less forced the Landers clan to accept me as Logan's wife back in Tennessee whether they wanted to or not." she said softly. "I didn't expect it. Logan and I were both resigned to it, being outcasts, you know. But Abel wouldn't have it. Even though he had never set eyes on me, He wrote every one of his brothers and sisters letters shaming them into accepting me." There were tears in her eyes, as she said, "Lectured them at length apparently on their Christian duty, he did. Aunt Mary showed Logan her letter. He said it was fourteen pages long, and referenced 22 different scriptures, and read like a legal indictment!"

I was dumbfounded that I knew nothing of any of this. "Well, that certainly sounds like Papa!" I smiled. "But Fanny... why? And why don't Jesse and I know any of this?"

Her look softened and she said, "Lizzie, how old are you and Jesse?"

"Why, I'm 25 and Jesse is 24." I answered.

She nodded thoughtfully, "In 1850 when Logan and I married, I was twenty-four years old. He was twenty-eight and old enough to know better, but he did it anyway. You and Jesse were- what- eighteen at the time. Much too young to be included in the family squabbles over a marriage, especially all the way over in Tennessee."

"But why was there a squabble?" I asked, bewildered. "It's not like you were too young..."

Fanny shook her head. "No, it wasn't my age," she said softly, "It was the fact that I was the daughter of a whore, and was already carrying another man's baby."

I felt my mouth fall open, and closed it quickly as I could, but Fanny nodded. "Exactly." She said. "And I know that some would say it's no excuse, but my mother and I were both victims of circumstance, and of men who were evil enough or weak enough to take advantage of those circumstances."

"What happened, Fanny," I asked softly, touching her hand. She froze for a moment, then took my hand and squeezed it.

"Did you see what just happened there, Lizzie? – How when you touched me, I froze for a moment?" she asked.

I nodded, and she continued, "I *hate* that I do that. But I do. I have ever since…. But wait, I want to tell you about my mama first. My mama and daddy were both from Bedford County, Tennessee. They both knew your daddy when he was a young man just come there, and they knew his family. My daddy was a – a – I guess you'd call him a dreamer. Kinda like Amon Bond, but without the common sense. He and mama both came from good people, not well-off, but decent folk. And my daddy he went to hear the talks when men like Mr. Houston, and Mr. Crockett, and Mr. Austin came to Tennessee to talk about Texas. Now he wanted to go to Texas, but Mama didn't. And they fought over it – a lot. I was old enough to hear and I know when the revolution started in 1834-35 he heard Mr. Crockett was gathering men to go fight. So one day, we woke up and he was gone. He'd left Mama a note. She had to get Mr. Henry, our neighbor, to read it to her. It said, "I'm sorry, Frannie, but I have to go to Texas to fight. I will send for you when it is safe." And he signed it "Love, Tom."

She paused, gathering her thoughts. "So my mother cried, and she waited. We did alright until my granddaddy died. He died in 1845 just before they announced Texas was a state. Mama, she figured daddy had died in one of those battles we heard about- the Alamo, or San Jacinto or somewhere in-between. But Mama never heard a word. And when Grandaddy died, he left a little money, so she decided we would go to Texas, her and us four children, and she would get work as a seamstress and try to find out what happened to Daddy. So we went by stagecoach all the way to a town called San Augustine in the piney woods of East Texas. We got a little house there, rented it with Grandaddy's money. Things were alright for a while, but then the money ran out, and mama couldn't get enough work from decent folk, and so finally to eat, she took a job waitin' tables at a saloon. She was too old be one of the "doves" there, but some of the older men, they liked her. Liked that she was kind and wasn't coarse actin'. And so, sometimes, a few times she would think a man was nice and was telling her true about having real feelings for her, and she would bring him home to meet us. There were four of us. I was twenty when we went and I should've stayed in Tennessee, but Lizzie, I wanted to protect her, to help you know? So I mostly kept watch on the younger children, and tried to keep my brother Ben from getting in with the wrong crowd. Of course he did. Ben disappeared in 1848. He was 19. It nearly killed my mama when we lost Ben."

"Oh, Fanny," I said, shocked to the core, "I am so sorry."

She nodded, "Me too." She sniffed, and pulled out her handkerchief, and blew, before continuing in a choked voice, "After Ben left, Mama, started drinking. She started bringing home some really scary men. Mostly, Ellie and Sarah and I would hide under the bed in our bedroom, in the dark, so the men would think the house was empty. Sometimes that was really scary too, because we could hear things. They would hurt Mama. I just knew that one day we would come out and find her dead. I knew it was all going to end badly. I was twenty – four years old, had no skills, no decent way to make a living, and I was terrified to leave that house because I was afraid for my sisters. But I was determined I would never let myself become what poor Mama had become. "

She stopped, unable to continue, and I said, "Fanny, it's all right, you don't have to –"

"Yes, I do," she insisted softly. "If we are going to be true friends, I want- I need at least one person I don't have to lie to. I-I want you to know."

So she took a deep breath and told me the rest- how her mother's guest one day had spotted her. How her mother had died at his hands trying to keep him off of Fanny. How he had then raped Fanny, while her two sisters remained hidden, terrified, under their bed. How

Logan Landers had been riding his horse down the street that night, on his way down to the Sabine River to catch the ferry at dawn. How he had heard her screams, and come into the house and killed the man with his bare hands. How he had nursed her wounds, helped bury her mother, seen her and her sisters moved to a safe place – a farmhouse on land he owned in Smith County, and how when it became obvious that she was carrying her rapist's child he had offered her marriage, and her child a name. She lost the child before the marriage could take place. But somewhere in all the horror, love had been born, so marry they did, and he took and her and her sisters home to Tennessee with every intention of building a life there.

"But, he had written to your father and to two other relatives before our marriage, and told them my story. So when we got there, everyone knew. They really took your father's words to heart and tried to be kind. My sisters both were able to find very fine young men who came to love them. Logan was generous enough to provide them with dowries, and they are very happy. So our time there served its purpose. But we both needed to be somewhere where most folks don't know. I know your parents know, and now you and Jesse will too. Will you keep our secret Lizzie? Please."

Shaken, and filled with sorrow for all this poor soul had experienced, I promised, "Fanny, you humble me with your trust. I promise we will keep your confidence and indeed we need not speak of it ever again, unless *you* need to talk. You and Logan can always come to Jesse and me for anything." I squeezed her hand. "Thank you for telling me."

"Thank you for understanding." She smiled, and said, "I guess I gave a pretty bad picture of Texas. It's not all like that. It is wild, and new, and big, and the parts I have seen are really quite pretty. I like the sound of the place we are going. I love rivers and the sounds of running water!"

"Me too," I exclaimed, and I told her the story, which she had not yet heard, about the Arms of God.

"Oh, Lizzie, I love that! I must tell Logan! He will too!" she smiled.

Two fussing babies demanded our attention just then, and as the afternoon passed in gentle companionship, I thanked God for my new friend and prayed that she and her family would find the shelter they needed in Los Brazos de Dios.

***** ****** ***** ***** ***** ***** ***** *****

For the most part, once we left the heavily wooded areas around Neosho, our route took us through gently rolling country, grasslands, with few trees except in the river bottoms. Once out of Missouri we saw few people, for Amon and Ben had chosen to bring us the shorter route through the Indian Territory of Oklahoma, rather than the longer more settled route south thru Arkansas and east through the piney woods. It was a risk, but some of the supplies we brought were sorely needed and there was also the necessity of getting there in time to meet the requirements of the land claim deal, which meant a crop planted and harvested this season.

The men were diligent in scouting the surrounding country for the small bands of Indian hunters who roamed the area, and we stayed far away from any of their nomadic villages, usually set up along a river bank. Our plan was avoidance rather than confrontation, and many nights we made cold camp to keep from being spotted. I had never lived on the trail before, and certainly the lack of comforts of hearth and home took some getting used to. But during that early part of the journey, the spring weather was mild and sunny, and the game plentiful. We took mostly small game caught in snares set overnight, the men wanting to avoid using their rifles, which would have announced out presence in the country.

We were careful and we were lucky. We managed to reach the crossing at the Red River without incident. We would cross into Texas at Colbert's Ferry. A few miles out Amon announced that we were now in country occupied by the Chickasaw Indians, a peaceable tribe who had come here many years ago from Tennessee. One of their number, a half-breed named Benjamin Franklin Colbert had bought and run the ferry since 1849. Mr. Colbert's property presented us with the first real bit of civilization since leaving Missouri almost a month before. We arrived at the entrance to Mr. Colbert's operation mid-morning on a hot humid day in mid-June. The wide rock entrance included an overhead sign proclaiming "Colbert's Ferry", and a large southern style white frame two story house commanded the hillside overlooking the farmland on our left. Black workers dotted the green fields and left little doubt as to Mr. Colbert's stance on current events.

Past the main house, which set in the middle of a big open grass yard, nearer the river was a large double log cabin. Upon arriving, we discovered it was a stagecoach station house and trading post offering numerous amenities such as a common sleeping room, a large dining hall and bar combination, bathing facilities, and a small general store. When we pulled into the stable yard next to the stage station two young Indian boys and two young black boys came out together to help tend to our stock. I was busily whispering to Jesse all the details I could about what I was seeing, when the door of the stage station opened, and a tall dark headed man with a handsome face and reddish bronze skin stepped out. He was dressed as any well-to-do businessman (or southern planter- it occurred to me) would dress, his suit and matching waist being of fine dark gray cloth, and sparkling white linen for his shirt. He greeted Amon Bond with great cordiality and it was obvious they were well acquainted. Jesse and I had just set feet on the ground when Amon brought the gentleman to us for introduction.

He shook Jesse's hand with enthusiasm and nodded courteously to me, and invited us to make ourselves welcome. Once Fanny and I were seated at one of the long dining tables with our two little ones and Henry and Benjamin for escort, the older men and Jesse withdrew with Mr. Colbert to "conduct business". I felt a brief surge of curiosity and wondered if they would get invited into the big white house across the way. Fanny was very quiet, and sat close to me. It was clear that being in the room with so many loud talking men made her nervous. There were several other travelers gathered around the long tables, all men, almost all cowmen and land agents from their talk. They seemed mostly to be headed either north to Springfield, or south to a town called Dallas. I remembered seeing it on the map of Texas in my father's study, about 75 miles east and north of our new home on the Brazos,

The food was simple but plentiful. Skillet cooked ham and fried potatoes and boiled greens, collard by taste, were served with a good strong coffee and sourdough biscuits. There was apple pie made with early fruit from the orchard I had spotted behind the big house to end the best meal any of us had had since leaving Missouri. We were midway through the meal when our menfolk came in and quickly played catch up in the eating. Afterward, full and sleepy, we walked across the road to the small shaded field where our wagons had been parked with our stock hobbled and grazing nearby. Our turn on the ferry would not come until early the next morning so we had a rare afternoon of leisure to enjoy.

We two couples headed for the sleepy refuge of our wagons, while Amon, Ben and Henry made camp in the shade of the surrounding trees near the supply wagon. Jesse and I settled against the pillows in the haven of our wagon bed. While Abby nursed hungrily, Jesse said with a smile, "I could hear the wheels turning in that brain of yours the entire time we were eating."

"You're a fine one to talk, Jesse Nutt," I retorted. "You've been like to burst with wanting to talk ever since you men got back from your time with Mr. Colbert."

"What I have will keep a bit," said Jesse. "You first."

"All right," I conceded, thinking where to begin. "First of all, even though Amon had spoken of it before, this place comes as a complete surprise. It's like an oasis of civilization, in a vast wilderness. Just the sight of cultivated fields again, after so much open country was a shock, and then that house, looking like something I remember straight off a Tennessee plantation, complete with the nigras in the fields. I was only ten when we left Tennessee, but I remember…"

Jesse nodded. "I know what you mean," he said. "Of course I can't see it but I can picture it as you describe. But what I refer to is the man Colbert. Henry says he looks like a brave wearing white man's clothes, which I guess he is. When he speaks it is with that broad southern drawl, straight out of the deep South, and that is certainly where his politics come from!"

"Obviously," I said, thinking of the slaves in the fields. "But he is an educated man?" I asked.

"Very much so," said Jesse. "He is a member of the Chickasaw tribe- one of the Five Civilized Tribes sent here to settle on government land by Andrew Jackson. He and some of the Cherokee men here have created a government structure and lifestyle here modeled on that of the white men they admired in Tennessee. They seek recognition and acceptance as a territorial government at the national level. So far Washington has turned both a blind eye and a deaf ear."

"So are they being courted and cultivated by the secessionists then?" I asked.

"Very astute of you my dear," said Jesse, with a grim smile. "Yes, that is precisely what is happening. Apparently all along this side of the Red River that is what is happening with both white and Indian landholders."

"And just south of here, across the river in Texas?" I asked, fearing I already knew the answer.

"I am not sure exactly," said Jesse, "From what I know, in many areas all over Texas there are groups of moderates like ourselves settling. Some were already there, and some have, as we know, been brought in by Sam Houston and others like him. Right now it seems those folks may be close to holding a majority. But if they do, it is a slim one."

"Which means the balance could tip either way." I whispered, with a sinking feeling. "Jesse, is it all for nothing? Have we moved from atop one powder keg to another?"

"I don't know, Lizzie," he said, honestly, "I hope not. At the very least, I hope our remote situation may be a buffer from the full scale violence of war, should it come. At most, we and people like us just may be enough to turn the tide, and keep Texas out of it, and maybe, if we get very lucky, stop it altogether."

"How so?" I asked.

"There are some who think if Kansas, Missouri, and Texas all hold for the union, the south won't secede. Texas really is the key. The south needs Texas ports and her manpower." said Jesse.

"And all this deep thinking as the result of a half hour with Mr. Colbert?" I asked.

Jesse shook his head, "Not entirely. You know of my correspondence with Senator Houston, and of Amon's network of contacts. But Colbert is flesh and blood – the whole situation personified. Yes, on

144

the surface he's a very courteous likeable fellow, but underneath....”
He shook his head again.

“What about underneath, Jesse?” I asked.

“Underneath,” said Jesse, “beats the heart of a warrior fighting for his people to be accepted as equals in the white man's world. He's already proven that he is willing to hold other people of color – black nigras and Indians from other tribes- as slaves, to gain acceptance into the world he wants to enter. What else might he and his friends be willing to do to further their cause?”

“That is a frightening thought,” I agreed, suddenly wishing morning would come sooner.

“It is indeed.” Jesse nodded, and added, “I think I am very glad indeed that over 200 miles of wilderness separate the banks of the Brazos River from the banks of the Red.”

“Yes, please God, that it will be enough,” I prayed softly, “Please God that it will be enough.”

    *****   ******   *****   *****   *****   *****   *****   *****

The sounds of galloping hoof-beats grew louder, and I spotted Henry hunched over his horse's neck as he angled in alongside the slowly climbing wagons. Jessie and I coughed as the dust swirled briefly around us as he reined in beside our wagon. “It's there!” he said with a huge grin, “This is the last big climb! At the top, - it just goes on, and on, forever! There's the mountain of the Comanche they told us about! And- and- it's just- just...BIG and -...”

His excitement and grin were both infectious, and we all smiled back at him, and Logan said indulgently, “Well now son, we are hurrying as fast as these poor beasts can bring us! Go on and explore a bit, and we will meet you at the top!”

Jessie touched my shoulder and said, "Are the beasts struggling much, Elizabeth? I can walk if need be. It seems our pace is slow enough."

"No," I said as I guided the big mules around yet another clump of brush, "We're over half way to the summit. It won't be long now."

The big horses that pulled our wagon were plodding doggedly up the hill, but seemed in no real distress. Thank goodness the rain that had followed us for two days to the north of Dallas had gone away in the last week, so the faint wagon trail we followed was firm ground and not mud. It had apparently been a good year for rain though. The country around us showed a fine healthy green even coming into the heat of summertime, and wildflowers scattered bright clumps of color all around.

Our wagon was lead today, so I could see Amon waiting for us at the top of the rise. At age 67, he was a dried up prune of a little man, but still vital. He sat straight in the saddle atop the coal black stallion that along with my mare was our hope for future good quality horse stock. He turned from the view and watched us approach, a smile lighting up his usually somber face. He turned to face west again, as I pulled on the reins to bring the wagon to a halt beside him. "There it is, children," he said softly, "Los Brazos de Dios- the Arms of God."

I raised my eyes from the backs of the horses before me, and gasped softly. "Lizzie?" said Jesse, reaching for hand. "What...?"

"Oh, Jesse," I breathed, "It is so beautiful."

"Tell me..." he whispered.

"Wait!" I said softly, and turned. I lifted three month old Abby from her bed, with a murmured, "Come here, love."

I placed her in her father's arms and laid my hand in her sweet soft curls as I swallowed, searching for words. "It's big." I said, with a little chuckle, "and- and green! We are way up high looking west, and the-

the view stretches out in front of us for what seems like forever. The land just rolls down from here in a gentle bumpy slope covered with green grass and little short clumps of trees here and there, and in the grass there's pale splashes of yellow and purple and pink- that's wildflowers. And there's places where you can see it's rocky too. White and bright outcrops, maybe limestone, all that is just spread out like a carpet for maybe three or four miles to a dark green line of trees growing close along both sides of the river. And some places it's just barely visible, and others it's wider and you can see the water – sparkling silvery blue in the sunshine- and it's crooked – all curves across the carpet of green. And a couple of places it curves so much it almost meets itself- and on the far side rising up as high or higher than we are now is a big flat-topped mesa or mountain, just the one, standing there with its' shadow falling down toward the river because the sun is getting low in the sky, and ri-right up the river from it, you can see two high spots with white bluffs that tower over the river bottom, and you can see the river flowing way up the country to the north, but not so far to the south, cause there's more hills that direction." I stopped for breath, and Jessie squeezed my hand.

"My Letha, you do have a way with words!" said my brother Henry said, his lean face creased in a smile, "Can you see our land from here, Amon? Are we going to get there today?"

"Yes, I can see your land, and mine too, but we won't make it there today," he answered. "Elizabeth, you said you see that second bluff overlooking the river, just north and east of the mountain? The land Abel and I planned for Nutt family land starts at the river bank there and runs back to the north and east along the river on the west side. The Landers claim will be just north of that up by that next bend you can see in the river. And my daughter and her husband have a little place on that little creek right between them. My claim is further north along that same line. So we will camp on the east side tonight, and like the Israelites cross over into the Promised Land tomorrow.

There is a reasonable ford a few miles north, so that is where we will head in the morning."

Logan and Fanny and Ben and their wagons had joined us at the summit, and there was a wave of excited relief that swept through all at the beauty of the land and the prospect of the journey's end. "Well, Pa, we'll not get *there,* If we continue sitting *here.*" observed Benjamin Bond impatiently.

"You're absolutely right, son," he agreed. Catching my eye, he raised an arm, "Let's move out!" he called.

I spoke to the mules, and the wagon tilted downward, as we began the last leg of our journey- our journey home.

Staking a Claim   August 1856

We forded the Brazos just below Stockton Bend early the next morning. It was a scary experience. The river was by far the largest we had crossed without using a ferry, and I could hear Jesse and Henry, who was handling our wagon, muttering to each other about ferry cables, and toll regulations, and water levels, and degrees of slope. Fortunately the rain had held off and I heard Amon saying "all we had to worry about was getting wet if we fell in".

I sat in the bed of the wagon, Abigail clutched in my arms. There was an absolutely terrifying two or three minutes when the wagon was actually floating with no contact with the bottom. I actually missed seeing anything as I sat huddled with eyes shut. Never has there been a more blessed sound than the sound of the wheel rims hitting the river bottom again. I opened my eyes and looked forward between the mules' heads at the grassy green slope that made up the bank on the west side of the Brazos. So like Moses in the Red Sea, and Our Lord in the waters of the Jordan, we had come through the waters to meet our destiny in this new land. And a fair and beautiful land it was,

There was a high bluff that towered over the east side of the river all along the sweeping curve of the river known as Stockton Bend. The valley of gently rolling almost flat land embraced by the arch of water beneath that bluff was where Amon Bond and the other families in our new community had made their foothold in this new land. While our land claims would spill out over the surrounding hills and valleys like the soon to be carefully cut and sewn pieces of a wildly colored patchwork quilt, Stockton Bend was our refuge in what was still a wilderness. Amon and that first group of settlers had all filed claim on all that land within the bend with the intention of leasing it or selling some of it to other settlers once they had clear title. With that in mind, they had first built dwellings and laid out farms for their own folk, and then Austen Yates and his friend George Griffith had begun building small houses set in the middle of each "kitchen plot" of land to be leased - 10 acres with enough space for a house, a barn, a field for kitchen crops and grazing for a small number of livestock. They also built – on demand – buildings for whatever business the tenant wished to engage in. So far, there was a small grocery, a couple of livery stables, a saloon out by the edge of the "town" and a shoemaker.

On the property that was to be leased to the Nutt family two cabins already stood with the foundation for Papa David's blacksmith shop already laid between them. The larger of the cabins would someday be for Uncle David and Aunt Sarah, Jacob, Abel, Susan and David, while the smaller was for me and Jesse, and Abby. The next two plats were to be leased to my parents, and whichever of my siblings were still at home and/or decided to come. Papa had sent plans with us for the house he wanted built. Papa knew it might only be a temporary home, but he wanted Mama to be comfortable, and he also wanted room for whatever gatherings they might wish to host. It was going to be interesting to see what Austen and George would come up with based on his plans versus the materials to hand. Logan and Fanny and their children were going to share the Nutt cabin with Henry until they could get their place found and built. Henry would of course supervise the building of our father's house, and move in there when it was completed.

We were just dismounting off the wagon seat in front of our new cabin, preparing to take our leave of Amon and Benjamin, when hoof beats sounded at the gallop coming toward us from the west. Amon's head snapped up, and Henry, Ben and Logan all touched hands to guns. Over the rise appeared a paint horse carrying slender dark haired man. Amon moved his horse forward, saying "It's my son, Ed. Something's amiss."

"Pa!" exclaimed the gentleman, reining his horse hard to a stop. "Thank God you're back! We've got trouble!"

"Ed, these are our new settlers- Jesse and Elizabeth Nutt, Henry Landers, and Logan and Fanny Landers. I don't see red Indians or a cougar chasing you. So what is this trouble that prevents simple civility?!"

"Sorry, Pa." said Ed, a bit subdued. He nodded our general direction and said, "Welcome folks! Sorry for my manners."

Logan spoke up and said, "That's alright Mr. Bond. What is the difficulty, if we may ask?"

Ed looked back at his father, who nodded slightly, and answered, "Pa, you know that plot of land to the west of us, that old man Davis tried to claim and found out somebody else already filed and got patent on it? Well the folks arrived three days ago- six families of them. They're from Georgia, and Pa they've got black slaves- ever family of 'em has at least two or three.   We've kinda nosed around and looks like about half adult black and half children- about thirty or forty in all. – Pa, you know how most of our folk feel about that, and most of the other folk in these parts, too. So far there's just been a lot of whispering and kind of a cool reception for those folks, but there's trouble brewing. Some of the younger men especially got a little much to drink over at Charlie's saloon. Tommy was in there at the time and kinda talked'em down, but if he hadn't been….." He shook his head worriedly.

"These folks own the land?" asked Jesse?

"Yeah," said Ed. "It's all in the name of their leader, a Georgia famer and stockman by the name of Rylee. It's his name on the patent. I asked."

"Well," said Jesse, "Just like in Missouri, slavery is legal in Texas. Man's got a right to have'em on his own place and his tenant's do too. Basically, we may not like it, but legally it is none of our concern."

"Jesse's right," said Amon, "I had hoped this wouldn't happen- that all who settled right here in this area would be of like mind on this. It would've made things a lot easier on down the road, I suspect. But son, it's his land and he can share and work it with whomever he wishes- just as we can ours. "

Ed nodded, but grimaced as he said, "Pa, Tommy and I tried to tell some of those boys over at Charlie's just that, but they won't listen to us."

Amon shook his head, and looked at us and said, "This is the kind of situation where I surely wish my good friend Abel was here to back me up. He is much better at handling this kind of conflict than I am."

"Amon," said Jesse, "forgive me if I'm overstepping here, but maybe it would be a good idea to invite this Rylee and his wife to dinner. You could have us since we're new too, and Tommy Lambert and maybe whoever is leader of the group that's upset. Let's all get to know one another as folks, and then maybe we can talk about issues."

"Now, Jesse, you surely do have a higher opinion of some folks self-control than I do," said Amon dubiously.

"Well, it is my experience that breaking bread together and having the women folk present tends to make folks look at each other as people rather than ideas and ideals. Sometimes it takes a bit of the edge off." said Jesse.

"Tell Sarah that Fanny and I will be happy to bring something to help with the food," I said, mentally inventorying our remaining food. I still have some of the apples we bought at Colbert's Landing so we can bring a couple of pies, and I'm sure we can stir up some corn bread also."

Amon nodded, "Alright then, I can see you folks are gonna just jump right in. I appreciate it. Lizzie I will send word to Martha about the guests and the food. Ed, you ride on over to Rylee's place and invite him and his missus to supper, tell him I just brought in some more new folks and thought it would be good for us to all get acquainted. Tell him we'll be hoping to see them at our place about an hour before sundown. That should give the women time to get the food ready. I'll go talk to Tommy and those other boys."

"Alright, Pa," said Ed Bond, "I hope this whole thing doesn't blow up in our faces."

"If it does," said Jesse, "It's on me. Maybe with a blind man and women present everybody can keep their head. I'll play that card if I have to."

Amon and Ed rode off, and Jesse turned to Henry and Logan and said, "You all are surely being quiet over there..."

"We were just enjoying watching you set us all up for an entertaining evening with our new neighbors," said Logan, with a grin.

"I've seen Jesse in action before," said Henry, "He's not quite as good as my father yet, but this will just give him some more experience!"

"You three are dangerous together!" I said, exasperated. "The last thing we need is for this evening to be 'entertaining', as you call it.."

"Now, Lizzie," said Jesse, with a grin as devilish as Logan's, "you know a good spirited debate never harmed anyone. Besides, I don't think it will even come to that. Not with you women there. The main thing is to show everyone that nobody here has horns and a tail. We can disagree on slavery with these folks and still be decent neighbors to each other. The touchy point will be if Rylee insists on making it an issue, or if he proves to be the type who mistreats his people. *Then* it could get ugly really quickly. And God help us all if any of his darkies ever try to escape. The dictates of conscience for all of us in that type of situation could get very complicated very rapidly."

"I just wish we didn't have to start out dealing with something like this," said Fanny.

"I know what you mean," I agreed, "But Fanny, if you haven't figured out yet that that is just part of being married to a Landers, you'd best learn now."

"You do have a point there Cousin," said Logan, "Come on gentlemen, let's get these wagons unloaded, so these ladies can jump right in with setting up housekeeping."

"Lizzie," said Jesse, "hold Abby while we get her little bed situated first, then she will have a safe place to be."

"All right," I said, taking her up into my arms. "Come Miss Abigail, let's go see our new house."

***** ****** ***** ***** ***** ***** ***** *****

The cabin was not that much smaller than our little cottage on the Nutt farm in Missouri. There was a porch across the front, and the door opened into a main room with a large fireplace that would be our gathering area and indoor kitchen as well. To the right was a doorway into a smaller low ceilinged room that would be our bedroom. In the great room was a ladder leading up to a loft area above the bedroom . That space under the eaves would be a sleeping area for our children as time went on, I hoped. Right now, sweet Abby would be cozy with us in our little room.

Henry and Jesse were unloading the wagon and I heard Henry instructing Jesse on distances and so on. Jesse's memory was amazing, and soon he was moving about with relative ease. "Lizzie!" he called from the bedroom.

I put down the apple I was peeling and went to the doorway, "Yes?"

"Do you want the bed facing the window or under the window? There's not room the other direction." he said.

"Oh, definitely facing the window." I said.

"You'll get the sun in your face in the morning," said Henry.

"I don't care. I want to be able to see out when we leave the shutters open." I said.

Jesse shrugged, and grinned at Henry, "We'd best do as the boss has directed."

"Pft!!" I snorted, "You gentlemen are making fine progress, but if you want this apple pie done for supper you'd best answer any further questions yourselves!"

"Yes ma'am," said Henry with a mock salute. They set back to work with great zeal, and by the time I had my pies baking in the new fireplace, the bed was set up with mattress and bedding and our special quilt in place. The clothing and linen trunks formed a neat row at the foot of the bed.

The wonderful wooden table with iron legs forged in his shop that had been Uncle David's wedding gift to us was reassembled and sitting in the place honor on one side of the main room. Its four matching straight chairs set proudly in place. My little rocking chair set in the corner between the front window and the fireplace. The only other piece of furniture we had brought with us, a mahogany wood settee with padded seat cushions that had come from my Grandmother

Shipman's family home was dusted off and set facing the fireplace. The wooden crates that held things like dishes wrapped in rags, our few books, a small supply of candles and holders, and all the kitchen supplies were neatly stacked along the back wall. Once unpacked, the little cabin would complete it's transformation into a home.

Jesse was standing with one hand feeling the stone of the fireplace. "What kind of stone is it?" he asked quietly.

"Limestone," I said, "It's pretty. Lightens up the room against all the dark of the log walls and wood floors."

"I'm glad they did the floors," said Jesse, "I know most folks just have packed dirt."

"It looks like good tight construction." I said, "Austen and Mr. Griffith did a fine job."

"Where did Henry go?" I asked.

"He went to unload his own stuff into the other house and help Logan and Fanny unpack as well." he answered. Then after a moment's hesitation he said, "Lizzie, come sit on the porch with me. With the cooking fire the heat in here is a bit much."

"All right, " I said, following him outside. "It will be a while yet before the pies are done. And Abby is finally asleep. She fussed the entire time I was trying to put those pies together!"

We sat down in the shade of the porch and leaned back against the rough walls of the cabin. "Methinks Abby has gotten used to being held most of the time while we traveled." said my husband with a smile.

"And whose fault would that be?" I asked, both my raised eyebrow and my smile in my voice.

"Oh, mine, to be sure," said Jesse, readily. " I admit it. I love holding her! We- communicate- my joy and I." he added softly.

"Yes, you do…" I said, reaching for his hand with a sigh. "It is good to be just us again. Does that sound horrible?"

Jesse shook his head. "No, I feel the same way. We are – home – at last. And it feels good."

"Even with the prospect of 'entertainment' this evening?" I asked, not sure whether to be serious or not.

He seemed to sense my uncertainty and squeezed my hand. "Even then," he nodded, "It will be all right Lizzie. I just have a feeling that all will be well."

"Well, I am going to hold you to that, Jesse Nutt," I said softly, as I turned into his arms.

***** ****** ***** ***** ***** ***** ***** *****

"Well of course you don't have to go, if you really don't want to!" I said to Fanny "I will miss you, but if you are sure- it would be easier to leave Abby with you…"

"Oh, yes!" exclaimed Fanny, "I would be so happy to keep her. She and Hugh- they keep each other company! And you know I get nervous around strange folk. Logan, he's not real happy with me for not wanting to go, but he understands. Bless that man, I don't know how I got so lucky!" She thrust the basket containing the three warm batches of cornbread into my hands. "Here, take this for Logan would you? Do you want me to take Abby now, or do you need to feed her first?"

"We just finished," I said with a smile. "I knew I had to do that before trying to make myself presentable. She's good and full and sleepy. So, go ahead and take her. Do you need Henry to come for her box cradle?"

"No," she smiled, "Logan was so impressed with yours he made one for Hugh as well. So she will feel right at home!"

"Alright then, Fanny. Thank you so much," I smiled, and then kissed the top of Abby's head as I handed her to Fanny. "We will come by and get her when we come home. Surely we won't be late."

"You be sure and pay attention," said Fanny, "I want to hear all about it! Try to keep our men out of trouble!"

"I'll do my best," I called as she started back down the path toward the big cabin, with Abby sound asleep in her arms.

Once they were out of sight, I quickly fetched fresh water from the well just off to the side of the house. "Jesse!" I called, "Where are you?" as I entered the house.

He came out of the bedroom just then, "I was trying to find the crate that has that box of cigars that Papa Abel sent to Uncle Tommy. He said Uncle Tommy loves a good cigar better than anything, so I was thinking the gift might influence his mood, and that of some of the others, should he be inclined to share them around."

I snorted in a way my mother would call unladylike, "Knowing Uncle Tommy, more than likely he will hide them instead. But it's a good idea nonetheless. Did you find them?"

"Finally," he nodded. "Funny, all those crates feel the same, and I am sure they look pretty much the same too. But I didn't have much trouble. I found the cigars by smell. Amazing how that is..."

"I know," I agreed, "just being around you and seeing how you notice things, it's made me more aware too."

"God blesses us with what we need Lizzie," said Jesse softly, "and with each other."

I touched his face gently, and then said, "Well right now we need to get cleaned up and changed into some decent clothes for tonight. Lord knows we don't want these folk to think we are something the cat drug in for supper."

"Lead on, Mrs. Nutt," said Jesse, with a grin, "I place myself in your capable hands!"

***** ****** ***** ***** ***** ***** ***** *****

Jesse, Henry, Logan and I arrived at Amon and Sarah Bond's home just minutes before the Rylees' appearance. We dismounted and I was smoothing my skirts after Jesse lifted me down from my side-saddle when Sarah and Amon came out on their porch to meet us. Their cabin was one of the double cabins with the dogtrot area in the center. A trestle table was set up in that sheltered area, taking advantage of both the shade and the cross breeze. We would apparently dine outside this evening.

"Oh, my dear, Elizabeth!" exclaimed Sarah Bond, "How good to see you again! We are so very glad to have you here at last! Welcome!" She smoothly took the pies from my hands and passed them quickly to a young woman I took to be a granddaughter or other relative, and then enfolded me in a warm embrace.

"And Jesse!" she turned and quickly relieved my husband of the bread he was carrying, and embraced him as well.

"Sarah," said Amon, "you remember Lizzie's young brother Henry from our dinner at Neosho? And this is their cousin, Logan Landers."

Both men nodded in greeting, as Amon said, "Logan, where is young Fanny? She is not ailing, I hope?"

159

"No, sir, thank you." Logan assured him. "She was tired though, and since the nature of this gathering is uncertain, we all thought it best if we left the children in her care for the evening. Being on the trail with two little ones has been a challenge, for certain!" He smiled ruefully.

"Ah, yes," said Sarah with a smile, "well I know that! Truth be told she will probably pray them early to sleep and then wallow in the sound of absolute blissful quiet!"

We all laughed, and Amon turned at the sound of a horse drawn vehicle approaching. Over the hill came a small wagon drawn by two matched black horses. "Ah," said Amon, "here they come."

"Where's Tommy?" hissed Jesse, "the whole point of this whole thing?"

"Damned if I know," said Amon. "He promised he and Sarah would be here, and would bring Charlie Smithers and John Dawson with them. They work for Tommy and are two of the leaders of that pack over at the saloon. Charlie owns the place and usually keeps a pretty good handle on his crowd there. This is unusual."

The wagon pulled into the yard, and one of Amon's younger sons stepped out to offer help with the animals. "Well, here we go," muttered Amon, "Look sharp."

Jesse took my hand, and I stood close, quickly and quietly describing my impressions into his ear, as Mr. Rylee got down, tossed the reins to Henry Bond, as if he were a servant, and stepped smartly around to help his wife to the ground.

Young Jefferson Rylee was a tall rawboned man with auburn red hair beginning to streak with gray at the temples and piercing blue eyes that missed nothing. His wife was everything he was not in appearance- tiny, dark haired, with olive skin and soft hazel eyes that reflected a disposition as quiet and retiring as her husband's was fiery. Of course her slow movements and quiet demeanor were

160

probably at least partly because she was also enormously pregnant and my heart immediately went out to her for having to endure the rigors of life on the trail in such a condition.

Amon stepped forward, bowed slightly, and extended his hand, "Amon Bond, at your service sir. Welcome to Stockton Bend!"

Rylee returned the courtesy, "Y. J. Rylee, likewise sir. Allow me to introduce my wife, Mary."

Amon introduced Sarah, myself and Jesse, and I noticed the sizing up look he gave Jesse, similar to the one he had given Amon. I saw the moment he realized Jesse's blindness, and the unguarded look of reappraisal that fleetingly crossed his face afterward. Good luck with that, I thought. I caught Henry watching the whole episode, and his eyes met mine just before he stepped forward to be introduced. He took his place next to Jesse and I turned to follow Sarah in leading poor Mary Rylee inside to sit down.

"My dear, do come inside and sit with us in the shade while we wait for the others to arrive!" said Sarah. I notice she gave Mrs. Rylee the one padded chair near the window, while she and I took our seats on a bench near the fireplace. Fortunately the cooking fire had been placed outside in the yard between Amon's cabin and the one occupied by one of their sons and his family. Some of the daughters and daughters-in-law were apparently supervising the cooking to free their mother to act as hostess. "We are so glad, Mrs. Rylee, that you and your husband could join us for dinner on such short notice."

"It is most kind of you to extend the invitation, Mrs. Bond." answered Mary Rylee, "We are still so unsettled that anything beyond a camp cooked meal will be a great treat."

"We too are just off the trail," I said, with great understanding, "It is a great blessing, to be received with such hospitality!" I smiled at Sarah Bond.

The older woman made a dismissive gesture. "I'm used to feeding such a crew, a few more is nothing to bother."

"So you have a large family, then?" asked Mary.

Amon's wife laughed, and said, "My dear, most of those settled in all these cabins around are relations somehow. I reckon Amon and I can count over fifty as kin right here in Stockton Bend. And now, with our dear friends arriving from Missouri, we just feel our family expanded!"

"We are much the same, Young and I," nodded Mary. "Most in our party are kin as well. Of course our own children are young still. Indiana, our oldest, is but twelve, and this one will be number five."

"We just had our first," I explained, "Thank the good Lord she arrived in April, before we left Neosho in June! I can't imagine being on the trail with a baby coming."

Mary placed her hands protectively on her huge belly, and grimaced. "I can assure you, it wasn't my first choice either. But Young was afraid if we waited for the baby, we couldn't come this year. And with the Homestead Act set to expire,…. Well , we made it, and none too soon either. I am due any day now."

"Do you have a good midwife among your folk?" asked Amon's wife, with interest.

Mary nodded, "We have my mammy with us. She delivered me, all my brothers and sisters, and all our children beside. What she doesn't know about birthing just hasn't happened!"

"Oh, that is good to know!" said Sarah. "Would she be permitted to come help if called? My young cousin Rebekah is increasing again, and she had a very difficult time with her last one."

"Well, now," said Mary reluctantly, "Young would have to say on that. He normally doesn't like the darkies leaving the home place much. But certainly if your kinswoman needs help, send word, and I will see if he can be persuaded."

I filed this little speech away for sharing later, but we were distracted from further female conversation by the arrival of Uncle Tommy Lambert and his two cohorts along with their wives.

Conversation over dinner was a little strained given that the men were all trying to be cordial without revealing anything. We all spoke much of our longtime ties to Amon and Sarah and their families. And Amon played the role of intrepid land seeker and wanderer very well. Logan spoke of his earlier ranching interests in east Texas, and why he had decided to come further west in pursuit of a larger, freer land and also to be closer to family. Young Rylee spoke of seeking greater opportunities as a younger son, and agreed with the possibilities offered by larger more open areas of land.

Jesse had been very quiet, listening intently, saying only a word or two now and again. Finally, over dessert, he said, "Mr. Rylee, did you encounter much civic unrest along the way from Georgia to Texas? " A civil and neutrally worded question it was, but almost impossible to answer without some sort of declaration.

Young Rylee turned his attention to Jesse, and smiled a smile that he would have never smiled had Jesse been able to see him, and suddenly it was just the two of them at the table. But it *wasn't* just the two of them, and my intake of breath was warning to Jesse, who was already aware he was baiting the lion. Young leaned back casually in his chair, and said pleasantly, "Why no, Mr. Nutt, none a'tall that I was aware of. Of course, you folk are more likely to know about *civic* unrest than I... coming from Missouri and all."

Jesse smiled pleasantly, but his eyes were the color of steel, and in that moment, had I not known he was blind I would have sworn he was meeting Young Rylee's gaze, and looking past the façade at the man's soul. "My brother Jacob and I would be more than happy to describe to you in whatever detail you prefer our most personal experience with the *civic unrest* perpetrated against the poor and free people of color in Missouri."

Rylee had the grace to look somewhat startled by the bluntness of this statement. The silence in the room spoke volumes, and in the presence of the ladies, Rylee had no choice but retreat, and said mildly, "A most unfortunate occurrence, I am sure."

Mary Rylee was pale as the tablecloth as she reached out to touch her husband's hand, "Young, I fear I am suddenly very fatigued. The heat is just too much. I must ask you to take me home. Mrs. Bond, you will forgive our hasty departure?"

"But of course, my dear," said Sarah Bond, trying her best not to look relieved.

The party dispersed quickly, and in relative silence- no one wanting to give the appearance of staying behind to gossip. We were mounted and out of earshot when Henty commented laconically, "Jesse, you sure do know how to end a party!"

Jesse was still tense and he was angry as I had ever seen him. But he had himself under tight rein. "Once he answered my question with a question, everyone in the room knew all we need to know," said Jesse tightly. "If the man stays here, and treats his people as I think he must, there is going to be trouble."

"Maybe he will realize that too," said Logan, soberly. "He seems to care for the wife a bit, so maybe he will reconsider and settle elsewhere."

Jesse nodded grimly, and said, "I pray you are right, Logan. Meanwhile, I must pray God will cool my anger. I hardly know the man, yet I despise what he stands for with every fiber of my being."

"Don't beat yourself up, Jesse," said Henry, "You couldn't see the look on his face as he drove away. Trust me, the feeling is mutual."

***** ****** ***** ***** ***** ***** ***** *****

Jesse Nutt wanted desperately to go for a walk. It was one of the things he missed most in this dark world where he had lived for almost two years now- the simple pleasure of just being able to decide at a moment's notice to get up and go out and simply walk somewhere or nowhere just because he wanted to. - To seek out new places and new experiences without advance planning and fear, and always having to be in the company of others. There was a certain joy in the solitude found in being alone in a natural setting that had always been very much a part of who he was as a young man. While he cherished the times spent with Jacob and Lizzie during those years, he also had very strong memories of hours spent walking the streets of Neosho at twilight and the banks of the river there as the sun came up, comfortable in the company inside his own head, and the sense of the nearness of the Creator who walked along beside him, present in the beauty all around.

He had awakened this morning to the sounds of mockingbirds making their raucous silly noise outside the bedroom window, and a warm breeze bearing the scent of wildflowers had stirred the air around him. He felt the warmth of the sun's rays on his face as it came up over the bluff across the river, and for the first time in a long time he had felt that restless urge to *move,* to go out and become one with the dawn and the birds, and the breeze, and the thoughts inside his head. In fact he had thrown back the covers, set his feet on the floor, and even risen to take the first steps toward the hook that held his clothes, before the conscious thoughts of his reality collided with the inclinations of instinct. He stood motionless there in the middle of the newly familiar room and for the first time in a long time felt a wave of sheer frustration and anger (partly unspent from last night) wash over him.

Vaguely he heard the front door of the cabin open and close and the sound of bare feet padding across the floor of the front room. They stopped, and then Lizzie's voice soft from the bedroom doorway behind him whispered, "Jesse?"

He forced himself to take a deep breath through his nose and let it out slowly, resignedly pushing his longing aside, turning to greet her and the day with the love and tenderness she so deserved. He found a smile and with it, "Good morning, Lizzie," he said softly, extending his arms as she walked into them. She returned his embrace and then drew back, and her fingertips touched his cheek, feather light. Even at that, her touch made him realize the moisture that was there. He started to draw back, as shame washed over him, but with gentle hands on his arms she would not let him go. "What?" she asked softly, "Tell me."

As always, he was totally incapable of being anything but honest with her. "I woke up, and the day seemed fine, and I wanted to take a walk." His kept his voice soft to not wake Abby, and was actually surprised when it broke and fresh moisture came to his eyes at the last word. The thing he loved most about his Lizzie was that she always understood *him*. Like now, she didn't protest, or start talking, or try to dismiss what he felt, she simply said softly, "Oh...." In acknowledgement, and embraced him again in wordless comfort.

A few minutes later, a knock on the door brought Henry with news on the progress at Uncle Abel and Aunt Sally's cabin, and he spent the rest of the day at the building site working one end of a two man saw with Henry on the other end. They sawed and Austen Yeats and Logan built walls with the logs they trimmed. It was hard exhausting work, but it was work he could do, and Jesse found his spirits rising as the day passed, buoyed up by accomplishment and the camaraderie of his fellow workers. They worked through lunch trying to get more done before the hottest part of the day. Finally, in the middle of the July afternoon, when the sun boiling down was making the sweat pour off in rivers, and between each log cut they were stopping to drink huge gulps from the water buckets, they stopped for a while. He and the other three men sat companionably down in the deep shade of a grove of live oak trees, the slight breeze and the shade a welcome relief. Cornbread left from the previous night's dinner plus the last of the apples bought at Colbert's made for a tasty late lunch. They ate slowly, conversing companionably. It was clear their thoughts were all still centered on last night's strange dinner.

"Well, gentlemen," said Jesse, "I confess to a certain curiosity. What did you think of our dinner guests last evening?"

"Damned if I know," said Logan, "For starters, I got the distinct impression that he was definitely looking us over as closely as we were examining him. Even before you and he went at it."

"Interesting that early on he hinted that somebody, and he wouldn't say who, "Suggested" he come here to settle..." said Henry.

"I didn't dislike the man at first," said Austen, thoughtfully, "He actually seemed like a nice enough fellow. I almost got the impression he felt he had been misled by whoever advised him to come here... But then that episode with you, Jesse, he just turned in a heartbeat."

Jesse nodded, "That was my impression too. Interesting how he was obviously discomfited, to the point of aggression, by the realization that not a one of us owned slaves or had any intention of doing so."

The sound of running footsteps brought all their heads up. The four men were all on their feet and reaching for what weapons lay to hand. Jesse gripped the handle of the ax in his hand and listened intently.

"It's young Amon, Austen's boy," said Henry softly, right next to him. Again Jesse nodded, and relaxed a little.

"Pa!" said the youngster, skidding to a halt. "Gramps sent me to tell y'all, those new settlers are leaving!"

"Leaving?" said Jesse. "You mean permanently?"

"Reckon so," said young Amon, "They've loaded all their belongings back up, hitched up all those wagons, and are down at the ford, headed east, back across the river!"

"East!?" exclaimed all four of his listeners almost in unison. With a chuckle at their like mindedness, it was Jesse who continued, "Are you sure it's all of them son? Did you hear any talk amongst them?"

Young Amon smiled- a wide grin that said he was about to make himself look very good in their eyes, "Well, as a matter of fact, I just walked myself right up to one of those pretty girls that I heard callin' Mr. Rylee 'Pa', and I set my feet heading in the same direction as hers just as if I had business down that way on the road, and I said, "Are you folks leavin'?" And she nods and says as how one of her papa's darkies found a whole bunch of natural springs on some of that land just the other side of the river a little to the south of here, and that her Pa- he told all them folks it would be better for them to settle over there because of the water supply but also 'cause he said it might be just as well to have the river between them and us- "to keep any hostilities from erupting" he said!"

"Well, my, my," said Logan, "Isn't that interesting?"

"That's not all she said," added young Amon, importantly, "She also went on as how her Ma was mighty unhappy about moving again, and that she had enjoyed the society of the ladies here last night, and that Mr. Rylee had promised her a fine rock house built by real stonemasons to get her happy again!"

168

There was a general laugh, as Jesse said to the boy, "Amon, the woman is nine months along, it's 100 degrees in the shade, and he is making her pick up and move again! Trust me, there is nothing going to get that man out of trouble anytime soon! Meanwhile, I for one am relieved that he had sense enough to see the lay of the land and withdraw. It will certainly make our lot easier. We will have to tell Davis to offer him a good price for his patent. We don't want him sending people back over here to work it."

"Agreed!" said Henry. He paused thoughtfully. "The next question I have is where does he plan to find stonemasons? – Or is that just big talk?" he asked.

"As a matter of fact," Austen spoke up, "there's a whole group of'em camped about 10 miles south on the river. Charles Bernard had dealings with 'em over at his trading post on the Paluxy. Says they're Scandinavian- where ever that is."

"Northern Europe," answered Logan automatically. He grinned, "Wonder how they like this weather?"

"Let's hope they're not recently arrived or we will be having a mass burial!" said Henry.

"Yes," agreed Jesse, "it surely is hot, which brings us full circle in this discussion. Does anyone think we should avail ourselves of the services of these stone masons in our community here?"

"Papa Amon says it's too soon," said Austen, "He says this land is good for farming but not the type of terrain and outlook we will want for an actual town long term."

"From what Lizzie has described, I am inclined to agree, " nodded Jesse, musing, "For one thing the bend in the river here, while wonderful for our current protection, would limit our options for growth in the future... We will want a piece of land high above the river, maybe on bluffs that will be visible for miles, and also overlooking a long expanse of the river to give us plenty of room to grow and build, and also have a view of the natural beauty Lizzie describes all around us.- A place with a view of both the valley below and the heights above, as she says."

"I declare Jesse," said Henry, gruffly, "sometimes I think you have better vision with no eyes than the rest of us have with ours that work..."

"Jesse, I know the place you just described..." breathed Austen, a look of wonder on his face... "It's about two or three miles southwest of here, just south of our cabin...."

"Really?" said Jesse, smiling at the notion. "You'll have to take us down there sometime, Lizzie and I, and Henry and Logan too. We'll want to write and tell Uncle Abel we've found his town for him!"

"I might just do that," said Austen, "sooner than you think!"

"Meanwhile," said Logan, "are we done for today? Henry and I have a little project we are working on at the cabin, and we'd like to get done before sundown."

"It's your Uncle's house," said Austen, "It's fine by me. Tomorrow same time then?"

They all agreed, and Jesse and Henry and Logan headed up the path toward the two Nutt cabins. Jesse walked easily between the two other men, his thoughts still on what Austen had said, when his two companions suddenly halted in mid-stride. "What the hell...?" said Logan.

"What is it?" asked Jesse, urgently. He'd been counting steps. He knew they were close to the cabins. "Is something wrong?"

"Well now, Jesse," said Henry, his voice telling Jesse he was grinning from ear to ear, "your wife has been busy today, and looks like she must've had some help from somewhere…"

He heard the sound of running footsteps coming nearer on the path. "Oh, Jesse," said Lizzie breathlessly, "you're early!" She took his hand and he could feel the excitement running through her.

"Well now, Lizzie," he smiled, "I can surely get these good fellows to take me away again and come back later if you wish!" He pretended to turn to go, and she grabbed his shirt sleeve.

"Don't you dare!" she said, laughing, "We've worked on this all day!"

"Who is we? And what is 'this'?" asked Jesse, catching her high spirits.

"Heck, I can see it," said Henry, "and I still don't know what it is!"

His sister threw him the killing look common to brothers and sisters everywhere, and then took her husband by the hand and said, "Hush, Henry Landers! And Jesse, you come with me!" She led him on up the slightly inclining path that he knew lead to the porch of their cabin. She stopped and placed his hand on the bottom of the rail to their porch steps. "Now, Jesse," she said softly, "where are we?"

"Well, I believe we are standing next to our porch steps," he said, a quizzical smile on his face.

"Alright," she said, "now turn around and face away from the cabin." He did so, and she said, "Now describe to me what I told you the view is from here," she said, the smile bubbling in her voice.

He searched his memory, seeking the picture she had painted in his mind. "The cabin faces east towards the river." Jesse recited cautiously, "and the land on either side has been cleared for a ways down to where one of the trials runs across from house to house all up and down this side of the slope overlooking the river. Our path continues on cut thin through the brush all the way down to the river bank where you go to do the laundry on those big rocks along the banks. And you said the brush and little trees have been cleared out all around and in between our three building sites here, so we can see the place where the blacksmith shop will be and the other cabin from our front porch, and they will be able to see us too."

"My, Jesse," Lizzie breathed, "you do have a fine memory!" There was some kind of rustling noise, someone handing her something, then she was taking his right hand and placing it around a pole? -of some kind. He started to reach out to feel it with his left hand also, but she grabbed it and guided it to the left to grasp .... a rope? "The staff is for balance where the path is uneven, and the rope is your guide for wherever you want to go. You can go all the way down to the river right along the rocks to where you can wet your feet. Or you can turn left at the path and go over visit Logan and Henry, or right and up the hill a bit to Amon's place. The ropes are strung on posts all along each way. We got pieces of spare rope from almost everybody on the peninsula. Once we got Amon's children and grandchildren involved, it took shape really quickly! Amon says it's not a bad idea for marking the main paths in the community for travel at night or in bad weather too. So... you can take your walks now Jesse, whenever you want to, and at least a choice or two for now. I hope you'll still ask me along....Every now and then..." She ended with a voice quivering with the strength of her love for him.

Jesse let go of the blessed rope and reached for her. He pulled her to him and heedless of the friends and family gathered round, kissed her thoroughly, and then whispered in her ear, "My dearest Lizzie, every step I take, you are there in my heart!" He paused, simply overcome with emotion. Gathering himself, he faced toward the happy sounds of both new and old companions, and said, "For each and every one who had anything to do with this, I say from my heart thank you. I am overcome... I promise you will find me a frequent visitor as soon as the pathway is marked to your door! Children, thank you so very much for your help to Miss Lizzie. We both appreciate your kindness very much! I shall look forward to sharing my new fishing spot with you down by the river!"

"Sarah Bond sent word that we must all come finish the left overs from last night," said Fanny. "Lizzie and I have got the babies all ready to go."

"Go, get Miss Abby," Jesse whispered with a grin, and a kiss on Lizzie's cheek, "I will be waiting for you at the turn onto the main path."

Her heart swelled with joy at the look of pure exuberance on his face. "Show off," she teased, "We shall look forward to walking with you, Mr. Nutt!"

Jesse listened to his wife's light steps on the wood of the porch, and then turned joyfully to the task at hand. Staff in hand, and hand on rope, he pointed himself to the east and went for a walk.

The Prayers of a Righteous Man – September 1856

September 22, 1856

Neosho, Missouri

Dearest Leatha and Jesse and Sweet Abby,

We were all so relieved to hear of your safe arrival at Stockton, and are heartened to hear that your journey passed with no great difficulty...

Abel Landers paused thoughtfully, quill poised just above the page, and stared out the window, seeing not the tall forests that surrounded the sprawling farmhouse where he sat, but the dark head of his beloved daughter bent over the page that now lay on his desk. He envisioned her seated at the rough cedar wood table near the white limestone fireplace in the tiny cabin she had so proudly described to him. He smiled as he remembered her vivid description of the encounter with Y,J. Rylee and her idea to make Jesse more able to make his way around the little community of Stockton Bend. He'd have to check with his contacts in Georgia and see what he could learn of that Rylee fellow, and pass it on.

He dipped the quill in the ink and continued -

With all the word we are getting of horrible violence and bloodshed along the Kansas — Missouri border north of us, it is difficult not to worry about how safe any of us may be in the months to come. I don't know how much you may get in the way of news down in Texas but events have continued to escalate with entire communities being burned to the ground and dozens of folk killed and injured So far most of the truly horrific actions have taken place over the line in Kansas. I am saddened to report that both sides are guilty of armed attacks upon the citizens who oppose their viewpoints, and most free blacks live in constant fear of capture and being sold into slavery. You may recall Lewis and Tempy Robertson, who worked for our family for many years, earning their freedom and getting established in life. When the trouble with free blacks being bothered here in Neosho arose, just prior to when you boys were injured, Lewis and Tempy sold their land here, and moved south to McDonald County. I recently heard from him that even that locale has become so volatile that he fears for his children's safety. So they have sold out and are heading west- to where he did not say. I sent him back word of your whereabouts in Texas and bade him seek asylum with you there, but have not heard back, so may have been too late with that information. He can neither read nor write so I am certain his letter to me was sent with great effort and was by way of a thank you and farewell. I shall pray that he and his family find a safe haven to live in the peace all deserve.

The news you send of progress on our dwellings cheers me greatly and makes this old man long to be on the trail coming to you. However, we are busy here. Between quietly making arrangements for the sale of my various properties, and being arbiter of the uneasy peace between my dear friend David and Henry, I have not lacked for occupation. Henry and Celina are behaving well enough in the presence of family, but privately are barely on speaking terms with those of us who are involved in the business of the farm. David is focusing almost entirely on the blacksmith business, trying to raise funds to finance the journey of so many to Texas. The farm will do well to support the family's daily needs over these next years with Henry and Celina getting their share as agreed. The younger children are all well and much involved in school and church activities when there are not chores to be done.

Jacob and David came by yesterday, and upon learning of my intent to write, bade me send greetings on their behalf. Jacob has taken to helping young David with his school work, having David orally recite lessons, and teaching him Latin as well as much about the natural sciences. They walk everywhere together, and are often seen in deep discussion over some topic or other. Some of the other boys tag along from time to time, and Jacob sometimes brings them here to talk of law and citizenship and how a Godly man should serve *his community. I am thinking working with the young ones has been good for Jacob, and I know all those boys hold him in high regard.*

I close this epistle with news that Frank and Phoebe are expecting again. She lost the last baby if you will recall, and Dr. Harding strongly advised her to not try again. However, the good Lord wills as he does, and so we share the news with gladness and hope, asking your prayers to the Almighty for a safe outcome for all. Sally has bade them to come stay with us so she can help with the care of young Abel Robert, as Phoebe is mostly confined to her bed. Frank has been beside himself with worry, so I have endeavored to keep him occupied by handing over more of the farming duties on my properties close to town. He is doing a good job there and is able to check on Phoebe often.

With prayers that this letter finds you all well and happy and safe, and with a special kiss for my most precious granddaughter - Abigail - I am

Your Most Loving Papa,

Abel Landers

Abel blotted the paper carefully and set it aside to dry while he considered the piece of news he had not included in the letter. Although doing her best to keep going and help Phoebe and look after the younger children, Sally was not well. She had forbidden him to say anything to the children, and she *was* doing somewhat better after being seen by Dr. Harding. A heart murmur, the doctor had called it. He had advised less physical labor, more long walks at a steady pace to try to build strength, and he had given her a tonic to try to do more of the same. But she still had spells of weakness and breathlessness from time to time.

Only once had Abel tried to talk with her about a change of plans. He was absolutely terrified of the toll just the journey to Texas might take on her. But Sally Landers had her own priorities and going to what they hoped would be the safe haven of north Texas with her sons and daughters before the whole nation went up in flames was at the top of the list. So she had forbidden him to speak of it again. Not speaking of it might allow her peace of mind, but Abel prayed daily for guidance from God, to tell him what he should do.

So far, the good Lord had remained silent, and so with a shake of his head and long draw on his pipe, Abel began the task of sealing the letter. A few minutes later, he was astride his favorite horse, heading for town, the letter tucked in his coat pocket. The new Oklahoma and Texas bound mail stage left for Springfield right after lunch. With any luck, he could get the letter on its way this very afternoon! Then it would be on to the monthly meeting between David and Henry, moderated by him and Jacob. "Well," thought Abel as he rode into the outskirts of town a bit later, "there was one thing he could be sure of… the afternoon would not be boring- "

He cut the thought off and reined the big black gelding sharply in. Around him, others also stopped to stare. Coming down the main thoroughfare toward him was a group of about twenty men on horseback. Rough and armed to the teeth, they rode tightly packed around but just behind the man who led them. Raw-boned and gaunt, with steel gray hair that covered both head and jaw with an unruly halo, his piercing eyes missing nothing as his party moved at a steady pace down the dusty street, John Brown looked every bit the avenging angel the abolitionist papers painted him to be. The caliber of men at his back spoke more of the true nature of his methods, if not his intent, and Abel felt a cold chill at the base of his spine that had nothing to do with the cool fall weather.

Instinctively he stiffened, bringing himself to his full height in his saddle. The movement, slight as it was, caught Brown's eye, and for a moment steel gray gazes locked, and Brown tilted his chin ever so slightly in acknowledgement as he came abreast of Abel's position. The pace of the ruffian group did not slow, and Abel let out a slow, long breath as the moment passed and he turned his horse to watch them go.

The letter in his pocket would have to wait. If Brown and his men were in the area, and spoiling for a fight, the local slaveholders needed to be warned. It was not that he was without sympathy for the abolitionist cause of course, but the kind of vigilante violence that Brown and his fellows practiced too often lead not just to freedom for the slave they sought to "rescue", but to death and wholesale destruction of their owners as well. Abel had no desire to see such a fate befall any of his neighbors, even those with whom he vehemently disagreed.

Brown and his band of men were headed east out toward Ed Wilkes place. Wilkes was a passionate abolitionist and was known to be sympathetic to the more violent measures being taken by Brown and his ilk, and so was likely providing some kind of shelter or headquarters to Brown and his men. Abel turned his horse to follow the band at a bit of a distance- although he too had land out this way and passed this way often. After a ten minute canter he came over a slight rise just in time to see the entire body of Brown's men riding brazenly through the front gate of Ed Wilkes place, as Ed and John Brown sat their horses nearby, looking on. They were expected guests then. Abel sat his horse well back in the trees and watched a couple of minutes longer as Wilkes and Brown engaged in animated conversation. Ed was gesturing broadly and he pointed north, obviously giving some sort of direction. The wind was favorable, and Abel caught the words "100 slaves" and the name "Rutledge" before Brown nodded and turned to follow his men, his look of grim determination more set than ever.

That told Abel all he needed to know, as well as all he was likely to find out. Brown was here, with his men, and their area of interest was somewhere north of Ed Wilkes place with a slave owner named Rutledge. In his mind's eye Abel reviewed the landowners up that way, as he turned his horse and headed back to town. David and Jacob, and Henry would be at his office by now, wondering what had become of him. He pushed the animal to a fast canter that would have him back to the town center in less than fifteen minutes. He glanced to the west. Two hours till sundown. That meant less than an hour and a half to get the word out. The Nutt land was first out that way, but of course they had no slaves. Next was the plot David had given Henry and next to it the farm belonging to Celina Rutledge Nutt's daddy and uncles. Beyond that was old man Wright's place and that of his son A.J., who was married to Abel's niece Elizabeth Nutt.

Henry's father-in-law, Tom Rutledge, and his brothers ran over 100 slaves on their combined lands, and the Wrights about 20- all belonging to the old man. 120 slaves. In Brown's view , 120 souls held in captivity by men who were disciples of the Evil One, Satan. 120 souls it was his God-assigned duty to rescue and save. – No matter what the consequences- no matter what the cost. Abel had firsthand knowledge of the consequences Brown's religious zeal had wrought in northern Missouri and Kansas a couple of years back. Entire farms, and two small towns burned to the ground and scores injured. Only five deaths, by some miracle, but Abel had traveled north to help one of the widows probate her husband's will, and he could still remember the lingering smell of smoke in the poor woman's hair when she had collapsed weeping in his arms when he arrived at the boarding house where she had taken refuge with her two small children.

As he rode, his mind churned with the choice for best course of action in the face of Brown and his band. By his count Brown and Wilkes had a force of perhaps thirty men at most. Unless he and David could muster the Nutt and Landers men in time, Tom Rutledge had few resources to call on. Rutledge had no sons, so Henry and Celina were his heirs, but his brothers and one sister all held shares in the huge Rutledge farm which in any other state would be called a plantation. All told he probably had fifteen white men on land populated by those 100 slaves. Of those slaves- figure 40-50 men who would have to be contained. Plus, the women and children of all races to be protected. Getting word to all the boys was going to be a challenge.

Fortune smiled on him as the town school was just letting out as he passed. He pulled up and searched the swirling mass of youngsters, until he saw some of those he sought. He hated to involve the young people in this horror, but right now he needed swift young legs, and healthy young lungs to carry his warning and summons.

"Nutt and Landers cousins!" he called, in his best courtroom bellow, "to me!" He caught a glimpse of jet black hair and called next- "James Rutledge, you and your cousins come here!"

In less than fifteen seconds Abel was the center of attention of nine sets of eyes. Young David and John Nutt and his own son William and the girls Sarah and Martha were the first to reach his side- their eyes wide with interest. Jimmy Rutledge was Tom's oldest nephew and at age 13 led his three younger cousins to stand near Abel's mount as well.

Abel turned his gimlet gaze on Jimmy Rutledge and demanded, "James, do you know where your Uncle Tom is working today?"

"Why, yessir, I do!" he said eagerly, "He and my Pa are helping my Uncle Ben put a new roof on his barn before the snows come."

Three Rutledge men in one place. Abel gave thanks to the good God, and nodded, "Alright, Jimmy, you boys go there as quick as you can run, and you tell your daddy and your uncles that you saw me, and that I said that a very bad man named John Brown and some of his friends just rode into town, and are planning to come and make trouble for your folks this evening. Tell him they will have about thirty men. They will most likely head for Tom's place first as that is where most of your slaves live. Tell Tom that I am meeting Henry and David Nutt in town and we will bring as many men as we can and be at his place by sundown. You got all that?"

The child's eyes were huge, but he nodded and with his cousins turned and ran toward the northbound road out of town. Abel turned to his own youngsters, and said, "You heard what I told Jimmy?" At their solemn nods he continued. "David and John go home and tell your mother I said she is to gather all the family there at the farm and bring them to your Aunt Sally's and my house in town immediately. Tell her I said to bring the horses but to leave the rest of the stock. I think they will bypass the place because they will have been told David doesn't keep slaves, but we will take no chances with our women and children in this." He paused for breath, and asked, "Got it?"

"Yessir!" nodded David and John, almost in unison.

"Then go!" said Abel, and as they too dashed away toward the north he called after them, "If you see any of your brothers or uncles, tell them we will meet there at the farm!" John waved in acknowledgement, and they turned away at a dead run.

Abel looked down at his own children, and said, "Will, go find your brothers Chris, Abel, and Daniel, and tell them to meet us at the Nutt Farm. Girls, go home and tell your Mother and Frank if he is there. Tell them guests are coming, and that Will is coming as soon as he finds the others. Will, it will be up to you and Frank and Jacob to protect and look out for the womenfolk and children." He held the boy's eyes for a moment, and said, "It is a sacred charge I give you all."

Will nodded and said, "I understand, Papa. Don't worry we will keep them safe." The boy hesitated another moment and then extended his right hand up to his father, "Godspeed, Papa."

Abel clasped his youngest son's hand briefly, and then gathered the reins, as he said, gruffly, "Godspeed to you too son. Now go!"

The children ran to do his bidding as Abel dug in his heals and headed his horse toward the center of town. Heads turned at the

181

unaccustomed sight of former state representative Abel Landers galloping through town. By the time he rounded the corner nearest his office, there were several men following him on horseback and more following as rapidly as they could on foot. He glanced again to the west, trying to judge the time. An hour- he thought- maybe a bit more. The approaching hoof beats had drawn Henry, David, Jacob and Jenkins down to the street level.

David Nutt met him at the hitching rail, reaching for the reins, even as Abel handed them down. "What's happened?'

Abel lowered himself to the ground, cursing mentally at the rheumatism in his knee that slowed his movements. Once on the ground though, he strode toward the steps of the building even as he spoke quietly, to David, "Trouble, my friend. We don't have much time. Let me only say this once." David nodded, squeezed his shoulder in support and stepped back to stand by with his two sons as Abel mounted the steps and turned to speak.

"Gentlemen!" he said, solemnly, projecting but not booming, already using his voice to calm the crowd to listen with thought and not heat. "Gentlemen, if I can have your attention. I speak to you tonight as a former state leader, and as your neighbor in lodge, in church, in community. As you all know, our state and our nation are in the midst of a great controversy over the holding of negroes as slaves." Just one sentence and the rise in tension was palpable, the under breath muttering audible. Abel paused and raised his hand once more for quiet. He let their eyes find him again, and continued. Many of us standing here have diverse opinions. But one thing I know we can all agree on is the safety and security of our community and our neighbors from outsiders who would do them harm." There, the street was still, he had them now. "I have reason to believe that the man John Brown and a band of his followers are nearby, by invitation of one of our own, and that it is their intent to attack the farms of slaveholders north of our town, burn their dwellings, destroy their crops, and assault their owners and their families, on the excuse of freeing the slaves they hold. Most of you know my stance on this issue, but hear this. I do not countenance the destruction of property or the injury of innocents or the unlawful execution of any persons without due process of law. And that is what these men intend. Make no mistake, these men are here do terrible things in the name of what they believe to be a Godly cause. Our goal must be to make them change their minds. Not through direct attack, but by forming a line of protection and defense they cannot cross without great cost. Whatever we here in Neosho, Missouri decide to do eventually about the grave question of slavery, let it be US who decide it, not some violent group of strangers from far away, who would kill and maim our innocent women and children without remorse. This is OUR town, and OUR county, and these folk, black and white, are OUR neighbors. Will we allow these outsiders, these ruffians to do them harm? If your answer is NO, as mine is, come with us now to David Nutt's farm. From there we will deploy to protect our neighbors from those who would do them harm. We believe the intent is to raid these farms within the next 24 hours. How many of you will join us?"

Of the twenty men gathered round, only two elderly gentlemen did not raise their hands. Abel nodded, and said, "Then gentlemen, I will see you at the David Nutt place before sundown."

He stood waiting for a moment as the men dispersed his eyes following one of the older men who climbed into a nearby buggy and drove away to the south. "You do know," said David Nutt at his shoulder, "that that is Percy Wilks and he is off to warn his brother, and I assume John Brown, that we will be waiting for them."

"Damn," said Abel softly, "I didn't see him till right at the end and by then it was too late. But David, we need the manpower. They have at least thirty men, maybe more, all armed to the teeth."

Henry and Jacob had been standing together quietly, listening. At last Henry stepped forward. "Uncle Abel, I know how you feel about all this, and I know you are doing this because of Celina and me. I want you to know I appreciate it and her folks will too."

Abel looked at him intently and said, "Henry, if I thought John Brown could go in there and free your folks' slaves and take them away to freedom without harming anyone else, and without wholesale destruction of property, I would be out there helping him do it, even old and decrepit as I am. But the man is a raving maniac, and his followers are mostly ruffians and fanatics of the worst sort. Innocent women and children don't deserve to die at their hands, or to have their homes and crops burned. THAT is why I am doing this, not out of any kindly desire to protect or condone your way of life. You would do well to remember that, and stay out of my way." With that he turned to David, and said, "I have to go to the house and get my guns. I'll take Jacob there with me. I sent word to Sarah to go there with your women and children. The rest of the boys are already headed to your place. I'll meet you and Henry there as soon as I can."

David Nutt extended his hand and Abel clasped it, as David said, "Bless you Abel! We will be waiting." David then turned to Jacob, "Son, I will depend on you to direct what is to be done if any are hurt. Tell Sarah and Sally to make ready."

Jacob was pale, but replied steadily, "Don't worry, Papa, I will take care of it." They hugged, and as he took Abel's arm to go with him he was stopped by his brother's voice.

"Jacob," Henry said, "tell Celina no matter what happens she is not to come till it is safe. A-And, if all should go wrong, t-tell her I love her, and I am – s-so sorry."

Jacob nodded and said, "I expect you'll tell her yourself soon enough. But if not, you have my word, she will be cared for- she and the children."

"Thank you, brother," said Henry, and turned on his heel to follow their father.

Abel grabbed his nephew's arm and pulled him none too gently toward the big gelding that was still standing, steaming by the hitching post. "Come," said Abel, "you will have to ride with me. I hate doing it to poor Benjamin after riding him so hard this afternoon, but there's no time. I can get a fresh mount at the house." He climbed into the saddle again with a stifled groan, and reached down for Jacob. Jacob found his grasp, and in seconds was behind him on the horse.

The house was not far, and five minutes later they were dismounting in the familiar stableyard behind the house. Jacob had a mental flash of vision of it as it had been that frigid night almost three years ago, when his cousin Henry and Abel had come to minister to him and Jesse. Suddenly he missed Jesse and Henry with an intensity that took his breath away. And even in the midst of the turmoil of the moment, his Uncle Abel stopped suddenly, and the hand on his arm gave a gentle squeeze. "I miss them too, son," said Abel, softly, "But I am also desperately grateful- that neither of them are here right now. Better the hazards of the frontier than the evil-mindedness of men." He finished grimly. "Come, we must hurry."

Inside the house was the quiet of fear, rather than the noise they both expected. Sally Landers met them at the door, pale, but obviously in command. She greeted her husband with a kiss, and then stepped aside to allow him to greet his sister, David's Sarah. Both women listened raptly as Abel recounted quickly the afternoon's events. "All the men are gathering at the Farm now," he said. "Frank and Jacob and Will will be here with you both and the other women and children. Is Celina here?"

"Yes, Uncle," said a voice from the kitchen doorway, "I'm here."

"Henry bade me tell you to stay put, niece," said Abel, with a small smile.

So pale, her freckles and red hair stood out like beacons, Celina, nodded, "Did he say anything else?"

In spite of the need for haste, Abel stepped over and took her hand kindly, and said, "He said to tell you that he loves you and that he will see you and the children here when this is over. – And he said to tell you that he was sorry."

"I know," she nodded, solemnly, "We both are, Uncle Abel. It is an awful mess. B-but he did it for me, you see. I am my parent's only surviving child- their heir. But only if we live by Papa's rules."

"I know child," said Abel gently, "We all do. Even David. It's the only way he could forgive, knowing that Henry did what he's done for love of you."

He turned and spoke louder, to be heard by all the listening ears he knew were nearby. "We are all family and we will stand with each other in this and in whatever comes. Stay here, and pray for us, and take care of each other. The other menfolk and I will be back as soon as it is over." With that benediction he reached for his Sally, held her close for a moment, kissed her thoroughly, whispered "I love you," as he touched her cheek. A moment later, the door closed and he was gone.

***** ***** ****** ****** ***** ***** *****

Hours later, David Nutt and Abel Landers sat side by side, rifles at ready, two of nearly sixty men who had come to defend the Rutledge home place. Almost half the men were family – Nutts, Landers, Shipmans, Rutledges, and Wrights, who might have been expected to support one another under even the most divisive circumstances. But the rest came in answer to Abel's call in town- neighbors and Masonic brothers, stepping up to say no innocent blood will be spilled today, not in our county, not on our land. As they watched the sun come up, a lone rider with a white flag rode slowly up the drive to stop directly in front of Tom Rutledge's big white house. Rutledge stepped out on the steps, his coal black hair and beard stark in the morning sun.

"You Tom Rutledge?" asked the man on the horse.

"I am," he answered.

"Well, John sent me to give you a message-" said the man, making sure both his hands were in plain sight. "He told me to tell you that today you are a lucky man. Today you get to live because of the kindness of your neighbors. Today you get to live because a good man chose to protect an evil one to protect the innocent. But that the day will come when the evil you do shall be no more in this land. The day will come when the people you oppress shall be set free to live on this earth as the children of God they are. And when that day comes you will have two choices- to get down on your knees before the Lord your God and repent of your sins and beg for his forgiveness, or to spend eternity being burned up by the fires of your own hatred and sinful vainglory. Today, as in the days of Sodom and Gomorrah, the just hand of God has been stilled by the prayers of a righteous man. But it will not always be so. God shall smite the wicked and destroy those who spurn his Holy Law for His Kingdom WILL come. AMEN!" With that, the man turned his horse , lowered the flag and rode away.

The sun rose over silence as Tom Rutledge continued to stand on his steps. Abel and David watched as an elderly Negro man, obviously a house servant, came down the steps. "Mr. Tom, " he said, quietly, "Miz Rutledge says to tell you if the fightin' be over, you should invite all these gentlemen in to breakfast. We has it ready for everyone."

Tom Rutledge startled slightly, as if awakened from a doze, and said absently, "Yes, of course, Elijah, I'll tell them." He hesitated a moment, and then said, "Thank you, Elijah."

The black man looked startled for a moment, and then with great dignity, bowed slightly, and said, "You're welcome, sir."

187

And they both turned and walked away from each other in silence. As Rutledge came down the steps toward them, Abel and David moved as one to meet him. Rutledge held out a hand to Abel, and said, "I guess you gentlemen heard. Abel, I do thank you."

Abel studiously ignored the proffered hand, and looked Rutledge in the eye. "I will pray for you Tom," he said quietly, "Give your wife my regards. We won't be staying for breakfast." He looked to his brother-in-law.

David Nutt stepped forward slightly, the bulk of his blacksmith's form towering over Rutledge. "For the sake of my son, who loves your daughter, I placed other sons in jeopardy here today. I tell you now, never again. If my boys and my friends must fight again, it will be on their own terms. Never again will I ask them to defend evil on your behalf." As he turned to mount his horse, he caught sight of Henry, standing in the shadows nearby. When his son stepped into the light tears streaked his face. He held his father's gaze for a long while, then face set, he turned and mounted the steps to stand beside his father-in-law as they watched the two men ride away.

It was almost three weeks later when silence reigned in the tiny little cabin at Stockton Bend. Elizabeth's voice stilled as she gently refolded the pages of Abel's two letters and slipped them inside her Bible to reread later. Jesse and Henry sat on either side of her, Logan and Fanny across the table.

Jesse spoke first, his fingers gently touching Lizzie's hand. "We will pray for your mother. And for Phoebe." She nodded mutely.

"They were very lucky," said Logan quietly. "You'll have heard the news that Brown is now in New York raising funds and being hailed as a hero. But the truth is the extremists on both sides are guilty of great atrocities all over Kansas and Northern Missouri. And if Brown gets the funds he is after this winter, he and more like him on the other side will be back next spring, to try again."

"God, I wish they could go ahead and come," said Henry, explosively. "If Henry is determined to throw his lot in with the Rutledges, then let him. Let them support him and Celina and their brood!"

"It's not just Henry Nutt and his family," Logan reminded him. "Phoebe certainly can't travel right now, nor your mother, especially not this time of year with the rains and cold upon us."

Jesse nodded in agreement and turned to Henry, "Speaking of the cold, did you get your chimney problem fixed?"

"Oh, yes," said Henry morosely, 'It pulls just fine now that we removed the raccoon."

"At least it wasn't a skunk," said Fanny, with a smile, "I understand one got in Amon Bond's root cellar, and now they are afraid their food will smell all winter."

"Skunk! Skunk!" shouted little William excitedly.

Whereupon both Abby and Hugh were awakened and domestic chaos broke up the conversation for a time.

Later, as she waited for sleep to come, Lizzie said quietly to her husband, "Jesse, do you think they will ever actually come? I miss Mama so much! And Papa too! And now, now I'm just afraid. Afraid they won't come, afraid Mama will die and I will never see her again! Afraid for Phoebe." Her voice broke, and he pulled her close and let the tears run their course.

Finally, when she had quieted, he stroked her hair gently and said, "Sweetheart, I can't promise you anything. The only thing I can give you is my certainty that no matter what happens, God will work his purpose out, and will be with us through whatever comes." He felt her nod wordlessly against his chest, and continued. "Lizzie I know now is not a good time, but we need to talk about money."

He felt her raise her head and knew that she was looking at him. "Alright," she said, "what are you thinking?"

"Well, as you know, we used part of your dowry, coming here and paying for this plot and cabin. There is about $300.00 left. We will need some to get through the winter, but Henry has spotted a couple of plots of good fertile river bottom just south of here that would be a good buy at $500.00. If we each pay half we can get both sections, and we either Henry could lease ours and give us an income or one of the other men will. I really think Henry wants to run cattle, so he may lease his bottom land out as well, to give income while he tries to build a herd."

"How much can we lease the land for?" asked Lizzie.

"Probably around $50 a year, in cash and crops," said Jesse, "More than enough to cover our expenses, if we are frugal. Your father is paying Henry and me a percentage to acquire land for him. We are planning to move forward with that when he sends us funds in the spring. Meanwhile we would like to get our own houses in order. Henry has confided in me that he has a particular motivation for getting established."

"Oh, really?" said Lizzie, wide awake now.

Jesse nodded and smiled. "She is very young yet, but Henry is convinced he has already found the only person for him."

"Jesse Nutt-" said his wife emphatically, "You are NOT going to get out of this conversation without telling me who it is!"

He felt her finger poking his chest repeatedly for emphasis, and grinned. He had distracted her from her earlier melancholy, as had been his intention. "Ah, I don't think so, Lizzie…. Henry would kill me."

"You will think killed, if you don't tell!" she said, her smile in her voice.

"Well, let's just say that someday there will be three sets of cousins married in the Nutt/Landers family if your brother has his way…" said Jessie.

"Three sets…? But who…?" Lizzie scrambled mentally trying to match the pieces of the suddenly very small puzzle. "Well, not – " She froze for a moment, and said, "Not your little sister Susan, surely?!"

Jesse nodded, the grin back, as Lizzie continued to stammer, "B-but Jesse! She's only what – fourteen!? And Henry twenty next month!? How could he even.... What could have even made him think...??"

"Well according to him, SHE proposed to him at our wedding," said Jesse. "Of course she was all of eleven at the time, and he turned her down nicely. But she took to following him around, and then, during time when Jacob and I were sick, they both ended up with the job of messenger between the two households. Since then, the relationship stuck, and before he left they made promises to each other. – After all, if they come in the spring of '59, Susan will be sixteen."

Lizzie nodded, and said, "Well, just as well they have to wait. She is *much* too young now. Still," she mused thoughtfully, "at that age I already knew it would be either you or Jacob."

"I will never forget that day in the clearing," whispered Jesse, "when Jacob asked you – to choose. I was so scared."

"Scared?" she said incredulously. "Of what?"

"That you would choose him, mostly." He answered softly. "When you reached out and suddenly we were holding hands, I wanted to shout for joy and weep at the same time." Jesse whispered, his voice breaking.

"I know," she replied, "Me too."

After a moment of silence, she continued, "I wonder how he is doing really. Jacob, I mean."

"Me too," said Jesse. "It sounds as if maybe teaching the young people is good for him. I pray for him every day."

"I know, me too." She smiled then, and said, "I pray for them all, That God will take care of them and bring them to us quickly, before War comes."

"Ah, Lizzie," said Jesse, pulling her tight against him, "at least our prayers are united- for you are right... War is coming, and soon."

***** ***** ***** ***** ***** ***** ***** *****

Jesse's words in the night proved to be somewhat prophetic the next morning. The sun had not yet completely cleared the rise on the east bank when hoofbeats sounded in large numbers from the west. Shouts of alarm came from the posted sentries and everyone scrambled from their breakfast tables to grab guns and ammunition and secure the openings on their cabins. Darkness descended as shutters were slammed over windows and door latches were secured. Eyes wide with fear watched through cracks and gun sights. Lizzie watched through the gunsight in the front window as Henry and Logan ran by on the path below, rifles in hand, headed up the hill, toward the western perimeter of the settlement, where the line of defense had long ago been fortified. There were pit traps and sections of pointed stake cross-rail fences, behind which a shooters trench had been dug, that stretched in a line overlooked by four sentry towers. Four men watched from those towers almost continuously, except in the very worst of weather. There had not been any trouble from the local tribes since the fortifications had been completed almost four months ago, Amon had told them, although raids had continued without pause further to the west.

Moments later the first shots sounded, and for the next half hour the sounds of horses, shouts and screams, gunfire, and the chaotic clash and thud of violent hand to hand combat were borne on the wind down toward the river. Jesse and Lizzie clutched their child between their bodies as they huddled beneath the window, praying, and waiting for what might come.

In time, the sounds began to grow less until the fading thunder of retreating hoofbeats announced the retreat of the natives back toward the west from whence they had come. Silence hung over the settlement for several minutes, the only sounds during those moments the wind blowing through the dry grasses, the constant gurgle and flow of the waters of the Brazos, and the gradual renewal of the chatter of the birds. Doors began scrape open, and steps sounded on dirt and wooden stoop as women, children, and others stepped out and stood with eyes and ears focused on the four paths coming down the slope to the community.

As the silence fell, Jesse and Lizzie relaxed their embrace, and Abby squirmed free. In a moment of lightning speed she was suddenly headed across the floor on all fours. Lizzie gasped, and Jesse reached for her again in alarm. "Lizzie! What is it? What's wrong?"

Caught between laughter and tears, Lizzie said, "She's crawling! Our precious, precocious little angel is crawling!" She scrambled to her feet, and ran across the room just in time to block the path to the open hearth.

Abigail stopped, bewildered at finding her way blocked by her mother's skirts, and looked up, w-a-a-y up to find her mother's smiling face towering over her. This new view of Mama so startled her that her rosy little mouth fell open, and she plopped backward onto her plump little behind.

Mama laughed out loud so she did too, and waved her arms up and down as her legs churned, ready for more action. Next thing she knew she was being scooped up into the familiar warmth of Mama's arms, and carried across the room to where Papa's bigger stronger arms waited. She gurgled ecstatically as Papa kissed her and held her cheek against his wet one. And though she couldn't yet understand the words, she heard the love and pride in his choked voice as he whispered, "Tell me, Lizzie, so I can see...."

194

***** ***** ***** ***** ***** ***** ***** *****

The native horsemen had been repelled with only minor injuries on the side of the settlers, and no real indication of what, if anything, had prompted the sudden attack.

"Horses is usually what they're after," said Amon Bond later that day, when he stopped by the Lander's cabin site. The four men, Henry and Logan Landers, Jesse Nutt, and his own son-in-law Austen, were making steady progress. The walls were up, and now Henry and Logan were working on the roof, while Austen had Jesse helping him pack the mud into the space between the logs. It was nearing the end of October and working with the wet mud was chilly work. Jesse shivered slightly as he plunged his mud covered hands into a bucket of clean water before reaching toward Amon to receive the still warm, buttered bread Lizzie had sent along with Amon. 'Grateful for something hot for their lunch, the men sat down on the bare planks of the floor near the fireplace in the unfinished house. Logan had built a small blaze to heat some coffee, and the cups were blissfully warm in their hands.

"Looks to be an early winter," said Amon, "Last two years, we didn't get this cold till far into November."

"Really?" said Jesse, in surprise. "I guess being used to Missouri, it just seems about normal for us."

Logan reached over to pour another batch of hot black coffee into his tin cup, as he said, "Yeah, I think you're right Amon. When I was in Texas for quite a while a few years back, we usually didn't even have any frost till around first of November, with the first freeze two to three weeks later. This all seems about a month early to me. 'Course we are further north, but not that much."

"Well, I know I will be glad to get that roof done!" declared Henry, "It was so windy up there today, a couple of times I almost lost my balance!"

"Yes," nodded Amon, "that north wind will bite right through a body. And blowing damp too. The river's up, that means rain up north, and headed our way, likely."

"At least most of our work here will be inside from now on," observed Jesse, "Once we get the windows in, with this fireplace working, we will have a real cozy time of it mudding the walls, and building furniture this winter. Then come spring, we can get started on Logan and Fanny's place, once they've got their land secured."

"I can't believe Abel had those glass windows shipped all the way from Springfield, and not a one of''em broke!" said Austen, shaking his head. "That must've set him back a pretty penny."

"He says he won't bring Mama, unless he knows she has a decent place to live," said Henry. "She's not well, you know," he added sadly.

Amon looked chagrined. "Why no, son, I didn't know. That's too bad. Your mother is a fine woman, and a fine helpmate to your Pa. Long as I've known Abel, he was just plum head over heels about his Miss Sally."

Jesse laughed, "That he is, Amon, that he is. And wouldn't deny it either. She is a very special lady with a great inner strength. Her daughter is very like her." He ended with a smile.

Henry looked up at his last remark, surprised. "You know Jesse, I always thought of our Leatha as being more like Papa, but now that you say that – she is much like Mama too, especially that strength you speak of."

"My Sarah is much the same," said Amon, "Not so much on the outside, for Sarah is quiet and almost shy in company, but she has that inner core of steel. Austen, your Frannie has that too."

"I think," said Logan, thoughtfully, "that it takes a strong woman to be willing to follow her man into these new areas of wilderness. We men tend to forget that from time to time. I marvel at my Fanny's strength. Amon, you and Austen don't know her story, and I'll not betray her trust by speaking of it. But she has been through hell and come back, and somehow remained whole. I not only love her, but admire her more than any one I know."

"Well," said Austen solemnly, "it seems we have all been similarly blessed in our choice of helpmate. Except for young Henry here, who has not yet chosen." He raised his cup, "Here's to Miss Sally and all of our special women who have followed us to make homes for us in the wilderness. May they be part of our lives for many years to come. And may young Henry here be as blessed as we are in his mate!"

There was a chorus of agreement as their cups clinked together, as the flames burned brightly on the hearth of what would soon be a home.

***** ***** ***** ***** ***** ***** ***** *****

Shortly after the turn of the new year, Sarah Nutt stood in her parlor and looked skeptically at her daughter, and said, "The man said the letter was for a Miss Susan Nutt, and I can tell that is correct, because I know what Nutt looks like, and name before starts with an S."

Susan reached eagerly for the bedraggled missal, but her mother held it tightly and shook her head. "Who is it from Susan, and why would anyone who knows you write you a letter?"

"Not everyone knows I can't read, Mama," said Susan reproachfully. "It's not something I shout from the rooftops, any more than you do."

A look of pain and sorrow passed over her mother's face, and Susan felt her cheeks burn with shame when her mother said softly, "That was unkind Susan, and unworthy of you. You know how hard I have tried to get your father to relent."

Susan grasped her mother's free hand and said, "Oh, Mama! I *am* sorry! I know you tried! And just so you know, I have a- a friend who has tried to help me a little! I at least know my letters and what some words look like. But we never got to the part about writing, though. I still can't sign even my own name!"

"Oh, but that's wonderful Susan, that your friend has helped you! Who is she? Is it someone from church? Does she live nearby? Maybe we could arrange for you to have more time together!" Sarah's face was wreathed in gladness, the mysterious letter momentarily forgotten.

Sarah shook her head sadly. "No Mama, that's not possible. M-my friend- went away." Her lips trembled and her eyes were moist.

"Oh, my dear, I am so sorry!" said her mother, assuming the worst. "I had no idea! We've been so wrapped up in this thing with Henry that I had not heard of any of the local children passing away!"

Susan shook her head violently, "No, Mama! Not passed away! Never ever even think that! He – I , My friend MOVED away! And I recognize the writing! That's all!"

Sarah was suddenly very still and looking at her fourteen year old daughter through new eyes. She sat down on the sofa, laid the unopened letter on the nearby table, and watched how her daughter's eyes never left that fragile piece of paper.

"Susan, come sit." she said gently, "Look at me." As the girl obeyed Sarah gathered herself.

"Your- friend," she asked quietly, "is a young man?"

For a moment the girl's eyes widened in fear, and she started to shake her head. But Sarah leaned forward and reached out and placed a gentle hand on her daughter's knee. "Susan, why are you afraid? Has he hurt you?"

Again the violent shake of the head, and the tears overflowed, "Oh, no, Mama, he would never ever hurt me! He's so strong and generous and kind, and he was so good to me when I was so worried and scared! And then, when things got better, we had such good times together. He talked to me like I'm a real person, and as if what I think and feel is important to him. A-and he knew about me not knowing how to read and offered to teach me! A-and t-then he told me that Uncle Abel was sending him to Texas! A-and I wanted to go too, but he said I was too young but that he would wait for me! A-and now he's gone and I miss him so much! And I'm so scared that h-he won't---- wait for me..." she finished in a tiny voice, and then sat silent, tears running down her face.

Sarah, after having had a bad moment or two early on, was now almost limp with relief as epiphany dawned. "Henry." She said softly. "You've fallen in love with Henry Landers."

Susan finally looked up, met her mother's eyes, and nodded. "We know I'm too young, but we know how we feel too!" She blushed, "Although I will admit, it was only me, at first...."

Sarah's eyes sparkled and she smiled down at her daughter and said, "Oh, really? Tell me."

Susan blushed again, a deep red. "I proposed to him, at Lizzie and Jesse's wedding three years ago!" She shook her head, "He laughed at me! And I told him he could laugh all he wanted, but that I had decided, and that someday- he would marry me!" She looked up and smiled sheepishly. "I was bossy when I was eleven."

Sarah bit her lip to hold back a grin, and said, "I gather something changed his mind?"

The tears were stopped for now, and Susan was remarkably composed as she recalled the grim months of her brothers' illness, and how she and Henry had been thrown together as messengers. They had both been grief-stricken and terrified, and faced with an adult level of responsibility, especially Henry, and they had supported one another, listened to one another, and advised one another. And they had fallen in love. Knowing she was too young, they had held on to their friendship, and kept their love as a secret promise. And then Henry Nutt had caused everyone's plans to be thrown topsy-turvy, and Henry had seen that his father, his sister and his best friend needed him to go to Texas. And together they had made the decision that he should go. "He was going to refuse if I asked him to, Mama," she said softly. "But they needed him, and here we would have only been frustrated – waiting for me to finish getting grown. So I told him to go. But that doesn't mean I d-don't m-miss him most dreadfully!"

The tears were threatening again, but Sarah smiled brightly at her daughter, took both her hands in her own, and said, "Susan Nutt, I am so very proud of you!"

"Really?" said her daughter in wonder, "I was so afraid to tell you and Papa! I knew you would think we were too young to know real true love!"

Sarah reached out and gently touched her daughter's cheek. "Oh, sweetheart, your Papa maybe…. But let me tell you a little secret…. I've known your Papa all my life. He was Uncle Abel's best friend even before I was born. He is ten years older than me. That means he was a young man of sixteen and I was a precocious *six* when I told him I intended to marry him!" She laughed heartily at the memory. "Your Uncle Abel offered to throw me in the lake like the little bitty perch of a fish I was, but your father… I remember him looking at me for a long moment before he laughed too, and said, "No Abel, best leave her out here on dry land. It'll save me having to catch her when the time comes!" And they walked off laughing like boys do, and me standing there on the dock fuming. It was ten years later, to the day, standing on that same dock, - that your Papa proposed to me."

Sarah looked up at that moment to see her husband standing in the doorway. His expression was that of a man trying to contain a variety of emotions, not quite knowing how to express any of them. In the end, love won out, and he stepped into the room, saying with a rare smile, "Yes, she had finally grown enough to be a keeper, and I knew one when I saw one!"

Susan, who had jerked upright upon his entrance, relaxed into a bright look of happiness at his expression, and said, "Oh, Papa! I am so glad you both know now! I hated keeping secrets!"

"Well, I do expect there to be no more secrets, Susan, " said David seriously, and then smiled again, gently, "but we will be more than happy to wait with you while you finish growing into a keeper! And with that in mind, what do you say we all take this mysterious letter over to your Aunt Sally, and let her get started on showing you how to tell what it says."

As his daughter threw her arms around him in a glad embrace, David looked across the top of her head at his Sarah, whose smile and glad tears were in that moment all for him alone.

She reached out to grasp his hand as she silently mouthed the words, "Thank you!" and then, "I love you!"

He pressed her hand to his lips and kissed it, and then said, "Ladies, come along. Let's go find Jacob and take ourselves over to visit Abel and Sally. Hopefully after reading her Letter, Miss Susan will bring us all up to date on all the Texas news!"

June 30, 1857

Neosho, Missouri

Dear Jesse, Lizzie, Henry, and Abby,

I take pencil in hand to write to you with apologies from all that we have been so long in sending word to you of things here. Uncle Abel especially begs your forgiveness, and bids me assure you that although they have both been ill this spring, that he and Aunt Sally are both well on the mend, and think and speak of you all every day. It has been a very hard spring for all of us here, as you will see, if you can decipher my poor hand. David has fallen and broken his writing arm — thus we are reduced to my poor efforts. David says it is readable, so I trust that the good Lord will give Lizzie or Henry good deciphering skills to share all the news.

It is with great grief that I tell you that our sweet sister Phoebe died in April, giving birth to a little girl who also did not live. Poor Frank is just devastated, and blames himself. Having been down a similar dark path I have tried to be of help to him and he is trying to find solace in the task of raising their boy, Abel, but it is hard for him and he is much in need of your good prayers, that he might find peace and purpose in his life.

Aunt Sally and Uncle Abel have both been very ill with a lingering ague, that has threatened to go into pneumonia but Reg Harding and I have fought hard to keep it from doing so. I am staying here at the house in town with them as is David, and we, along with Chris and Mary looked after them and supervised the younger children. Uncle Abel is out of bed now, and is working from home, trying to get caught up on legal work. Aunt

202

Sally is still very weak, because of her heart, but is improving daily and I feel I can give you some assurance of her recovery.

Papa and Mama send their love and bid me tell you all is well with them. Henry and Celina have been very subdued and cooperative since the incident last fall with John Brown, which is a blessing, because with Uncle Abel ill I am not sure how we would have dealt with it if there was trouble.

Henry, your letter to Susan in January caused quite a stir which I am sure you will hear more about soon. Suffice it to say your secret is out, and everyone is glad to think that there might be a wedding to celebrate shortly after we arrive in Texas. Papa bids me to tell you to write to him of your plans via Uncle Abel, and that he is trusting in your continued honourable conduct until he and Mama deem Susan old enough to marry.

Papa and Chris Landers have worked together to make sure all the crops are in and all the farms operating well. Fortunately most of the unrest continues to be well north of us, although we do have bands of ruffians riding through often, which keeps all law-abiding folks on edge.

We are glad to hear that your Indian troubles have subsided a bit. Hopefully the rumors we hear of trouble along the Texas – Oklahoma border will not reach down your way. It is said that the man you mentioned- Colbert by name- is among a group encouraging more Indian unrest to try to keep white folks confined to the east part of Texas. Good luck to him on that, as we hear of plans to open up land as far west as the Pecos soon.

Well it has taken me most of the day to write this. I hope you will forgive the untidiness of my hand. David should be able to write soon, and Abel will likely send news as well.

Give Logan and Fanny our regards, and know that we all think of you often, and pray for the day we can be together again.

Your loving brother,
Jacob

***** ***** ***** ***** ***** ***** ***** *****

September 17, 1857

Stockton Bend, Texas

Dearest Mama,

It was such a relief and joy to at last receive your letter last week. You have been much in our hearts and prayers these many months, and we give thanks to God for your recovery and pray that you will take great care of yourself as we all continue to count the months and days until we can be together again.

Jacob and Papa shared with us earlier about the difficult time poor Frank is having and we are so glad to hear from you that he has moved back home with his little Abel, but having a little one myself, I pray you will let others do the chasing, and limit yourself to providing the comforts of Granny's lap! Our Abby is walking everywhere now, of course, and it is only moments like this when she is napping that I get an occasional moment to sit undistracted.

Jesse is so good to help, but the more active she becomes the harder it is for him to be sure of her safety. But she does love to sit in his lap while he sings to her the hymns of our Lord, and they often keep me company in my chores with their musical time together. As we both know, I have no voice or gift myself, but I do so love to listen, as Jesse has a fine voice, and the songs a message of joy and comfort that lifts the spirit.

We are happy here, Mama. Jesse has been most gratified with the amount of work he has been able to assist with in the building of the cabins, and he and Henry and Logan have made a good team in securing land for us all to work here in this new place. The pieces of land that Jesse and Henry have secured so far are three plots adjacent to each other. It is all prime river frontage that does include the bottom lands, but also higher ground overlooking a beautiful view of the river and the valley to the south. There is also, from almost everywhere, a view of the great mesa known as Comanche Peak. It is the highest point for many leagues around and is also a sacred place to the local Indian peoples. Many times a year we see smoke rising from great bonfires as they make some kind of ceremony up there on the mountain.

We are so eager for you all to come and join us in the land. We are coming to love it very much, and definitely feel that God has brought us here to make a home. There are hardships aplenty, but also great joy in being a part of a beginning. Amon and his family are proving fine neighbors and Fanny and Logan are so good to be with as well. But Mama, I do not think they will stay with us here forever. There is restlessness in them both, and they seem very reluctant to commit to the purchase of land for themselves. Logan has friends in south Texas in the cattle business down there and corresponds with them often. I think that may well be where they will decide to settle someday.

Selfishly, I hope they stay- at least until you all can come. I miss so much the fun of having the whole family together. I know that will probably never be again, but if I have my Jesse and Abby, and you and Papa, and Aunt Sarah and Uncle David close by I shall be content. We had a letter from Jacob and then one from him and David both. It sounds like he has made progress at last and is planning to come to Texas with his folks when you all come. Jesse and I had both wondered what his decision would be.

Again, take care, Mama, and know that we are counting those days till you may come to us.

Your loving daughter,

Leatha

***** ***** ***** ***** ***** ***** ***** *****

Neosho, Missouri
January 25, 1858

Dear Jesse, Elizabeth, and Henry,

Well at long last we enter the last months of what has become our exile here in Neosho. It is a great sorrow to me to see this area which we came to with such dreams nearly twenty years ago so torn asunder by the strife that is born of our pending national tragedy.

Here we now see open suspicion of neighbor for neighbor, we have various factions refusing to engage in trade with one another, and we find our civic and religious institutions reduced to mere shadows of themselves as members splinter into small groups pitted against one another in their zeal to uphold their version of the Right. People are afraid of both the stranger and each other. Widows and orphans, the victims of vigilante attacks across the border in Kansas, and in the strife-ridden counties to the north, appear in our community destitute and yet afraid to ask for help for fear of yet more reprisals because of the point of view of husbands and fathers already dead at the hand of their political adversaries.

The orphanage and the churches help where they can. Many, including your mother and me, have taken refugees into our own homes. And we lock our doors and guard our stables at night lest the lawless bands of self-appointed executioners come to our lands seeking either sustenance to be confiscated, or opponents to be slaughtered. Atrocities abound on both sides, and rancor and suspicion, and outright hatred soil the very fabric of our community relations. They say war is coming. I say war is already here.

David and his obligations are what hold us here now, and he and Sarah have begged the rest of us to depart with haste while they remain behind to take care of what they must. But I cannot bring myself in conscience to do so, and your mother will not go without me. And the younger generations are so divided among themselves that it is uncertain which of them would choose to leave and which will choose to remain.

We ask your prayers for us all, that we might remain in safety while we do that which honour commands, and find the pathway straight when the time comes to leave. May the blessings of the Lord be upon you always my children.

Your most loving Father,

Abel Landers

***** ***** ***** ***** ***** ***** *****

"I never in my wildest dreams," said Jesse, with a groan, "thought I would be a blind man pushing a plow." He stretched his aching limbs before the fire, and leaned back gratefully as Lizzie's strong hands brought relief to his neck and shoulders.

"I never thought I would pull the horse in front of one, either," said his wife, "But with three sections of land to get ready for planting and half the owners not here yet, there's no other choice."

"Did I understand right that we are going to plant corn? And not cotton?" asked Lizzie.

Jesse nodded. "For this year at least. Some of the fellows who have been here longest may do some cotton this year, but for those of us with increasing numbers of mouths to feed and limited cash resources, planting something that can feed both humans and animals, or be sold for cash really makes a lot of sense."

"Thank God Fanny and Logan decided to stay another year!" said Lizzie. "I don't know what we would have done if Fanny weren't here to keep Abby while we work in the field," said Lizzie. "There's no way I could watch a two year old, and help you at the same time."

"I miss the little minx when she's not here at night though," said Jesse with a smile.

Lizzie sighed, "I do to," she agreed. "But I must admit I am so tired tonight I can barely move."

Immediately he rose, and took her into his arms. "Ah, Lizzie, I am sorry. Here I am sitting letting you minister to me!" He kissed her gently and then turned her toward the chair. "Your turn," he said, as he began to massage her neck and shoulders.

She signed and he heard the smile in her voice as she said, "You're right. That does feel good! We can take turns!" There was silence for a moment, and then she said, "Jesse, what do you think the real reason is behind Logan and Fanny not wanting to stay?"

"I don't know, Lizzie," said her husband, thoughtfully. "I think it's as much about Fanny not being comfortable around a lot of people as anything else. I tried to talk to Logan about it once, telling him that there were plenty of areas just west of here where they could be as alone as anybody could want to be. But he kept saying that whether they stayed or not had to be Fanny's choice, and that he wouldn't take that away from her. That was the reason he gave me for deciding at the last minute not to lease our land."

"I think she will always be afraid that if some folks found out about her past, they would condemn her for it. Maybe even want her put in jail," said Lizzie.

Jessie nodded, "I think so too. But I also think that she thinks further west she will have a better chance of keeping Logan out of the war that's coming. And in that she is right. At this point who knows what way Texas is going to swing. Secession and war are coming, no doubt about it, and although I still believe Sam Houston will do everything he can to keep Texas in the Union, he is just one man. And lots of people in this state disagree with him."

"I heard from Rose Massey from over at Comanche Peak Post Office that there is talk of trouble up around Dallas between factions. I hope our folk don't drive right into that now that it looks like they may come this fall."

"Abel said they were going to try to avoid bigger towns in general on the way down. He figures whatever comforts they might find are outweighed by the risk of stepping into a hornets nest."

"Isn't it sad that it has come to that?" said Lizzie, drowsily.

"Yes, it is," said Jesse, as his hands stilled. "But God willing, they will arrive in the fall or next spring, and we can know the great joy of being together again! Meanwhile, Mrs. Nutt, you are asleep on your feet! Come on to bed. We've more to do tomorrow!"

***** ***** ***** ****** ***** ***** ***** *****

Neosho, Missouri

September 3, 1858

Dear Jesse, Lizzie, and Henry,

Uncle Abel and Papa bid me write to you all as they are all very busy with preparations for our journey to you. Jacob is helping me remember everything I am supposed to say, and helping me to know how to say it.

There has been a lot of discussion about who is coming with us to Texas and who is staying behind and Papa is really mad a John right now because he wants to stay behind with Henry and Celina. He wants to finish school and go to college, and he is afraid he can't do that in Texas. Mama says he must stay if he wants, that his education is important. Papa is not happy but I think he will give in to Mama in the end.

Henry and Celina and John are staying, as is Lizzie and Henry's old maid sister Phoebe Landers, who teaches school out at the orphanage. I think she is sweet on Brother Farmer, but Jacob says I must mark that out - that it is what you call a plate tonic relationship, which means they aren't lovey dovey. The other old maid Polly Landers is staying too. Mostly 'cause she and Phoebe live together and she has taught at that same school forever. I didn't think Chris and Mary Landers and their kids would come, but they are and so are our Elizabeth and her husband A.J. They were gonna come later, but things are so messed up here they decided to sell their land and come. A bunch of his folks may come later. Plus all of us younger ones are coming. Papa says to tell Jesse that we will be a group of twenty to twenty-five all together and that we will need Papa Abel's place and at least three more cabins if possible and we should be leaving here around September 15th.

Jessie, Papa said to tell you that he and Mama are going to go ahead and come for the winter, and get things settled there. They will have to come back here in the spring to sign everything over on the land. Papa wanted to just go ahead and do it, but Henry is holding him to the letter of their agreement that they have until March to get out. Mama says they have to do it this way as she will not let Aunt Sally travel to Texas without her along to help. Jake says it is all a mess and damn Henry's sorry hide for doing this to Mama and Papa. Don't tell Jake I told this - but I heard him tell Henry last night that he hopes he and Celina both "rot in hell for what they have done to our family."

We hear there is much unrest around Colbert's ferry but are praying for the best. If all goes well, we should arrive sometime around the middle to the end of October. We hope it doesn't get cold early this year. We can hardly wait to see you all! We are finally coming to Texas! See you soon!

Love to all,

David and Jacob

*****   ******   *****   ******   *****   ******   *****

Five and a half weeks later, Logan, Henry, Jesse and Lizzie stood on the bluff overlooking rows and rows of freshly harvested land stretching down to the river upstream as far as the lay of the land would allow them to see. Across the blue waters of the Brazos they could see the fields of the Rylee land interspersed among plots of pasture populated by the occasional cluster of cattle. In one of the fields slave workers were clearly visible as they finished the harvest.

Henry looked down that way then resolutely pulled his gaze away, back to their own fields. "I can't help but be proud of what we've accomplished here," he declared, "We got it done and we did it ourselves in good time, even minus the resources some others had."

"That would be using our own sweat rather than that of slaves?" said Jesse, bluntly.

"Yes," said Henry quietly, "that it would be. And damn proud of it, I am," he said, his eyes fixed on the people in the fields across the river. "You know, Jesse," he continued, "there are some things you are blessed to not have to see every day.

Jesse nodded, "No doubt, Henry, no doubt." Even as he spoke, he felt Lizzie stiffen beside him. "What? What is it Lizzie?" he asked, turning toward his wife in concern.

Her grip on his arm tightened. "Look, Henry! Wagons!" And sure enough, off to their left, north of the Rylee fields, was the spot where the trail from the east came up over the last rise and took a gently sloping turn north and down toward the ford just below Stockton Bend, about two miles upriver from where they sat. Appearing over top of that rise was a string of wagons, led by two men astride two large horses, one black and one bay. "It's them!" she cried excitedly, "I can see Papa and Uncle David! A-and, oh my, so many wagons!" She stared in disbelief as Logan said, "Good Lord! Did they bring half of Neosho with them?!"

"I count fifteen wagons" said Henry, eagerly. And looks like they managed to bring quite a few head of stock with them as well! I didn't expect that!"

"We must go to the ford and meet them!" said Jesse excitedly.

They all headed for their mounts, and were soon travelling at a good pace northward toward the low water ford just below Stockton Bend. Almost there, they met up with Amon Bond and his sons Ben and Ed, "Is it them?" asked Amon. "Austen sent word that he'd seen a big party come over the rise!"

"Yes, it's them!" said Lizzie, her eyes dancing with excitement! "Oh, I wish we had Abby with us!"

Hoof beats sounded, and another horse appeared, ridden by Sarah Bond and a bouncing dark haired moppet. "Miss Abby wanted to come meet her grandparents!" said Sarah with a smile, even as Lizzie maneuvered her horse over to take the little girl onto her lap. "See Granny!" she announced loudly.

"Oh, yes we do we, sweetie!" said her Mama, with a bright smile.

"Let's go, then," said Jesse, as he held his horse close beside Lizzie's. And so they all turned toward the waters of the river and went down to welcome their family home.

Together For a Season, Fall 1858 – January 1859

My heart was nearly to burst with joy as I looked round the crowded room in my parents' new cabin. My mother and my sister-in-law Mary sat beside me and Fanny at long last, and Papa's big booming voice rang out as he regaled the men with tales of their journey south from the Red River. For miles they had been shadowed by a group of Indians who had appeared on their flank almost as soon as they left Colbert's landing. Then the Indians had evaporated upon the approach of a body of Texas militia who had stayed with them until they split off just outside of Dallas. That partnership had turned out to be an amiable one, with the militia officers coming to share fireside conversation with the Landers and Nutt men in the evenings. "They were mostly East Texas fellows," said Papa David, "and an interesting mix serving together and managing to stay focused on the task at hand- monitoring the Indians- in spite of major differences among them on the politics that surround everything. "

Jacob nodded, "True Papa. That Hennis fellow, now he was an odd sort. Roman Catholic, family in Texas since '35, and vehemently anti-slavery, yet hates the Indians with a passion. It's personal with him. Seems his sister's daughter was romanced by an Indian and ran off with him." He was still thinner than before, but his color was good, and he seemed much more the Jacob I remembered, keen and intellectual, still a student of people just as his brother was. And still with the same magnetism for small children. Abby kept scrambling from his lap to Jesse's and back again. I really should intervene but they both seemed to be getting a kick out of the back and forth. God, it was so good to see them together again....

It was my poor brother Frank who worried me now. Both Mama and Papa had written more to us of how hard he had taken Phoebe's death, and the loss a day later of the little girl she had carried. He obviously was still in that same depressed mind set all these months later. He sat, cadaverously thin and silent, as alone as one can be in a room full of people. The only time he showed any expression at all was when his little son Abel came running over and crawled into his empty lap.

Logan responded to Jacob's tale thoughtfully, "Well, you know that kind of thing isn't all that uncommon. There are several of the older frontiersmen who live out west of here, who keep Indian wives."

"And then there's Charles Barnard's wife over at the Trading Post at Glen Rose Mills. She was captured as a young girl, and lived among the Indians for several years. She had been married to an Indian and bore him a child before Charles and his brother found and rescued her."

"Was she terribly traumatized?" asked Mary curiously.

"I'm sure it was horrible at the time," said Sarah Bond, seriously, "but she is really very matter of fact about all now. She says some of the women especially tried to be kind to her in their way."

My mother shuddered, "Well, we shall pray to the good God that none of us are ever faced with such a tragedy."

"But surely it would be different if you fell in love...like that Hennis girl did," said Susan, who had not let go of Henry's arm since arriving.

"I can't imagine such a thing," said her mother, with an indulgent smile, "But perhaps it could happen..."

215

"Well, not around here it won't," said Papa David, sternly. "You girls are to steer well clear of any savages who might come into town to trade, you hear?"

"We don't get much of that here," said Jesse, "They do over at Barnard's, but so far they mostly leave us alone."

"Not always though. The Comanche especially, will still try a raid if they see someone being careless with their horses," said Amon from his seat by the fire.

"What about other stock?" asked Abel Nutt, who was now a very grown up and darkly handsome nineteen year old.

"So far," said Logan, "they don't seem to have much interest in anything but horses. That could change if we had drought years where game became scarce."

"Well, right now we don't have such large herds that monitoring will be a huge job," said my father, "but I expect that may change rather quickly. We've brought some prime breeding stock and I know from our letters that both Henry and young Abel, along with some of their younger cousins plan to make that their primary focus over the next few years."

Henry nodded, "That's right, Papa," he grinned, "now that you old men are here to do the farming, we young folk aim to stay out on the open range and away from the plow!"

"You'll come home every evening to eat the food produced by those plows quick enough, I reckon," said Mama Sarah, with raised brow.

"Now, now," said my father, "each to his own gifts, children!" a twinkle of pure joy shining in his eyes. "We're all together at last! There'll be plenty of hands to make all of our labor light work!"

"Speaking of all together," said Jesse, "Now that we've all caught our breath, and everyone has seen the cabins, we need to start unloading. Uncle Abel, Papa David, do you have a final plan of who is going where?"

"Well," said my father, "Chris and Mary and their little ones are to go in the northeast bedroom upstairs here, and Frank in the room next door with his little Abel. The other two rooms up there are our Abel and Will in one and our Sarah and Martha. Sally and I are going to partition off the end of this room into a bedroom and study for now. Maybe we'll move upstairs in a few years, if we aren't too old and decrepit." He smiled at my mother, but I could see the wistfulness flicker in his eyes. He had written me months ago about how hard it was for her to do stairs now. And God love him, this was his way of seeing she didn't have to.

Papa David said, "We'll all be at our place of course. Sarah and I and young Susan will share the bedroom space, while Abel, and David take the "dog trot" space. Jacob will sleep in a corner of our main room."

"Yes, Uncle David," said Henry, "I told Jake he will like that spot next to your big fireplace- I've had my bed there for almost three years!"

Aunt Sarah frowned, "Henry, I wish you would stay! I feel like we are pushing you out, after all you've done for us."

"Oh, no, Aunt," he answered, more than a little proudly, "I am already moved into my own place. I have built a little cabin down on the land along the river that I have in my name. I've already got a nice little herd of about 20 head of cattle and looking to buy more."

"And Jesse and Abby and I are snug in our little cabin right between your two bigger ones!" I said with a smile.

"Well, alright, gentlemen," said Logan, "sounds like we have a plan. Let's get to it."

***** ****** ****** ****** ****** ******* *****

It didn't take long for all our folk to settle into the busy routines of daily life on the Texas frontier. The menfolk and boys rose early and spent their days hunting, fishing, tending the stock and baling the hay for the winter, and those who were able took their turns in the rotation keeping a sharp eye out on the sentry line up above the settlement.

The women did what women have done from time immemorial. We cleaned, washed, mended, sewed, cooked, took care of barn stock, and gardens, and watched our small children. We visited and helped one another, and waited for our men to come home.

The weeks passed and as they did certain patterns of our lives began to immerge. My father had almost overnight, through nothing except the remarkable force of his own personality, become the de facto head of the Stockton Bend Community. It was a position long held by our friend Amon Bond, and I watched worriedly for signs of resentment on Amon's part. I said as much one afternoon to my mother, as we sat sewing companionably before the big fireplace in her and Papa's cabin.

"Oh, my goodness, no!" said my mother, with a smile, "It was what Amon wanted from the beginning. You see, Amon is a good man, a smart man, an educated man- although not so much formally as your father. But Amon – he loves starting things, your father- he – his passion is taking a community and helping it grow- much like raising a child. Amon loves the excitement of the new baby, but my Abel- for him it is seeing it grow, mature- bonds form, the people and their lives and dreams and how it all weaves together to become that – that thing called community. It's hard to explain ..."

I nodded eagerly, "I understand, Mama. It's that part for Jesse too. – The people part...."

218

Her face softened, "Yes, I know… That's why…. Well, you know what we hoped for…." She finished softly, her voice trailing off.

I nodded again, saying. "God works in mysterious ways, Mama. To an extent I never dreamed possible, it's happening anyway. Jesse is so good with all the folks around, and somehow, I think because they see him as a fair-minded, moral man, but not a threat to them, the gentlemen come round and confide in him- talk about things- seek his thoughts- much like they always have Papa. And I see them doing it together, even here. Why just this last week, when Tommy Lambert got crosswise with Jim Davis about that bull getting in with his cows – Papa and Jesse were just out for a walk, when Tommy shows up, all hot and bothered, and Papa and Jesse just calmly walked on over to Tommy's pasture, sent young David over to get Jim Davis, and they settled the whole thing amicably right there on the spot!"

She nodded and laughed, "Yes, I heard all about that tale! And yes you are right. God is gracious. Jesse and Jacob are both able to do so much more than I ever dreamed. I am having such fun working with Jacob in the morning teaching some of the younger children their letters and numbers. I declare that man does have a gift of patience for working with the little ones!"

"I can hardly wait for Abby to get old enough to come!" I said. She is so smart. I have been reading to her and Jesse since before she was born!"

"I am so glad! It is a joy you can all share!" she said sincerely.

"Speaking of sharing," I said softly, "How are you, Mama?"

She sat very still for a moment, as if deciding how to answer. "I'm alright, sweetheart." She said softly, "The trip here was difficult, but your dear Father, and everyone else worked very hard to see to it that I did not over do. And sweet Mary, Chris's wife is wonderful. She doesn't let me do very much of anything around the house! Your father and I are very blessed. We are surrounded by a loving family, we both get to do pretty much only the things we love with the people we love. And I love our early morning rides together. We haven't had the time to do that since we were first married!" She paused, and then reached for my hand. "You must always try to do that, you know. Make time for you and your husband- just the two of you! Sometimes it is hard, with life, and chores and children. But it's oh so important!"

I nodded my agreement. "I know what you mean, Mama! Jesse and I take pleasure in some of the strangest things- as long as we are doing them together!"

Later that night, I lay in bed, smiling as I thought of my parents- still savoring and hoarding that time spent together after all these years. Somehow, it did not occur to me, until weeks later, that they were indeed using that time together for the most precious of all purposes. They were using it to say good-bye.

***** ***** ***** ***** ***** ***** ****** ******

It was Christmas Eve night in our little cabin in Stockton Bend. I had just finished putting the goose Henry had brought us earlier in the day into its pot to bake all night in fire on the hearth. As I washed the last of the utensils, Jesse came out of the bedroom, and pulled the door gently to with a long sigh. '

"Is she finally asleep?" I asked quietly.

"Lord, yes, at last!" he said, shaking his head, but smiling all the same.

"She is one excited almost three year old!" he added, as he took his seat on the bench by the hearth.

I smiled too, and said softly as I moved to sit beside him, "She's not the only one!" I breathed a contented sigh, as I leaned against his shoulder. "At last we are all together again and I feel like we are all finally home! It is as if this Christmas will mark a new beginning for us all for all Christmases to come!"

He nodded and said, "I think everyone feels that way, Lizzie. Anon Bond was up at Uncle Abel's place this afternoon, bemoaning the fact that we don't any building big enough for the whole community to come together to celebrate Christmas! I am thinking a church-raising may be in the offing come springtime. But meanwhile, your father is up to his usual organizing and scheming…. and I must say he has not lost his touch!"

"Oh dear Lord, what is he up to now?" I said. "The mind boggles…"

"Well, do you remember back when we were little, before there was a church in Neosho, how Papa and Uncle Abel would make Christmas come for all of us after supper on Christmas night? How we would exchange our presents just before the meal and all us children would play while the womenfolk got the table ready. And then Uncle Abel or Papa would say a special Christmas grace, and after supper we would all gather round the fire and sing carols and one of them would tell the Christmas story…." His voice drifted off as he remembered.

"Oh, Jesse, we are truly going to have Christmas!!" I exclaimed. "How wonderful that this will probably be the first one Abby remembers!"

He nodded. "We're all to gather at the big house of course. Tommy Lambert has loaned Logan his guitar. Logan and I are both a little rusty, but I think we can pull it off!"

"You're going to lead the singing?" I asked, thrilled.

"Yes, and Jacob is going to tell the Christmas story!" He laughed. "Papa actually told him that if he'd had to do it from memory all these years, he saw no reason why Jake couldn't do the same!"

I gasped, "What did Jacob do?"

"Well, Lizzie, there was this moment of just dead silence, and then he started to laugh. And then all the rest of us started to laugh too, and O God, Lizzie, I would have given anything to have been able to see his face! And somehow he knew, because next thing, he was next to me, and threw his arm around my shoulders just like the old days, and said, 'Brother, you'd best go get that walking stick of yours and take us away! We've got some rehearsing to do!'" Jesse stopped, overcome.

There were glad tears in my eyes too, as I squeezed his hand, and whispered, "Oh, Jesse, at last! He has made his peace! Oh I am so glad, so very glad!"

And so it was that as we all gathered round the two long trestle tables set up in the great room of my parent's cabin, my father stood at head of one, looking out over the thirty-one kinfolk come to celebrate together. He cleared his throat loudly, in his best courtroom manner, and as he waited for silence, I saw his eyes meet my mother's and soften, as the corner of his mouth twitched with a secret smile just for her.

And he began as he had begun that fateful day over five years ago, "Children. I call you that because all of you belong to my dear friend David and me in one way or another. We are- all of us here – family. And here we are together again at long last. At long last we are come safely home to this new land where a great river flows- its waters and the protection it gives us and even its very name- El Rio de Los Brazos de Dios- a daily reminder to us of the Faithfulness and Goodness of our Lord. We come together tonight to celebrate a miracle – the miracle of Our God come to dwell among us to live as a man. - To live and die as one of us. - To be always with us. Our presence here together today is a testimony to the constant and abiding care of our Lord and Saviour. And so we give thanks to you O Lord for the bounty you have poured out upon us. We ask you to bless this food for the nourishment of our bodies, and our lives that we may live them to your service. In Thy Holy Name we pray. Amen."

Our great Amen was followed by a joyous and noisy feast. My goose was joined by several chickens and a ham that had been sent to Papa by none other than Jeff Rylee. Jesse had muttered something about checking it for unusual ingredients, which earned him a swift kick under the table. As dinner began winding down, and we were clearing the table, I handed Abby to my mother and bade her go sit in the rocking chair near the fire. I saw my father catch Papa David's eye, and he in turn leaned over and said something to Jesse who, along with Jacob had moved to two chairs sat on either side of the big fireplace. The space in front of the hearth had been cleared, I saw Logan reach quietly for the guitar he had borrowed from Tommy Lambert as Fanny settled with their little William and Hugh near his feet.

Jacob reached over petted Abby on the head, and then reached down and gathered Chris and Mary's youngest into his lap. Henry and Susan, the two lovebirds, sat together on the settee near my mother. Papa David and Mama Sarah sat next to my father at the head of one table while the other adults, Chris and Mary, A.J. and Elizabeth settled onto the trestle benches. Frank, still hollow eyed- even after all these months, found a place for himself and his little Abel next to Papa. As Logan began to quietly play some chords, conversations softened and finished quickly. Jesse's brothers Abel and David, led, as the older children came from their various corners of play, and began to take their places on the floor in front of the brightly burning hearth. My little brothers William and Cal came to stand with me against the rough log wall as Jesse began to sing in a soft clear tenor:

Oh, come all ye faithful, Joyful and Triumphant,

O come ye, O come ye to Bethlehem.

Come and behold Him, born the King of angels.

O come let us adore Him, O come let us adore Him,

O come let us adore Him, Christ the Lord!

We all joined in on the second and third verses, ending with the chorus once more, echoing the call to all the earth to come to the manger. And then in the flame-lit quiet of that cold December night, as the waters of the Brazos flowed round the great curve of Stockton Bend, Jacob began,

"And it came to pass in those days, that there went out a decree from Caesar Augustus, that all the world should be taxed. (And this taxing was first made when Cyrenius was governor of Syria.) And all went to be taxed, every one into his own city. And Joseph also went up from Galilee, out of the city of Nazareth, into Judaea, unto the city of David, which is called Bethlehem; (because he was of the house and lineage of David) To be taxed with Mary his espoused wife, being great with Child. And so it was, that, while they were there, the days were accomplished that she should be delivered. And she brought forth her firstborn Son, and wrapped Him in swaddling clothes, and laid Him in a manger; because there was no room for them in the inn. And there were in the same country shepherds abiding in the field, keeping watch over their flock by night. And, lo, the angel of the LORD came upon them, and the glory of the LORD shone round about them: and they were sore afraid. And the angel said unto them, Fear not: for, behold, I bring you good tidings of great joy, which shall be to all people. For unto you is born this day in the city of David a Saviour, which is Christ the LORD. And this shall be a sign unto you; Ye shall find the Babe wrapped in swaddling clothes, lying in a manger. And suddenly there was with the angel a multitude of the heavenly host praising God, and saying, Glory to God in the highest, and on earth peace, good will toward men. And it came to pass, as the angels were gone away from them into Heaven, the shepherds said one to another,

Let us now go even unto Bethlehem, and see this thing which is come to pass, which the Lord hath made known unto us. And they came with haste, and found Mary, and Joseph, and the Babe lying in a manger."

With the end of the story, Logan began to play the sweet chords of a song a man from Germany had shared with him and my Father many years ago. Papa David, my father, Jesse and Jacob began it together,

"Silent Night, Holy Night, All is Calm, All is Bright,

Round yon Virgin Mother and Child,

Holy Infant so tender and mild.

Sleep in heavenly peace, sleep in heavenly peace."

***** ***** ***** ***** ***** ***** ***** *****

It was almost a month later when the sound of frantic knocking caused both me and Jesse to sit bolt upright in bed, shattering the cocoon of warmth in which we were slumbering. Between us, Abby- assaulted by both frigid air and horrific noise- launched herself into her father's arms. I was reaching for the loaded revolver on the bedside table when a hoarse voice shouted, "Leatha! Jesse! Papa and Mary say you've got to come! Mama's took bad!"

I was vaguely aware of Jesse speaking quietly to Abby, as I stumbled to fumble with the bar on the cabin door. "Will," I called, "I- We're awake! Just a minute!"

My teeth were already chattering when I opened the heavy door and more ice cold January air sliced into the cabin. I grabbed the shoulder of Will's coat and pulled his lanky body inside. Slamming the cabin door quickly shut against the wind, I shoved the bar back in place.

My 18 year old brother William leaned back against the door, shoulders hunched with the cold, but it was the tears glistening on his face that turned me to ice inside. "What is it, Will? What's wrong with Mama? Is it her heart again?"

He nodded his head, "I think so. Papa said he woke up to her thrashing and moaning and saying her chest hurts, and she can't get her breath. Papa called out for help, and we all came running. You know Mary's taken care of lots of sick folks, and she took me and Cal aside and told me to come get you. She said to tell you if you wanted to see Mama a- alive you better come quick. She sent Cal to get Henry, and Rob to get Aunt Sarah and Jake. She said maybe he would know somethin' to do."

Suddenly, Jesse arm was there, pulling me close. "Lizzie, It will take too long if Abby and I come. Go now with Will, and send someone back for us when you can. We will be fine."

Blindly I nodded, and moved away from his warmth to begin putting on another layer of clothes, before donning my cloak. "Will, get the fire going for Jesse, and leave some extra wood within reach. Jesse, there's milk from last night in the pail on the porch, and the leftover bread is in the keeper. "

"We'll be fine," Jesse assured me. "I will pray, Lizzie," he said, holding my cloak for me. He pulled me quickly close, and his lips brushed my hair, then Will had me by the hand, pulling me out into the cold, windy darkness.

Several minutes later, we stumbled out of the cold and into the warmth of the big main room of my parent's home. The curtains that surrounded my parent's ground floor sleeping area had been pulled back to give more air. Jacob was already there with Mary and Uncle Abel by the bed, Aunt Sarah right behind him. Frank and Rob were herding the younger children back up the stairs, as Chris came to meet Will and I at the door.

"Jake says it's her heart, of course," he said softly. "He said if he had access to certain medicines they might help, but probably not. He's had Mary try to give her coffee- says sometimes that helps, but so far nothing has. They brought the little ones down – she wanted to see them. Now she's askin' for Polly and for you. Reckon she wants to say..." He stopped- unable to continue.

I felt a bewildered panic as my legs started carrying me to my mother's bedside. How could this be happening? My mother, so much the light in our family for so long, who was always there – sensible and calm and steady, how could any of us do without her sure confidence in each of us? And Papa – she was his due north- amid all the tempests of his eventful life. How.... - And suddenly I was there, and Mama's eyes were open, looking at me. "Leatha-," she whispered through blue tinged lips.

I gripped her hand, so suddenly frail, in mine. "Yes, Mama, I'm here!" I said, willing the tears to stop so I could see her dear face.

"You and Jesse," she said, "You must help Papa. Keep e-everyone safe..."

"W-we will, Mama," I said, hardly able to speak. Suddenly there was a hand on my shoulder, and Jesse was right behind me as I knelt by my mother's bed.

"Don't worry Aunt Sally," said Jesse, "We'll be right here whenever he needs us."

She closed her eyes and drew a rasping breath. "Polly? Phoebe?" she whispered, her voice barely audible.

Gently my father moved in front of me and took her hand from me. "Sweet Sally," he said, "our girls Phoebe and Polly stayed in Neosho, remember. They are helping Brother Farmer raise all those orphans."

My face was buried against Jesse's chest, and his arms were tight around me. Papa kept talking to Mama in that soft choked voice I had never heard from him before.- Words of love, comfort, assurance. Finally, the harsh gasping grew less, and then stopped. There was a rustle of sound and I turned in time to see Jacob gently touch her throat, then turn to my father, and say softly, "She's gone, Uncle."

"Thank you, Jacob, Mary....children...." my Father said, in that same soft choked voice, "Please, go a-and warm yourselves b-by the fire. We- I need..."

Since I was closest, I gave him a brief fierce hug, and somehow managed to say, "Of course, Papa. Come on everyone..." and clutched Jesse's arm as I moved blindly away toward the big fireplace on the other end of the room. "H-How did you get here? W-where's Abby?" I asked Jesse, struggling to focus.

"Papa came right after you and Will left," Jesse said softly, "He knew Will was coming for you, and when Mama left with Jake he got dressed and came to fetch me. Francis took Abby upstairs with his little Abel."

I looked toward the stairs, and saw Sarah Nutt heading purposefully up, along with my cousin Susan. Uncle David was speaking quietly with Mary and Christopher and Abel Nutt, and Rob, Will and Cal were huddled nearby. I looked again toward the stairs, and saw Jacob and Henry headed toward Jesse and me. Henry was red-faced and his eyes wet with tears. Jacob, by contrast, was pale, and dry-eyed, but his face softened as he spoke, "Lizzie, I am so, so sorry."

Jesse's arm was strong about my waist, and I struggled for a steady voice as I reached out and lay a hand on Jacob's arm, "I know you are, Jacob. A-and I thank you for coming and doing what you could."

He shook his head. "It wasn't – Lizzie when it's like this, there's really nothing... There's a new drug – called digitalin- sometimes it helps, but usually not with sudden severe things like this."

It was at that moment that the curtain pulled back, and my father stood there. His eyes scanned the room and fell on Jesse and me, and he said, "Jesse, I wonder if I might have a moment?"

"Certainly, Uncle," said Jesse. "Jacob, will you stay with Lizzie?"

"Of course, brother," he said, and Jesse gave me a gentle squeeze and let Henry take him to my father.

With his leaving, suddenly I felt very hollow inside. Jacob must have sensed this, because he said, "Lizzie, I think we both need to sit down."

"Yes, please," I agreed, deliberately telling my feet to take us toward one of the benches at the big table.

Henry came and joined us. "Papa sent me away," he explained, "Said he needed to talk to Jesse privately." He sounded a little hurt.

At a loss, I said nothing, but Jacob said, "I suspect Uncle Abel wants to talk to Jesse about the burial. I heard him and Papa and Jesse and Amon talking about where they think the permanent county seat should be located someday, and most of the land is part of what is in Jesse's claim. So if we are going to start a burial ground it needs to be over there, I guess."

"Oh," said Henry, hollowly, "I hadn't even thought...."

Jacob shrugged, "Well, I know when Amon's daughter almost died in childbed in the fall, it came up. Made them realize they needed to go ahead and have a plan. Never mind that the state legislature has not got anything but possible secession on their minds. They couldn't be bothered to do something peaceful like form a new county."

"Lizzie," said my sister-in-law Mary kindly, "would you like some coffee? Gentlemen?"

We all took coffee, and I dazedly thought I should offer to help her wait on everyone, and suddenly I realized that I was used to my mother doing just that and asking me to help. My eyes flooded, and I struggled to stifle the sob that caught in my throat. I clung to the cup of coffee, and focused on it like a lifeline. I was conscious of Henry and Jacob continuing to talk, but was not paying much attention to anything but my inner turmoil. Once again, just as I was feeling totally adrift, Jesse's hand touched my shoulder and I was anchored once more.

My Uncle David had brought him to us. "What did Papa want?" asked Henry.

"Well, several things he wanted my thoughts on. Most importantly for now, what to do about a cemetery." explained Jesse. "I suggested that Papa and Amon and I call together some of the men in the morning and go look at a couple of places, and see if there is agreement. Then, since the river is too high right now for Brother Joe to come from Comanche Peak, he asked me if I would say the words for Aunt Sarah, and lead the prayers. I told him I would be honored to do so." Jesse's voice broke then. He was sitting with his arm about my waist, and I laid my head on his shoulder, once again blinded by tears.

Jacob spoke for us all, when he said, "Jesse, I know that would please Aunt Sarah to no end." He turned toward Papa David and Henry and said, "Papa, why don't you see if you and Christopher can get Uncle

Abel to go upstairs and rest for a while. My sisters Sarah and Susan and I can take charge of the little ones. That way Mama can come down and help Mary and Lizzie with what must be done. Then Henry why don't you and Frank take the rest of the boys over to our place and get a little shut-eye before the sun comes up. We've still got a few hours yet."

"A sensible plan," nodded Uncle David. "Jesse, you and Elizabeth bide here a bit. My Sarah will come for you in a little while, Elizabeth."

"Thanks, Papa," said Jesse softly, for both of us. "Come, Lizzie, let's move over to that settee by the fireplace. We can be comfortable there for a bit."

Numbly I led Jesse to the settee. As we sat down, Jesse pulled me close in his arms and pulled my long cloak around us. The combination of strength and warmth melted that numb frozen feeling deep inside me, and I closed my eyes to join him in the darkness as the pain washed over me and finally, I gave way and wept.

***** ****** ***** ***** ***** ***** ***** *****

We laid my mother to rest in a clearing ringed by a grove of post oaks, atop a bluff overlooking the Brazos River. Some of the women were upset because it was almost two miles from our little settlement of Stockton Bend, this ground Amon, and my father, and Uncle David and some of the others had chosen. But I alone of the women was with the men that bleak January day. Jesse and Jacob both declared that I had to come, and be their eyes. So we rode with the men that day, me riding double with Jesse while young David did the same with Jacob.

Shortly after my Father's arrival, he and this same group of men had ridden all over the area, and they had met with other groups of men from other settlements, and they had discussed several possibilities for the site of what they hoped would someday be the county seat of a new Texas county carved out of the hills and bluffs along the Brazos. One of the preacher men from over toward Fall Creek had taken to calling the theoretical town Bethlehem as a joke – since all the "wise men" were searching for it, and the name had begun to stick, with everyone in the area now using it to refer to the new town.

Of all the possible sites, I knew there was one dear to my father's heart. It was a place he and my mother had found when they were out riding the morning after they crossed the Brazos. Always early risers, they often enjoyed an early morning ride together as a private time before seeing to the demands of family and business. My mother had told me of that first morning in this new land in the Arms of God, when they had come to the crest of a hill that sloped gently down to the top of the first of a series of great white bluffs that overlook a commanding view of the Rio de los Brazos de Dios as it runs in a broad sweeping curve in front of the great mountain of the Comanche. She told me of how the sun came up just at the moment they came to the top of the bluff, and the green of the hills and the blue and silver of the waters in the sunlight formed a view that took their breath away.

So it was to that bluff that my father brought us that cold January morning. We, his offspring, bore witness to the promise he saw there. And later, on that same day, we sunk our roots deep into the dark Texas soil, laying my mother to rest atop the bluff where she and my father reaffirmed by their presence their love for all of us and for each other.

 Jesse's voice was strong and filled with confidence in God's Great Promise, as he reminded us all of Home:

> Jesus said - Let not your heart be troubled: ye believe God, believe also in me. In my Father's house are many mansions: if it were not so, I would have told you. I go to prepare a place for you. And if I go and prepare a place for you, I will come again,

and receive you unto myself; that where I am, there ye may be also. And whither I go ye know, and the way ye know.

Thomas saith unto him, Lord, we know not whither thou goest; and how can we know the way? Jesus saith unto him, I am the way, the truth, and the life: no man cometh unto the Father, but by me.

And so we speak together the words of praise and comfort the Lord gave to his servant David:

The LORD is my shepherd; I shall not want.

He maketh me to lie down in green pastures: he leadeth me beside the still waters.

He restoreth my soul: he leadeth me in the paths of righteousness for his name's sake.

Yea, though I walk through the valley of the shadow of death, I will fear no evil: for thou art with me; thy rod and thy staff they comfort me.

Thou preparest a table before me in the presence of mine enemies: thou anointest my head with oil; my cup runneth over.

Surely goodness and mercy shall follow me all the days of my life: and I will dwell in the house of the LORD for ever. Amen.

Let us pray.

Heavenly Father, in sure and certain hope of the resurrection to eternal life through our Lord Jesus Christ, we commend to you Almighty God our sister, Sarah Ann, and we commit her body to this ground made holy by thy presence here with us today; earth to earth, ashes to ashes, dust to dust. The Lord bless her and keep her, the Lord make His face to shine upon her, and be gracious unto her; the Lord lift up His countenance upon her and give her everlasting peace. Amen."

"Lizzie?" my sister-in-law called from the open cabin door, "are you here?"

"In the bedroom!" I called, "Changing the linens!"

"I help!" Abby proudly informed her, as she came through the doorway.

"I bet you do!" Mary said with a smile, touching the top of Abby's black curls as she entered. She stepped over to quickly help me tuck the final corners and pull up the quilt. "Lizzie, I've come because I'm worried about Papa Abel." She said in her direct way.

I nodded, and motioned her toward the fire in the front room. "There's coffee," I said, "Come and sit." I picked Abby up from the bed, runny nose and all and headed for the fireplace in the front room.

I settled Abby in the big wooden box Jesse had built in the warm corner, and then Mary and I settled by the fire coffee in hand. "Tell me." I said, and took a bracing sip of the strong, hot liquid.

She settled a moment, taking a deep sip of the coffee, "Oh, Lizzie, I knew- all those years, when she wasn't really well – I knew what her going was going to do to him! And I know you miss her desperately too- we all do, but Lizzie- he's just lost – you know? Every morning he gets up just as they always did, and he gets on that horse of his, and leaves. I've had David follow him just to see, and sure enough he goes to that bluff and sits by her grave for hours. And when he does come home, he goes in that study and shuts the door, and doesn't say anything, or see anyone, until we finally summon him out before dinner each evening. He eats because I make a fuss if he doesn't, and sometimes in the evening he does make an effort with the little ones- taking one or two in his lap, and asking about their day. But for any of us…-, If we try to start a conversation – he just says he's tired and going to bed… can it wait till tomorrow…." She shook her head, "Lizzie, I know it's only been a couple of weeks, but….. Well, you've always been one of his favorites…. Has he talked to you at all?"

Shaken, I shook my head, and fighting back my own tears, I said, "No, but I haven't talked to him either. – Abby and I have both had a horrible cold, and I didn't want to come around the other children. We're better now, but we have been staying close here. Jesse and Henry have been working on mending tack out in the barn these cold days, with Jesse just trying to stay well, and I have been only putting one foot ahead of the other these last days myself."

"Oh, Lizzie, honey, I am so sorry! And here I come, your first dose of company, and bringing nothing but more troubles! You should have sent word. One of the girls could have come and been company and helped out, too!"

"I know! But I was too busy feeling sorry for myself to even think of it!" I admitted sheepishly. "I missed Mama so much these last two years, and then to have her here, and – and then…" My eyes filled, and my nose started to run, again…. The next thing I knew I was in Mary's arms. After a minute or two, I found my poor much used handkerchief and reached again for some measure of composure. "Oh, Lord, Mary, I am so sorry. I just cannot seem to get myself together either. For sure I am not the one to lecture Papa when I cannot even control myself!

But I will tell you who has helped me a great deal, in spite of what you see, is Jesse. And I think he might could help Papa. He has been so good to me and to Henry too, these last few days." I stopped, thinking, and said, "Does Henry know about Papa?"

Mary shook her head. "He spends most of his free time over at the Nutt's with Susan these days, and working – he's usually out at his place, or over here with Jesse. We see very little of him except sometimes he is with us for supper. He's sleeping out at his place now."

I nodded. "I knew that. And I know he's a horrible cook. So I try to feed him when he is here too. Maybe with Mama Sarah and you and I all working at it, we can keep him fed till we can pass him on to Susan!" I said, managing a smile.

"So you think that die is well and truly cast in spite of her being so young?" said Mary, dubiously.

"Yes," I said, "I do. I've spoken to them both about it, as had Mama and Papa, and Aunt Sarah and Uncle David. There's no budging either of them. God knows they both come by that stubbornness naturally! Lord help any children they might have!" I smiled ruefully, "I am a fine one to talk...."

"Well, yes," said Mary, smiling too. "You do have some experience to draw from...."

I sighed, suddenly remembering what had brought her here. "Speaking of stubborn...- poor Papa! I know he is just ... as you say... lost. But we must help him find his way back to us. Mama wouldn't want him to give up, or to not take what joy he can from life! In fact, she would be lecturing him sternly on being made of better stuff than this...." I found myself smiling. "I can hear her now..."

Mary chuckled sadly, "Yes... me too, Lizzie." We stood a moment hearing that loved voice in the silence, then she handed me the cup and said, "I've got to get back. I left laundry soaking. Thank you for the coffee. You'll speak to Jesse, and maybe Henry too?"

I nodded. "Yes, Mary. Thank you so much, for – for taking care of all of them! I know Mama felt easier, knowing you had it all in hand over there…. Especially our Sarah and Martha. They are both still so young…"

She nodded, "Yes they are, but they are both old enough to help out too. And both good with little ones. Why don't we ask young Martha if she would like to come over here and help you out from time to time? There's so much you have to do to help Jesse keep the place going, and she could help with the house and Abby, especially as she gets more active…."

I started to say no, really I did, but then I realized…. Martha might need me as much I needed her. So I nodded, and said, "Bless you, Mary! Yes, let's ask her. I think it might be good for both of us."

"Wonderful!" she said, and reached out to hug me, runny nose and all. "We will look for you and Jesse and Miss Abigail for dinner tonight! And Henry too. Let's get everyone together, and see how it goes."

I shook my head, "Let's make it tomorrow night instead. Give this cold one more day, and we can finish off this stew I already have started tonight."

"Alright, but tomorrow night…. For sure…." she said, firmly.

As she headed down the path, I turned to Abby and said, "Come here, young lady, it's time to get Papa and Uncle Henry some lunch made!"

As I began to gather up some midday fare for my men, I mulled over all Mary had said. By the time I had Abby and I bundled up and we headed for the barn, I had the beginnings of a plan. "Ah, Mama," I thought, with a smile, "you knew didn't you, that he would need us all? It's why you taught us so well. Thank you, Mama. We'll try to make you proud!"

***** ***** ***** ***** ***** ***** ***** *****

The barn was warm, in spite of the cold outside. It was built almost as tightly as our cabin, by the same capable crew, and our two horses, milk cow and assorted chickens resided very comfortably. It also gave the men a good place to work on projects throughout the winter months. Abby slept comfortably on a bed of clean hay, while Jesse and Henry and I ate our midday meal of bread, butter and grape jelly, and talked of Mary's visit.

Jesse and Henry both sat silent for a moment after I had finished the telling of Mary's report. Jesse reached for and took my hand and squeezed it gently as he began, "We're all still grieving. But Lizzie, your parents, they – they had something special. My parents do too. As do we. We are blessed to have a family that believes in love matches. Most people don't, you know. Marriages are arranged for all sorts of reasons- land, politics, survival, and most folks try to find love and respect after the fact. But our folks, they were lucky to find love first, and they've let their children do the same. But more than that- Lizzie my parents love each other, but their relationship is still very different from what your parents had. My father loves my mother, but he is still "the boss", or at least she lets him think he is!" He smiled and then continued, "But Uncle Abel and Aunt Sally- they had – I guess you would call it a partnership- somehow they saw each other as equals – like you and I do." He paused. "Do you have any idea, Lizzie how rare that is? I know most folks think we share so much because we have to- because of my blindness. But, Lizzie, one of the things I did back when I could see, during those years growing up in Neosho, was watch your father and how he lived his life. And that included how it was between him and your mother. And I said to myself- I want that someday – that singleness of heart and purpose with another person. And I got lucky. God heard my prayer and gave me you. And when I think of what it would be like... to lose you..." His voice broke.

Stricken, and touched, I found myself unable to respond except to cling even tighter to his hand. Finally he found his voice and continued hoarsely, "Yes, Lizzie, I will talk to Papa Abel, and I may not be able to do anything other than weep with him as he remembers her, but I will try. And I will pray God gives me the right words."

Henry had set, silent through all this- watching us. And when he spoke he too was hoarse with emotion, "Lizzie, I know what you mean about missing her all over again! I know a thousand times a day it seems I will think of something I wish I could tell her. I did get to talk to her a long time about me and Susan, and I am so glad of that. She had talked to Susan a lot on the way here, and she was a big part of why the parents all agreed we can marry as early as next year. So my Susan and I, we both already miss her very much indeed, but like Jesse, I can say that we want the kind of marriage that Papa and Mama had, that you and Jesse have."

"Oh, Henry," I said, my heart full, "I am so, so glad for you, and Susan too. I know I am not Mama, but anything I can do or that Jesse and I can do to help you all, you know we will."

"I know," said my brother gruffly, "And as for Papa, I think Jesse, that what he needs is to be busy. You know Papa, always before he had his politics, his town projects, his people he was looking after.... I think maybe now is not a good time for him to be .... retired. I think he needs to be involved...."

He stopped because Jesse was suddenly grinning. "What?" said Henry, a trifle suspiciously.

"Yes," I said in what I recognized as my mother's tone, "What?"

"I had a visit yesterday…. While you were napping, Lizzie," he said almost apologetically, "from Amon Bond."

"Oh, dear God," I said, again in my mother's voice, "What is he up to now?"

"Well, he came to me with some interesting news," said Jesse. "He had a copy of a newspaper from Dallas dated just last week. He read it to me- the whole thing from cover to cover."

"Oh, really?" I said, "And what great bits of news did it contain?"

"Well," said Jesse, "It seems that our friend Senator Houston is in the news again. After two terms as senator the pro-slavery elements in the state legislature have finally succeeded in ousting him from the Senate, and are sending up Jim Hemphill instead."

"Oh, no!" I said, disappointed. "That will surely be one less voice of sanity at the national level!"

"True," Jesse agreed, but continued undismayed, "However, the paper indicated that the Senator is already making other plans."

"What plans?" asked Henry, eagerly.

"Oh, just a little something that will be sure to thrill the members of our wonderful state legislature to no end. Citizen Houston has cast his hat into the ring in the upcoming race for Governor of our fair state. And he is asking that all Unionists rally around to get folks of like mind registered to vote, and to the polls come August 1. It should be an interesting race, and we are so far flung and far from the county site that I would imagine that Judge Burk will be only too glad to have someone assist with voter registration in these remote areas. And I am thinking that we all know just the gentleman for the job!"

We were all grinning now, and I said to my brilliant husband, "Mr. Nutt have I ever told you...I like the way you think!"

***** ***** ***** ****** ***** ***** ****** ******

That evening, Jesse walked over to Amon Bond's place to get the copy of the newspaper. Upon his return, I seized the battered pages to read for myself. We ended up reading the whole thing again after we were bundled up in bed, and by the time we had finished my cold-weakened voice was hoarse again, from reading aloud.

"Jesse," I croaked, "correct me if I am wrong. But doesn't that whole paper- all the articles, I mean,- seem just a little bit biased toward the pro-slavery side of things? I mean, maybe I am being overly sensitive, but it sure seems that way to me."

He nodded, "Oh, you're not imagining it, Lizzie. That paper is run by a group squarely backed by the secessionists. I hate using it as a source of information, because you have to wade through all their slanted perspective and spouting of propaganda to at least get the nuts and bolts of the truth of what is going on." He grimaced, "Unfortunately, it's the paper we usually get first around here, so we are stuck. Charles Barnard will usually get an Austin or San Antonio paper about a week behind this one. He reads it and then sends one of his boys over to Amon with it. And Amon is good to share. We usually get together after lodge each month and spend a couple of hours - some of us, going through what is happening."

"So that's what you all are doing!" I said, enlightened. "I wondered what on earth went on in lodge that could possibly take so long!"

Jesse laughed. "Well, now you know! Anybody that has gotten and newssheets or interesting correspondence brings them, and we all share! It is amazing really, who some of us correspond with regularly. - Your father especially. I'm surprised if he doesn't already know about Houston. He hears from him pretty often. Just as he did from Tom Benton, until he passed away. Did you know his wife fell ill and passed away only a few months after their visit to us?"

"Really?" I said, surprised. "She seemed such a vital and energetic woman... You just never know, do you? Lord, Jesse, in some ways that seems a lifetime ago..."

"Yes," he said quietly, "it was. In lots of ways. But Lizzie, I do feel strongly that your father has work to do yet. We will all need his wisdom to guide us through the coming years. He, and Houston, the elder statesmen of that generation – the first born of a new nation - they feel those bonds of Union so keenly, have fought for it all their lives. We desperately need men like that right now."

"Mary didn't say anything about Papa not reading his mail....But then with the weather, we may not have gotten any lately." I said. "I know he got a letter from Polly right after the New Year."

"Well, either way, I am going to ask David to take me to the bluffs tomorrow morning if it's not just pouring. We can still do dinner tomorrow evening, but I want to see what I can do just me and Uncle Abel..." said Jesse, "There's some things he needs to hear. And best from me."

"Thank you, Jesse," I said softly, "for loving us so much."

"You're easy to love, Lizzie," he replied, turning toward me and putting gentle hands in my hair. "Now put out that candle, and let me show you."

***** ***** ***** ***** ***** ***** ***** *****

The bright morning sun actually felt warm on Jesse's face as he and David rode down the path that was rapidly becoming known as

Stockton Bend Road. "David," said Jesse, "When you followed him down here, did he acknowledge your presence?"

"No," said David, "I didn't go close, just sat back at the top of the fields and watched, from back in the trees. But I think he knew I was there."

"Why?" asked Jesse.

"Because once, after I had been there for a while, he got up, took his hat off, and turned and stared right at where I was. He stayed that way a long time, maybe three or four minutes, then he turned back around, put his hat back on, and sat back down with his back to me again."

"Yes," agreed Jesse, "You're right then, he knew you were there."

"But," said David, with a maturity beyond his eleven years, "he didn't invite me down. He didn't say come sit with me. So, I didn't force it."

"No-o-o," said Jesse, "and for you it was the right response, unless the need had been urgent." He was quiet a moment, and then continued. "David, today, what I want to do, is I want you to take me to the closest point under cover, and then I'm gonna get down, tie my horse, and you get me pointed right. Then I want you to leave. Really leave David. That's important. What I have to say to Abel is just between us."

"But, Jesse," protested David, "What if he…"

"He's still Uncle Abel, David," said Jesse, firmly, "He won't let any harm come to me."

"Well, all right then," said David, "stay close. We gotta circle around…"

Minutes later, they stopped in silence, and David touched Jesse's leg. Jesse reached down and squeezed the strong young hand, and then swung down from the saddle. He pulled down his walking stick and tucked it under one arm as he felt his way forward to secure his reins to a nearby branch. He turned toward what he thought was the meadow, when suddenly David hissed from behind, "Jesse, he's coming."

Jesse smiled briefly, and nodded, and said softly but aloud, "Thank you, David. You can go now."

"All right, Jesse," said David as he turned his horse, "Take care."

Jesse turned toward the sound of approaching footsteps, and waited. A few steps more, and the footsteps stopped. The seconds passed, the cold crackling sounds of the winter woods all around. Jesse breathed in the cold damp smell of the woods, and caught just a hint of something else, the sharp tangy smell of his uncle's pipe, mixed with....whisky? His nostrils flared again as he breathed deeply, to make sure. "Abel..." he said in greeting, for only the second time in his life meeting his uncle man to man as equal, with no title, no honorific. "Whisky?"

Jesse heard the surprised intake of breath, mingled with some kind of snort- of amusement? "Jesse," said his uncle gravely, acknowledging the greeting. "Yes, whisky. But only a sip or two against the cold." A soft chuckle, "She'd come back and tongue lash me but good, if it was more!" He paused before continuing. "We fought that battle once and for all over thirty years ago, my Sally and I. We both saw what that path could do to a man, and I made her a promise then. I'd not besmirch her memory by going back on it now."

Jesse nodded, relieved, and said, "What then? Do you think she would have you here- like this? Worrying your children. Neglecting the duties you are called to? Acting as a sentinel where she is no more? Do you honor her in that?" He stopped, afraid he had said too much too soon. Damn! He hated this darkness, this not being able to look into a man's eyes and see his soul! But he heard the sharp intake of breath and knew he had touched a nerve.

The silence stretched long, and then a footstep, and a firm hand on his shoulder. "So, Jesse.... You have come to be my rescuer, eh? Well, come then, and let us sit in the sun where it is warmer. And you can tell me what is on your mind."

So they went and sat down in the light and the warmth, and Jesse told him. And when he was finished, he became aware of the surrounding hot spicy aroma, and realized Abel had lit his pipe. The silence of the winter outdoors was broken by the occasional burst of birdsong, the rustling of the blowing leaves, and the grinding noise of teeth on wood. Jesse bowed his head to hide his smile, as he heard that glad noise. Faster and faster, and then a sigh as Abel inhaled and then breathed out the fragrant smoke.

"Well, now," said Abel Landers, as he turned from past memories, to ponder future possibilities, "Let's see. We'll need to send word to the various communities to send representatives. We'll have to have a meeting. And I will send a letter to County Judge Burk. Tell him we can get the voters signed up. Have to be on the up and up about it, and signup everybody, even Rylee and his bunch...." The teeth were going full force now. "But how to campaign for Sam... that's the kicker. We'll have to be canny about that."

"Maybe we can let Sam do most of his own campaigning," said Jesse. "The man is a phenomenal speaker.... As long as there are newspapers reporting his speeches, we can read those around.... at lodge and such."

"True, true," his uncle agreed and plans began to take shape and form. Hours later, as the family gathered for Mary's supper, they all looked up to see Jesse and Abel riding into the yard, accompanied by Tommy

Lambert who they had met on the trail back. All three men were engaged in animated conversation.

Lizzie took one look and turned a brilliant smile on all the dear ones gathered. "Well, Mary, looks like maybe one more for supper. Jesse and Papa are at it again, praise God!"

Jacob came up beside her and said softly, "Lizzie, put me and David next to Jesse if you would please. I think it's time for a little Nutt Brothers campaign alliance to be formed."

"Oh, really?" I said, delighted. "Politics? You?"

"Well," said Jacob, "last time I checked, a fellow didn't have to see to have ideas and to teach. I think we've got some talking to do, and David and I can do that as well as anyone!"

"Consider it done," I said softly, with a smile in my voice, as we all surged forward to welcome my father home.

***** ***** ***** ***** ***** ***** *****

Bright and early the next morning a brisk knock sounded on the cabin door, just as Jesse finished buttoning the collar of his shirt. He quickly pulled up his suspenders, ran his fingers through his hair, and called out, "Just a minute!" He turned and with the precision of memory reached for his daughter who had been sitting on the bed watching him dress. "Come on, sweet girl!" he murmured, as he picked her up. "Let's go see who that is so early this morning!"

He reached the door, and said, "Who is it?"

"It's Papa," said his father, and Jesse immediately flung the door wide.

"Come in, come in Papa!" he said, holding on tight as Abby began bouncing excitedly, saying "Ganpa, ganpa!!" in enthusiastic greeting.

Jesse could hear the smile in his father's deep voice, "Well, look who is feeling better this morning! Here, son, let me take her before she jumps and lands on her head!"

Jesse released his daughter to the embrace of her "Ganpa" and turned toward the table and benches near the fire. "Come sit, Papa. Would you like some coffee?"

"Oh, that sounds good," enthused his father, "It is surely bitter cold out this morning! Where's Lizzie?"

"She is in the barn doing the daily hunt for where the hens have hidden the eggs," he said. "According to Lizzie, we have the most devious group of fowl to ever inhabit a barn. We have a very nice setup with boxes for them, etc. as you well know. But apparently the feathered ladies rarely use the boxes, preferring instead to make my wife labor for her reward by laying their eggs all over the barn in the most unlikely spots."

"Hmmm," said David, "that's not normal…. There must be something they feel is threatening them near the boxes. Have you checked for snakes, and so on….?"

"Well, *I* haven't, of course," Jesse replied, with a grin, "but Lizzie swears she has…. Maybe you could take a look while you are here?"

"Be glad to," said David, "But before I do so, let's speak of something else. I started to go straight to Abel with this, but you've been here longer, and have actually met the man, so I thought you might have more insight. Abel and Amon are sending out invites to men they want to help with organizing this voter registration thing. Now I don't know the politics of the men involved, but I have figured out where most stand around here. Do you think Abel is making a mistake not including Jeff Rylee on the leaders list?"

"He's not on the list?" said Jesse in surprise, "That's strange, because Abel specifically mentioned that we needed to include him and the pro-slavery folks, and be even-handed in our efforts."

"Well, now, of course I wouldn't know," said David, gruffly, "not being able to read the list or the letters myself. But, your brother Abel is who mentioned it to me- that Rylee wasn't on the list and should be."

"What does Abel know of Jeff Rylee?" asked Jesse, puzzled. "I can't think how he would hardly even know of the man, much less advocate for him."

"Well, being a happily married man, and (sorry) blind to boot," said David, with a smile in his voice, "you wouldn't know that Rylee's oldest daughter is quite a beauty. Just about all the young, single men hereabouts take great notice of her whenever they come over here to shop. I understand Abel is now a local hero of note- because he has been actually spoken to by the young lady."

"Oh, ho," said Jesse, "the plot thickens! Well Lizzie tells me that Abel has grown into a fine looking young man, so maybe the attraction is mutual?"

"May the good Lord forbid such a thing!" said David, vehemently. "It would be Henry and Celina all over again!"

"I'm sorry, Papa," said Jesse, dismayed, "I hadn't thought…. Well, surely including Rylee in our councils would only encourage further contact between our folks. Maybe reason enough to leave well enough alone,"

"Now, Jesse," said his father reproachfully, "you know neither your Uncle Abel nor any of the rest of you taking leadership in this thing have the luxury of letting personal preference or feeling get in the way of doing what is right and ethical for our political process."

Jesse was silent a moment, considering. "As usual, Papa, your counsel is wise. We need to go and talk to Uncle Abel, and find out why Rylee is not on the list- he should be as basically opposition leader. .Then we can go forward from there.   There must be some piece of this puzzle we are missing...."

"Alright, son.   Let me go see what varmint I can find that is scaring your chickens, and then we will go on over to Abel's and figure this out."   David Nutt refastened his coat and was out the door with a blast of cold wind, leaving his son pondering what it was that even those with eyesight could not see.

*****   *****   *****   *****   ******   *****   *****   *****

Engulfed as he was by the competing odors of Uncle Abel's pipe and his father's cigar, Jesse Nutt was fairly certain that he might not be the only person not seeing clearly in his uncle's study that afternoon. When confronted with the question of Jeff Rylee, Abel had snorted loudly, and said that Rylee's participation in or cooperation with the voter registration drive had "been taken out of his hands" and that the ball was now in Rylee's court and they would all just have to join him in waiting to see what happened.   And, he added mysteriously, either way there was bound to be "hell to pay".   Joining Jesse and their father and uncle in this so far most uninformative meeting was Jacob.   Jacob, being new to this circle of political intrigue, was naïve enough to inquire precisely what kind of payment might be required to hell and on whose behalf.

Jesse winced, and mentally ducked, bracing for the explosion he recognized was coming.   "I had in mind,' Abel began calmly enough, "to approach Jeff Rylee, whom I have not yet met, privately. – Perhaps call on him at his home, where we could speak candidly and clearly without prying eyes, and without any need for posturing or bravado on either side.   It was my hope that I might convince him to help us be sure that everyone has their say in this thing.   Well, first, I get Tommy Lambert and his saloon keeper in here this morning, telling me they won't help recruit voters and will boycott any election if Rylee and his people are allowed to be involved- as if that makes a lick of sense!

250

And then, just when I THINK I have them talked round to my way of thinking, there's a knock at the door, and in walks YOUR SON-," he roared. At this point Jesse heard his father groan, and knew Uncle Abel must be right up in his face, and listened with mounting chagrin as he continued. "YOUR SON, on his nineteen year old high horse, telling me all about how we should have included Jeff Rylee on our list, and that he deserved to know about the meeting, and that HE HIMSELF had taken care of that for us, by sending a handwritten notification himself via Miss Indiana Rylee, to request her father's presence to "join our counsels about the upcoming election"! AND that he had already received the courtesy of a reply, delivered in great haste less than two hours later. This reply, which I have here in my hand is addressed to ME, and reads as follows:

February 17th, 1859

To: The Honorable Abel Landers, Stockton Bend, Texas etc,

From: Young Jefferson Rylee, Rylee Farm., Texas etc.

Dear Sir,

Your nephew Abel Nutt has most graciously informed of the political meeting to be held at your cabin Wednesday next, and has suggested I might wish to attend. Because of the fairness of character exhibited by this young man in the issuing of this kind invitation I am delighted to inform you that I and a group of friends of similar interests are making plans to attend. We look forward to interacting with our neighbors in discussion of the way to best make our voices heard in the context of the upcoming gubernatorial election.

Yours most sincerely,

Y. J. Rylee"

There was a moment of absolute silence, broken only by the crackle of the fire in the nearby hearth.

Finally, David Nutt spoke, "My God, Abel. I am so sorry. I knew my Abel was up in arms about this and I told him I would speak to you. I had no idea-…. That he would….- This…" He stopped, obviously at a loss for words.

Jacob spoke up. "Papa, it's not your fault. You had no idea that Abel would take it upon himself…."

Jesse, as in days of old, jumped right in to continue the thought, "Yes, and Papa you did tell him that we would look into it. He should have waited."

"Well, he didn't," snapped his uncle, "and a helluva mess he's created in the process. Tommy and Charlie left here talking about gathering up men to come to the meeting to, and I quote, match Rylee and his men rifle barrel for rifle barrel, and Amon Bond is breathing down my neck trying to decide whether we should send word to Joe Robinson, Charles Bernard, and Pleasant Thorp to not come for fear there's going to be a confrontation of some kind. And then there's Mary- wanting to know if we should evacuate the women and children from nearby houses in case there is gunplay….."

"Good Lord, what a mess!" said Jesse, shaking his head. He paused a moment, and then turned toward where he had last heard his Uncle's voice, and said, "Well, obviously we can't let this situation that young Abel has created stop what we are trying to do here. So the question becomes- how do we fix this?"

In the quiet of the room, Jesse heard the teeth on that pipe again. "You're right, Jesse," said his uncle, calmer now. "You're right. We will deal with young Abel later. David I will leave that to you- to impress on him the possible consequences of his impatience…"

There was another pause, and Jesse ventured, "Basically we have three groups or factions here that we have to decide how to address- Rylee and his men, Lambert and his people, and the leaders coming from the other communities."

"Yes, that's right," agreed Abel Landers, "and if we fix the problems with the first two, then there's no reason the third group even need to know about this little fiasco."

"Oh, they'll likely hear of it," said Jacob, "you know how that is, but hopefully they can hear it from us, after the fact. The straight story with a totally uneventful outcome."

"Yes, one can hope," said David. "Abel, your plan was to have this meeting consist of yourself, Amon Bond, Jesse, and who else?'

"Well, Robinson, Thorp and Bernard from the other communities, and Lambert because he leads a certain faction here, and then Rylee to represent the slave-holders in this part of the county. And he wouldn't have been entirely alone. Some of the folks Robinson represents over at Comanche Peak Post Office own slaves too." Abel summarized, "But that was all. Plus I figured that you and Jacob would join us too. So a small gathering of maybe ten to twelve men total. The idea was to get to know one another, talk about the logistics of getting people registered in each of our areas and how long that might take. Inform everybody about the necessary forms for reporting and what information we have to have. And talk about ways to inform the public about ALL the candidates running. Later of course we would need to talk about the logistics of the actual vote in each community as well. But that would come later. The idea was that this would be the first of a series of meetings. That we would format a plan, submit it to the county judge for approval and then be the leaders responsible for implementing our plans in our various areas, and eventually to tabulate and submit the election returns in the format required to the county and the state."

253

"Well, Uncle," said Jesse, "why don't we try this. Why don't you stick with the plan. Ride over to the Rylee place and ask to see Y.J. Tell him that in his enthusiastic efforts to help, Abel may have given the wrong impression. Tell him the plan, - small meeting, just a dozen or so men. See if you can't get him to agree to come- not alone, but with just one or two friends. Then, depending on how that goes, you and I can go and talk to Tommy Lambert and get him to call off the war and come to the meeting, and hopefully the others can come as planned, none the wiser till after the fact..."

"I'm not sure I like the idea of Abel riding over to Rylee's alone," said David.

"Since when did I need a nursemaid?" snapped Abel.

"Not a nursemaid, Abel," said David quietly, "a friend. And someone to watch your back, because stranger things have happened...."

Jesse heard the pipe being cleaned and then very deliberately placed on the desk. Finally his uncle said, "Alright David. You can come. He stood, and said, "Well, gentlemen, there is no time like the present. Let's fix this." He paused in the doorway, and said, "Jesse, since David is coming with me, I want you and Jacob to find young Abel, and I want you to explain to him what almost happened here- what could yet happen. And you impress on him that if he is a grown man he has a responsibility to think of the consequences of his actions. Tell him if he has a problem with a man, any man, better to approach the man directly, not maneuver behind his back. And most of all, tell him that love for a woman can make a man do many a foolish thing, but that the love of the right woman can make a man wiser than he ever dreamed. He'd do well to mind the difference."

***** ***** ***** ***** ***** ***** ***** *****

And so it was that twelve gentlemen gathered in the big room in my father, Abe Lander's cabin on a cold night in February 1859. Y.J. Rylee and his brother came and were greeted courteously by most of the gentlemen present. Jesse reported almost total silence on the part of Tommy Lambert- who he said Papa David described later as being swelled up like a toad. The concept of a drive for voter registration was met with great enthusiasm by all present and Papa agreed to chair their committee and correspond with the appropriate county officials. As those gentlemen met, Sam Houston was still in Washington, waiting for the government turnover on March 5th that would give Jim Hemphill his long desired Senate seat. While he waited, the political machinery, even in our far reaches of the Texas frontier, began to grind.

Amid all this focus on politics and community, there was family business to attend to as well. Papa David and Aunt Sarah left on horseback with Abel along to help with the pack animals and protection for a grim and grueling trip to Neosho and back to sign the final land transfer papers and receive final payment for the farm. Traveling light and stopping only when they must to rest people and livestock alike, they were gone only seven weeks. By the time both they and Sam Houston had returned to Texas in April, voter registration was well underway. Throughout the state, men like my father and his cohorts held meetings, sent out appeals, and even traveled door to door and farm to farm, seeking out voters.

The voters in Texas were being presented with an interesting choice. Our current governor, Hardin Runnels, was a vehement state's rights pro-slaver and secessionist who had defeated Senator Houston in 1857. There's was a long standing and bitter rivalry that spoke to the very core of differences between the two factions dividing our nation. Sam Houston was first and foremost a gentleman and a patriot. Runnels by my measure was neither, and on top of that was a horrible administrator who had allowed horrible abuses and conflicts to arise between the Texas militia, the Union army and the reservation Indians out in West Texas. That conflict was rising to a boil again and a call had gone out for more militia volunteers. Much against his father's wishes, Ed Bond left in early May to answer that call. The Indian troubles were worse this year than at any time since our first year in Texas. Ed had declared that he wanted to DO something and so had joined up. Jesse and I were afraid he was but the first of many of our young men to go off to battle. But still we labored on, in the hopes that by the votes cast in the upcoming election we might yet stem the tide of chaos.

Sam Houston was running a clean campaign, refraining from dwelling on the controversial and divisive issue of slavery. Instead he focused on his record as a statesman, administrator, strong military man, and his love of Texas and her people. He appealed to the good people of Texas with stirring speeches that spoke of our many blessings as a people, the great opportunities offered to us as citizens of Texas and of the United States, and of concrete plans for ending the Indian troubles, and providing the people of Texas a safe and secure and prosperous place to live their lives.

All those working to sign up voters remarked how eager most men seemed to be to cast their ballots. There was a sense among many of the importance of this election, and all the newspapers we saw were predicting turnout would be high. The county Judge over in Buchanan was ecstatic that the men of our areas were willing to do so much of the work necessary to get votes cast in all areas of the far-flung county. A stickler for detail, my father had personally ridden the trails to each community to review registration results and election site setups.

Election Day, August 1, 1860 dawned scorching hot and muggy, but just after dawn the first men began to trickle into the open door of the big Landers cabin. Every one of them was greeted personally by Papa, who thanked them for coming, handed them their ballot and directed them to the big long dining table to cast their vote. I read Jesse and Jacob's ballots to them and circled the names as they instructed. My father certified the ballots officially cast and we dropped them into the sealed ballot box that had been sent by the county.

Traffic was steady all day, with men coming by to vote as they went about their day's business. Mary and I passed out glasses of cool cider brought up from the cellar, and Jesse and Jacob sat most of the day on the front porch visiting with the men who came and went.

Finally darkness fell and my father declared the polls closed. Young Abel Nutt and Benjamin Bond were designated to make the long ride to Buchanan to deliver the box of ballots. They would be gone two days if the weather held. As they rode away toward the river ford, Papa David and my father joined us on the porch.

"Well, Abel, that is a job well done, no matter what the outcome!" said Papa David.

"Yes," said Papa, "and thanks to each of you for all your help. We did our best for Sam and for the state, and I think most every eligible soul in this community voted. We can be proud of that."

"Yes," said Jacob, "we even got the ones we knew were against us to vote! Nobody could ever accuse you of not being fair-minded Abel, and that's a fact!"

My father laughed and said, "Well, Jacob from time to time I've been accused of that and much worse I assure you. But I do think we did good work here. You folks did notice that Rylee sent his people a few at a time. He has really been surprisingly cooperative through this whole thing.- Especially considering young Abel's impetuous action early on."

"Well, what did you expect Abel?" asked Papa David, "After what you said to the man?"

My father actually looked abashed and I said disbelievingly, "Papa! What did you do?"

"Well, if you'll recall David and I went over there knowing that Jeff Rylee had been given the impression in the beginning that we were trying to exclude his folks from registering and voting. And you would think that after we managed registration as well as we did that he would have gotten the picture that we are all in this together and that we were trying to be sure of every man's right to vote his conscience unimpeded."

"Ah, but Abel," said Jesse, "we must remember that there are those who specifically DON'T want that- on both sides"

"Right you are, my boy," agreed Abel, "and they have been hard at work on both sides of the river these last weeks trying to stir things up. Tommy Lambert and Charlie Smithers going on and on over there at the saloon that we don't need any slavers coming over here to cancel out our votes, and how wouldn't it be too bad if "something" happened that would keep them from coming...."

"Oh, dear Lord," I breathed, "Papa that's not- ....well, it's not who we are!" I said explosively.

Papa patted my arm and motioned me to sit. "Now, now Lizzie, we all know that. And Tommy Lambert knows it now too, if he didn't know it before...."

"It was Amon, you see, him being kin to Tommy by marriage and all that..." said David, "He rode over to the saloon with Austen and some of the other boys, and they took Tommy and Charlie out back and had a discussion with them about the meaning of Democracy, and as Abel here described it, a clear demonstration of the consequences of not participating in the democratic process in a gentlemanly manner."

"Papa!" I exclaimed, "that's not who we are either!"

"The hell we're not, Lizzie!" said my father forcefully. "Either we have a free democratic process in this country or we don't! Either we stand up for the right of EVERY man to vote his conscience or we don't. It doesn't matter if we agree with them or not, it is their right to cast their ballot, and to do it unmolested! If the men of this community have to be forcefully reminded of that, then so be it!"

"Abel," said Jesse, with a bit of reproach in his voice, "she's on our side, remember?"

There was a moment of embarrassed silence, and then my father smiled sheepishly, and reached our gently to touch my cheek. "Ah, Lizzie, I do apologize! I did forget my manners. Your mother would remind me that there is a lady present!"

"It's all right, Papa," I said with a gentle smile, "I understand now." I paused considering, "So…. Uncle Tommy got his lesson, but what about Jeff Rylee? Surely, there was some "stirring up" going on over there at his place too, given the situation?"

"Yes," agreed Jacob, "what we were hearing down by the general store was that Rylee was going to arm his men and come over in force!"

"And what a recipe for disaster that would have been!" I exclaimed, "Although, I must say I can understand why he would feel the need, given what I am sure he must have heard…."

"Yes, well, that is where your father comes in, again," said Jesse. "See he and Papa went to see Jeff again, just as they dd last spring before registration."

259

Uncle David nodded, and said, "Yes, and Abel told him point blank that if they came in force that he could not vouch for the consequences, and that most likely there would be a bloodbath that would stain the history of this community for evermore."

"And as Elizabeth so eloquently put it a bit ago," said Abel, "I said to him: This is not who. we. are! – So I made a suggestion and a promise. – I told him to come himself, and to send his men- three or four at a time across the ford to cast their ballots. I invited him to sit with Amon and me on the porch outside in a show of community cooperation, and we posted sober, armed Masonic brothers at intervals along the path from the ford to the Big Cabin to assure the safety of all who came to cast their ballots. They weren't obtrusive about it, but they were there. And Jeff's men knew and Tommy's men knew it too. In this community, we had a free and democratic election- for everybody. That's who we are!" he ended his tale.

"Oh, Papa!" I said, with a smile, "I am so proud of all of you!"

"Well," he said soberly, "we did discuss the fact, Amon, Jeff, and I while we sat there on the porch, that we were likely going to have to the same thing again, a year from now, when we elect a new president...."

"Well, what is the saying... we will cross that bridge when we come to it...?" I said, wearily.

"Yes," agreed Jesse, "along with "sufficient unto the day is the evil thereof...."! I am just relieved we got through it with no bloodshed. Now we just have to pray that we get a good result!"

"Yes, this state needs a man like Sam Houston." said my father soberly. "We need him very much indeed."

***** ***** ***** ***** ***** ***** ***** *****

One boiling hot day toward the end of August, as Stockton Bend lay virtually immobile from the stifling heat, a lone rider passed unchallenged through the sentry line and appeared drooping at the Nutt family cabin. The rider of the poor horse appeared in equally sad shape. His clothes had been of decent quality once, and his wide brimmed hat might have been custom made, but the mustached face beneath the brim was gaunt and once removed it was evident that the hat had held in place a rugged bandage wrapped about his head. Other similar wrappings were in evidence on his arm and upper thigh. He was not known to me, but apparently was to the men. My father and Uncle David had been joined that afternoon in the shade of the Nutt's dogtrot by Jesse and Jacob and Logan and Henry. I was helping Sarah with snapping beans to be put away for winter while Susan and Fanny and my sister Martha sat on a blanket under a nearby tree mending socks and shirts quietly while watching over our napping toddlers.

We all looked up at the sound of the approaching horse, and the men all stood when the creature and its rider turned to come into the yard. Moments later, Papa and Uncle David got a better look at the face and burning eyes under the wide brimmed hat, and leaped forward to meet the pair as they came to a halt in front of the cabin. Papa David was reaching up to help the poor man dismount while my father and Henry both reached for the horse's bridle, although the poor animal looked more likely to collapse than to bolt.   Logan was talking rapidly and softly to Jesse and Jacob and I caught a name- Garland- Peter Garland. Jacob was already half out of his chair when his father called for him, as he and Papa half-carried, half-walked the man over to drop limply into the rocking chair recently occupied by Uncle David. The hat fell off and it was then that the bloody bandage on his head was fully revealed.

Henry grabbed a mug and poured it full of the cider the men had been drinking for refreshment, and Papa held it as the man drank a few swallows before shakily reaching up with one hand to try to hold it for himself. Jacob had knelt beside the rocker and had hold of his other wrist. "Easy now," said Papa, "I've got it. Just relax, Pete, and get your breath."

David Nutt laid a hand on the man's shoulder and said firmly, "Pete, you remember my son Jacob from lodge, right? He's had some training as a medical man. Let him check you out."

It was measure of the man's state that he nodded and laid his head gingerly against the tall back of the chair, eye's closed, and submitted to Jacob's ministrations. A few anxious minutes passed, as Jacob quietly questioned the man as he learned what he could by touch and feel. I went to stand next to Jesse just off to the side and in front of the man in the chair. "Lizzie,"asked Jacob quietly.

Wondering silently how he and Jesse could both do that- know I was nearby when I hadn't touched them or said a word- I answered quickly, "Yes, Jacob?"

"How's his color?" he asked, quietly.

I saw the man's eyes dart quickly and alertly from me to Jacob. "Better now," I said, meeting the man's eyes, "and more focused and alert too."

Jacob nodded. "The head wound, messy as it is, and the arm wound seem to be healing okay. But I feel heat and swelling around the leg wound. I'm going to raise the bandage. You tell me if you see redness or other discoloration."

"Alright," I said softly, remembering not to nod. Funny how even after all these years that urge just never quite went away.

My quick intake of breath told Jacob most of what he needed to know, he learned the rest with a gentle manual probe, and a couple more quiet questions. In the end he turned to face the gentleman. "Pete, you know this leg is inflamed and headed toward something a lot more serious if you don't take care. Now are you gonna let me and Lizzie tend it while you tell us what has happened, or are you gonna be a stubborn fool about it, and end up with gangrene?"

The man named Pete nodded, and said grudgingly, "Might as well let you tend it. This story is gonna be a while in the telling anyhow." He leaned his head back against the back of the rocker for just a moment eyes closed. Then he gave a long sigh, opened his eyes and visibly gathering himself he looked toward Jesse, and said, "Jesse Nutt, they say you're the closest thing to a preacher man of God they have round these parts this side of the river. That being so, I hope you will pray for me as I have, through a grave mistake, caused a great wrong to be done which can never be made right. I'd have no regrets at all those I punished had been guilty of what I believed them to have done. But now I have learned that is not the case and I must live forever in the knowledge that I have spilled, and caused to be spilt, innocent blood. Once you have heard my tale you must tell me whether the Lord can ever forgive this thing or not....."

He stopped, overcome again by some strong emotion. And Jesse knelt down next to Papa, who still held his friend's free hand, and placed his hand on the man's knee. "If you have truly asked forgiveness, then the Lord has surely given it." Jesse assured him with quiet confidence.

My father spoke next, and quietly too, "But, Pete, there's no judgement here, only brothers and friends. Tell us what has happened, and we will help if we can."

Some of the tension left the pale face and the man nodded again, "Well, I'd begin by sharing the news that I heard while on my here. Sam Houston has won the election for governor. It was to spread that news that my men and I set out on Thursday last – word having come from from a state militia man traveling from Austin through our town of Stephenville carrying orders for the men at several outposts to the west. We were headed to Bernard's Mill down the valley of the Paluxy when a man known to me, John Lavender by name, hailed our party, and told us he had been shot at while peaceably making his campsite the night before. He declared to us, without any urging from us, that the shots were fired by a hunting party of Caddo Indians from a Caddo village nearby and that they were known to him. He further declared that they were wearing war paint, and appeared to be bent on mischief. He claimed they stole his horse, while he pretended to be shot dead. He was on foot and did indeed have the mark of a bullet graze right along the side of his head- the wound fresh.

So upon his direction we set off in pursuit of the Indians. Now you all know I have strong feelings about the savage nature of the red men. I was but nine years old when I saw the Comanche kill my father in our barnyard with my own eyes. So I was most alarmed, as were my neighbors that there should a party of them been upon murder and mayhem residing in the country so near our homes. Bill Powell sent one of his boys back to town with warning. Bill and I and the rest followed their trail for some time, becoming more and more alarmed as we found several hair ribbons and pieces of jewelry along their trail- leading us to believe that they either had or had had at one time a female hostage with them. That being the case we felt a great sense of urgency to find them in hopes of saving the poor lady from a horrible fate!"

All of the men's faces were grim and set, and I knew mine must be the same, imagining the woman and what she might have already experienced. Garland took a swallow of ale, and continued, "Shortly after that we lost the trail. But Bill Powell declared he knew of a bunch of Indians that had set up a pretty big camp only about a mile from where we were. Well we figured that had to be where they were headed. So we hightailed it over there as fast as we could. And there it was, a full blown Indian encampment, and there was a group of horses down by the river being watered like they had just been ridden in, and several braves standing around one of the central campfires. It was right at dusk, and we were afraid of losing the light, so we went in guns blazing."

Logan's head snapped around from where he had been tending to the horse, and he said, "Without knowing where the hostage was?!" The sinking feeling in my stomach was suddenly such that I had to step back and find the cabin wall for support.

"I- I know," said Garland, nodding, his eyes cast down now. "Fortunately for us – and unfortunately too– there was no hostage. There wasn't any war paint either. But it was too late when we realized that too. The – the braves they fought back, even for all we had caught them totally off-guard. A couple even got off a few shots. One of the Powell men was killed." He stopped, his eyes full, unable for a moment to go on.

We all waited, silent, and I could see the knuckles on his hand whiten, as he held fast to Jesse. "W-When it was o-over and all was quiet, they were all dead. A-all, e-except t-two little girls and t—the two o-old squaws who were in the teepee with them. We'd n-never known they were t-there except w-when I-looked up at the e-end, one of'em was standing there in the door of the teepee- b-big brown eyes staring at me, a-and I looked down a-and I realized – I-I'd j-just s-scalped h-her mother – r-right before her eyes!" He collapsed sobbing against Jesse's chest, even as my knees buckled, and I suddenly found myself sitting on the ground my back against the cabin wall, as I buried my face in my hands, trying by instinct to hide from the sight of the image in my mind.

Stunned silence, broken only by the sounds of the man's gasping sobs reigned over the little gathering. Suddenly, from behind me, a thready voice gasped, "L-Logan, I-I c-can't b-breathe!" It was Fanny, backed hard up against the big tree, eyes big as saucers, one hand blindly groping the air, and the other drawn up in a fist up against her chest. Her face was stark white, red freckles and hair a glaring contrast. Logan grabbed for Jacob, and they were at her side in three strides each, followed by my mother-in-law, a wet cloth in her hand. Papa David followed, scooping Abby and little Hugh up in his arms and motioning Susan and Mary and little Willie to follow him into the cabin.

I knew I should follow them, but I remained frozen, mesmerized by the tableau of my father, Jesse and the poor sobbing form of Peter Garland, all still huddled together around and in that rocking chair less than ten feet away. Faced with three different crisis situations happening all around me, I was literally frozen immobile, not sure who needed me most.

As always, somehow Jesse knew. "Lizzie?" He said softly. The next thing I knew, it was my father's strong hands, pulling me gently up, and taking me to my husband, and pushing me into Jesse's arms, even as he gathered Peter Garland into his own. The four of us huddled there, essentially motionless for several minutes. Sheltered in Jesse's strong embrace, I struggled to wipe the horrific images Garland had described from my mind. I was torn between horror and compassion. Finally, in the silence, I realized the sounds of sobbing had subsided. I sat up, to find Peter Garland looking at all of us through hollow eyes. In a soft voice, barely more than a whisper, he looked at Jesse and spoke, "So even blind as you are, you can see- we- we made a-a mistake. It wasn't them at all. B-but by the time we knew, I-it was too late. They – they were no more. S-so I – I ask you, is there God's grace for a man who has done these things?"

Jesse very gently reached out and touched Peter's tear-soaked check, and then placed his left hand on Peter's shoulder and reached out, felt, and grasped Peter's right hand in his own. "Do you believe in Jesus Christ as your Saviour and Lord?"

"I do indeed, sir," whispered Peter Garland, in a soft but steady voice.

"Our Lord has promised us that where two or more are gathered in his name, He is present also. And since we are here, brothers and sister in Christ together, Abel, Jesse, Elizabeth, and Peter, we come before our Lord with our heartfelt petitions together. So my brother, Peter, make now your Petition to Almighty God."

Whether he knelt deliberately, or whether his legs simply wouldn't hold him, Peter Garland was suddenly on his knees, and all of us with him.. In a clear steady voice he said, "Lord I know you have heard my confession to you and to these good people. I pray thy lovingkindness and forgiveness for leading my men into sin, for unjustly killing innocent people and for acting in the heat of anger and rage against those unable to defend themselves. I ask your forgiveness oh merciful God, and I ask that you teach me greater wisdom and less heat so that I may not sin against thee in the future. I ask this all in the name of Jesus Christ our Lord. Amen.

Jesse waited a few heartbeats and then whispered to Peter, "My friend and brother, I share with you the words of Holy Scripture which assure us that if we Confess our faults one to another, and pray one for another, that we may be healed. God promises us that the effectual fervent prayer of a righteous man availeth much. And we are promised that when we confess our sins, God is faithful and just to forgive us our sins, and to cleanse us from all unrighteousness. And so Our Lord tells us to go and sin no more. Amen."

After a few moments, Peter nodded, and said, "I do thank you my friends. I am sure that news of this tragedy will be widespread. I only ask that you share the truth of it when you can. Meanwhile I am most afraid that once the larger Caddo and other tribes know, this may cause great unrest and seeking of revenge by all the tribes. It is for that reason that I must go, to warn others in the country north and west, where the Caddo are numerous, that danger is near, and why.

Continue to pray for me, if you will, for I am in dire need." He made a move to rise, and with Jesse and Papa's help, stood swaying on his feet.

"Won't you stay with us, at least overnight?" said Papa, worriedly, "And let Jacob finish fixing that leg while you rest?"

Peter Garland shook his head gingerly, even as he glanced over to where Logan and Jacob were still administering to Fanny. "No, Abel, I've caused enough trouble for you good-folk as it is. I'll be alright, and others are in danger." He walked slowly to his horse, and climbed aboard. "Take care my friends, and thank you. Jesse, especially...." He broke off as Jesse dismissed his thanks with a shake of the head and a wave of the hand. "Thank the Lord not me. I'm just the messenger sometimes!" He said with a small smile. "Take care!"

As he rode off, Uncle David came out of the cabin and headed straight for Jacob, Aunt Sarah, Logan, and Fanny. We headed across the clearing to the shade under the trees as well. Logan was sitting with Fanny in his lap, with Jacob holding one of her wrists. "That's good, Fanny, just keep focusing on breathing slow breaths, and counting as you breathe in and out. Logan's gonna keep counting for you. I'll be back in just a few minutes. I've got to go check on the others. Squeeze my hand if that's okay." Apparently she responded, because he nodded, and rose.

"You go, son," said Sarah, "I'll stay here with Logan and Fanny. I'll call if we need you."

"Thanks, Mama," he said as he turned toward us and took a couple of tentative steps. Papa David immediately reached out and laid a hand on his arm. "Here we are, son." He said quietly. "Let's take a step over here to the cabin and let's all catch our breath." He led Jacob, and I led Jesse, and the moment we reached the dogtrot and placed their hands on a chair back, they both collapsed into a chair and leaned forward head in hands in remarkably similar gestures.

Papa exchanged a look with Uncle David, and my uncle nodded and disappeared quickly into the house. He reappeared seconds later with bottle and two small cups in hand. He poured quickly and thrust the cups into his sons' hands. "Drink it slowly, boys, and let yourselves settle a bit."

"Whisky?" said Jesse, in wonderment. He sipped and added, "And damn good whisky, too! Where on earth did this come from?"

"I bought it from Tommy Lambert to give to Abel if Sam Houston got elected," said my Uncle. "It just seems like maybe under the circumstances, you boys might need some of it first, before the rest of us."

"Good, lord," said Papa, "that's right. He said that first, didn't he? At the time it didn't even register! Well, thank you, Jesus! That is great news!"

"Yes, it is!" agreed Henry, "but dear Lord, what of the rest he told? The Indians are going to go crazy! There won't be a safe place west of the Trinity!"

"We're going to have to re-think some things around here for a while, I'm afraid," said Papa grimly. He looked at Henry. "Those of you wanting to live full time out on your land- I'm just not sure if that's going to be wise."

Henry nodded, "I know. I'll come back in at night for the time being. But days – I'll go when I can. I have a house to finish. And speaking of Susan...." said Henry, heading for the cabin door.

Uncle David nodded, and said, "Go on in, and reassure her and Martha that all is well, but tell them to keep Logan's youngsters inside till we see what's to do with Fanny."

"Papa," said Jacob, his voice slightly hoarse from the whisky, "if Willie and Hugh could stay here tonight.... That might be a very good thing."

"I was just coming up to suggest the same thing," said Aunt Sarah, stepping into the shade of the dogtrot. "Logan is taking Fanny home now, and wanted me to thank you Jacob for knowing what to do. He said he'd be much obliged if you and I would check in on them later."

"Peace and quiet and calm and the security of her own home are exactly what she needs right now," said Jacob, quietly.

"What's wrong with her?" asked Papa David, with concern.

I gave a long sigh, and said, "Fanny had a very sad life, before she met Logan. She saw a lot of horrible things and I suspect hearing Mr. Garland's tale and seeing him so distraught brought it all back to her mind."

Jacob nodded, "Yes, and sometimes, if someone has been very shattered in their mind before, having that all brought back up triggers not only an emotional reaction, but a physical one as well. It makes sense now. Logan was trying to tell me, in the heat of the moment out there and it wasn't making much sense, but now...... well, he indicated this is not the first time this has happened, but that it's never been that bad before."

"Poor girl," said Uncle David, shaking his head. "Logan should have kept her back in Tennessee. This life out here is hard, even for a strong woman."

Papa nodded, "Well, David, that's true. But I know something of why they left Tennessee, and it seemed like the right decision at the time.

We've just all got to help him take care of that little lady. She's a fine woman, and deserves some happiness in her life."

"Speaking of taking care of folks," said Aunt Sarah, "Is Peter Garland going to be alright?"

Jesse sighed, and spoke pensively, his voice also hoarse, "Physically he'll mend, but in his spirit..." He shook his head, "I don't know, Mama. When a man loses himself to violence like that.... If they are at heart a good person.... it weighs on them. We must all remember to pray for him, and for all the others involved."

Soon there were various versions of the Caddo Indian Massacre, as it came to be called, flying through the gossip mills all over North Texas. The name alone is indication of the judgmental nature of most of those accounts, most of them spread by a frightened population looking for someone to blame for any increase in trouble with the Indians. However as the months passed the country just to the north of us exploded with a wide range of Indian blamed troubles that appeared to have little to do with the actions of Peter Garland and his little band. Yet for a long while they received the brunt of the blame anyway.

There was a brief respite from the scary reports from all around during the coldest part of the winter. Shortly after the first of the year, however as the weather began to warm, both the natives and the white population began to grow restless in ways that made us take every precaution possible with regards to the safety of our people and settlement even as we waited with baited breath for the next newspaper or traveler to come our way. And while we waited, we watched the skies for a visitor that never came: rain.

Word came via newspaper of numerous Indian raids to the north and west. In Erath county alone there were five major incidents that spring of 1860. Many injuries and horse thefts were reported, and in

May came word that a white woman had been raped and killed by a group of Indians of unknown tribe who had raided her farm and found her there alone. Everyone became even more cautious, if that was possible, no one left home alone, all households armed, no one traveled the trails unaccompanied, no one fished or walked by themselves.

Crops were planted but without rain the harvest was meager. The river ran lower and lower, and the fords became numerous and shallow. Amon and Papa added patrols along the river banks to guard against attack from that direction. The newspaper brought word of the upcoming Presidential election, and the field of candidates described seemed more and more certain to mean disaster for the Union. While Jesse and I personally (and secretly) admired Mr. Lincoln's stance on many issues, we were terrified of what the consequences of his election might be. Our friend Sam Houston, encouraged by my father and many others, briefly threw his hat in the ring, but lacking the financial backing to effectively campaign nationwide, he withdrew rather than split the southern vote.

By summer the state and the nation was simmering on the brink of explosion in more ways than one. In Texas the pro-slavery and anti-slavery factions had already started a war of politics and propaganda designed to pit neighbor against neighbor, creating an atmosphere of suspicion and distrust almost as deadly as the actual exchange of gunfire. The country was parched, tempers short, and the brittle stubble of crops in the fields and dried up prairie grasses in the pastures made the very land where we lived a literal tinderbox waiting to burst into flames.

And burst into flames it did. There were horrible grass fires all over the state and most particularly in north Texas. And all across the state, rumors began to fly and were reported in the most sensational way in some of the politically driven newspapers – rumors that blamed this faction or that faction for setting fires to intimidate or drive out different groups of voters. One particularly virulent set of articles written and supposedly investigated by a young reporter from Dallas, claimed that several fires in Denton and Parker counties just north of us had been set by abolitionists to try to destroy the farms of several prominent area slave owners. People became terrified of their neighbors, and even in Stockton Bend these reports stirred up trouble and suspicion.

Papa was suspicious of the reports but determined to maintain peace in our area. He and Uncle David and Amon worked with the men from the surrounding communities, holding frequent Masonic lodge meetings where all brothers were welcome and could deliberately leave their differences at the door. Joe Robertson and a couple of other ministers traveled to the various communities preaching and holding revival meetings in an effort to draw people together. And when the word came in the late summer that it had been admitted that most of the news stories had been fabricated and that in particular the Denton fires had been witnessed to be caused by lightning, there was in many communities a hearty round of "I told you so's", accompanied by an almost universal sense of righteous indignation.

But all was not gloom and doom. Our community and families hosted two joyous weddings in spite of the over 100 degree heat. In June, my youngest sister Martha married Ed Bond who had returned safely from his service with the Indian fighting militia. In July Henry finally got to marry his Susan. Both young couples already had a house and farm ready for them, but also maintained close ties to the little settlement at Stockton Bend, where homes were regularly full of guests from the outlying farms when the Indians were restless nearby.

As the date for the fall elections drew near, Papa and the men once again did their due diligence to see to it that all were registered to

273

vote. Sam Houston had written to Papa regarding his thoughts on the coming ballot. He was convinced that if Mr. Lincoln was elected, that most of the southern states would secede. If this happened it was his intention to do everything he could as governor to prevent secession, for he believed that without Texas' ports and manpower any rebellion would be short-lived. He also believed that our best chance for avoiding disaster was the election of Mr. Douglas, a southerner. He believed if that happened that perhaps a breathing period could be bought, during which reasonable men could once again seek a negotiated compromise that would lead to the phasing out of slavery over say the next twenty years – giving the economy of the south time to adjust to the change. And allowing the Negroes to buy or earn their freedom over time.

While not the ideal to which most of our families aspired, it seemed to most the approach most likely to avoid war. I do not know how any of our men except Jesse voted that day in the cold driving rains that had finally come to our part of the state, but vote they did. And once again our state and the nation settled back to wait for the results the new year would bring.

The news came in stages, bits and pieces, coming blow by blow over the next few weeks – In the month of January- Lincoln elected, the secession one by one of each of the states in the deep south, the admission of Kansas to the Union as a free state, and all the while Sam Houston and the state legislature locked in a political stalemate over the fate of Texas. Finally in the last cold days of January, 1861 the Democrats called a rival ad-hoc state convention, voted to secede, and forced the legislature's hand. The vote to secede came on February 1, 1861. A two month battle ensued as Sam Houston held fast, refusing to sign the documents joining the Confederacy. Finally on March 28, 1861 the legislature found the votes to force his resignation. The next day, after a brief meeting with his successor, our friend rode out of

Austin for the last time. Before he left he sent a brief message to my father. The text of that letter will be forever emblazoned on my heart.

My dear friend,

Our cause is lost. Mr. Lincoln has offered twice now to send federal troops to subdue the legislature and insure the success of my efforts to keep Texas in the Union. However, my conscience tells me that would result in a bloodbath that would spawn open warfare upon our streets and worse still, into many of our homes. I cannot be the instigator of such a fate for the citizens of our beloved State. Join me in prayer for Mr. Lincoln and for Mr. Davis and for all leaders on both sides that they may see the wisdom of negotiating a rapid and fair peace and the quick and peaceful restoration of the fair Union for which so many have given so much. Meanwhile, we must also pray for the safety of our sons and the security of our homes, for my friend, the hour is upon us. – We are at war.

Boys in Gray 1862

I had finished putting away the last of the dishes from supper, and banked the fire in the kitchen to try to make it cooler in the cabin for sleep later on. I took a tiptoe by the little back bedroom to check on Abby. She was off to dreamland as only an almost five-year-old can be, her sweet black curls framing her face and her new "Dolly" clutched close. At last, I stepped out on to the front porch, my eyes automatically seeking Jesse in his big rocking chair by the door. He wasn't there. He was standing at the west end of the porch. There was stillness about him that I hadn't seen in a long time. I walked silently over to stand beside him. There were tears on his face glistening in the last rays of the setting winter sun. Silently I placed my hand over his on the porch rail.

"I would give all that I am and all that I have or ever will have, just to see her face- her smile- just one time" he said softly.

"I know," I whispered. It was all there was to say, except, "You will see us all Jesse, when God takes us all Home."

"And you know I know that," he said, squeezing my hand, and then taking it as he turned to walk back across the porch. "And mostly, you know that I am reconciled to it. B-but sometimes..." He sighed deeply. "Come sit, Lizzie. We need to talk."

I wondered at the tone of his voice, but before I could ask, he continued as we sat. "Funny, I started that train of thought being grateful. Being grateful to God for the gift of my blindness! Being grateful and then feeling guilty for it!"

"Grateful? A-and guilty?" I questioned, bewildered. "Jesse whatever do you mean?"

"Grateful that my blindness will keep me from being forced to fight in this accursed war!-...And guilty for feeling that way knowing that mostly likely my own brothers will be!" he said fiercely.

I gaped at him. "Forced to fight in the war? Who? What do you mean?" I asked.

"By the Government of the Most Sovereign Confederate States of America," he spat. "Of which we are now a part and citizens of this past year!"

"B-but they can't force someone...." I stammered

"Yes, apparently they can, or will soon according to Sam Houston." said Jesse, grimly. "Your father got a letter from him yesterday- a warning- much good it will do. Withdrawn as he is these days from politics, Houston apparently still has friends – or spies- in high places. He says the CSA legislature is set to pass the first ever conscription bill on this side of the Atlantic sometime this spring. Unless something drastic happens in the next few weeks, the idiots are finally beginning to realize that this war is not going to be some quick one or two major battle skirmish- or even as some predicted a one massive battle bloodbath. It is shaping up to be a very bloody, ugly, long drawn out nightmare indeed. And both sides are already going through men like water! Another major battle and the Confederacy will have no choice. Word is that every man between the ages of eighteen and thirty-five will be required to serve three years unless physically disabled or mentally incompetent. Houston also said they are already working on an exemptions bill that will create a way out not just for only-son status, and essential workers like train engineers and miners, but also for those who can afford to buy or pay substitutes or send slaves to fight in their stead!"

"But that means that the wealthy... oh, dear Lord..." I sat down quite suddenly, and continued in horror, "...can send slaves to fight in their stead!?! Oh, Jesse, surely not!"

"Apparently so," said Jesse sadly, "He says that volunteerism simply is not supplying the manpower they have to have to conduct the war, and that they see no way forward except to ignore individual rights and states rights to follow the European practice of drafting men into the service, willing or no. Houston says Georgia and Virginia are threatening to pull out of the CSA if the exemption clauses aren't written into law. Many of the wealthy planter families apparently want this war to defend their lifestyle, but not at the cost of putting their sons on the front lines!"

"But they are willing to put other people's sons out there? Or their slaves in their stead? But that- that's just..." I was searching for a word.

"Unconscionable is what I would call it," said Jesse, bitterly. "But yes, that is exactly what is going to be happening. Especially in those states where the registration/conscription boards will be predisposed to use the exemptions heavily..."

"Like the two you mentioned- Georgia and Virginia?" I asked.

He nodded. "At least here at the local level we can assure that every one is treated fairly according to the law, which for most of us .... is going to be a very bitter dose to swallow."

"You mean… all of them…?" I said with growing horror, as the list unrolled itself in my mind: My younger brothers Henry, Abel, Will and Cal, Abel Nutt, Henry Bond and his brothers, Ben, Ed, and Amon Jr., Austen Yeats, the Lambert boys, the Morris twins, and some of the older men – Jesse and Jacob's age and older- A.J. Wright, my brothers Chris and Frank, and many more- most with wives and young children… I swallowed past the lump in my throat, "Dear God, Jesse! It will decimate our community! And yet, may God forgive me, I just want to weep with gratitude that you and Jacob…. Oh, Jesse! The Lord does work in mysterious ways! Who would have ever thought…?"

He nodded soberly, "You understand now what I meant earlier…"

We sat in silence for a moment, and then Jesse said, "Your father had a copy of the census made before George Massey turned it in. – And no, I don't think that's legal, but nonetheless he has it. In 1860 there were approximately 3800 souls recorded as being here in Johnson County. About 1200 in the area designated Comanche Peak Post Office. Of those, our best estimate is that over 200 men will be eligible to be conscripted. That means 1 of every 6 people, over half of those are fathers with young families, who will have to be looked after and cared for. The good news is that we have a lot of able bodied robust middle aged and older men and lots of family groups. That will make it easier to see that no one is forgotten. Your father has already started meeting with the leaders in the other communities in the Comanche Peak area, making sure they have the information and making sure we are working toward every family of women and children left behind will have at least two men who can be on call for whatever they need. Some families have boys just below the age limit. We know they may be called next year but we are hoping not. In our own families – your brother Chris is 36 thank God, and Frank is 37. But Henry and Logan both have young families. The younger men – your brothers Will, Bob and Cal Landers, and my brother Abel are all still single. That's six at least this go round from our folk. But Lizzie, when Abel was reading the names to me- some folk- the Chambers have nine men on that list- nine! Tommy Lambert has two sons, and Amon three on it!"

"Surely they won't take so many all at once?" I said, and then, 'Jesse, what if it's not enough?"

"Then they will take more- both older and younger, next year," said Jesse, grimly. "And Lizzie, we know- we know some of them- probably many of them – won't come back. The reality is the South can't win this thing. If sheer bull-headed stubbornness alone would do it- yes. But the Union has more manpower, more weapons, more money, more manufacturing capability. And God help us, we jumped the wrong damn way, in the end. If we had stayed in Missouri.... who knows – it might have been different. At least we would have been fighting for what we believe in."

"Jesse, can't they refuse? Or go back to Missouri and fight for the Union at least?" I asked.

"Abel and Papa and I talked a long time about that yesterday. And we called the boys in- the seven who are our own. Every one of us finally agreed. We have claimed Texas as our home. We voted in the last election here. It was our duly and legally elected representatives who voted to secede. We may not agree, and we may have hoped to ride this thing out as neutral parties. But if called to serve by our duly elected government, there is no honorable recourse open to any of us, but to serve. That means that once our boys are committed, whatever we can do here at home to support the war effort we will do. Your father said it best-"We may not be able to ensure victory for the Confederacy, but if through our efforts we make it possible for just one more soldier to survive to come home to his family we will have done our duty before God and man. The soldier whose life we save could be one of our own."

***** ****** ***** ***** ***** ***** ***** *****

Two weeks later another letter arrived, sent by way of a Cherokee Indian. The Indian had stopped at Charles Bernard's trading post to the south, and asked where he could find the great white father from Missouri known as Abe. Charles apparently sent him to us without hesitation.

His arrival at Papa's front door caused no little stir. He had been stopped by the regular patrols set each day to watch the approach to Stockton Bend. Their purpose continued to be early warning of approaching Comanche or Caddo war parties. The advent of one lone Cherokee caused notice but not alarm and he was escorted to my father's house by one of the Lambert boys, with lots of help from all who saw them pass by. Jesse and I were working in our garden when the growing group approached. "He has a letter for Mister Abel," called Jimmy Lambert, as their horses passed our fence.

"Maybe we should go," I said to Jesse, after hastily describing the unusual messenger.

He nodded, "Yes, we'll stop for Papa on the way." So it was with Jesse and Jacob present, and Papa David and I looking on that Abel ceremoniously received the thin one page note of correspondence from the solemn Cherokee. "The Raven sends greetings to his friend Abe Landers," announced that dignified gentleman.

Papa received the Indian gentleman and the letter courteously inside his cabin and nodded as he said, "I thank you for delivering it sir. Does the Raven require a reply?"

The Indian shook his head, "The Raven say tell my friend I am watched and may not write again. He say he hope you and your sons much good and blessings from the White God. I return now to the Raven. He old man now. Need friends."

Abe nodded solemnly, "Tell the Raven the White Chief Abe thanks him for his friendship, and that I will pray for him."

The Indian nodded, and silently walked out of the cabin, through the gathered crowd and mounted his horse and rode away.

Papa shut the front door firmly behind him and came over to the table near the lamp as he broke the seal on the letter from Mr. Houston. It was written in a hasty scrawl, short and to the point. "Dear Abe, Just received word that conscripts will be forced to sign on for three years. Right now volunteer's term of service obligation is only 12 months. Have heard from friends in Buchanan that Johnson County is forming two volunteer units under their brigade- one cavalry and one infantry, both mustering in Dallas, under the command of Colonel George Sweet. Strongly recommend you send men who are ready to Dallas by March 1 to enlist for the 1 year of service. Time may be extended, but likely only one year more. God willing this will end by then. Will keep you apprised as I am able." It was signed simply S.H.

It was February 20th. A spell of bitterly cold weather had given way to almost spring-like warmth. Rain was coming. If they were to reach Dallas in time, our men would have to leave quickly. Papa looked at Uncle David and said, "Send out the call through our Masonic brethren. We must meet tonight. Tell them to come here. Tell Abel or Henry what is happening and send one of them to tell Joe Robinson over at Comanche Peak Post Office. They may want to send their boys too. Tell him our boys will be coming across the river by sunrise on the morning of the 22nd, if any of their lot want to travel together."

Uncle David nodded and left. Then Papa turned to us. Jesse and Jacob, you boys come with me. We've got lists to go through. And Lizzie, get with your Aunt Sarah and put together some refreshments for the gathering tonight. We'll probably have close to sixty men here."

"Will the womenfolk be coming?" I asked. I thought not, but wanted to be sure.

My father shook his head. "No. Not tonight. This will be a long night with hard decisions and recommendations to be made. If what I was told a few days ago holds true it appears that Rylee is set on coming. According to what Logan has heard he and his crew want to apply to have their slaves go instead of anyone in their households...."

"Oh dear, God, can they do that?" I asked.

"They can if they want to go back to Georgia or Virginia. Those are the only two states so far whose legislatures have passed that particular exemption." He answered.

I shook my head. "If I were in charge of this thing their boys would be the first to go. After all, it's their choice we are all being asked to defend."

"I am sure that argument will be made," Jesse said dryly. "Meanwhile, we need to send all Abel's women and little ones over to Papa and Mama's cabin."

"We'll be ready," I assured him. "Have Susan bring the younger children over to us for the night. You will need all the room you can get here."

He nodded, "Thank you, Lizzie."

I kissed Jesse and squeezed Jacob's hand. "I'll be praying." I said softly.

"We'll need it." answered Jesse. Then turning away he said to my father, "Come uncle. Let's begin."

***** ****** ***** ***** ***** ***** ***** *****

There were no killings in Stockton Bend that night, although there were quite a few heated words exchanged in that meeting of men at my father's house. Jesse reported the whole thing to me later, although some of what was said was not meant for female ears. Rylee and his friends were there, and left early after Abel and Pastor Joe

283

Robinson from Comanche Peak assured them that should conscription come, they would be in the same draft pool as everyone else, and their slaves would not be acceptable substitutes.

A local conscription review board was formed. My father was chair, and Jesse and Jacob, Joe Robinson, Charles Barnard, and Pleasant Thorp were selected to serve. It was hoped that we could avoid using them if enough men could be encouraged to volunteer. But they were ready for that hard task if need be.

And so it was that I stood between my father and Jesse, with Abby clinging to my waist as first the first group of our men left just before dawn on February 22nd 1862. Jacob stood with Uncle David and Aunt Sarah just the other side of Jesse. Amon Bond, stood grim faced the other side of Papa, his wife Sarah weeping at his side. Fanny and Logan stood just behind us along with Henry's wife Susan, my widowed sister Sarah and all the younger children. My brother Frank and young David Nutt stood just behind Jacob. Frank held his little boy Abel in his arms. At the front of a column of just over 40 men from Stockton Bend alone were our eight dear ones- Henry and Benjamin Bond, Austen Yeats, Jesse's brother Abel Nutt, and four of my brothers- Bob, Henry, Cal, and William. We stood at the ferry landing and watched as they swam their horses across the river, leaving its protection as the sun rose in the east. Silent tears glistened as the sun struck my father's ashen face, and for the first time I remember thinking that he looked old.

One month later, after receiving an urgent letter from Henry that what they were hearing was that conscription would be official by mid-April and duty stations would be assigned, the scene repeated itself, as twenty more Stockton men set out to meet up with the Brigade at Clarksville, Texas before it headed east toward the fighting. Ben Bond, Logan and my brother Frank led that group. My father watched his nephew and his fifth son and those with them leave and then silently turned and got on his horse and rode off to the south toward my mother's grave. I watched him go, my heart already broken. Uncle David followed my gaze, and said, "I'll follow in a bit Lizzie. I imagine he needs a little time."

"Thank you, Uncle David," I said in a choked voice. "He is lucky to have a faithful friend like you."

"Ah, Lizzie," said Uncle David, with tears in his eyes, "I'm the lucky one, to have a friend like him." He kissed me on the forehead, and turned to Jesse, "You boys take everyone over to our place. Your mother needs her family around her. I'll go fetch Abel home. We'll be back for dinner." He walked over to his horse, which I noticed he had ready nearby, and rode off to the south, to comfort my father, his friend.

***** ****** ***** ***** ***** ***** ***** *****

The official letters arrived from Richmond via the county clerk over in Buchanan – the county seat of Johnson County at the end of April. There were roughly 4000 souls recorded on the 1860 Census of the County. Of those, someone somewhere had determined that 600 men could be raised from here as soldiers for the CSA. The Comanche Peak Post Office area was given the quota to meet of 180 men. My father was gratified to be able to send back word that of the 180 listed, over 100 had already enlisted. He provided names, muster dates, ranks and units to the beleaguered county clerk, and was assured our region would receive "proper credit".

As the fighting picked up and burst into flames to the east, here at home a different kind of war began to emerge- the mad scramble to get more households consolidated and more non-combatants lined up to help care for animals, plant crops, and carry on with day-to-day living. We were so blessed in Stockton Bend to continue to have a large group of older men who were still able bodied and active. We also had large families who had boys old enough to help out with the men's work. Crops and daily chores were quickly taken over, and

285

women folk were still able to focus on the care of the sick and the young.

But the truth was- everyone was trying not to think about the real and immediate threat that hovered over the western horizon – the Comanche. With most of the men, and many of the firearms gone, and women living alone in isolated cabins with several young children, many of our neighbors were shockingly vulnerable.

Henry's wife Susan and their little George had moved in with Aunt Sarah and Uncle David, so their cabin now housed six souls. Papa had a house full already, with my oldest brother Christopher and his Mary, their two children, my two youngest sisters, and my brother Frank's little boy Abel.

Jesse and I had offered to take someone, and young David Nutt stayed with us on occasion, but we were hoping for another baby, and once that happened Abby would move up to her own room in the tiny little loft. Many other households had combined seeking safety and help in numbers. But there were still many women and children alone in cabins scattered across the river valleys of the area.

One afternoon in mid-June Jesse and Abby and I were walking in the late evening, along the riverside path that now ran pretty much the whole length of Stockton Bend. We had been cordially greeted by several of our neighbors and were nearing one of the places where the path sloped down to meet the river at one of the low water fords that came into use this time of year. My mind and conversation were focused on the questions being asked by seven year old Abby about the path of the evening star when Jesse interrupted me with a touch on the arm, and a hushed, "Lizzie-".

I immediately froze and drew Abby closer to me. "What?" I questioned softly.

"Horses- coming across the ford. I hear them." He hissed.

Immediately upon hearing his first words, I looked frantically around for the nearest cabin or cover. "Come back, Amon's place is just over the hill."

"No time," said Jesse, "they're coming."

He was right, I could hear them too, now. "Come on," I breathed frantically, propelling both him and Abbey into the nearest clump of cedar brush. It was prickly and pungent, but we watched blessedly unseen as a half-dozen Indians rode, bold as brass down the path before us. I had my hand over Abby's mouth desperate to prevent any hint of sound. As I watched, the Indians stopped silent just below Amon and Sarah Bond's cabin. In the dim light of the lingering dusk I watched in silent horror as one brave dismounted and disappeared in the direction of the barn behind the house. Not a sound reached our ears, no dog barked, nothing. Two minutes later the brave was back, leading a horse, apparently the object of their intentions. He remounted, and the entire band passed in front of us once again, returning silently to the ford, and departing as clandestinely as they had come.

When they were safely away, I turned to Jesse just as he turned to me. He face was grim and furious, "A horse, right? They just stole a horse!" He was speaking softly, but his voice still crackled with anger. "They just waltzed in here, into the midst of our community, while there was still light enough for anyone but me or Jacob to see, and stole a horse! And no one saw them in time to raise an alarm. No one was paying enough attention to even notice the sound of six horses coming across the river within a stone's throw of a cabin! Where are the damn sentries? Doesn't Amon even own a dog! What if you had been walking home alone, and hadn't heard them in time?! What would have happened then?!"

"Jesse," I said, gripping his arm, "stop it! You're scaring Abby!" And it was true. She was staring at her father with wide eyes. This anger was something he showed so rarely that in all her seven years she had never seen it. He immediately softened, and took a deep breath, before squatting down in front of Abby. His voice was very soft and gentle, as he said, "Abby, sweetheart, I am so sorry. I know you were already scared and I didn't mean to make it worse. I was just upset and worried because you and your mama could have been in danger, and I don't like that." He paused for a moment, and then said, "Will you come to Papa, and let me carry you up the hill to see Uncle Amon?" He opened his arms and immediately found them full of daughter. He gave a groan as he stood with his load. "My goodness you are getting to be a big girl!" He shifted to get his bearings. "Lizzie, take my walking stick, would you, and point us in the direction of Amon's place. We've got some serious talking to do."

A few minutes later we were startling the elder Bonds with an evening knock on their door. Moments later, with only the briefest of explanations, two of the older grandsons were dispatched to call an emergency meeting at my father's house. Less than an hour later, and just minutes ahead of the first men of the community, we arrived at my father's front door. I had thought that Jesse had cooled off a little bit, but I discovered I was wrong.

He knocked on the door, "Abel! It's Jesse and Lizzie. Open up! We've got trouble."

Almost immediately the door opened to reveal my father's face, startled at the abrupt summons. "Jesse! Lizzie! Come in! What is it? What's wrong?"

"Who is supposed to be on river sentry duty this evening?" snapped Jesse.

My father was understandably caught off guard, and said, "Well, now Jesse, I don't know. I'd have to-"

"By God, you'd better find out!" shouted Jesse, "And whoever it is- I want him thrashed!"

"You'll mind your manners, and remember how to speak to your elders," snapped David Nutt, as he came through the front door, "or you'll find yourself being the one thrashed!'

At the sound of his father's reprimand, Jesse froze. Visibly shaken, he closed his eyes and breathed in deeply. His eyes opened and he turned toward my father and bowed his head, "I am sorry, sir. I meant no disrespect. I-I a-admit to being badly shaken by events earlier this evening. Events that make me question the safety of my family in this community. I lashed out without thinking. I apologize."

My father's face was grim but his eyes were soft with compassion as he replied, "Thank you, Jesse. For a surety I know what it is to be afraid for those we love. Come in children, and tell us what has happened."

"There are more men coming," said Uncle David, "Amon's sent word to summon a town meeting."

My father nodded, and focused on the matter at hand. "Lizzie would you go, tell Mary we'll need all the women and children upstairs, to make room down here. And if you could see that there's coffee...?"

"Don't worry Papa," I assured him, "We'll see to it." Before leaving, I turned and spoke quietly to Jesse. "It will be alright." I said softly. "*We* are alright. Your keen ears heard them coming. You kept us safe!"

He pulled me to him in a quick fierce hug. "Thank you, sweet Lizzie! Now go. We must do what must be done to fix this."

I squeezed his hand and headed for the fireplace to consult with Mary, Abby at my heels. Behind us more male voices sounded as more men arrived. Mary and I moved quickly to put on multiple pots of strong black coffee and set out all the cups we had. Then we stole quietly up the stairs to join the slumbering children.

Abby had clutched at my skirts the entire time since we had arrived at the house. Now I took a few minutes to quietly reassure her and say our nighttime prayers. She appeared to take comfort from that and crawled contentedly into bed with her cousins and was soon sound asleep.

Mary and I quietly crawled into the other bed fully clothed, and huddled together, ears straining, listening to the gathering of men below.

In the end, when all the shouting was over and John King's oldest boy, who was all of fifteen, thoroughly and loudly chastised for his neglect of his sentry duties, the men reached a sobering and daunting conclusion. There was not much that could be done. Depleted as we were, there was simply not enough manpower available, even with the grown women added in, to effectively watch every foot of river bank every hour of every day. The roaming patrols would continue, but a twenty–four hour a day watch would be placed on each of the fording places – right now there were three. Beyond that there was little to be done. And so life continued, and as we worked and struggled our minds often wandered, thinking of our men, gone from us over four months now. How did they fare. What horrors were they facing? Why hadn't we heard anything lately? Would we ever see any of those precious faces again? At the end of each long day, we did all we could do. We prayed.

***** ***** ***** ***** ***** ****** ***** *****

For once the men had all come to our front porch to gather. It was the longest day of the year in this year of our Lord 1862 and our porch was the only east facing outside shade on any of the nearby cabins, so they had come, hoping to be out of the humid heat of the blazing sun, and still outside to catch any breath of breeze that might come along.

I had served up lemonade made from the last of the precious lemons I had on hand. With all the trouble down Galveston way, Mr. Borden reported produce not locally grown would be in short supply for the foreseeable future, and also staples like sugar and coffee and tea too. So I told the gentlemen to enjoy their refreshment while it lasted. Never before have I seen it take so long to drink a glass of lemonade!

My father and Papa David had come, along with Jacob, and Amon Bond had appeared a while later, declaring himself searching for male companionship, his home place being almost totally overrun by womenfolk and small children.

On a clear day we could not only see the river directly in front of and below our cabin, we also set on enough of a rise that we could see the low-water ford the Indians had used just a few days before. It had been a hot, dry June for us, although we heard there had been much cool and rain to the east all spring. The desultory rumble of conversation stopped suddenly, as young David came running up the path from the sentry post announcing, "Wagon coming!"

All heads turned and Papa David rose from his seat to go stand with his son at the porch rail. "I think it's one of Rylee's darkies driving. They were just over here yesterday, stocking up. Must've forgot something."

A few minutes passed, then David said, "That's strange... he didn't turn toward Borden's. He's headed up here!

At that, there was suddenly a palpable tension amongst the group on the porch. They all rose, and Amon and Abel lead the procession down the path to the road, where we waited in silence as the wagon approached. The driver had seen us and skillfully brought the wagon to a halt at the foot of our path. He touched his hat and nodded respectfully, as he announced, "Beggin' your pardon, sirs. My mastah, Mr. Jeff Rylee, he says I'm to find Mr. Amon Bond?"

Amon stepped forward putting a hand on one of the horses. "I'm Amon Bond. What is your business with me?" When Amon spoke, there was a sound from the back of the wagon, and we all realized in that moment that something or someone was hidden in its deep bed.

The Negro nodded, and said, "I'se got your boy here, suh..."

The poor man got no more out before we all surged forward. Going round the end of the wagon, Amon took one look, and gasped, "Henry!" as he leaped into the wagon bed with the agility of a much younger man.

We all heard the weak voice saying, "Papa? Papa? Is it really you?" followed by the sound of hoarse, heartbreaking sobs.

Immediately, Jacob was pushing his way toward the wagon bed. Many hands reached to guide him and propel him up into the wagon to kneel with Amon beside Henry's filthy, emaciated form. The stench of illness and infection was recognizable even well back where I stood with Abby clutching my skirts.

My heart clenched in fear as I remembered another time, when another wagon had brought tragedy and disaster to me and mine. Jesse's voice sounded from the hubbub at the back of the wagon, saying sharply, "Jacob! Be careful!"

Heads whipped around to see Jesse standing there in the path, white faced. There was a heartbeat of silence, and then Jacob shook his head, and said softly yet clearly, even as he reached out to feel the filthy cloth of Henry's uniform, and gently lay his hand on Henry's heaving chest, "It's still who I am, brother. I can't change that.." And then he turned to his patient with that fierce concentration of the physician, seeking answers by touch, smell and sound, murmuring quick words of comfort and inquiry that only Henry and Amon could hear.

I picked Abby up, and made my way quickly to Jesse's side. He stood among the others, silent at the back of the wagon, stricken to muteness by Jacob's statement. As we all watched, Jacob, using his hands and Amon as his eyes, did a quick assessment of Henry's condition. But when Jacob leaned close to ask something of Henry, and Henry made muffled reply, Amon reacted with an involuntary cry of distress so great that we all surged forward, and my father too belied his years with his vault into wagon to be suddenly beside his friend. The crowd around us was growing as more folk spotted the strange wagon on the path and came to see what the fuss was. Young David followed my father, instincts taking him to Jacob's side, even as Papa pulled a distressed Amon away. For a moment we all assumed that Henry had died, but then Jacob raised his voice slightly, "Lizzie, are you here?"

I moved forward toward the back of the wagon immediately, saying, "I'm here. Jacob. What do you need?" Jesse was gripping my arm to keep me from going too close.

"I need clean water and some hot coffee if you have it. And a blanket you can spare. The rest can wait till we get him up to Amon's."

"He's not-?" asked jesse, still gripping my arm.

"No," said Jacob, "he's made it this far. I expect he'll be alright eventually, with care." He dropped his voice, "He just told us, Ben and Ed died in Little Rock." He hesitated, and then continued, "We lost Frank there, too.- I'm so sorry Lizzie."

There was a collective gasp at his words, then a stunned silence descended. "Lizzie, sweetheart" said Jesse quietly, "give me Abby, and go get what Jacob needs. We'll be right here."

As I hurried up the path to the cabin, literally blinded by tears, I realized my mother-in-law was right behind me. "We saw the wagon and men gathered from our place, so I came down to see what was what."

"Did you hear-?" I asked, my voice breaking as we climbed the path.

"Yes, Lizzie," she answered, briefly, her own voice choked as well. "Poor little Abel! And O Lord, your father and Amon and your sister Martha! Lord, after losing the baby last winter, now this!"

I led the way through the open front door as I nodded, tearing running down my face, "She is so very young! Oh, how I wish Mama were here! But at least she has become close with our good-sister Mary. She has really been a mother to the youngest ones, since Mama passed. I-I guess Mary and Chris will take little A-Abel now!" I strode into the bedroom, and threw open the lid of my trunk at the foot of the bed. Reaching inside, I grabbed our spare blanket and thrust it into Aunt Sarah's hands. "Here. Take th- this." I stood still for a moment, struggling to focus, to think.

Decision made, I moved next to the hearth in the main room. There was a half-pot of coffee left from breakfast still hot on the coals. I pulled a battered canteen from its hook on the nearby wall, and carefully poured the hot liquid into it. I fastened the cap tightly and passed it to my aunt as well. Grabbing an almost full bucket of water from its place by the kitchen sink, I lead the way back outside and down the path toward the group and wagon still gathered on the trail below.

Jesse had moved to stand near the front wheel of the wagon. He was speaking to Jacob who still knelt beside his patient in the wagon bed. David was next to him, obviously helping where sight was needed. Tommy Lambert was up at the front of the wagon, speaking quietly to the driver. Papa and Amon had moved out of the wagon and were standing with Uncle David in the shade of a nearby tree, their backs to the gathered men standing grim faced and silent a few yards away. Uncle David had his arms around both Papa and Amon's shoulders and my heart ached as I remembered that it was just two years ago that Amon and Sarah had lost two of their daughters within weeks of each other. One of those daughters had been Tommy Lambert's wife.

Suddenly my arms ached to hold my sweet Abby, and I moved quickly to the back of the wagon and thrust the handle of the water bucket into David's outstretched hands. I turned abruptly away, not even waiting to see the rest of the supplies delivered by my mother-in-law, and mindlessly rushed the few steps forward that drew me by sheer instinct to appear suddenly at Jesse's side, startling both him and Abby as I reached out and grabbed her unannounced and none too gently from his arms. I clutched her to me as my eyes filled and I staggered blindly a few steps away to stand motionless, my wet face buried in the little girl softness of her hair. A great sob welled up in my chest for mothers and fathers and daughters and sons, and brothers... even as a part of my brain registered with chagrin Jesse's startled exclamation of, "What-? Wait-!"- and then immediately, a fearful, "Abby? Lizzie?" My mind shoved all that away, driven by an instinct older than time itself, demanding that one scent filled moment.

Then I became conscious first of the agitated murmur of voices behind me, then the sound of a footstep, and then my husband's gentle touch on my shoulder. My next conscious awareness was the warmth and strength of his arms around Abby and I as he silently embraced us both.

Another breath and his strength had anchored me yet again. Abby squirmed and I relaxed my hold and kissed her puckered brow before saying softly, "Oh, Jesse, I'm so sorry! I don't know what-..."

He stopped me with a gentle kiss to the forehead, and said, softly, "Of course you do.... Sons and daughters and mothers and fathers.... And brothers... and love and loss...."

Dumbfounded, I gave a tear-choked sputter. "How- how do you do that, Jesse Nutt? Read my mind….know….."

And he smiled that gentle smile I loved so, and murmured as he touched my wet cheek, "And the two shall become one………. I know, Lizzie, I know…."

A wave of blessedness and peace washed over me as I turned with my family to join our loved ones in a strange mixture of grief for those we had lost and joy at the one spared to return to us. In my heart I knew, even then, that there would be many such moments in the fiery wrath of the years to come.

And so it was that I gripped my husband's hand tightly the next day as we stood with so many others on that bluff where now some dozen members of our community lay with my mother in their eternal sleep. Three small crudely carved stones now lay embedded in the soil between my mama and tiny little Amos Bond and his aunts. Jesse's voice rose, carried by a gentle breeze toward the encircling arms of the Brazos,

"Father we come here today to commend to your eternal love and care the souls of our brothers Francis Landers and Edmond and Benjamin Bond. We pray that you will in your mercy receive them into your heavenly kingdom. We thank you for their sacrifice, and we pray that you will lead people toward the path of an end to all war and of peace for our nation and for all mankind. In Christ Jesus' holy name we pray. Amen."

Empty Arms and Heavy Hearts 1862 - 1864

Word came in August that Logan Landers had been killed by the Indians while fighting the Comanche with the State Militia out in West Texas. The news shattered poor Fanny. She never spoke again after her initial cry of anguish. Uncle David and Aunt Sarah took her and her two little boys into their cabin so that Jacob and Aunt Sarah could care for her. She lingered there with them until November, her light growing ever dimmer like a lamp that has used the last of its oil and slowly dims, then flickers and dies. Jacob found her one day, seemingly dozing in a chair. But her sleep was that of eternity, as if she had simply left this world to follow Logan to the next.

Grieved by the loss of my friend, I hardly took notice of my own doings until sometime in January, I felt a queer fluttering in my belly, and counted the days and remembered the turning cycles of the moon. And so it was that I greeted Jesse that evening with glad news, news of new life growing with the New Year. In spite of the war, in spite of the grief, in spite of everything, we rejoiced…. But it was not to be….

I awoke still in Jessie's arms. He must have felt me stir, because his hand gently stroked my hair, and his face tilted down toward mine. "Lizzie?" he whispered.

"I'm here," I managed. I wished he would take my hand so maybe I could squeeze his. I wanted to reach for him but the effort of moving seemed quite beyond me still. But the cold feeling had gone at least and along with it that feeling of becoming disconnected from my body. I was very sure I had almost died. I had been bleeding so badly. I remembered the pain and the tearing feeling and the feeling of hot blood between my thighs. I remembered the agonizing pain as first Mother Sarah and then Jacob, when her strength had failed, had kneaded my belly endlessly, trying to slow or stop the bleeding. I remembered praying to God, begging him to let me stay, to be with Jesse and Abby who still both needed me so much. And I remembered the sound of my husband's voice begging the same deity to let me stay. With those two memories I gave thanks, and reclaimed my ties with things of this earth. I hurt, but it was a dull physical ache that I knew would pass. Still- in my weakness, my gratitude was mingled with a searing sadness for what was lost.

"Jesse?" I whispered, "I'm so sorry." My heart broke remembering the feeling of that tiny life leaving my body too soon.

His arms squeezed gently, and he shook his head, "Oh, my sweet girl, it's not your fault, it simply was not meant to be." He paused and swallowed , "God has let me keep you and our sweet Abby. For that I can offer nothing but heartfelt gratitude!"

There was a stir nearby and a hand on my forehead, accompanied by a sigh of relief. I struggled to open my eyes enough to focus as Jacob felt for the pulse in my throat and said huskily, "Welcome dear Sister, to the land of the living. You scared us badly you know." He tried for a smile that didn't quite make it, and said, "The Rylee's midwife has come and gone. The bleeding has stopped. But you must be very still, and rest and heal for the next week or two."

I nodded, "Don't worry," I said softly, "I will be good. Right now I'm just so tired..."

I felt Jesse tense, and Jacob's hand on my wrist, just before he squeezed my hand, and with a real smile this time, said, "It's alright, Lizzie. Jesse and I know you are much too stubborn to give up and leave us now! You just relax and rest. And if you wake and need anything just say so. We'll be right here." I felt Jesse relax, so, I did too, and this time slid into darkness made light by their strength and love.

When I woke again, Jesse was gone, but curled up next to me was his new assistant. Even before my eyes opened, I recognized the scent and presence of my eight year old daughter.

Abby was laying close, fast asleep, her head on my shoulder as always. I smiled, and this time found the strength was there to pick up my hand and touch her raven-black curls. Her eyes opened, and she smiled at me. "Good morning, Mama"

"Good morning, love." I said softly. "Are you my nurse today?" I asked.

"Only for a little while," she said. "Granny is here, but she went to get fresh water. She said to tell you if you woke up that she would be back directly, and would help you get clean and change your gown."

"Oh that will feel good!" I said, as I began to be aware of other morning things that also needed to be taken care of.

"Where's your Papa?" I asked.

"He and Uncle Jake and Grandpa Abel and Grandpa David went over to visit Grandma Sally at the cemetery," she said.

My aunt Sarah picked that moment to walk in. She had obviously heard Abby's innocent remark. One look at my face and she bustled Abby out quickly with orders to go across to her and Uncle David's house and bring the sewing basket she had left on the kitchen table. I hadn't the strength to reach out to her, but next thing I knew she was on the bed next to me holding me as tears ran silently down my face. "It was a little boy," she said quietly, answering the question I had no voice to ask. "He was perfect, just too small. It was just too soon." she said, kindly.

I nodded, and whispered, "I wish I could have seen him."

She was still for a moment, and she said, "Oh, Lizzie, I am so sorry. Of course you do. That is my fault. W-we've been so afraid for you, and Jesse has been so distraught…. Well we just didn't think, that's what. I ask your forgiveness for not telling the boys to wait a bit." There were tears in her eyes too, as she added softly, "If it's any comfort at all, they've put him right next to your dear mother. I'm sure she is watching over him for us all."

Wordlessly I nodded, as I leaned weakly against her. After a bit, she squeezed me gently and said, "My dear girl, I know it is hard, but life will go on. And you've a husband and little girl who need and love you desperately. So let's get you cleaned up and feeling more yourself before the men folk come home."

I nodded agreement, and even managed a shaky smile for Abby when she returned. Sarah let her help me get into a fresh nightgown, and she was very proud of herself when she brought me a bowl of warm chicken broth Sarah had helped her prepare. I managed to eat a bit, and then lay back against fresh pillows. I went to sleep waiting for Jesse to return.

I awoke sometime later to find Jesse and Abby together inhabiting the rocking chair next to the bed. Jesse was holding my hand, but was fast asleep. Abby, on the other hand, was awake. She smiled at me from her perch cuddled against her father's chest. I smiled back, and without thinking discovered that some of my strength had returned when I found myself holding my finger to my lips, warning her to stay quiet. She winked at me conspiratorially, and in a few moments I drifted off again, feeling God's healing grace begin.

***** ****** ***** ***** ***** ***** ***** *****

In May, 1863, just as I was beginning to feel myself again, we got the mixed blessing of yet another of our own returned to us much debilitated- not by injury but again by illness. My youngest brother William arrived like his fellow Henry had months before- filthy, emaciated, and with a deep bone-jarring cough that had Jacob fearing pneumonia at best and consumption at worst. Fortunately, time and tender care proved enough for both men to make some recovery. Both would most likely suffer from a lifelong weakness of the lungs, but they were alive and with us, and we were grateful.

During the summer and fall of 1863 the Confederacy finally got a decent mail service operating for a time. After over a year of silence, we began to hear from some of our men. The letters were scattered and sporadic, but taken all together, along with the newspaper accounts we began to get a picture of how the war was progressing. In the case of the south, from the beginning, progress was in reality a misnomer. During the first two years of the war the south went through men like water, losing men by the thousands – not just on the poorly conducted battlefield, but to illness, disease, cold and neglect, and equipment failure.

In early August, the newspapers brought word of the death of our friend, Sam Houston at his home in Huntsville, Texas. The obituaries from the Texas newspapers remarked much on his lack of enthusiasm for the Confederate cause while the few northern papers that trickled through my father's pipeline reviled him as a great hero in the end too "cowardly" to stand up for the Union. These unjust judgments grieved us deeply, for the man we knew had given his all for the love of the people of Texas, and was a man of fine character and true Christian convictions. As my father so succinctly put it, "Sam deserves better."

Ironically for us, Missouri had been the last state to secede, and did not enter the war until November, 1861. We finally got word that Jesse's brothers, Henry, and the twins- Robert and John had been caught up in the first draft and were serving in Tennessee, where some of the bloodiest fighting was. Papa David at long last got a letter from Henry Nutt in October of 1863, telling of his incarceration in a

Federal Prisoner of War Camp near Chicago. The bitter cold and horrendous over-crowding made illness and disease rampant, but he still expressed himself thankful to have survived the nightmare of Tennessee, and hopeful that by the time he gained release the war would be over. John and Robert had also been captured and were somewhere in the same prison, but he had no direct contact with them since their arrival.

The same week we heard from Henry another letter came. It was to Papa from my middle brother Rob. He too was a Prisoner of War being held by the Union but in what he described as a hellhole of a place near New Orleans, Louisiana. Constant humidity, heat, and mosquitos were the enemies now. The men there were also living in overcrowded, horrible conditions, but like Henry Rob expressed hope that the war would end soon and allow him to come home with no more battle.

Susan got a short letter from her Henry, who by virtue of being out on patrol had avoided capture with Rob and others from our area. He had seen Abel Nutt in the recent fighting but not since, so could not verify his well-being. The war in Louisiana, where he was, had descended toward chaos on numerous occasions, and the company command had changed several times. The new fellow appeared more capable, he said, and was hoping things would calm down enough for furlough time in the New Year. There had been some talk of it, so he closed with words of love to Susan and their two babies, the youngest whom he had never seen, with great hope to see all soon.

And so our little settlement continued to wait and pray, ever hopeful that the nightmare of war would end quickly. We came together to eat meager fare and sing carols for the children at Christmas, but joy was very hard to find in those days. And as the New Year came, we listened with dread for the sound of Indians from the west and the hoof beats of messengers from the east, as the fury of war continued to engulf the land.

***** ****** ***** ***** ***** ***** ***** *****

A knock sounded at the cabin door. Jesse hesitated as Caesar growled briefly and then ended with kind of a squeak. Not quite sure what to make of that, he felt quickly for the shotgun that leaned against the wall nearby. (Even a blind man could run off someone with a shotgun, he reckoned.) He pointed the gun carefully at the floor and walked toward the door. "Who's there?" he called, as he reached the latched door.

"Jesse!" said a hoarse voice, "It's me, Abel!"

With an exclamation, Jesse made himself carefully place the gun in the nearby corner, before hurriedly lifting the latch. As soon as the door came open he found his arms full of hairy, bearded, sweaty, dirt and mud covered brother. Heedless of it all, they clung tightly to each other for several seconds, until Caesar, recognizing his old companion, let out a glad yelp, and launched himself with enough force that they both staggered sideways.

Jessie listened to man greet dog with a combination of tears and a big grin on his face. At last the ruckus subsided, and he reached out a hand to help Abel to his feet. "Brother! We thought you were in Louisiana! What a wonderful surprise! But what brings you back to us?" He stopped suddenly, and felt anxiously of Abel's arm. "You are not wounded?'

"No Jesse," his brother assured him quickly, "I was, but I am sound now." He hesitated, and Jesse's stomach knotted with dread. "But I- I bring h-hard news." His voice broke and Jesse felt him sway.

Quickly he grasped his brother's arm and led him to the chair. "Here, Abel. Sit, and let me get you some refreshment. You must be exhausted!" The fact that Abel made no protest, and sat without speaking told Jesse just how bad the news must be. Jesse concentrated on gathering water and towels, and then bread and cheese and a cup of hot fresh brewed coffee, bringing all to his brother in silence.

Once Abel had washed himself, and eaten and drank a little, Jesse sat down across the table from him and took a deep breath, and said softly, "Tell me."

"Henry is dead. – Killed in April at the battle of Mansfield in Louisiana. We won there, but he was in the first line of Calvary that went in. They took the most casualties of the day. I-It was bad Jesse. Most of the first line were shot off their horses and t-then trampled underfoot. So m-many weren't even r-recognizable. I-I tried to find him, really I did-." His voice broke, and Jesse felt for and found his hand across the table and held on tight. "Fi-finally I found his horse. Its leg was broken. I shot it. A-and I got Henry's spare belt, and his saddle and blanket. But they wouldn't let me keep them. - Nothing but the belt. I wanted something to – to bring Susan..." He fell silent, and Jesse held on, silent, as Abel squeezed his hand so hard the bones ground together.

Ah, Lizzie, Jesse thought, in agony! And sweet young Susan, and Papa Abel! Oh, how many hearts would break at this news! Finally, after a bit, the grip of Abel's fingers eased, and Jesse prodded softly, "What of the others? Were they there? Do you have any news of them?"

Abel nodded, "Alive, as far as I know. I saw Young Cal and Rob, who had gotten exchanged out of New Orleans somehow. They were both grieving Henry, but were otherwise alright. A couple of days later I heard that they were in a group captured by the Federals a few days after the last skirmish. Rumor has it that now the prisoners are all being shipped north to Chicago. They say conditions are harsh, but at least they are out of the fighting for now. If I hadn't left when I did, I would have been taken with them." He paused. "I've been temporarily discharged, due to being shot twice in the leg." At Jesse's exclamation of alarm, he hastened to add, "It's mostly healed up now.

I stopped in Waco and let a surgeon friend I met last year patch me up. Rob Curtis served with the brigade until he was shot himself in the middle of trying to remove wounded from the battlefield early in war. Lost his leg, but still a brilliant surgeon. He got all the pieces of shrapnel the quacks at Mansfield had missed, and made me stay with him till he was sure the infection was gone. I may always limp, but I figure I owe Rob that I still have my whole leg."

"Well, thank the good Lord for his gift," said Jesse, fervently. "I am glad you are home brother! So, you won't have to go back?"

"I don't think so," said Abel, quietly. "I pray not. I was told to report to my local state militia group when I became able-bodied again, and I will do so. But I am hopeful I can stay in the area."

"Ah, that is good," breathed Jessie. "Well, brother, I think we will find most of the family over at Mama and Papa's place. Lizzie and Susan are both there I know, helping Mama sew a quilt. Let's take your news to them first." He rose with a sigh. "Then, you and Lizzie and I will go up the hill to tell Papa Abel." He paused, and shook his head, "Frank and now Henry, dead, and Rob and Cal prisoner... Thank God you are safe brother!" He unashamedly embraced Abel once more, and then the two men headed down the path to their parents cabin, hearts heavy with their news.

***** ****** ***** ***** ***** ***** ***** *****

I held my good-sister tightly, as sobs racked her body, and could hardly see for the tears blinding my own eyes. Henry, Sweet, stalwart, steady Henry, who had stood by Jessie and me through so much, who had with a wisdom beyond his years helped Jesse find himself again as a man. He and Jesse had worked together to build our little cottage in the woods of Neosho, and he and Logan had together helped Jesse relearn so much and invented new ways for him to help and be a part of the building of our new homes and community here.

305

Many were the times during those early days of darkness, when Henry would find me, hiding in the forest or the barn, to cry tears of grief and frustration where Jesse wouldn't hear. Many times he simply held me and reminded me that we weren't alone. But Henry was a doer, and he almost always set out immediately to help Jesse and I look for solutions and reminded us that there was help to be found. Oh, I would miss that brother of mine so much.

But more than that, I knew my Father would miss him. Papa loved all of us children fiercely, but it was Henry and Jesse who had grown up to become also his friends. I released Susan into her mother's arms and turned to Jesse. He held me tightly while I wept, and when I finally looked up, his face was also wet with tears. I struggled to get my breath, and finally whispered, "We have to tell Papa."

Jesse nodded, and went to speak to Abel and Papa David. Minutes later we were headed up the path. Jesse held my hand tightly as we approached the big cabin on the hill. Papa had seen us coming up the path, Jesse and I followed by Abel and Papa David. (I had left Abby with Jesse's mother, knowing she was too young to understand the doings of grief.) He stepped out on the porch and watched us come, his face set like stone. Our faces and Abel Nutt's presence told the nature of the news we brought. I went to him, kissed his cheek gently, and gripped his hands, as I said, "Papa, it's Henry."

His eyes closed, and opened again, full of moisture, and he nodded. "Come inside, then, children, and tell me."

"Jesse?" said his Uncle Abel., "will you ride with me today?" The voice came from the doorway of the cabin. Jesse had heard his approach up the path through the open door and recognized his step. Abel limped a little now, his bad knee finally freezing into the immobility of old age. But he still rode out every morning, weather permitting, and Jesse often joined him on days when field work didn't beckon.

Jesse loved their rides. The freedom of the saddle and the conversations with Abel were a precious remnant of the life he had lost, and while he was grateful for all he had been given and spared, he was only human, and often came to their rides together as a thirsty sojourner to an oasis in the desert. His uncle understood that, and indeed shared much of Jesse's sense of loss for what might have been. So he too cherished these times with his nephew and son-in-law.

As they rode out this particular spring day, Abel sensed pensiveness in Jesse that reflected his own feelings about many things, and Abel resolved to bring it up- to see if perhaps they could help each other. They rode for a long while in silence, the fresh, bright air of the Texas spring morning a balm to their troubled souls.

As usually happened on these rides, when they basically gave the horses their heads, through sheer habit they came out of the trees onto the open pasture land that they hoped would someday become their permanent town site. They dismounted and staked the horses near the bluff, and walked through the tall grasses to sacred spot where some of their loved ones lay, with their eternal view of the wide sweeping valley of the river.

Before they left for the war, Abel's sons had gifted their father with a stone bench that they had set near their mother's grave. Now markers for two of them plus a beloved nephew lay in the hallowed ground at his feet. Abel sat down with a weary sigh cut short as Jesse moved not to sit beside him, but to gently touch his shoulder, and then take a few unerring steps to squat and place his hand upon the stone that marked his own son's tiny cradle of eternal sleep.

Abel watched in silence, his heart pierced anew, as Jesse raised a tear streaked face toward him and said in a choked voice, 'We both have sons to mourn here now, Uncle. When Lizzie and I come, I-I feel like I have to be s-strong...." His voice broke on a sob, and through the dark tunnel of his grief, Jesse heard his uncle's voice saying gruffly, "Come here son." He reached toward the voice, and found himself next enfolded in his Uncle's arms as they shared for a while the grief of fathers for sons.

After a bit, they ended once again in silence, but now sat side by side, facing toward that sweeping panorama of El Rio de los Brazos de Dios. And Abel sighed again, and said with regret as his eyes soaked up the Promise in that beauty, "Ah, Jesse, I do wish you could see the view... It is.... a Comfort."

And Jesse smiled, and answered quietly, "Oh, but I can, Uncle. I've seen it clear as can be ever since our Lizzie brought me up here the day we buried Aunt Sally." The breeze caught his dark hair as if in a caress as he spoke. "You and the some of the others had decided on the grave site, and had walked away a ways to talk to some of the Stockton men about the town you and Sally had dreamed about, but Lizzie and I - we stayed here." He was smiling softly, thinking of her.

"And I said to her- as I always do- Tell me, Lizzie. Let me see! - And she always does. She has such a gift for words, and she- she paints me a picture so I can see it in my mind clear as day! So, you see Uncle, whenever I come here, I see it too! The bright sparkling blue of the river stretching out its arms in a long sweeping bend beneath foothills that roll gently up to the broad flat mesa of the mountain of the Comanche...." He paused a moment and said, "Yes, every time I come- I do "see" it, and you are right... it is... a Comfort."

This time the silence was the sound of the Peace brought only by the Creator settling on the two men. "So," said Jesse, "what can we do? Anything?"

"I don't know, Jesse," answered Abel, honestly. "The cause of the South is well and truly lost. We have no ports save Matamoros, which is in a foreign land, our supplies are dwindling to non-existent, and we have gone thru men like water, sacrificing over a quarter of the sons of a generation to a cause we cannot win. And yet to surrender without a negotiated peace is give up thousands more to the gallows of treason, and our cities and towns to the mercy of the swords of the conquerors. Our leaders continue to hope to somehow gain the upper hand, if not to win, to at least secure a negotiated peace that will allow the men who have fought and served to keep their lives, their freedom, and their full rights as citizens."

"But the cost of that is lives and money," said Jesse grimly.

"Yes," agreed Abel, "and we have little of either left to give. We, personally in our community, have sacrificed the lives and health of fully a quarter of our number if you count the wives and children who have perished even with what care was ours to give."

"What about funds?" asked Jesse. "God knows I have none, and I assume most in our community and others across the land are much in the same straits. We have land, and some stock, and our crops, but precious little if any cash."

"Indeed," Abel said, as he pulled out his pipe. Jesse caught the smell, and suppressed a smile and fell the uplift of his heart as they passed from mourning into the good work of thinking. Abel continued, "The newspapers are begging folks to donate to the cause in any way they can. Old jewelry – especially gold, is especially being sought after, but also there are a few factories- small places- producing hats and belts mostly – that are seeking people to peddle their products out here on the frontier, and in Mexico, to folks who have any cash to pay. The idea is that they produce the items out of materials donated or already on hand, and therefore only shipping fees come out of the money collected. The end seller gets to keep 10% for their trouble, and the Cause gets about 80% of the cash collected. That then translates to mostly ammunition and food for the troops."

"God," said Jesse, shaking his head, "that can't produce much!"

"Enough from the first batch that they are recruiting folks for selling a second go round." said Abel. The smell of pipe smoke grew stronger, and Jesse heard the chewing begin. "I've been giving it some thought, and I think we might do a little project here. With summer upon us – you and young William could make some rounds to the far flung farms offering hats for sale and also checking on folks and finding out what kind of help they need to get their second planting in. "

"Well, we could do that, I guess," said Jesse, "You think Will is up to it?"

"Well, that's just it," said Abel, "In fine weather it'll get him out in the fresh air, and riding will build some strength gradually but an easy pace doesn't require the stamina or the brute strength that preparing the fields or working cattle does."

"True," said Jesse, "and we could seek shelter or not go out if storms were threatening." He paused and then said, "And...?"

"Well, meanwhile I plan to put the women folk about gathering up any oddments of jewelry they might have or know of. I figure if I put the women folk on it, it works better than if the men all had to go and ask their wives to turn it over," said Abel in a dry tone.

Jesse let that sink in for a moment, and then he began to laugh. "Abel, you do beat all!!! Only you would be devious enough to think of it that way!!" He shook his head grinning. "What else?"

"Well, now, boy," said his uncle, "it's your turn. I shouldn't have to come up with the whole plan by myself!"

Jesse thought for a few moments rapidly considering and rejecting any number of ideas. "Well, we could spread the word to the surrounding towns and areas. Especially the jewelry idea- we could tell Pete and he could send word to Stephenville and Weatherford, you and Joe Robertson could send word to communities on the east side of the Brazos and on over Buchanan way. And get others to do the hat thing too- in the areas too far away for me to cover. I can't see there's much else we can ask of folks that wouldn't be asking them to give up what they need to survive. There's not much except the bare necessities that anybody has right now."

He paused for a moment and then said, "Not to change the subject, but have you heard that Jeff Rylee has now sent all but 3 of his male Negroes to fight. He kept two older men and one house slave who is crippled, but the others are gone. Of course he still has their women, and I am told is using them in the fields."

"Damn, Jesse, you must have ears like a mole!" exclaimed Abel, "How and where do you hear these things?"

"You know," said Jesse, thoughtfully, "it's a strange thing. Lizzie and I have often commented on it. When you're blind or deaf – to some folks it sort of makes you invisible. I mean they act as if you've lost all your other senses too. I can't tell you the number of people who- once they realize I am blind- feel called to speak more loudly than normal, as if I might have trouble hearing them too. Or people who don't know us- when we walk into a shop- and the clerk will address the whole conversation to Lizzie as if my mind was defective or I was deaf and mute as well. It's very strange. And oh does it make my Lizzie furious! For instance, there is a store over in Comanche Peak that she refuses to give our custom any longer after the clerk made the mistake of asking her permission for a purchase I was about to make! Oh, Lord, Abel, I wish I could have seen it when she exploded and gave that man a tongue lashing he's not likely to forget!"

Abel laughed and said, "I would've liked to have witnessed that myself. Her mother was like that, my Sally. Wouldn't take anything off of anybody, and woe betide anyone who offended someone she considered hers!"

Jesse nodded, "Well, anyhow, to answer your question…. One day last week I was out walking and decided to step into Charlie Smithers' place for a drink of ale. I was sitting there at the bar in plain sight, while some of Jeff Rylee's cattle hands were sitting at the table behind me. And they discussed all about Jeff's slaves, his crops, his cows, his finances, his personal life, all right there within my hearing. Now personally, I came close to sending Jeff a note that he ought to fire the lot of them and why, but I didn't want to make problems when we need none, so I refrained."

"Well, I must admit, that is interesting. Of course all his slaves are supposed to be free anyhow, but I don't suppose he has bothered to inform them of that." said Abel, "I suppose I won't assume that he is well fixed to make a donation then, but I shall ask anyway!"

"Just don't mention to our Abel that you are going or he will want to tag along. Come to find out he has corresponded with Miss Indiana the entire war. Papa is just fit to be tied. But you mark my words, there's going to be a match there whether Papa particularly likes it or not. That is why I absolutely agree that whatever we do, we need to include Jeff Rylee in the loop. I would suggest using Abel for the hat thing, but as you know, he is already busy using his pay he has saved to buy land north of here, and he paid Susan a good price for Henry's cattle. Have you found a buyer for their land yet?"

His uncle snorted, and said, "I offered it to Abel, and at a good price too, but he had his heart set on that piece upriver and I can see why too. The man he got it from had plans of running a ferry across the river there- it's a good place for it – and Abel says he had already completed about fifty percent of the works for it. So there's a livelihood there that is even more promising than the cattle."

"Well," said Jesse, "Jacob and I would like to buy it from Susan, if that suits. We have enough put back between us to pay cash. We are going to lease it out to Henry Bond to farm for now, and my land next to it as well. It will be a steady income and the land will be there in our name when the time comes to talk of a town. Papa just acquired the piece on the other side of mine, so that's a big part of your town plat right there. Tommy Lambert got Austen Yeats claim when word came of him being killed, so Lord help us – he is who we'll have to deal with for the rest."

"I've known Tommy for a long time. Almost as long as I've known Amon," said Abel, "He's a maverick for sure, marches to his own drummer, but he's a community minded man. He'll work with us when the time comes."

"If you say so Uncle," said Jesse, dubiously. Then he brightened, "Well, Abel, I guess I need to go and tell Lizzie I am about to become a hat salesman!"

Abel stood and led the way as they headed back to their horses. "I'll send off for the hats right away," he said. "I'll need Lizzie and your mother to help me with this jewelry scheme. And maybe we can get your father to fashion some lock boxes for us to use to ship what we collect in cash and jewelry to Richmond!"

313

"And just how do you plan on getting this treasure from here to there?" asked Jesse, as they mounted up.

"I will have that all addressed by the time we get to that point!" declared Abel.

"In other words, dear uncle, right now," said Jesse, with an impish grin, "you don't have a clue!"

***** ****** ***** ***** ***** ***** ***** *****

As it turned out, I ended up travelling with Jesse to sell the hats that summer, as my brother William had already agreed, in spite of his still uncertain health to help Abel with his burgeoning cattle business, and young David or "Lee" Nutt as he now liked to be called was helping Papa David farm his land. We left Abby in the care doting care of her grandmother, and went forth on horseback, pulling a pack mule loaded with our stock of fifty hats and our supplies for "camping out". Truth be told we were often offered the hospitality of the farms we visited, so we spent few nights out in open camp.

Jesse proved an able salesman and the people eager to make some contribution to the war effort, however small. But the expenses of our supplies ate up our share of the meager take, so our personal profit from the enterprise equaled exactly zero. But we actually had fun. It was enjoyable to meet and visit the folk on the outlying farms, although many were suffering from the long absence of husbands and fathers. Jesse, or Uncle Jesse as the settler children began to call him was a popular figure as some of the youngsters on the remote farms had never seen a man in his prime, only the elderly men and young boys too old and too young to have been called off to war.

When we spent the night at those remote homesteads, we shared whatever sparse meal was available, often supplementing what the goodwife had on hand with some of our own supplies. After the meal, Jesse would sit by the fire while the lady and I did our womanly chores, and the children of the house would gather round him, curious and drawn to this strange creature in their midst. And he would charm them with stories- some funny tales that brought unaccustomed peals of laughter, and some tales from the Good Book. And he always ended just as he did with our Abby singing them to sleep with some hymn to our Lord, sending them off to dreamland with the assurance of God's love.

I comforted many a mother brought to tears at the sound of their children's happiness, or at the sound of Jesse's beautiful tenor singing their babies to sleep. Some of them wanted to talk and some were tight-lipped and stoic about their fears. So in each home, we did what we could, brought some assurance of the concern and support of the wider community, and at every hearth we prayed with them, that the war would soon be over and their men be brought safely home.

Through it all I kept notes and accounts, not only of our sales, but pages of information about the situation and needs at each household. These I gave to my father upon our return at the end of June. We were all a bit appalled and dismayed how many had gone without help all this time, simply because we did not know they were there. To give Papa, and Uncle David, and Amon, and all the others credit- they had done the best they could, but now they set out to do more. My father sent an update to the county to amend the dependents pension lists to try to get the women monetary help. And the men and older boys spent the remainder of the growing season trying to help those households that had been missed get the help they needed to bring in a harvest and be set for the coming winter.

The money we raised and the jewelry collected were sent via Jeff Rylee's brother to a cousin of theirs who lived near Richmond. It took two months and several hair-raising experiences to get it there, but arrive it did and we received a most cordial form letter thanking us for our contribution to the "Glorious Cause". Privately, Jesse and I felt the money could have probably been spent better right here at home to help those in dire need. But we knew our feelings would likely be misunderstood by some, so we kept our own counsel.

Upon our return, Jacob came over to visit and share our dinner. Abby and Jesse were sitting on the porch together when he arrived, and he joined them there in the cool of the evening shade as I finished dinner. I listened to their conversation as I mashed the potatoes, and added some final seasoning to the greens.

"Where's David?" asked Jesse, "I expected he might come with you."

"You mean 'Lee', don't you?" asked Jacob, with a grin. "That would be our brother who has become enchanted with the fact that Papa's grandmother was a Lee, and that we are umpteenth cousins, 4096 times removed of the great general!"

"You're joking, right?" said Jesse, incredulously.

"Ah, would that I was," said Jacob with a sigh. "He's sixteen year's old Jesse, and Lee has been a prominent heroic figure on the national scene for most of his life. You can't blame the boy. Plus it inspires awe in some of the other boys- who I might add are also sixteen."

Jesse chuckled and said, "You're right brother. And, truth be told, if I had been in the same place as Lee, with the same agonizing choices to make, I don't know what I would have done. There's nothing about this whole war- what came before, what we've endured these years, or what's bound to come after – that has been or will be easy. I don't know that our country will ever truly recover from what has been wrought here."

"Agreed." said Jacob sadly. There was silence for a moment, and then he said, in a much lighter tone, "But you were asking about our dear brother, "Lee"....well, he's at home. He won't be leaving anytime soon."

"Is he ill?" I asked through the open doorway, concerned.

"Not unless you consider a sore backside, wounded pride, and being the laughingstock of the whole town an illness…" said Jacob, struggling to keep a straight face.

"Let me guess- the sore backside was courtesy of Papa…." said Jesse, with a rueful grin.

"Pre-cisely," said Jacob, mysteriously.

"But why did Uncle Lee get spanked," asked Abby, curiously. "I didn't know big boys got spanked."

"Only when they are very, very stupid," said her Uncle Jacob, seriously, "And even then, only when they talk back to their father in the telling of it."

"Uh, oh," said Jesse, struggling now himself to remain solemn.

"Is this suitable for young ears?" I asked Jacob, wishing he could see my glare.

"Oh, yes," he said. "I seriously doubt the situation is likely to happen to young Abigail here, but perhaps she will learn from it the value of paying attention to one's surroundings."

"Do tell," said Jesse, gathering Abby close. "We're all ears!" Abby giggled and I struggled to suppress a similar reaction.

"Yes, do tell, Jacob," I said, coming out to the porch. "Supper will keep for a bit. I want to be sure I hear this cautionary tale."

"It would be so much more fun if he were here," said Jacob, with true brotherly relish. "But here it is…. About a week ago, the south end sentry was old man Rankin. God bless him he means well, but you might as well put me out there. The man can't see ten feet ahead much less keep watch over a hundred yards of river front. And not only that, in order to see, you have to be awake, and he sleeps most of his shift. They try not to use him, but that particular night there had been a fire up in one of Henry Bond's barns and half the community was still over there, and they were shorthanded, so bless him, Rankin volunteered. Well it's like the Indians *know* when he is down there. So here they come, across the river, and right up the main trail and make off with a half-dozen head of horses and two milk cows."

Jesse groaned, "Good Lord, Abel and I have been trying for two years to get him out of the rotation. So... the Indians came and went unmolested. So then what?"

"Oh, no," said Jacob, "*Not* unmolested....because our intrepid younger brother, "Lee", and his merry band of young valiants were at that very moment coming home from Henry's place just in time to see the aforementioned Red Indians taking off with our precious livestock! So with a tally ho and shouted charge they gave chase. The Indians fled and disappeared into the darkness. Having observed their direction to be westward our stalwart sibling predicted they were headed for that divide over by the Paluxy between here and Erath County. Determining that with cunning they might take a shortcut and reach the divide more quickly than a larger party of warriors herding livestock, off they went, without a word to anyone, disappearing into the night in pursuit of their fleeing foes.

Near dawn they reached the place of their intended ambush, and in an abundance of prudence and caution they unsaddled and stake tied their horses some distance away down the hill, while they climbed up to hide among the bushes to await the arrival of The Enemy. That arrival happened shortly when the Indians and a large group of about 30 horses and some unknown number of cattle burst upon the scene in such a way as to so frighten the staked horses that they all broke free and were swept along with the rest of the stampede right on through the divide, followed by their new Indian owners. And thus our young adventurers were required to return home on foot, covered in dust, their only trophies of war the leather saddles they carried upon their backs."

"Oh, dear," I said, struggling not to laugh out loud. Jesse had no such compunction. He roared, "Oh, Jake, can't you just SEE it! Oh, that is just priceless! Oh my God, poor guys, having to walk all the way back from Paluxy…." He stopped, and his eyes got big, and he struggled for seriousness, as he said, "Wait- you said they left without telling anyone…. So everybody thought…."

Jacob nodded, "Yep. When it was discovered that the horses were gone, and Rankin reported hearing a ruckus as they rode out of town, and the boys were nowhere to be found, we all thought they'd been taken. Papa and Uncle Abel, and Amon and Tommy, and about thirty other men took what firearms we still have and every available horse, and headed out after them. They met up with the returning young intrepids about six miles out. They all stayed on their horses as the boys told their tale. According to "Lee", Papa waited until the end, and then he looked at Uncle Abel, and then said to the whole lot- 'I will expect to see you at the fence behind my shop upon your arrival back in Stockton Bend.' And the whole body of men turned and rode off, leaving them to walk the rest of the way home."

Silence reigned, and slowly we all began to grin again. "It's not funny," I said, "But it is!!! Oh, Jacob- it is!"

"I am never," said Jesse, evilly, "going to let him live this down!"

"Me neither!" said Jacob, with a totally impish look I hadn't seen in years. "When we are eighty and he is sixty-five, I swear we'll still be telling this story!"

Abby giggled, and said, "Can I ask Uncle David to tell me about what happened to his horse?"

"Oh, yes, love," said Jesse, "Please do!"

"You miscreants are corrupting this innocent child," I said, getting into the spirit of the evening.

And so, the next morning, upon seeing her Uncle David, standing, staring morosely at the single horse still residing in his father's corral, Abby, my dear sweet child, said, "Uncle David, what happened to your horse?"

I reported to Jesse that I had never in all my days seen quite that particular shade of red.

***** ***** ***** ***** ***** ***** ***** *****

Abel Nutt was called up again in October, but managed to get the conscription board to see reason, and served for a couple of months with a state militia unit taking a group of Indians to the reservation in Oklahoma. As he said, the trip wasn't bad, and the pay he received welcome, although there was talk that some places were beginning to refuse Confederate script.

As the new year came and the Confederacy sank further and further into chaos and ruin, my father revealed to those closest to him his most closely guarded secret- the five hundred dollars printed by a bank in Chicago, Illinois, held in secret to see his family secure at the end of the war. When the end came and the Confederacy was no more, we would have that money to buy seed for crops, horses and cattle for our use, and food for our tables. We all quietly thanked God for his foresight as we waited for the end to come.

Remote as we were from the corridors of power, we received the news of the end all of a piece, on April 22nd, 1865. A rider sent from the county seat at Buchanan arrived first at Comanche Peak Post Office and later the same day came across the ford into Stockton Bend. He had apparently been given direction, for he did not stop until he reached my father's cabin. The man was dirty, unshaven and exhausted. Upon inquiry he informed us that he had been on the road travelling from town to town for two days. With him he brought copies of news articles from papers in Dallas and Galveston. The first article reported the surrender of General Robert E. Lee to General Ulysses S. Grant on April 9, 1865. The second told of the cold blooded murder of Abraham Lincoln, the President of the United States by John Wilkes Booth, an actor and southern sympathizer on April 14, 1865.

In the stunned silence that followed his announcement to the crowd gathered in front of my father's porch, the sound of the running waters of the Brazos were a reminder that time marched ever onward. The long nightmare of war was finally over, but for those of us who survived and for the nation – a new battle – the battle for unity – had just begun.

A knock sounded at the cabin door. Jesse knew it must be family or friend since none of the dogs had sounded an alarm. "It's open!" he called, feeling glad for the company with Lizzie gone to help his mother and the other girls with the last of the canning for the winter.

"It's me!" called his father-in-law, as he entered. "I've got a letter from Bill Shannon down in Austin, and another from the Governor!"

"Throckmorton wrote you himself?" said Jesse, "Why? What's Shannon done?"

"Made a damn political statement with us, is what he's done!" said Abel Landers, with an irritated sigh, "and Throckmorton, poor man, is furious. But in the end there's nothing he can do really."

"I gather the legislature *is* meeting, in spite of the fact that Congress has yet to sign off on President Johnson's order readmitting us into the Union." said Jesse, not even bothering to make it a question.

"Oh, yes," said Abel, "everything's in full swing down there in Austin. And the Southern Democrats are trying to run the show as if we won the damn war, passing a constitution that gives the blacks practically no rights, refusing to repudiate the act of secession, and so on…. While the Moderate Republications like Throckmorton are trying to get them to at least pretend to acknowledge the demands of

Washington, and not do anything so utterly stupid that it will cause Congress to nullify our readmission and send in troops and declare martial law!"

"Good Lord," said Jesse, "that could start the war all over again!"

"Oh, I think Congress could send enough firepower to keep that from happening, but only at the cost of hundreds, maybe thousands of lives, and livelihoods." Abel paused, and then said softly, "You do know, Jesse, that Congress could order every man who fought for the Confederacy arrested, imprisoned, and put on trial for treason. And every politician who voted for secession too. Legally they have more than sufficient grounds. The peace that Lincoln and now Johnson have offered us is amazingly lenient. And these fools are too radicalized to realize it!"

"I gather from what Lizzie and I read in the papers that Congress is not so benignly inclined?" asked Jesse sardonically.

Abel cleared his throat, "Um, you could say that... And yet this fool legislature continues to persist in doing things that just baits them to intervene! And now this thing with Hood..."

"Hood, as in General John Bell Hood?" asked Jesse.

Abel caught himself nodding, and said quickly, "Yes, the very same. Now, I know Jesse, that I don't have to defend myself to you, but just for the sake of clarity, you do know that I respect John Hood. He may not have been the greatest military mind ever produced, but he was a good leader of men, and a patriot to the cause he believed in, and I greatly admire him for that, but he is allowing himself to be used. Even if it is unintentional, I still find it distasteful. Hood was in Austin for a week just after the start of the legislative session. Shannon and some of his cronies made arrangements for him to be honored by both houses of the legislature- invited to come sit at the bar- as they say – in each chamber for a day. Hood accepted and came, and so charmed all those fine gentlemen of the Democratic bend, and not a few of the moderates too, and got the pump all primed – so to speak. And now, the senate and house, after at least some discussion begging to reconsideration, have passed a resolution for one – single – solitary - new county to be formed, and named, by this first post-war, supposedly reconciled with Washington, legislature. That new county, carved out of the entire western part of Johnson county, is to be formed forthwith, and has been given the name of Hood County, after the great (I'm quoting here) war-chieftain, John Bell Hood, of Texas, and it's county seat is to be styled Granberry, after Hood's stalwart companion in the fight, General Hiram Granberry, also of Texas."

Abel paused for breath, and Jesse asked quietly, "Did Throckmorton veto?"

"Of course he did!" said Abel. "He had no choice. His veto of this bill, and his written pleas to Congress asking for time to persuade the legislature to modify the more belligerent stances taken in the new state constitution, is the only thing between Texas and armed invasion. The Senate and House vote this week whether to override his veto or not. Shannon proudly assures me in his letter that they have the votes to override the veto and as he says, "acknowledge these great leaders of our late and glorious cause"!"

Jesse shook his head, "What a quagmire! Like you, I dislike our people's desire for our own county with more local government being used like this as a political tool. Especially when it is part of a stance that could have such disastrous consequences for the whole State and yes, the Union, in the long haul." He got up from his chair to pace the room he knew so well, as he thought further. "But the truth is, Uncle, this news of these names will not be badly received by the citizenry at large. In fact most will probably think the choice a popular one rather than a legislative one. Many men from this county fought under these two men, and most I believe harbor a favorable feeling about their leadership. Few except those like ourselves with some knowledge or experience in government would even stop to think of the political consequences, and the bigger picture."

Abel smiled, ruefully, "Unfortunately they may find themselves living in a world created by those consequences without even understanding why, then. But you're right. Why, if his veto is overridden, there is no reason why Throckmorton's objection would even become public knowledge. And as for the reasons for it...-, folk would much rather continue to think of the government of the Union as some evil ogre, rather than ever admit that we might have done something to justify their "wrath and indignation" against us."

"I declare, Jesse," said Abel, "you have at least slowed me down. I was all set to publicly repudiate the names and say we wanted no county under those terms. But on further thought, I think we must accept this as an opportunity to move forward in our own journey to effective local government. We will do the best we can with that, and let the larger drama play out as it will. There is naught we can do regarding that really. – Other than pray....."

"Amen, to that Uncle!" agreed Jesse, "Amen to that."

***** ****** ***** ***** ***** ***** ***** *****

At the very end of November, Uncle Abel received another packet of letters from Austin. In one of the packets was an embossed copy of an official proclamation, establishing Hood County, Texas – the raised Great Seal of the Sovereign State of Texas affixed thereto. The was also a letter from the governor, official this time, appointing him- Abel Landers – as the first county judge, and thereby chief executive of the brand new county of Hood. There would need to be an election held quickly for things like county commissioners and a sheriff .... All done under the shadow of continued uncertainty as to what was going to happen in that great circus known as Washington D.C..

A series of meetings was held in Acton, Stockton, Thorp Springs, and Glenrose Mills, in lieu of a formal county-wide election- since voter eligibility was a question still very much up in the air. Jesse traveled with his uncle to most of those meetings and as he listened he not only marveled at the older man's stamina, but also at his ability to get others to see the reasonable path and the larger picture. The inclination of the men to elect to leadership positions the men who had so recently lead them in battle was understandable, but Abel over and over reminded them of the looming constraints most likely coming from afar. He welcomed the participation and leadership of former soldiers in the process, but preached the wisdom of allowing that older generation of non-combatants to serve as community leaders – county commissioners and such for a while longer, allowing the younger men to focus on rebuilding lives and livelihoods so disrupted by the recent years of conflict. Abel consulted with leaders in each community and chose four older men of strong leadership reputation as commissioners for his police court. C.C. Alexander and Wilson Barker from the area near Glenrose Mills and Barnard's Trading Post, John Meek from over along the Paluxy, and Joe Robertson, the fiery preacher from Acton, were all eager to serve to promote the interests of the folks in their various parts of the county. C.C. had been county judge over the entirety of Johnson County for a time a few years back, and so was a good source of information and comradery to Uncle Abel in the daunting task at hand. There was only one major disappointment. Abel had encouraged Peter Garland to run for commissioner. Garland had recovered from his ordeal, and had gone on to be a great help to the settlers of the whole area, by leading well organized and disciplined patrols to help quell the threat from the Comanche who still refused to leave North Texas. Abel had thought his expertise might come in handy, but alas the sad incident in his past had colored the response to his candidacy. Abel and Jesse both hoped that would change with more time.

***** ***** ****** ****** ****** ****** ***** *****

While all this politicking was going on, the Lord saw fit to bless our war weary little community is a very exciting way. All through the years of our time in Stockton Bend some of us had gathered most Sunday mornings for prayer and singing either in one of the cabins or if the weather was fine we met in the shade of the little grape arbor David Nutt had planted next to his and Sarah's cabin. During the war numbers had dwindled, and so it was that in the fall of 1866 we were down to about a dozen who still gathered faithfully. Joe Robinson would preach for them a few times a year, and Jesse and Jacob and even my father would share thoughts on scripture from time to time. But we all yearned for the time when we could have an ordained man of God to shepherd them.

And so, one fall morning, there were only ten who had shown up. Sarah Nutt, Jacob, Jesse, Abby and I comprised fully half of the little congregation. We had sung a hymn, and read some scripture from the Good Book, and Jesse had led a prayer. During that time a young man had come and taken a seat on one of the benches in the arbor. He had joined enthusiastically in the singing, but had remained silent during the reading and discussion of the scriptures.

We were preparing to dismiss, when Jacob said, "Wait a moment, everyone. I think we need to talk about what we are doing here." There was silence, and he continued. "I think we need to consider – now that the war is over and it is safer to travel a bit – disbanding our little group here and maybe travelling to Acton/Comanche Peak to worship. No offense, but I am hungry for some true preaching and to be a part of study of the word led by someone with greater knowledge of such things than ourselves. I would like to move that we disband our group here and try another course."

"I agree, Jacob," said Mama Sarah. "After what we have all endured these past few years we are in need of Spiritual Food, more than we can give each other."

There was movement from the bench behind us, and the young stranger tentatively raised his hand. Mama Sarah saw it, and turned to him with a welcoming smile. "Hello, young man! We are so glad you stopped to worship with us! I'm sorry about the depressing nature of our current discussion! We certainly don't lack for a love of the Lord. We just lack in numbers!"

The young man smiled, and said, "I can certainly see that ma'am. I greatly enjoyed the singing. And your discussion of scripture was most thoughtful. May I ask, sir," he said to Jacob, "why you have not sought the services of a minister for your group?"

"We have tried, sir," said Jesse soberly. But our resources are so meager right now. My father-in-law has written to leaders of both the Baptist denomination and the Methodists, seeking to find some interest from either in establishing a congregation of the faithful in this place. But the ravages of war have greatly thinned the ranks of men called to preach God's word, and right now both groups are hard pressed to find shepherds for the flocks they already have."

The young man started to speak, then hesitated. Mama Sarah looked at him keenly, and having raised seven sons, she saw something there. "Young man," she said directly, but gently, reaching out to touch his sleeve, "are you a preacher?"

He swallowed once, and then as if making some kind of great decision, he nodded, and said, "I once was shepherd to some folk in the middle of the cornfields in Georgia, ma'am that's all. I've got a little schooling and studied with a couple of fine men of the Baptist faith. But .... It's been awhile...,and I reckon I've been waiting for God to tell me if it may be time for me to take it up again."

Sarah Landers Nutt said, "What's your name, son?"

"It's Chandler, ma'am. J. D. Chandler," he said, smiling.

Mama Sarah returned the smile, with one that suddenly reminded me very much of my dear father, when things were exactly like he wanted them. "Jacob," she said, looking down at her son, "You can just take that motion of yours back!" Then she turned back to Mr. Chandler, and stuck out her hand and said, "Will you preach for us, sir?"

"What- now?" said the young man, startled.

"No time like the present," said Jesse, encouragingly.

A delighted smile spread across J. D. Chandler's features, as he grasped Mama Sarah's hand, and said, 'W-well, yes ma'am, I will." And on that day our little band officially began the first church of our Lord in this place, with Mr. Chandler as our shepherd. It was but the first of many changes to come as the world began to move again.

*****   *****   *****   *****   *****   *****   *****   *****

When the dust settled, in January of 1867, and the men met at Abel Landers' cabin in Stockton for the first ever meeting of the Hood County Commissioners or Police Court, Jesse, Jacob, Abel, and David Lee Nutt were among the thirty or so observers gathered to watch. After discussing the consensus built at each of the far flung county meetings, the crowd was pleased to hear Abel announce the election of one of the new doctors in the area, D. K. Turner, as county treasurer. Gideon Mills, a literate Scots-Irish farmer from over Paluxy way, had been chosen as tax assessor and collector, and John Morris, a miller from over near Walnut Creek in Acton, had been picked as clerk for the district court.

In spite of Abel's advice to the contrary, the other two persons elected were former Confederate Officers. Jesse could not help but be pleased at A.J. Wright's election as county sheriff. A.J. had married his older sister Elizabeth, way back in 1850 in Neosho, and Jesse knew he was grinning like an idiot remembering their wedding. Lizzie had been one of Elizabeth's bridesmaids, and Jesse had seen her for the first time that day as something more than his sassy and fun cousin. He struggled to straighten his face and focus as the last elected official was announced. Relative newcomer Alex McCamat, who had fought with one of the Indian Protection regiments out in West Texas with several local men, was the new county clerk. He was a surveyor by trade, so Jesse figured that made sense for him to have that office that dealt so much with the affairs of land ownership.

"Well," said Jacob, as the meeting dispersed, "I think Uncle Abel has put together a good team of men to lead the county going forward."

"Yeah, well I just hope the fellows up in Washington will decide to see reason, and just leave us alone." said his brother Abel. "I, for one, am weary of fighting, and just want to get on with my life."

"Well said, brother," said Jesse, "We must all pray it will be so. I know Abel was disappointed that Peter Garland did not get elected as one of the commissioners. He ran but got precious little support. Too many folks forget all the good he's done, and just remember that disaster with the Caddo's. Ah, well, maybe he can serve in some capacity later—after more time has passed." He allowed Abel to lead him outside through the mass of men, to the path. "Will you all come home with me brothers? Mama and Lizzie said they will feed us all if I bring you home! Uncle Abel is coming too, as soon as he can get free. Then we can rehash it all again as we share with the women-folk!"

"That brother," said Abel, "sounds like a plan!"

***** ****** ***** ***** ***** ***** ***** *****

Less than three months later, in April, a big packet of newspapers and letters from Austin arrived for Abel Landers at Comanche Peak Post Office in Acton. By the time they reached his home the newspapers had been devoured by two different deliverymen, who moved quickly to spread news of the 1867 Reconstruction Act passed by the United States Congress throughout the county. Abel Landers made the mistake of opening the large, very official looking packet from the new Governor Pease in the presence of Uncle Tommy Lambert, who was visiting his office when the packet arrived. A day later, as dusk fell on the little community of Stockton Bend, it was becoming ever more obvious that all hell had broken loose.

Abel Landers 16' by 30' cabin was by far the largest building in Stockton Bend, but now that it was being asked to double as the county courthouse and headquarters, its size was hardly adequate to contain the thirty to forty men who gathered there on a regular basis. That was especially true today, when it was not just thirty men but thirty *very angry* men who filled the little courtroom to capacity and more.

"Well, I say we need to go down to Austin and shoot the whole lot of 'em!. They got no right comin' in here and telling us what to do!" shouted Andy Shropeshire.

The crowd of men gathered roared their approval, and another voice shouted, "A.J. Wright is our duly elected sheriff! If Jack Hightower agrees to this, he's no better than all them carpetbaggers in pretty clothes! I say we find a rope and let him and his friends see what it feels like to swing from the end of it!"

Abel Landers stood and banged his gavel on the table at one end of the room and tried to shout above the fray, "Order! I will have order in this court!" but he was getting old now and his voice didn't carry like it once did.

David Lee Nutt leaned over to his brothers and said, "If they leave here like this it'll be a bloodbath, and there will be hell to pay!" He was shouting to be heard over the din.

Jesse touched Jacob's hand in silent question, and Jacob squeezed back in answer. That was all Jesse needed. "Show us to the door David…, now!"

Thinking they were about to flee, David moved quickly to comply. "Where's Abel?" shouted Jacob.

"He was up by Uncle Abe, but he's seen us." said David loudly. "He's coming."

They reached the door, and to David's surprise his brothers turned and stood in the aisle of the tiny courtroom, blocking the path to the door. Abel came and took his stance by his brother Jesse's left side, and David, realizing what they were about, mentally consigned his soul to God, and moved to stand by Jacob's right side. At that moment the crowd turned as one, ready to boil its way out of the courtroom and into the mud that passed for streets, and came face to face with two blind men, a teen-aged boy, and a war veteran – one of their boys in gray - all silently blocking their path.

The front man, Herman Jackson by name, skidded to a halt, and when he got his feet back under himself demanded, "Ah, hell, Jesse! What're you boys doin'?" The crowd behind him quieted.

"Well," said Jesse Nutt, "Near as I can tell, we're keeping you gentlemen from committing suicide."

"Suicide!" shouted a voice from the rear of the crowd, "It ain't suicide if we string old Hightower up with his own rope!" There was a general roar of approval and the crowd surged forward a step before Jesse answered back.

"You're right, Ed!" he agreed. "That would be Murder!" He raised his voice just slightly. "And every one of you fine folks would, with that single act against the Laws of God, be sentencing yourselves to be convicted and executed for murder by lynching. And, I might add, to fiery fate promised in the Good Book as well. Now, just personally, I'd call that a really thorough job of committing suicide."

The hubbub died down, and Jesse could hear the sound of shuffling feet. He had them now- if he could keep them long enough to get the job done. "Gentlemen, I put this question to you. Until this day, this moment of learning of his appointment by the state as sheriff, was there a man among you that had a complaint against Jack Hightower?" Two heartbeats of silence, and, "Is there any man among you that prior to today would have called him a dishonest, cowardly, or evil-minded person?" Two more heartbeats, "Is there any man here who knows anything about Jack Hightower, our neighbor - and a man of our community - that would make him unfit to be elected to the office of sheriff, had he chosen to run for that office?"

"I wouldna voted for him," stated old Dick Blevins loudly.

"I didn't ask who you would have voted for," snapped Jesse, "I asked if anyone knew him to be unfit." Jesse drew a breath and sent up a prayer. "So... my friends - let us re-examine the situation at hand. First, gentlemen, and I ask that you hear me with all sobriety- first and foremost- *we lost the war.* We are in fact a conquered and occupied people. But we are also a blessed people. We are blessed to live here in this far outpost of civilization where the heavy hand of the conqueror has been but little felt. Because of the remoteness of our situation, the government in Austin has had difficulty finding people of any qualification willing to come here to do their bidding as government officials. Therefore they have been forced by providence to be satisfied with disallowing from elected office only those men who were officers for the Confederacy during the recent conflict.

Those men have not, for the most part, been arrested. They have not been prevented from returning to home and family and the pursuit of prosperity. They are simply, for a time, being barred from holding public office. We are fortunate that only two of our duly elected public officials find themselves in this situation. We could have been forced, like many of our comrades in other states, to bear the indignity of the government of strangers. We could have been forced to conduct our lives under the watchful eye of armed invaders. But here, in this haven we call home- this valley of the Brazos, we are simply asked to accept as our sheriff- one of our own, a neighbor, of decent character and honest intent. We are also being asked to find among our own number another qualified man to act as clerk of record for both district and county. This too can be one of our neighbors, someone we know, and trust. We should get down on our knees and give thanks to God that it is so. Is Jack Wright an able man? Yes. Would he make a fine sheriff? Yes. And perhaps someday, when a little time has passed, and the wounds of our great national tragedy have begun to heal, he can run for office again. But meanwhile, we have appointed as our sheriff a man of good character, a man we can trust and support, a man who deserves a chance to do his job unmolested.

We came to this place to build a new legacy for our children, and our children's children. Let us not make murder and lawlessness and mob-rule the foundation of that new legacy.

Go home, gentlemen. Let Sheriff Hightower serve his term of office with our peaceful support. Let Judge Landers figure out what will work best for him – so he has a clerk that will meet his and the county's needs. Go home and give thanks for peace, my friends. - For surely, in these last bloody years, we have had enough of war."

Jesse stopped then, listening for the silence that would signal success. The silence lasted for 10 heartbeats before Abel Landers banged his gavel, and declared in his best courtroom voice, "Gentlemen, I hereby approve the appointment of Jack Hightower as Sheriff of this county, and I hereby appoint Jesse Franklin Nutt as the official County and District Clerk for Hood County Texas. He will be assisted in the performance of his duties by former County Clerk, A. S. McCamant for the duration of his time in office. This court is now adjourned!" The gavel sounded again, and so it was.

***** ***** ***** ***** ***** ***** ***** ***** *****

The river was running fast. We could hear it coming round the bend, from the front porch of our cabin. It had rained for the last two days, adding to the quagmire of mud that passed for streets and roads in our little community.

Jesse and Jacob were still in high spirits after the great courtroom showdown (as it was being billed) the day before. "Well, Lizzie," said Jacob, "how does it feel to be married to the Official County Clerk of our brand new Hood County?!"

"It feels fine," I said with a smile. "Of course, I told Mr. Clerk here it would be even better if this fine new county actually had money collected, so said clerk and his assistant could actually be *paid!*"

"You are talking to the wrong county official, ma'am." said Jacob. "I believe the fellow in charge of the money end of things is going to be Gid Mills. He gets to collect the taxes!"

"Well, now speaking of money," said Jesse, "Jacob – how are you fixed right now?"

"Me?" said Jacob, "Well brother if you are in need, I have about $14 put back from the Land leases."

"Yes, that is about what we have put back as well. I have eighteen dollars and 22 cents to be exact. Now that it is spring we will get lease money again, but that has to last a long time - until March of next year. Still that would be plenty to get us through," mused Jesse, "but...."

At his hesitation, I decided a nudge was in order. "Jesse, ask him," I said, "You know you want to."

"Jesse?" said Jacob.

"Old Jim Borden wants to sell out his grocery, " said Jesse. "I was thinking we could buy him out."

"Us? Run a grocery?" said Jacob, incredulously. "Now, I can tell the difference between a potato and a peach, or a sack of flour and a sack of salt. But what about the things in boxes or jars or those new-fangled tin cans Lizzie read to us about from the New York newspaper somebody left over at Abe's?"

"Well, now I figure to begin with most things we can sort by touch and smell, but the money end of it is where we will need help. Lizzie can help out some, but she has Abbie and the house to care for as well." said Jesse, "The truth is we would need a third partner, someone we could trust totally."

"Are you thinking of David?" asked Jacob.

"I am," said Jesse, "But Jake on the face of it what kind of offer can we make the boy? He's smart, capable, and personable. Why should he limit his horizons going in with the likes of us?"

I had been trying to read the Good Book, and finally I just could not stand it another second. I said, "I think you two fools need to stop worrying about what you can or cannot do, and start worrying about what the good Lord has given you to do!"

Jacob said, "Now, Lizzie, I hardly think that the Good Lord cares overmuch about whether or not we open a grocery. In fact," he continued, with a melancholia that still surfaced from time to time, "I often wonder just what it is he would have us do."

It had been a long time since we left Missouri. Years of frustration finally, may the Good Lord forgive me, just boiled over and I said, 'For ten years – 10 years!!! – I have watched you two – the two boys I loved as a girl, the husband and brother I have loved as a woman – I've watched you struggle with the hand you've been dealt. I've seen you searching for answers- for ways to contribute, to feel yourselves men. I've watched and searched and prayed right along with you every day. And I keep looking for the visionary young men I once knew. Remember I was there with you when we sat on the rocks by the river, fresh from watching the town square being built in Neosho. I remember what you said about how a man could come from nothing, but with the right knowledge and vision he could go west and build something- a legacy – you called it Jesse. And Jacob you talked about building community, and how people should care for each other. And you both talked about making a whole fresh new place into something that would last- not just a farm or an outpost in the wilderness, but a community with businesses, and churches, and schools, and good government. And when Amon first went - you said that if we came – if my father and others like him were going to build something here- you vowed to be a part of it. Not just bystanders but a *part.* Well I know, for a long time, you both have felt God has taken that dream away. But what if He hasn't? What if He just wanted to see how badly you want it? What if He is waiting to see if you really have the courage to make it happen? In – in spite of everything…. "

I stopped then, appalled at myself. Silence reigned, and for the longest time none of us even moved. I was trying to figure out how on earth to undo what I had just done when Jesse spoke. "Well now Elizabeth, perhaps you can ride over to Papa's place and see if young David can come hear our proposition? I believe the three of us have some work to do."

Less than an hour later, I returned with word that David was in the midst of helping his father shoe some horses, but would be over directly. Meanwhile, Jesse and Jacob were discussing the distressing state of public opinion regarding the quality of Mr. Borden's groceries. I had a rather strong opinion myself, and did not hesitate to express it. "If you gentlemen intend going forward with this venture, you have simply got to do something about the quality of goods! Everything he has in that dank, dark little hovel he calls a store is either water logged or moldy! It is just terrible!" I said with a passion born of hard earned money spent on items that turned out to be mostly unusable and/or inedible. "I declare I do not know how he has stayed in business for this long!"

"No competition on this side of the river, for one thing " said Jacob. "Right now the nearest competition is across the river at Comanche Peak Post office. And folks can't afford to pay the ferry fees plus the price of groceries, so that doesn't count."

"According to Jim, who is aware of the problem, by the by, the reason is that all his goods come overland from Houston, right through all that rainy wet country, plus crossing several rivers to get here." said Jesse informatively. "We will have to use those same suppliers at least in the beginning. But over time, I would like to check getting supplies from the north, maybe Springfield. It's not much further, the roads are better, and I do still have contacts up there from before the war."

Jacob nodded, then caught his own foolishness, and said, "That's a good idea. I can contact some folks in St. Louis as well. But whichever way we go, we'll need to keep it quiet that we are buying from that direction. "

"True," said Jesse, "Of course all this is moot, if David doesn't agree."

At that moment, a black horse emerged from the wall of trees and brush that marked the edge of our household plot about 50 yards away. Its' rider was none other than young David, or Lee, as he had become known in this community. David Lee had grown into a likely looking young man, and was already, at eighteen, catching the eye of several young ladies. I hoped starting this new enterprise would cause him to slow down on that front.

Jesse cocked his head, listening. "Is that you, Davy?" he asked, not recognizing the horse's gait.

"Yeah, it's me, Jesse," he answered, as he dismounted. "Hey, Jake! Lizzie!" He nodded my direction.

"What's with the new horse?" asked Jacob, a small twitch pulling at his lips.

David turned beet red. "You know dang well what's with the new horse, Jake. We hadn't been able to afford to get another one as long as the war was goin' on. Plus this is the first decent one that Papa got a chance to offer on since..."

"Ah, Davy," chuckled Jesse, "at last you can put the great Indian Chase behind you!"

"Lord, I hope so!" he exclaimed, "It is very irritating that Some People," he glanced over at Jake, "Have to keep bringing it up!"

"Well," said Jacob, cheerfully, "How about we give them something new to talk about?"

"Such as...?" said David Lee, understandably cautious, although he was grinning as he said it.

"Jacob and I are thinking of buying out Jim Borden, and going into the grocery business. But we need a third partner, someone who can help keep the books and write out bills of sale and such, as well as help us select and buy merchandise, and so on. We wondered if you would consider it? There would be a $10 initial investment each. If you don't have that, Jake and I can probably front what you need, but barely. We have lots of ideas already, but we would proceed slowly until we learn the business and build some capital. And all three of us would have to agree on any decision. I'll not allow it to be a source of division, ever," vowed Jesse. "I would draw up a formal agreement, and we would sign before witnesses. That way we all know what's what. And we could all agree to stay the course for at least a year or until we run out of money. But not to put more money in- except if we all agree – for expansion." During the first part of this speech, David Lee just looked dumbfounded, but then I could see him starting to think it over.- Seriously.

"Well, brothers," he said, "you all have certainly taken me by surprise. But...." He paused for a moment, clearly thinking intently, "I truly appreciate the honor you do me with the offer. I think the three of us, plus Lizzie here have made a good team before. I suspect we can do it again." He stood up straight, and said, "Gentlemen I would be honored to be included in your company, and will do my utmost to be worthy of the trust you are showing. I only have $5 to put in, but I will certainly contribute that and consider myself a junior partner if that will be sufficient. Perhaps when it comes time for our first expansion, I could fund that to purchase an equal share later on?"

"That sounds agreeable to me," said Jacob, nodding at David Lee, "Jesse?"

"Yes," said Jesse, "shall we shake on it then?" There were handshakes all around, and a hug or two as well.

"At LAST!" I was thinking, and I knew the Good Lord's hand was in the mix when the next thing David Lee said was, "Okay, my first question is – what do we have to do to find some groceries to sell that aren't WET?!" Yes, I said to God, as I looked out over the rolling river, and felt His mighty arms enfolding us. Yes, I whispered, with a silent smile, this was going to work out just fine indeed.

Epilogue

A Promise Fulfilled – Granbury, Texas – Spring 1893

The first rays of the morning sun bathed the limestone white and the newly washed plate glass windows reflected the white and red of the new courthouse tower and roof against a deep blue sky. Taller than any of its neighbors save the center of justice across the street, the new building stood waiting silently at the corner of Crockett and Bridge streets. The last nail had been nailed, the last piece of flooring laid, the new fixtures and merchandise had all been carefully placed. And now, at this early hour, as the bright spring sun came over the eastern horizon, three men stood alone on the north lawn of the courthouse, waiting.

The two older men stood tall and slender, unbowed by advancing years. Between them, as he had been for the last almost 40 years, the younger man stood, his eyes gleaming with unshed tears. "Tell us, David," said Jesse, simply. "Let us see her." And with the ease of long years of practice he did- describing the solid strength of the gleaming white limestone walls, the marvelous expanses of the front window glasses and how they reflected all that they looked upon. He described the wonderful ornate stone work at the top of the front façade, and the sheer presence of the building on its proud corner lot. He read the big sign newly mounted across the center front reading "J. and J. F. Nutt Groceries", and read off the types and quantities of goods displayed in those wonderful huge front windows. And finally, in the end he grew quiet for a moment, and taking each of his brothers by the arm, he ended by saying, "Here, come with me. There's one last thing I want to show you."

Leading them across the dusty street, they stepped up on the limestone rock of the sidewalk. A few feet more, and he said softly, "They finally installed the iron entrance plates last night. Feel.... " The two hesitated a moment, and then knelt, reaching out with sensitive fingers. Slowly they traced the raised letters engraved there. "J. and J. F. Nutt Building 1893". With tears glistening on his checks Jesse reached for his brother's hands. "She was right." He whispered, "My Lizzie was right all along."

Jacob turned his face toward his brother, and smiled. "Yes, she was, wasn't she? Hard headed woman…"

"What?" said David, "What do you mean?"

"I remember the night well," said Jacob, "It was nigh on thirty years ago. We were all sitting on the front porch of Jesse and Lizzie's cabin after the war was over…"

"Yes," agreed Jesse, "trying to decide what to do. Whether we dared to even consider trying a – a business venture. Whether it was fair to ask you to hitch your wagon to ours…" said Jesse, with a nod toward to David.

"And Lizzie, she sat there listening all quiet like for a while, and then, slam! She snapped that Bible shut that she was reading, and she said, 'I think you two fools need to stop worrying about what you can or cannot do, and start worrying about what the good Lord has given you to do!' " Jacob said, "And me, being a simple bachelor, I tried to ask just what she meant by that, and well-…"

"She let us have it!" He smiled softly, and set back on his heels, remembering. "She said, 'For ten years – 10 years!!! – I have watched you two – the two boys I loved as a girl, the husband and brother I have loved as a woman – I've watched you struggle with the hand you've been dealt. I've seen you searching for answers- for ways to contribute, to feel yourselves men. I've watched and searched and prayed right along with you every day. And I keep looking for the visionary young men I once knew. Remember I was there with you when we sat on the rocks by the river, fresh from watching the town square being built in Neosho. I remember what you said about how a man could come from nothing, but with the right knowledge and vision he could go west and build something- a legacy – you called it Jesse. And Jacob you talked about building community, and how people should care for each other. And you both talked about making a whole fresh new place into something that would last- not just a farm or an outpost in the wilderness, but a community with businesses, and churches, and schools, and good government. And when Amon first went - you said that if we came – if my father and others like him were going to build something here- you vowed to be a part of it. Not just bystanders but a part. Well I know, for a long time, you both have felt God has taken that dream away. But what if He hasn't? What if He just wanted to see how badly you want it? What if He is waiting to see if you really have the courage to make it happen? In – in spite of everything.... "

"I remember she stopped for breath about then..." said Jacob with a smile.

Jesse nodded, "Yes, she did. And for the longest time you could've heard a pin drop on that porch that night."

"Well- what happened then?" asked David, softly.

"Well, as I recall," said Jacob, "It was Jesse, being a dutiful husband and all, who finally answered."

"What did you say, Jesse?" David queried.

"I sent her to fetch you," said Jesse, his fingers once again tracing the letters on the plate. "I said it looked like we had some work to do."
***** ****** ****** ***** ***** ***** ***** *****

The sun was setting now, as the grand opening of the new Nutt Brothers Mercantile Store and Building drew to a close. The last hand had been shaken, the last sale made, the last toast drank, and the three bothers stood once again on the courthouse lawn soft in the glow of the new gas street lamps. The townsfolk had all gone, but they were not alone. They were joined now by two smartly dressed ladies. Lizzie stood proudly between Jesse and Jacob and Sudie was in her usual spot- at David's right side.

"Well my dear ones, it has been quite a day," said Jesse, "Thank you all, - for everything."

"Yes," said Jacob, "It was just about perfect."

"Lizzie," said David, "I understand we have you to truly thank for this day."

Elizabeth Nutt looked up, startled, and said "Whatever do you mean?"

"We told him today about that morning on the front porch," said Jesse, with a wry smile.

"Ah," she said, in immediate understanding. "Well, I really can't take credit. Sometimes the good Lord uses us, but the words are all His. That particular moment I felt His presence with us – as I surely felt Him here today."

"On that note, and in the spirit of the day, I am reminded of what we read at home last night." said Jesse, "Do you remember Elizabeth? A fitting couple of thoughts to end our day....."

"Oh, yes, I remember," she said, lifting her gaze to the sparkling new building and the darkening night blue sky above. "We read first from the Old Testament – from Kings – And the word of the LORD came to Solomon, saying, Concerning this house which thou art building, if thou wilt walk in my statutes, and execute my judgments, and keep all my commandments to walk in them; then will I perform my word

345

with thee, which I spake unto David thy father: And I will dwell among the children of Israel, and will not forsake my people Israel. So Solomon built the house, and finished it.

"And then," said Jesse, "from Romans- our favorite....

Who shall separate us from the love of Christ? Shall tribulation, or distress, or persecution, or famine, or nakedness, or peril, or sword? As it is written, For thy sake we are killed all the day long; we are accounted as sheep for the slaughter. Nay, in all these things we are more than conquerors through him that loved us. For I am persuaded, that neither death, nor life, nor angels, nor principalities, nor powers, nor things present, nor things to come, nor height, nor depth, nor any other creature, shall be able to separate us from the love of God, which is in Christ Jesus our Lord."

There was a moment then – of total stillness, followed by moment of grace as they all breathed "Amen", and in the quiet of the evening, carried on the gentle breeze, came the sound of flowing water – a reminder of where they stood - forever encircled by the Arms of God.

Afterword

After reading any work of Historical Fiction, one question the reader invariably will have is how much of this is true? The other is usually - how many of these people are real?

Well to answer the second question first- I used very few fictional characters here. Almost every named person did actually exist. There are six minor characters who are fictional- the slave, Elijah, owned by Thomas Rutledge; the saloonkeeper, Charlie Smithers; the Indian who brought letter from Sam Houston; the slave belonging to Jeff Rylee who brought Henry Bond home; and the two men- Herman Jackson and Dick Blevins- who were part of the rabble at the county meeting toward the end. Everyone else is based on a real person of the same name.

As for the story – almost all of the events and relationships are based on at least some shred of provable fact. The two MAJOR fictionalizations are these: the actual cause of Jacob and Jesse's blindness and the close ties of the older men to Sam Houston and Thomas Benton. First – the cause of Jesse and Jacob losing their sight was given in one historical source as an infection of the eyes, and in another source as a mishap. Most Nutt family relatives say they do not know but had thought it might be some genetic defect, but one that did not appear to have been passed down to later generations- so they really had no clue. So I took two out of three theories, combined them with the chaos of the times, and got the resulting storyline. Whatever the cause, we know that they did quite suddenly and totally lose their sight within weeks of each other at that particular age. Whatever the cause- the drastic effect on their lives and relationships would have been just as catastrophic.

Second- the facts surrounding Sam Houston's and Thomas Benton's work for the Union cause, and attempts to settle the frontier with pro-Union, anti-slave leaning folks is part of the historic record. Also, Sam

Houston, David G. Nutt, and Abel Landers all were young men in Tennessee about the same time- during the 1820's. Given the smaller populations and cluster of settlements at that time, it is quite conceivable that their paths could have crossed. The facts regarding David and Abel's turning away from the owning of slaves is also well documented. The saga of Sam Houston's failed first marriage, relationship with the Indians, his battle during those middle years with alcoholism and his later embracing of the Baptist faith are also a matter of record. So these are pieces I used to construct that part of the story. When I did it I really agonized over whether I was wandering too far afield. Imagine my surprise, when much later in the process I discovered that there had been at least two letters exchanged between Sam Houston and Amon Bond during the early to middle 1850's. The content of those letters is not known but they are listed in the index of Houston's correspondence. So, maybe not so much fiction as I thought!

This book is just the beginning of the tale. There is so much more to tell, both historically and personally for these characters. It is my intent to tell the rest in two more volumes that will carry the reader to the end of David Lee's life in 1929. There is a lot of story there- but as you see in the Epilogue here, the major truth of the *whole story* is their steadfast witness through the entirety of their lives, as they remained ever Faithful stewards of the legacy and community they hoped to build. Their witness to us all is the ideal of finding the path that will allow us to live forever "Safe in the Arms of God". May we in our turn be as Faithful.

PICTURES

David G. and Sarah Landers Nutt

Abel Landers shortly before his death. Sadly there is no known photo of Sally Shipman Landers.

The Nutt Brothers: David Lee and Jacob (Standing) and Abel N. and Jessie F. (seated) – Photo dated about 1880 – some fifteen years after the end of this book.

This picture is of Jesse and Elizabeth – about 1880.

David Lee and Sudie Nutt about 1880.

Ben Colbert

Sam Houston

Thomas Benton

A. J. Wright

Gov. James Throckmorton   **State Senator Bill Shannon**

Lt. Gen. John B. Hood   **Lt. Gen. Hiram Granbury**

The NUTT HOUSE

TOWN SQUARE
GRANBURY, TEXAS 76048